LAST DAYS OF A TOYSHOP

This Large Print Book carries the
Seal of Approval of N.A.V.H.

LAST DAYS
OF A TOYSHOP

ANNABEL JOHNSON

THORNDIKE PRESS

An imprint of Thomson Gale, a part of The Thomson Corporation

Detroit • New York • San Francisco • New Haven, Conn. • Waterville, Maine • London

LIBRARY OF CONGRESS CATALOGING-IN-PUBLICATION DATA

Johnson, Annabel, 1921–
   Last days of a toyshop / by Annabel Johnson.
      p. cm. — (Thorndike Press large print clean reads)
   ISBN-13: 978-0-7862-9372-8 (alk. paper)
   ISBN-10: 0-7862-9372-1 (alk. paper)
    1. Young women — Fiction. 2. Large type books. I. Title.
   PS3560.O37134L37 2007
   813'.54—dc22
                                       2006038427

Published in 2007 by arrangement with Annabel Johnson.

Printed in the United States of America on permanent paper
10 9 8 7 6 5 4 3 2 1

*DEDICATED TO
TOMMY,
DAVID,
AND ESPECIALLY
EDGAR*

■ ■ ■ ■

St. Louis

■ ■ ■ ■

ONE

Fear was so strange a sensation she could hardly put a name to it. She was just aware of a pervasive imbalance, a loss of orientation that was new to her life. Walking in the dark of night Terry began to define it. Not some little scare — as a child she'd been frightened of cats. When she was ten she had been worried about getting leprosy after her mother had read her *The Black Arrow.* Nervous her first day of junior high school. But nothing like this nauseating twist of the heart. It made everything seem ominous — the air so cold it was sharp enough to cut glass, the stars overhead heavy with glitter, the sound of a dog barking hysterically over on Gannon, barking at that thing in the shadows you can't quite see. From far down the street came the tap of a night stick, Officer Wells walking his beat, bouncing his wooden club off the sidewalk to let the neighborhood know that the law was in control. A reassuring sound, but the terror in her heart could not be banished by a kindly cop.

The black silence of the hour allowed the echoes in her head to ring with bright anger. *"Henry, please, I really wish . . ." ". . . Marj, I don't ask a whole lot of you. This shinding is important . . . customers will all be there . . . I might even get a chance to land the Chase Bag account . . . honor to be invited . . ." "But it's New Year's Eve, I hate to leave Theresa alone . . ." ". . . can survive for one night on her own, the girl is almost eighteen, for Godsake!"*

Terry had seen her mother wince at the blasphemy. In a spasm of guilt she blurted out something — "I'll be fine. I'll go over to Dixie's, we'll see the year in together."

Shivering, she walked faster, skidding on the occasional patch of ice. People had shoveled their walks, but earlier the afternoon sun had caused the snow to melt and run. Now frozen again, it made the footing treacherous. Which is why she'd worn . . . a horrid panicky giggle rose in her throat, *whoever heard of wearing tennis shoes on New Year's Eve? Dixie will scathe me.* In the undertow of desperation, she had a wild

10

impulse to rush in and blurt it all out, share the misery, what are best friends for? But this was one secret she couldn't spill. *Hey, Dix, what does it feel like to come from a broken home?* Her stomach clenched up tight as a fist.

A memory made her want to cry inside, a mental snapshot of the doll house. Way back in the bad early Depression days, no money for Christmas presents, her father had built the thing out of scraps of plywood, finished it with stucco and filled it with cardboard furniture. Her mother had contributed one room of beloved antiques from her own childhood — they'd given her the richest Christmas of her life. Of course, eventually she had outgrown the house and they had taken it downstairs to make room for a new vanity with a full-length mirror. Then one day when the furnace was being converted from coal to oil one of the workmen had dropped a heating duct on the little bungalow and caved in the roof. A broken home.

Snow crunched underfoot as she cut across the yard toward the ramshackle old place that stood at the far end of the street. Perched on the edge of a new neighborhood of red brick duplexes, Berensen's house was a throwback to rural times, set under giant elm trees, winter-bare now. Beyond the ample front porch, light showed in the downstairs windows, another isolated glow far at the back of the house upstairs, Phin was home. And he too was beyond asking for any advice. The one subject never discussed in all their bull sessions — the three of them, could talk until they dropped but never about marital breakups. Years ago Mr. Berensen had walked out on them, leaving his family penniless except for this shabby old barn of a house.

Terry came to a stop in front of it, shrinking inwardly, half minded to turn around and go back. To what? A home still vibrating with anger and resentment and disgust? *Too many arguments these days, all about me, I don't get it.* Putting the questions aside, she stomped her tennis shoes free of snow, clumped up the warped steps onto the porch and straight on in, thrusting through the front door, slamming it behind her.

"I am going to hate 1941!"

Sitting cross-legged on the hooked rug in front of the fireplace, Dixie looked up from a game of solitaire and gave her a dark grin. "I told you that last week." Spectacularly ugly, the girl had a mouth like a gash, a hard bony jaw and gleaming eyes set deep beneath the black hair which scattered across her brow and down over her ears to her shoulders. Turquoise satin shoulders, her mother had grabbed the robe cheap from the will-call down at Sonnenfeld's. The golden earrings, too, were a benefit of Fran Berensen's job at the department store. They glittered as Dixie shook her head. "That awful kerchief makes you look like Tess of the D'Urbervilles on a bad day." Old joke. Back in junior high they had tried to concoct a name which could be derived from the loathsome "Therissa" and it had worked for a while until the teacher assigned Thomas Hardy for a book report. After that, the name "Tess" had garnered a chorus of snickers from the kids. She'd had to settle for Terry after all.

Shucking the rabbit-fur coat, she saw Dixie shuffling the deck and pleaded fervently, "Oh, no, not again!" In the week since Phin gave her the fortune-telling book Dix had read everyone's future a dozen times, each prediction worse than the last.

"Everything up to now has been practice," she announced. "This is the real thing. It's New Year's Eve, your future begins tonight. Don't look so long-suffering."

"Like I told you a hundred times, I don't *want* to know my future." The fact was,

Terry did feel some extra portent in the air. The far corners of the big drafty room were drenched in shadow, the two lamps giving off a meager glow that barely lit the rug where the two girls sat across a spread of cards.

"Pick one."

The three of clubs. *It even looks like me, narrow and dark and curly on top.* Terry ran a hand over the wreckage that the permanent wave had left. Maybell Queal, their next-door neighbor, had bought the machine to give home perms and make some pin money, but as her first guinea pig, Terry had suffered. Even Dad had been outraged, *the girl looks like some kind of Fiji Islander.* To drive off the jitters, she burst into a random spate of words. "This time, forheavensake, get me a boyfriend. Nothing fancy, I don't need a prince charming, just somebody who would take me dancing next New Year's Eve."

"I gather Ozzie didn't come through?"

"Well, of course he asked me. But did you ever dance with Oz? He thinks he's tackling some quarterback. Anyway, his whole family is at a neighborhood function. You get in a room of South Side Dutch doing the polka and you feel like you've been hoofing it with the elephants."

"Okay, you want slim and suave and elegant, how about Van Johnson?" Dixie was laying out the cards in a square around the trey of clubs, which looked like an orphan in a world of hearts and diamonds.

"Hey, I'm going to be rich."

"Hate to tell you, but they're all upside down. Except the jack, he's one of the worst villains in the deck. 'A slick-tongued devil and he lies with ease, he's got more women than a dog has fleas.' Watch out for that one, he's right off your left elbow."

"How about that king of hearts?"

"That would be your father, but he's upside-down too, so walk carefully around him this year."

As if I don't know.

"There's your mother, she seems okay." Dealing the second rank in a wide pattern around the first, she frowned. "Wups. Jack of spades, full of evil plans, steer clear of him even if he's handsome as a lord. Mmm. . . . jack of hearts, but he's a long way off, you probably won't meet him until you get to college."

"Forget that. I'm not going."

"Oh yes, you are. Madame Svengali, she see everyt'ing. You will spend nine long

15

months wearing pleated skirts and twin sweater sets and saddle shoes that make your feet look like mating guinea pigs."

"Where does it say *that?*"

"I don't need cards for that prediction. You will go because your folks make you, you will hate the college, you will break the rules, you will call down the wrath of authority and you will eventually go up in smoke. 'We hold these truths to be self-evident.' "

She knows me too well. "Enough of that, let's read your future."

"No need." Dixie shrugged, a little too carelessly. "I already know what I'm going to be doing. I've applied to Pratt Institute."

"That place in New York?" *And she never told me, she never even told me.*

"I sent them my portfolio. I asked for a scholarship. But even if they won't give me one, I'll go there anyway as soon as we kick this lousy high school. New York is where fashion design begins and ends. You've got to learn the trade there, even if you start out at a sewing machine in one of the shops."

Terry found herself grinning furiously. "That's swell. Does your mother know about it?"

"She's in favor. In fact she wrote her cousin in Brooklyn who runs a bakery. He'll give me a room in their apartment upstairs if I'll help wait on customers on weekends."

Everything figured out, everything settled. "But what about Hollywood?" Ever since their paper-doll days, Dixie had talked about designing clothes for the stars. She'd done a whole wardrobe for Judy Garland. "Those boxy suits they put her in are terrible, she's too short for padded shoulders."

Now she shrugged. "I'll get there eventually. Hey, you want to see my new sketches?" Scrambling over to the sofa she rummaged behind it, that sofa which once had been a treasure ship where they'd sailed all over the world on rainy days. Dragging forth a sheath of drawings, almost shyly she spread them out on the floor under the lamp. A long way from paper dolls, they filled whole sheets of butcher's wrap, dashing, insolent designs drawn with hard, sure strokes of the charcoal. You could almost feel the surge of inspiration racing from tangled head down scrawny arm to quick fingers. They were all signed with a single fierce word: *Dixi.* "Phin suggested I leave the 'e' off. In Latin, that means 'I have spoken.' What do you think, too sassy?"

17

Terry fought down a hard twinge of envy. This, *this,* was the thing missing in her life, a driving desire, a focus, an — ambition. With that, you have a weapon to fight them off, the parents with their own ideas of what you should do and be, *oh yes, our daughter is studying to be a concert pianist,* or the teachers with their silly narrow notions, *I strongly advise you to take chemistry, it will come in handy when you study to be a nurse.* None of them conceived that you might possibly want to choose for yourself —

"Well, Pete's sake, *say* something!"

The sketches. She was still staring at Dixie's drawings. "They are completely wonderful. I love them. You'll get a scholarship, I'd bet anything."

"I sure hope so, I don't have rich relatives to pay my tuition." Just a touch of snideness in the remark. A little envy at Terry's rich Virginia grandmother.

"Well, don't wish for any," Terry told her in heartfelt tones. "They give you money to go to a school you can't abide, to study for a career you can't handle and don't want. They are the source of all my tribulations."

"Good word, you got it from Shakespeare?"

"From Phin. What's he doing anyway?

18

Why isn't he getting his fortune told?" All week, his forecasts had grown grimmer and bleaker with every turn of the card.

"In a way I guess he is. He's sitting up there in front of that blackboard, trying to figure out what his life is going to equal after he graduates." Phin, their elder, was soon to be bestowed with a degree from Washington University. "The fellowship came through."

"Well, that's great!"

"Only he has to choose a major right now. For post-grad work you have to narrow it down."

"Like — how do you mean?"

"Don't ask. And don't ask him. Especially don't ask him about his new girlfriend."

"Phin has a *girl?*"

"Somebody he met at that night school class he teaches over in Maplewood."

Nobody tells me anything. Terry floundered again into the great unknown that seemed to be rushing at her. They had always planned that she would marry Phin to keep him in the family. Dixie was up and on the move, heading for the stairs. She followed, up the creaking uncarpeted treads, dim wallpaper with scenes on it of English fox hunts, but so faded you could hardly make out the horses. Through an unlit bedroom, they proceeded onto the big glassed-in porch at the rear of the house.

A sunny room in summer, now hung with curtains of blackness in the far corners, while a single cone of light from the overhead lamp shone down on the big wooden work table, which was bare. Very strange, the whole room looked odd. It was too neat, no books stacked on the floor, the chair free of junk, no papers overflowing the wastebasket, no crumpled yellow tablet sheets. The big blackboard had been erased except for a single equation:

$$\textbf{Phineas} + \textbf{\$} = \textbf{X}$$

Contemplating his conundrum, the boy sat with elbows hitched onto the table. He was swathed in a huge green wool sweater with cuffs that hung loose and shapeless. *I gave him that thing years ago. Looks awful. But it was my first big knitting project, twelve years old, I didn't know how to do ribbing. Or hide the ends.* Sprigs of green wool sprouted here and there like seedlings, somehow in keeping with the tuft of wheat-colored hair that sprang from the crown of his head, the rest of the harvest spreading out and down around his ears, across his broad brainy forehead. Phin bore no resemblance to his sister, who was the image of her mother. Terry assumed he must take after his departed father, gangly, with the long bones of a good horse, face dominated by a noble nose and an uneven mouth that was almost painfully revealing. It worked and twisted as he stared at the equation he had set out. When he came aware of the girls, he looked at them with eyes as complicated as a wind-swept sky.

As if their coming had settled the matter, he nodded. "Electromagnetics."

The word meant nothing to Terry. Electric, as in electric trains, one of which circumvented the big shadowy room? What did that have to do with magnets, which you use to pick up iron filings off a piece of paper in physics class which she never understood half of?

"What happened to metallurgy?" Dixie demanded in accusing tones.

"It's all part of the same discipline," he told her, standing up, tilting slightly to the left because of the shorter leg, a leftover from a bout of polio when he was eight years old. Going over to the bookcase he found a volume and brought it back to her, flipping the pages, finding one. "With electricity you can do all kinds of things to metal. You could call it the science of electro-magicality." When Phin made a joke only one edge of his mouth kinked up.

"In that case," she said, "I have a jar of pennies you can change into gold, we'll all be rich."

"I think you have to sell your soul to the Devil for that. I'll settle for a good alloy." He went to the blackboard and erased the question mark, took the chalk and wrote **II r$_2$**. It had always been a favorite symbol of his, denoting the mystery of the number that stretched out into infinity without ever being solved. "The possibilities go on and on forever. Just think of taking the first step on such a trip?" Excited as a little kid, he went over to the set of controls and threw a switch.

Across the doorway a magnificent drawbridge lowered majestically to click into place and make the connection that allowed the train to roll out of its station. The handsome Lionel engine chugged slowly around the room, across the wall of windows, all of which opened straight up and down and had not caused any difficulties. Up a 2% grade, carefully engineered when he was all of fourteen years old, it ran on a trestle past the bookcases, through the village in the corner. Terry had fashioned the houses out of match boxes and the trees out of twigs lavishly adorned with flour and water paste which she'd painted green when it hardened. Dixie hadn't helped much, that was the time she was learning to use the sewing machine, creating stylish flannel nightgowns because the material was cheap. Telling them the intricacies of putting in a sleeve, while Phin created his own dream from an old Erector set. Both it and the train had been early gifts from an uncle in New York who had been "filthy rich" before the stock market crashed.

Now the magnificent engine was on the downgrade, barreling home, into the train yard where a signal changed from green to red as its arm came down. The Rock Island Rocket rolled to a stop. The drawbridge creaked slightly as Phin raised it. They watched in a silence that had, for Terry, become significant. It was as if they were seeing it for the last time. Saying goodbye to all those memories.

Darn Dixie and her darned fortune-telling cards and darn Phin for giving them to her.

"Would anybody like some fudge?" Nervous, oddly obsequious, Dixie led them back downstairs.

In the antique kitchen Terry took over — Dix was a monumentally bad cook — stirring the squares of Baker's chocolate in the blue enamel sauce pan atop the ancient gas stove while Phin emptied the bottle of Karo into the mix. Dixie had gone to the icebox for butter.

"We're low on ice."

"Truck skipped us last Wednesday," Phin explained, "not enough business out this way any more. Everybody's buying refrigerators. Sis, bring the vanilla?"

"Any nuts left?" Terry inquired, hopefully.

"Uh-uh. We barely had enough for Mom's Christmas pie. They're so darned expensive," Dixie added, dolloping butter into the pan.

"Where is she tonight, your mom?"

In disgusted tones Dixie said, "She's gone on a date. She went dancing with the Horrible Hatter."

"C'mon," Phin scolded mildly, "she's earned it. She always did like to dance. Anyway, he's not so bad. Wholesaling ladies' hats is a respectable job."

"Brown shoes and white socks and a green overcoat, you tell me that's *respectable.*"

"Poor guy may be colorblind, you don't know." Phin was always ready to give anybody the benefit of the doubt.

A date? Terry absorbed the thought, trying to picture her own mother going out on a date with some man. Couldn't. But when you're alone, maybe you need to make new friends . . . the lump in her throat was harder and hotter than the ones she was beating down in the fudge. In a fury of effort she whipped it smooth, at least a pan of candy wasn't going to get the better of her. "Bring me a cup of cold water, Phin."

"Ah, the soft-ball test." He did as she asked.

Dropping a teaspoonful of the mix into the water she worked it with her fingers, the way her mother had taught her, how long ago? Back when she was about eight. "It's done," she pronounced.

Phin was ready with the buttered pie pan.

"Cut big squares, big big chunks," Dixie directed grimly, "I want a big fat piece."

"It's got to stand a few minutes first." The only place Terry could boss her best friend was at stove-side. They gathered waiting and, again, one of those silences developed that had to do with night and the wind outside, the waning hours of a year.

Around the windows the red-checkered curtains stirred slightly in the draft, the old house creaked. The linoleum on the floor still showed the scuff marks of roller skates — they'd had to teach Phin how to skate again after he got over the polio, but he couldn't go outside in the cold, so it was the kitchen or nothing. Their mother never said a word.

"Do you realize," Dixie's voice was a little strained, "that this is the last New Year's Eve we'll be mere juveniles. By next year we will be high school graduates, we'll be grown-ups."

"You mean I've been a grown-up for four years and didn't know it?" Again Phin got that little quirk of mouth.

"You were born grown up," his sister informed him. "That's why you didn't notice. Now you're through college you're positively — adult."

"What do you want for graduation?" Terry hardly knew where the question came from, it wasn't the kind you asked of people as poor as the Berensen's.

"I want some nylons," Dixie's answer was instant and specific. "You know, those new stockings they invented? Sonnenfelds' got in a bunch of them the other day, Mom took some out of the box. You ought to *feel* them, they're heavenly. Only expensive — they cost two dollars and fifty cents."

"For a pair of stockings?"

"Well, don't blame me. It's because the Japanese are bombing China or something, there just isn't any more silk and cotton

26

wrinkles so bad . . ."

Phin wasn't interested in the Japanese. "How about you, Bunch? What's your big wish?" The nickname had happened long ago when he'd been trying to teach Terry the multiplication table and she had declared that eleven-times-twelve equaled "a bunch."

She hesitated now, afraid that putting words to it would diminish the dream. "I want a car."

Dixie exploded in rude laughter. Even Phin chuckled around, his shoulders hunching and jumping. "I created a monster." He had taught her to drive last summer, helped her get her license, a fact her own parents didn't even know. "The madwoman of U.City, she'll be racing her tomato-red convertible down Delmar Boulevard scattering pedestrians right and left."

"Okay, laugh, but that's what I want and sooner or later I'm going to get it."

Phin was quick to sense the slight injury in her tone. "Sure you will. Can you afford one? I mean with that big bank account?"

Actually Terry didn't know how much was in her savings, her father preempted every gift check and deposited it for her, saying some day she would be glad he did. "I'll never see a penny of that until I'm twenty-one years old, I guess. Dad says he's got the right to manage my money." An old argument between the child and the man with the blunt clumsy fingers that wrote the checks in their family and kept all bank books in a locked drawer of the spinet.

"Well geeminy cripes!" Dixie was always two inches away from saying something really crude. Digging a piece of fudge out of the pan, she shoved it deep into her mouth, mumbling past it. ". . . your money, you ought to take him to court . . ." The Berensen father had been a lawyer. "Who knows, there might be a hundred dollars in there."

More than that. Terry had got a $25.00 check from her grandmother for Christmas, and there was always one on her birthday, fifty dollars a year. It had started the time of the bank failure back in 1933. The Mercantile hadn't gone under, their savings hadn't been wiped out. But her Grandmother Hamilton was sure they were living in poverty and began to send the checks twice a year. What the sum might be now she couldn't even imagine.

"How much does a car cost?"

Phin was considering it soberly, but Dixie kept on guffawing, with fudge all over her teeth. "You couldn't afford it, believe me. Anyway, your dad would have ten fits." Which was true. Henry Miller didn't even drive their old Dodge to work, but took the bus unless he was going to see out-of-town customers.

"Listen, Bunch," Phin told her dead-serious, "you hang onto your savings. In college they make you buy a lot of extras, books and lab fees, all sorts of stuff. It costs a fortune." Which was why in spite of his scholarship he'd taught remedial math at night school for years.

"But I don't want to spend my money on a dead frog." Cutting up her amphibian in biology had been one thing she swore never to do again. In fact her whole senior year had been hung with warning signs. *Who needs to learn French? Ancient history is never going to matter in my life.* What she did intend to do next semester was take typing. You never know when you might have to get a job. If her father walked out . . . And with that thought a flood of despair returned like a high tide sweeping up over her, drowning everything else. Watching Dixie cram another piece of fudge in her mouth, she said, "I need to get on home."

"But it isn't midnight yet."

"Who cares?" She was already on the move, back to the living room, yanking her old fur monstrosity off the coat rack, *they can't make me take this thing off to college!*

Phin was pulling on his windbreaker. "I'll walk you."

Leaving Dixie behind, a little puzzled, they went out into the cold dark. "Watch the steps," he said tucking a hand under her arm. "Bunch, are you worried about something? You seem pretty upset. Is your mother okay?"

"You don't need a darned fortune-telling book, you read minds."

"Not really. I saw her on the street the other day, she looked sort of pale — I don't know, she seemed sad?"

And Terry almost spilled it all right then and there. Ever since his polio days, Phin and Marjorie Miller had been close. Knowing that his own mom had to go to work, she had come over day after day to make lunch for the spindly kid laid up in bed. While the two six-year-old girls hung around the edges of the room, she had fed him hot soup and kind words. "You will walk again, you must not doubt that."

Now he nudged her. "Come on, Bunch, I can keep a confidence."

"Mother and Dad have — problems," she

blurted. "They fight a lot. Like tonight, over whether to go to a company party. And they fight over me, I don't know why." Her voice cracked like thin ice. "When I try to talk to them they just shut up."

"I know," he said quietly. "They go in the bedroom and close the door."

"Mother, if I even ask her any questions, she starts to cry. I guess I shouldn't keep saying how I really don't want to go to college. But I don't, Phin. Or at least I wouldn't mind taking courses at Washington U. If I have to go clear off to Virginia, I'll be lost."

The sound of their footsteps rang loud on the still air. In one of the yards a branch of a tree cracked under the weight of ice. Houses all dark, most folks were out at some festivity this special night. Terry shivered, with inner chill, with a sense of strangeness as if she'd never walked this neighborhood before.

"How did it go," he mused, "that thing Miss Baker liked so much? 'Not till we are lost . . .'?"

"That's from Thoreau. 'Not till we have lost the world do we find ourselves.' It's always on her final exams."

"That's the one. Maybe you're about to find yourself." Somewhere a firecracker went off and the dog over on Gannon went

31

into a new hysteria of barking. "Wonder who you'll be. Maybe a hounded noble-woman, Tess of the Baskervilles."

In spite of herself she snickered. "More like a homeless waif, Tess of the Hoover-villes."

"Anyway, happy new you." Off in the night, horns were blatting, and far away across the rooftops a burst of fireworks lit the darkness.

The year 1941 had moved in, ready or not.

Two

An irrational guilt held her momentarily suspended above the piano keyboard, her fingers flexed — those stubby fingers that could barely reach one key over an octave. If you kept a proper arch your span got smaller. Square hands, like her father's, they were made for milking cows. Jaw set, Terry braced herself, smashed down hard and fast on the big opening chords of the Concerto, sending them cascading down the keyboard like a muddy torrent. *Did it!*

After the wild opening passage the music settled into a rippling stream, as she rushed on, reading the notes as automatically as words in a book while her mother turned pages expertly. "You're doing fine, darling, beautiful, beautiful."

So, of course, she fumbled.

With a sour plink she sat back, feeling the creep of perspiration under the ruffled pink dress. She never did see why she had to put on Sunday clothes for a Tuesday afternoon music lesson. It was because Madame Arquette always dressed to the teeth in black silk and sequins, garnet pendant, dentures and wig and traces of a small mustache. And she too was lavishly damp, didn't use enough Odoro-no, leaving behind an atmosphere of sweat and pachouli that even a half hour later lingered in the small room.

Just an antechamber wedged between kitchen and staircase, it had been intended as a library. The built-in shelves now held stacks of sheet music, books on harmony and counterpoint, thick lives of the composers. The Baldwin upright was positioned squarely in the bay window so that the student imprisoned could look longingly upon the free world outside the glass. Bare now, the elm trees, but in summer the green grass was as tempting as if sent by the Devil himself.

Terry didn't really believe in the Devil, but she did think there was a God and sometimes wondered why he had deliberately bestowed her father's hands on her instead of her mother's lovely long agile fingers.

"Try it again, darling. From the start."

I'm never going to make it, I'm just going to disappoint everybody again. "Mother, I don't feel ready for this. Even Madame Arquette thinks I should stick to the Chopin Nocturnes or maybe a Beethoven Sonata." And if He was up there, God knew she could hardly handle those.

"Madame is a sillybones." Marjorie Miller had a laugh like small silver bells on a Christmas tree. "She's the best we can afford, but she's no Paderewski herself. I think the Concerto frightens her."

That was true enough, Terry acknowledged. When the old girl had played the opening, to demonstrate the proper way, as she always did, she'd missed notes right and left.

"But it's hard, it's really really hard, even the quiet part."

"You'll be great, I know you will." And that was the trouble, Marjorie had such high expectations, they shone in her eyes, green and luminous as the ocean. Her delicate face was of the sea itself somehow, fragile as a shell, and with that same toughness, enduring the tides of life. The wealth of honey-blond hair had gray streaks in it, but it rose to the chignon as proud as befitted an aristocrat. "You were born to be a musician, my dear."

A Hamilton mustn't fail, and that's what this

is all about. In a convoluted twist of conscience, Terry had already foreseen that any inability to exploit this mythical talent would mean a loss of identity, her own and her mother's, and that was somehow linked to the precarious state of their family.

Straightening her back, taking a deep breath, Terry attacked the opening page again, but this time Grieg did her in, she floundered under the weight of his chords and conceded defeat. "It's my fingers, Mother, they are too short, I can't manage the opening, and when it comes to the cadenza — even Madame couldn't handle that."

"That's why she's a teacher, dear. You are much more gifted than she will ever be."

"But I'd hate to flub up like I did at the recital." It came blurting out before she could stop it. The Black Key Etude had exploded in sour notes when she couldn't make the arpeggios. Her mother seemed to cringe at remembered consternation. The small lines appeared around her mouth as if she had been holding them at bay and they had crept up on her.

"That was a bit of stage fright. You're a year older now." Marjorie tried to steady the quaver in her voice, but tears were turning the blue eyes the color of salt water.

"Mother, please don't cry!"

"What the Sam-hill is going on here?" The man who stood in the kitchen doorway was short and square-set, beneath the dome of a shiny scalp fringed by thin gray hair. Still in a heavy brown wool overcoat and galoshes, he was weighted down by the huge sample case he carried in one hand, must have come straight in from the garage. "Marjorie, stop that. And you, girl, whatever you've been whining about, get over it and go back to your scales. You can just stay at the piano an extra hour."

Overriding the inaccuracy of his accusation, Terry panicked at those last words. "Dad, I can't. We have a history final tomorrow, I have to study for it."

"Henry, she's been doing very well, really. We just had a good, good lesson and she's going to be playing Grieg's Concerto. Don't mind me, I was — I was thinking back to another time, made me cry a little. It's not Therissa's fault. And of course her schoolwork is important . . ." she was steering him out of the room, back to the kitchen. ". . . needs to make the honor roll, so they will allow her an early entrance into the music program at Gloucester next fall."

". . . too confounded soft on the kid . . ."

37

There it was again, that tone of disgust. Left alone in the silence that was still dissonant with cross words, Terry read the music to herself. *What's an audition like, anyhow? They don't want to hear you play the whole thing? Maybe I'll never get to the cadenza.* Or maybe the music director would go straight to the most difficult part and demand to hear her execute it. If he didn't permit her to enter the program as a freshman it would mean a whole wasted year, an expensive year to be doing English and biology and what would the Hamiltons think of their money going for that?

With wretched madness she thought, *Maybe for the audition I should just play "Happy Days are Here Again."* That's how it had all started, this fable that she was a musician. Mother loved to tell the story.

"It was the first time I'd been home to Virginia since Therissa was born. There she was, this adorable little four-year-old, crawling around on the big Persian rug — it's my grandmother's rug, very old, brought back from the Middle East by my grandfather on a clipper ship. Redford was playing the Steinway, he was always clever with music, dashing off popular songs. It was a political year and everybody was singing 'Happy

Days are Here Again.' That's when we noticed my baby, down there under the piano, keeping time to the music, beating out the rhythm on the rug with her tiny fists. Reddie was tickled half to death. He picked her up and put her on his lap, they were playing chopsticks together in a matter of minutes. She learned so fast, he got excited and held her high above his head. 'This child is a born musician!' he told us. It was like a revelation."

Dear Uncle Redford, the inventor of my life.
Terry had only seen pictures of him since then, but he looked every bit the great-great-grandson of a Revolutionary patriot, the fair-haired youngest member of a noble family, adored by his sisters, the pride of his parents. His only fault was that he had remained unwed and never produced progeny. They commented on that frequently, much to his amusement.

But the fact was, the branches of that tree were supposed to grow sweet fruit. Terry felt the weight of it — her mother's ambition to add to the family's glory with a concert artist, I mean, what else can a girl do to distinguish herself? Never be leader of men like Uncle Chalfont who was a state senator, or a noble judge like Uncle John. Even Reddie had been an officer in the

United States Navy before he shattered his ankle in a polo game. A family of heroes, ready to support their own in any worthy endeavor, which is why they were financing her whole career that she might carry the Hamilton pride into the concert hall.

Shuddering, Terry went back to the first page and that smash-bang opening. Then hesitated as other sounds disturbed her concentration. Bicker from the kitchen rose louder, plates rattled, silverware clashed. She moved back from the piano and went out there into a spate of words that swamped the cheerful yellow room. Her mother was mopping up a glass of spilled water — Terry took the dishrag from her, thankful that for once it wasn't about her. Henry was protesting that the pork tenderloin was too expensive while Marjorie countered softly with the fact that there was no bone in it, therefore no waste. The only waste, Terry thought, was appetite. They managed somehow to eat in sullen silence and she was relieved to clear the table finally, while her mother seemed to fade into the shadows, soft footsteps on the stairs. Her father took refuge in the front room, turning on the radio from which H.V. Kaltenborn's high carping voice complained about the day's news.

Always warning about war. It irritated Terry, everyone harping on war when the President had promised never to take the country there again. How could he? Nobody would stand for it, people shuddered at the thought of another catastrophe like the World War. She couldn't imagine what it was really like, but the movies were bad enough. The battle scenes from *All Quiet on the Western Front* and the manic laughter of Louis Wolheim in *What Price Glory?* Even as raw as they were, those movies had made her father sneer. "What do they know about what it's really like on the front lines?"

He knew. He'd been there at the Argonne. In the bottom drawer of the dresser was a medal, but he never showed it to anybody. Something terrible had happened to him over there, a thing called "shell shock" which she didn't understand, they didn't put that in the movies. But her mother had warned her once long ago: "Your daddy still gets spells when his head rings with the sound of the artillery, it makes him upset, so just leave him alone, be kind and walk softly."

Terry polished the glasses vigorously, green glassware obtained one at a time on "dish night" at the Tivoli Theater all through the Depression. The one escape they had, every Wednesday, to lose themselves in the magical movies. Lately, Terry had grown more aware of the fact that everything she knew of the world came from those motion pictures, and it made her uneasy, as if she should get moving, go forth and learn what was true beyond the Hollywood make-believe, *and don't expect real men to look like Tyrone Power.* Her mouth took on a twist of cynicism. She'd heard the heavy clump of footsteps on the back porch.

He knocked and came on in out of long habit, Ozzie Turner. The kitchen seemed to expand to receive him — six-feet-four with powerful shoulders that rose upward into a thick neck which sloped straight up to the crown of his crew-cut head. A broad pink-cheeked face with broken nose and flat blue eyes, Oz's countenance was an oasis of in-nocence.

"Sorry I came early. Go on, finish your dishes. I just needed to get over here and learn about the Civil War quick before tomorrow. Are you going to eat the rest of those peaches?"

"Help yourself." She handed him a spoon.

Digging into the can with it, he carefully lifted a bite to his mouth, rumbling with pleasure. "My mom won't buy canned peaches, she says we can't afford it if I'm going off to college. I mean what can you do with them, they get these ideas? I told her, I can't even pass high school. But she doesn't listen, you know mothers. Say, your folks won't mind me finishing these up?"

"They wouldn't notice if you stripped the refrigerator clean and then ate the wall paper."

"Oh. Having problems, huh? I remember how that used to be." His dad had died of T.B. a year ago, leaving two kids. The Turners were living off a meager insurance policy and the bounty of an extended family. "What I did, I went out for football and had practice every weekend, y'know, whether there was scrimmage or not. I hated it when they argued. Always about money. That's why I don't care much if I pass history, because if I don't I'm gonna join the Navy and see the world and never have to worry about money again. They feed you pretty good in the Navy."

"You're going to pass," she informed him sternly. "Whatever you do you'll need your high school diploma." Sitting down at the table she opened his history text. "You've got too much stuff marked here. You can't remember all this."

"Yeah, okay, that's what I need, for you to tell me which is important. I mean Kettler keeps talking and talking and I take notes and I underline it in the book, and when a test comes I forget my own name." He plunked down opposite, the kitchen chair squeaked in protest.

From the front room came new sounds, Amos and Andy, her father's favorite show. He found it humorous when *they* argued, that silly affectation of Andy's, ". . . ah-wah, ah-wah, ah-wah . . ." Roars of laughter from the audience.

"Okay, here's what you need to do," she began. "Mr. Kettler says it will be an essay test — that means he's only going to ask two or three questions and you're expected to write pages on each one. Something like: explain the attitude of the Copperheads."

The big face crumpled. "*Ohmygawsh!* Who were the Copperheads?"

"They were the northerners who didn't want to fight the South. Wait a minute —" she found the page in the book and dog-eared it. "Read that later, it's the kind of question he likes. The point is, if you don't know the answer, write what you do know, write all around the edges, put in everything you can think of, just write! Try to fill the

44

blue book if you can. He may forgive you for not knowing one thing if you prove you know a lot of other things, see?"

"I don't know a lot of anything," Ozzie groaned. "My head isn't made for this, Terry. I wish I could just go into the Navy and sort of get started on my life. Only Mom says if I do that I'll learn a lot of bad language and wash a million dishes."

"And she's hundred per cent right, m'boy." Henry stood in the doorway, blinking as if the lights were too bright. He wandered over to the refrigerator. "Got a touch of indigestion, do we have any milk?" He brought forth a dish of yesterday's custard and a piece of celery left over from Sunday's stuffing. It was too limp to crunch, but he seemed to relish it as he went on, in that high authoritative tone. "Yes, indeedy, you will peel bushels of potatoes, mop acres of floor, wash enough dishes to fill a boxcar. That's how we traveled, you know, by boxcar: *Forty hommes and eight chevaux.* Except when the *chevaux* were mules, the *hommes* were lucky to get out alive."

Ozzie looked at Terry and grinned. They had heard all this many times.

"Y'see, there wasn't no water on those boxcars. Mules are crazy anyway, but you get a thirsty mule you got a real sit-chee-

45

ation. When the train stopped you were supposed to take 'em down to the water tank. Big round tank about yea high, hundreds of mules ahead of you, find yourself faced with a wall of mule rumps."

You must let your father tell his war stories, it's his catharsis.

"Well, sir, I took two of the beasts by the halter and tried to lead 'em to the tank, at which point" — big gulp of pudding — "they smelled that water and took off like a couple of Mack trucks. You don't hold back a mule, son, don't even try. When we get to the tank, one heads east, the other goes westward-*ho!* Which leaves me plastered smack-dab up against the backside of a whole new mule."

That I never was even introduced to. Ozzie's lips moved with the words, he laughed his big chesty guffaw right on cue.

As always, Terry was embarrassed when her father had to be humored in front of others, even a friend like Oz. Quickly before he could start another story she said, "Well, thank goodness those days are over. As they say, it was a war to end all wars. We'll never have to go through that again."

Her father stared at her as if he had just noticed she was in the room. "You'll never

46

have to go through what again? Miss Smarty, what the devil have you ever been through?"

"I just meant the country," she stammered.

"Yeah," Ozzie jumped to her defense. "President Roosevelt won't get us mixed up in anything bad."

"Oh, you think so? Well, don't bet your piggy bank, boy." Henry Miller's face sagged into a sneer. "Old F.D.Rooster is dying to get us into the fight."

"You think so, sir? Do you think we'll have to go whop the Germans again? I mean, I kind of wish we would. It must have been pretty exciting, all those big guns shooting —"

Aghast, Terry made small signals, *don't go on with that.* Oz had never wandered off into questions about guns.

He didn't notice her warnings. "How about it, I bet you fired some of them howitzers, didn't you, sir?"

As if the boy had turned into a stranger, Miller eyed him coldly. "There were no guns in my sector." Stiffly he turned and went off down the hall, the new Christmas slippers going *queep queep* on the parquet.

Oz frowned at Terry. "Why are you giving

47

me dirty looks, for pete-sake?"

"I wanted you to shut up about guns. Don't you know my father was shell-shocked?"

"No!"

"Yes. He was a complete wreck. My mother was working for the Red Cross at the docks in New Jersey. He was in the hospital there, she found him wandering around on the street, shaking like he had a high fever. She took him back to the hospital and took care of him for weeks until he began to get over it. That's when they got married. Only it was a long time, she said, before he could talk about what happened over there, and then only the mules. Never guns."

"But he just said there weren't any."

"Oz! He was in the artillery. The Argonne was a nine-day bombardment that never stopped. That's when he lost most of his hair. He used to have hair as thick as mine."

The boy heaved a long breath. "I heard about them trenches, the mud and all. That's why I'd join the Navy before I let 'em draft me."

"Draft? Oh, for heavensake, you don't have to worry about that for a couple of years yet."

"Heck you say. The paper told how they

might lower the age to nineteen. I'll be nineteen in July."

"Well, they'll defer you if you're in college, so let's get back to the books."

But now as they settled at the table there was an uncomfortable presence in the room, a ghost of things to come. From the distance an organ was playing the theme song from *One Man's Family.*

THREE

A travesty. In English class the word had been part of a vocabulary assignment which Miss Baker had illustrated by references to Charlie Chaplin. A parody, she said. Now the term came home to Terry with a bang of comprehension. It was bloodred fingernails an inch long, huge junk earrings, fake eyelashes and heavy lipstick at ten o'clock in the morning. More than that, it was the smile, like a mask, ingratiating and nervous and insincere.

"What's the matter, hon? Don't you like it?"

"Uh — not much." Rigid in the grip of draped green sateen, Terry stretched her face into a broad phony apologetic grin, feeling her whole childhood come ajar. After all these years when she had thought of Fran Berensen as "Dixie's mother" or as the neighbors put it, "that poor woman," it was a revelation to discover a human being

50

desperately playing a role. *If I get a job will I have to pretend to be somebody else all day?*

"How about the dotted Swiss?" Eager hands held up another prom gown. "What's the matter, Terry, you look kinda rocky, hon. Need a glass of water?"

I need to breathe. "I'm fine, really. I just came off without any breakfast." She had wanted to do this day's shopping alone. "Do you have anything a little more — uh — grown up? This is for college next fall."

"Of course. I've got several lovely gowns." Gathering the puffy-sleeved monstrosities from the rack, Fran rushed from the fitting room.

Putting on her best show, as if I were Mother, falling all over herself to please me — goshsake, I'm only a kid, I'm Dixie's friend, remember?

Of course, it was the checkbook she was trying to please. These sales clerks worked on a commission, just as her father did. Terry wondered what he was like out there on the road, did he have to put on a face and crawl to the customers? It must leave a bitter taste, she thought, beginning to understand why he retreated behind the *Post Dispatch* every night when he came home. You would need to get your bearings again, maybe just yell at people for a change. She warmed toward him in sudden sympathy. Must be a terrible responsibility to put food on the table for a family. Maybe it was too much of a burden, maybe that's why there seemed to be cracks opening up, moments when there was a kind of desperation in his bleak eyes. *What would we do if he left us? How could I ever make enough money to be sure Mother always had her pork tenderloin and sweetbreads and soft cheese and —*

Her stomach growled. She'd had no appetite for Grapenuts this morning. Waking to a silent house, she remembered it was her father's Saturday to drive the Southern Illinois route, where minor manufacturers bought small amounts of printer's ink for their cookie boxes and flour sacks, oat meal, sugar, whatever needed a label printed in World Exposition Inks. Nickel-and-dime stuff, he called it, but it had bought tea for Mother's breakfast during the dark days.

When Terry had gone to her room this morning with a tray, there had been only a slight stir under the sheets, a shake of the tousled blond hair. "I don't really want a thing, thank you, dear."

"Then I'm going downtown shopping. There's that Valentine's Day sale at Sonnenfeld's."

"Ummm . . . you go on, darling. Fran . . . take good care of you."

A friendship that went back years, it was a strange bond between the young wife and the beleaguered Jewish mother. At first it had just been Hamilton *noblesse,* with Marjorie Miller instructing the bridge club: "Don't you dare sneer at Mrs. Berensen for going out to work. She's a very admirable person." Then, during Phin's bout with polio, their acquaintance had deepened into an unlikely affection, Fran the small dark product of thousands of years of persecution and Marjorie the light, ornamental scion of the aristocracy that had done the persecuting. Somehow they respected each other beyond their differences.

"I think your mom will like this one." Fran was back with an armload of yellow taffeta.

Dutifully, Terry slipped into it, though she hated taffeta for its rustle and wrinkle and those wet spots that show so darkly. "I think it's a little too tight under the arms."

"Oh, sure, that piano-thing. I forgot. Your mother told me the sleeves on your clothes have to be loose. I'm so sorry she didn't feel well enough to come along today."

"She'll be fine with whatever we pick,"

Terry assured her from the depths of the taffeta. Once she got it off she sighed with relief to be rid of the heavy folds. "Anyway, this is not my recital dress. I have to look for one of those too. It was just an idea I had, to try on a few evening gowns. I mean, there will be dances off at school." *If I go. It's foolish to buy clothes now when I might not go.*

Head cocked, Fran looked her up and down as she stood there in her slip.

"I can't get over you kids. Dixie's wearing a bra now — doesn't need it, she's such a skinnymarink, but she says it gives her clothes a better shape. If you ask me, it's all in her mind." She flashed a grin that was totally real for a minute. "Now you are going to need one, another year or two. Listen, hon, do you mind if I sneak a ciggie?" She dug in the pocket of her tunic, an elaborately embroidered dark maroon silk garment, the newest thing in afternoon wear, according to the Sonnenfeld's ad.

"Those are great earrings," Terry lied fervently.

"Yeah, aren't they swell? But too old for you. I could find you some nice little pearly tear-drops. Are your ears pierced?"

"Gosh no! My dad thinks I'm too young."

"Well, don't rush it. They make your ears

ache, the big ones. But that's all the rage this winter, the gypsy look. We're expected to model all the new fads, you know."

"Fran, I was wondering: do you think I could — not now but next summer — could I get a job here, do you think?" It burst out before Terry thought it through. "I didn't discuss it with Mother yet, but I'd like to make a little money to buy school clothes and all."

"And you'd get a discount too. It makes sense, hon. Who knows, there might be an opening in the shipping department." Fran blew a final thin stream of smoke and stubbed out the butt in an ashtray, then dumped the ashes quickly into a small container which she kept in her pocket. "Why don't we look for that recital dress. Isn't that coming up soon, your trip back to Virginia?"

"Actually, yes." Terry didn't want to think about it. Left alone again in the fitting room she wandered around the small cubicle, glanced behind a screen in the corner and jolted to a stop. It hung there as if it had been waiting for her: wine-red velvet, simple lines, glorious flowing skirt that fell to the ankles straight from a tight bodice — *no straps!* Awestruck, Terry took it into her arms. *Happy Valentine's Day.* She was halfway into it when Fran came back.

"I hope this one isn't taken?" she said anxiously over her shoulder.

"Uh — no, I got it out for another customer who — here, hon, you're not doing it right. It goes like this, you have to sort of push it up and hold it while I zip the zipper, but I got to tell you this is way too sophisticated — oh Gawd! It fits you like a glove. Makes you look twenty years old, your mother would skin me alive. I'm sorry, I just can't sell it to you." It cost Fran a lot to say that.

"Maybe I couldn't wear it right now, but next fall there are bound to be formals off at school. Evening receptions."

"Of course there will, but those colleges have pretty strict rules about how to dress. This is way too décolleté for most of 'em. I know girls going to Bryn Mawr and Briar Cliff, and I got to tell you, sweetie —"

"Fran, pleeeeze. How much?"

"Well, it's on sale, a really great price, only twenty-nine-ninety-five. But —"

Terry did some rapid calculations. With her entire February allowance in her pocketbook, plus a few dollars left over from January — "I can manage it," *if I don't eat a candy bar all month.* "I'll pay for it myself, Mother won't even know until I spring it on her later. I'll pick the right time." *And my father will never see it at all.* Staring at herself in the mirror, Terry saw a stranger, full of dignity, maturity, even grace. Slowly she said, "I really . . . need . . . this dress."

Fran's loyalties wavered, but her eyes were doing rapid calculations, of right and wrong and a customer of the future. "Okay, kiddo. Just don't tell your mom I sold it to you. Now let's try to get you fixed up for that recital."

Slipping out of the red velvet reluctantly Terry allowed herself to be clad in a knee-length blue silk sheath with raglin sleeves, plenty of room to reach out to both ends of the piano. "It's very nice. That one you can put on Mother's account and send out to the house. This one, I'll take with me." She gathered the red velvet to her as if it might be snatched away.

Riding home, the big box took up most of the next seat, but the bus wasn't crowded. In fact Terry felt isolated from the known world, in a new place where she made decisions, kept secrets. A wave of panic stirred in her heart, but it was her mother's own fault, not caring enough to get out of bed on this morning when they had planned a day of shopping, the kind of day they used to relish together.

I'm glad she didn't come. She wouldn't have let me buy this gown. Even as she thought it, Terry felt a twinge of guilt. Not very brave, not really ready to go off on her own and darn the consequences. Of course you always knew you would leave home some day, but mostly you expected it to be on the arm of a man. To have to fend for yourself alone — it was a frightening prospect, even as it excited her.

As the bus passed her house, Terry shrank lower, though shades were drawn across the windows of the brick bungalow. At eleven-thirty in the morning Marjorie was probably in the kitchen heating a can of soup for lunch. Saturday, there wouldn't be any soaps on — that was the favorite thing for them in summer days, to listen to *Our Gal Sunday* and *The Romance of Helen Trent, which asks the question: can a woman find love at the age of thirty-five or even beyond.* Terry couldn't imagine what she'd feel like if she was unmarried at thirty-five, didn't want to speculate even.

"End of the line." The bus driver had said it twice, holding the door open.

"Oh, gee, thanks." Terry leaped up and out into the bright cold February afternoon, walking fast for the ramshackle building at the far end of the block. Berensen's old barn looked even more dowdy by day. At the steps she hesitated. Dixie could be merciless, especially about clothes she hadn't designed herself. *But she'll like this dress. She's got to, or* — Or what? An odd thought skidded across her mind: in a few months she and Dixie would be thousands of miles apart, her opinions wouldn't matter. Marching firmly across the porch, she let herself in at the front door, poised to field any criticisms that might come.

"Dix?"

"She's not here." Phin's voice came from afar. "I'm out in the kitchen."

Bravado draining away, Terry trooped down the hall to find him in the big sunny room, his long frame bent over the ironing board. Glancing up from his chore, he took note of the dress box. "You been shopping, too? Sis has gone off to find some new shoes for New York."

"That's great, you need to reward yourself for passing finals. She did pass, didn't she?"

"Squeaked through. I suppose you got all-A's again?" Phin took personal pride in his pupil, having labored mightily when Terry was in the eighth grade to impart the mysteries of Algebra and Geometry.

"They were questions I knew." She dumped the box on a chair and draped her coat over it. "I kind of flunked with Ozzie, though. I was trying to get him through history, the way you did for me and math. But he didn't make it. He read the main question wrong. Kettler asked us to compare the general weaknesses of the North and the South and Oz thought he meant the Generals'. He wrote that Grant was a drunkard and Sherman a mad man and Lee didn't have any. Weaknesses, I mean. He only filled one page of his blue book, so Kettler had to hand him a D-minus, which was really a gift. Last time I saw him, Oz was about to go join the Navy. I don't know how to help somebody study. You were always good at that . . . heavensake, what are you doing?" She suddenly realized it was his Sunday shirt he was toiling over, what he called his "white-polite".

"I've got a meeting with some of the faculty down at the University. I want to step up my program and get my MA in one year. I figured I should look neat and studious and so forth."

"Well let me!" She took the iron from him. "You're putting in wrinkles that weren't even there to begin with."

"Much obliged. These electric irons don't disperse heat as well as the old flatirons you warmed up on top the stove."

"So what's the big hurry, to get the degree? Won't you be carrying a heavy lot of courses?"

"I can handle it, that's what I've got to convince them. Point is, I ought not to waste any more time in school at all. I should be out there getting a job. Mom has been working so hard for so long, it's my turn now. But she won't hear of it. She says if I get the MA it will mean a better position and more money eventually, and she's right, of course. Also, the Fellowship will pay all my tuition, I'd be crazy to turn that down. But we need so many things, like a new roof and a new furnace, not to mention a refrigerator." He was squatting in front of the icebox, peering in with a frown. "The ice man missed us again. We ate up all the leftovers for dinner last night. I've got to go to the store this afternoon. But there's still some bacon and eggs. How about a little breakfast for lunch?"

"Swell. I'll fix it. I really don't want to go home yet." Terry hung the shirt on a hanger and went to turn the stove on under the black iron skillet. "Phin, you always knew you wanted to be a mathematician. But what would you do if your mom had this notion you should be something else, like, for instance, an actor? Go on stage and be famous — suppose she had her heart set on it? What could you do? What would you tell her?"

He hitched a hip on the oak table and considered the problem. When Phin thought, he did it the way other people scrub floors, on his knees mentally, going over every inch until he was satisfied he'd got in all the corners. Of course he was familiar with her problem; he and Dixie had lived with her miseries for years.

"I reckon," he said, "I would give it a try, but it wouldn't work. I could memorize *Hamlet,* but that wouldn't make me Maurice Evans. You need some extra dimension to turn yourself into a character and make it stick. I don't have that. Which would become obvious to my mom, in time, and she would back off. I remember once she thought I'd be a basketball player. Took me to games. 'See how everybody claps when you make a basket?' Of course the polio finished that. You can't argue with a leg that's a half-inch short."

"My mother could. She pretends my fingers are as long as Bach's — they say he could span twelve keys. His *Art of the Fugue* is almost impossible to play. Grieg's *Concerto* isn't that bad, but it's still way over my head. And what worries me is, those people at the audition, the head of the Music Department and all, they're going to know I'm floundering around. They're not going to let me into their program my freshman year. I can't bear what that will do to Mother."

"Yeah. You hate to fail your parents." He dug into the heap of scrambled eggs and bacon. "When's this thing coming up?"

"Easter vacation. We're going to my grandmother's house in Richmond and drive from there over to good old Glow-cester College."

"You better start calling it 'Gloster'," he advised.

"I don't want to call it anything." Tasting the bacon she caught a faint rancid flavor. "It's not just Mother, the whole Hamilton family honor is riding on me. They even sent us money for the plane trip." Picking up the plates to take them to the sink, she said, "Phin, what holds an airplane up?"

"Aerodynamics," he said. "Is that your audition dress in the box?"

"Aero-what?"

"It's the principle of flight. The dynamics of air flowing with such speed under the wings that there's enough pressure to lift the plane off the ground. Kind of like a kite."

A swift vision raced across her mind, of the time when her father had created a kite out of some brown wrapping paper and a few thin dowels. He had showed her how to hold the sticks together while he connected them with strings and folded the paper over, while she made a long tail out of knotted rags. They had flown it together out on the big hill, where a new block of houses was now going up. She still remembered screaming with delight as it swooped and righted itself and almost hit a tree, but he jerked the string and the kite sailed on. A wonderful day . . .

She shook it off. "Okay, but how do they get the plane down again?" The kite had eventually done a nose-dive into the ground.

"They cut back the engine, reduce the speed and set it down."

"How do they keep it from crashing?"

Phin was folding the ironing board. "That's the principle of aero-dy*land*ics. They tilt the flaps on the wings and the plane floats to earth." He floated the clumsy thing out of the kitchen onto the back porch.

"My brother being weird again?" Dixie had appeared in the doorway, triumphant with parcels, and a hatbox which she took to the table as if it were gold. "I'm glad you're both here to witness the birth of my new personality." Taking forth a turban she thrust her long hair up under it, stuffing all the ends out of sight, leaving her bony face framed in folds of lavender and purple silk.

Phin considered her critically. "Your new personality going to ride a camel across the desert?"

"I knew you'd scoff," she said airily, "but I intend to make a coat like a caftan and start a new trend."

"New York will be at your feet." He glanced at her narrow black pumps with the extreme high heels. "Better buy some sturdier shoes."

Terry was still staring, aware of a dawning skepticism. The turban was not really becoming, it was too soft and beguiling for Dixie's tough personality. It would make people turn and look, but not in admiration. They might even snicker behind her back. To realize such a thing was so close to blasphemy she was speechless.

The elfin face broke into a grin. "You're

gawking at me as if I were a stranger. You've paid me the ultimate compliment. That's just what I hoped to achieve, a whole new image."

"Oh, you've done that," Terry managed. A sudden gust of wind took the house in its teeth for a brief shake. No winter blast, this felt like spring. Glancing out the window, Terry saw a spiraling of dead leaves, two dish towels flapping madly on the line.

"That looks like the season is turning," Dixie smiled, a secret look. "I'd be on the next train out of here if I had the money."

Phin dug in a pocket. "Will three bucks and forty-six cents help?"

Terry shook her head. "Don't look at me. I spent my whole February allowance in your mother's department at Sonnenfelds this morning."

They turned as one to look at the dress box on the chair.

Dixie's face grew avid with curiosity, eyes glittering, tone imperious. "Show!"

"Uh — it needs some alteration, it's too long and —"

"And the dog ate your homework. Quit stalling. Open it up or I will."

Fumbling the string, Terry undid the knot and lifted the dress out, letting it fall loose in a rush of shapeless red velvet. "It looks better on."

Dixie seized it and held it against herself. "My God, it's strapless."

Terry marveled at how easily some people can swear. She had tried it, in private, but "God" and "damn" just didn't come out right.

Phin was inspecting the dress, as always interested in mechanics. "What holds it up?"

"This scrim." His sister turned the bodice inside-out. "See how stiff that is? Good thing, too, she might sneeze and there goes the ball game! Of course it's way too old for you." Dixie handed it back. "Put it on."

Terry felt the heat flood into her face and then it was replaced by a strange boldness. "No, I think I won't. I will wait until until I get old — really old — before I model it for you." Turning to Phin she said, "Can I please hang this in your closet for a few days? As soon as Mother's out of the house I'll find a place to hide it at home. I want to spring it on her at the right moment."

"Good idea," he agreed, and his eyes were telegraphing a kind of congratulation, while Dixie had pinked up under her swarthy skin.

With a flip of the chin, she said, "Well, all I meant was, you never had much practice being somebody you're not. It takes more than a dress, it takes *hutspah*."

"Or, as we goys say, 'nerve.'" Terry marched off leaving the kitchen unusually silent.

In the scrambled bedroom that led to the sun porch she picked her way across to Phin's closet, careful not to bump into the odds and ends. He had rigged up some gadget to demonstrate something, a rod hung with steel balls, and on the chair was a tall stack of *Popular Science,* while the wall was covered with a map of the heavens. In the closet, above a scattering of tennis shoes, all with holes in the soles, she found a place to hang the gown behind his second-best suit, a brown-wool garment she had never seen him wear.

As she threaded her way back past the scuffed old dresser, she saw a framed photo, a studio portrait of a young woman. Phin's new girl-friend that Dixie had mentioned? For a minute she studied it, wondering what qualities in a woman would attract a man like Phin. The lady wasn't beautiful, but she looked totally at ease with herself, no special styling to the long dark hair, no plucked eyebrows or false lip line, no jewelry. In that quiet face the main ingredient was determination.

An odd feeling surprised Terry — she was

jealous. She envied that girl her certainty, her poise. Whoever she was or would become, it was certain that she would never be a travesty.

FOUR

Disruption in French 301. One minute they were gabbling in horrible accents about "le homework" and the next, Miss Wolsey was tapping her staff, a souvenir of her trip to Paris years ago. A silly thing with ribbons only to be used on special occasions, it brought them to a startled silence.

"Attendez, s'il vous plait." Her version of the language was heavily laden with a Missouri Ozark twang. A great pear-shaped woman in an acre of beaded black silk, she was proud to have acquired a genuine refugee. "Today we welcome a new student to our school who comes to us from Austria by way of Switzerland and France and — where did you finally depart from, Rudi?"

"Lisbon," the boy said. A short, stocky kid, rigid hip and shoulder like a toy soldier with greased black hair slicked across his pale brow, he wore a double-breasted dark wool suit buttoned almost to his stiff collar and red bow tie.

"Looks like somebody cut his throat this morning," Dixie muttered in Terry's ear.

"Class, this is Rudi Klein. I'm sure you will make him feel welcome in his new home." She clapped her tiny plump hands, making almost no sound. Dutifully, the class applauded. Rudi bowed from the hips like a wind-up doll. Something about the way he carried himself exuded a superiority that insulated him from concern as to what these lowly Americans might think.

"Rudi, do tell us about your thrilling escape across the Alps," Miss Wolsey babbled.

"Vas not so thr-r-rillink," he rolled the "r" at her with a little sneer. "Vas more like smellink. Ve hide in a tr-r-rash tr-r-ruck down under garbage where cr-r-rossing guards wouldn't look. Aftervard, ve had to the clothes throw avay. But vas vort it, ve stayed alive." In spite of the heavy accent his English was careless and fluent.

"From there you went on to Paris, I understand." She invested the word with a kind of holiness. "How did you manage to elude the occupation forces?"

With a slight smirk Rudi launched into a spate of French that was so rapid and colloquial nobody in the room understood it, including Miss Wolsey.

"You say you walked . . . ?"

"Non, non, non. Not 'march'," he said, "marché. Le market, ve vorked selling le fromage vermouillé."

"Cheese," she explained to the class. "Vermilion . . . ?"

"Vormy," he corrected her with a wicked grin. "Mit vorms crawling, werry nutritious, vorms."

"French class just got a little more interesting," Dixie observed *sotto voce*. Aloud she asked, "Do they persecute Jews there the way they do in Germany?"

"Paris iss in Germany now, ja?" His contempt for them all was growing more evident. Miss Wolsey blushed for him.

"And then your family went on to Portugal?"

"The papa and mama stay behind to join Underground. Meinself vas sent on to Bordeaux vere I am in fishing boat, hide in hold vith fish all the vay to Bilbao, more stink." He spoke the word blandly, aware that it was raw to them. Even the boys never dared used vulgarities except in secret snickers in their locker room.

Growing redder by the minute, Miss Wolsey spouted some clichés about the horrible Nazis and the courage it took to fight them (presumably to run away from them too) and ended by saying they were all lucky to have Rudi as a classmate, clapping her little hands again. The rest of the class joined in without enthusiasm and Rudi took a seat in the front row.

Off in the rear, Dixie groaned privately, "The little brat speaks three languages, he's going to make us all look stupid."

"I'll bet they give him the title role in Cyrano," Terry said. She had already been chosen to play Roxanne in the excerpt from the play that they would perform in April. "I'll look like his mother."

As the class gathered their written homework and passed it along the rows, Rudi leafed through his new copy of *Columba,* scanning it the way other kids read the funnies. Pages, Terry thought, that had cost her hours of study to translate. It produced a kind of revelation, that there really were people who spoke and read French the way she did English, without effort. It suddenly made France a thousand miles closer, a lot more real than the stack of postcards which Miss Wolsey always passed around at the beginning of the year, the Eiffel Tower, Notre Dame Cathedral, the Arc de Triomphe, the Louvre, all in flat black-and-white photography and remember the spelling, there will be a quiz. Now, Paris was a montage of vivid pictures of wormy cheese and smelly garbage trucks and people furtively stealing around the city at night, in the sewers, like Jean Valjean or somebody. Hiding in fear that armed men would snatch them and — what? What could they do to a fourteen-year-old boy? Her imagination boggled.

About then they became aware of the hall monitor, hanging around the doorway half-in and half-out. When Miss Wolsey noticed him he said loudly, "Terry Miller is wanted in the office." Making it sound as if there were a price on her head.

By the time she had gathered her books and followed him out he was already twenty yards down the hall. His acne-studded cheeks worked as he chewed a wad of gum that almost interfered with his smirk. "Your father is here."

And now she writhed with a whole new set of anxieties. He had come to tell her goodby, he was leaving them forever. Or he had found the red velvet evening gown — she had transferred it to her brand-new college trunk in the attic, nothing else up there, no reason for anyone to snoop around. Why would he go looking in her luggage? Why was he even home? He had left early for his northeast route, around Hannibal. He should be a hundred miles away. *Whatever the matter is, it's probably my fault.*

Nervous, she edged into the office aware of Henry Miller standing at the window looking out at the raw February sky. Hands in the pockets of the heavy black wool coat, he was breathing in big sighs as if he had been running. The principal came to greet her with an arm around her shoulders.

"Don't be scared, Terry, everything is going to be all right."

Which frightened her more than anything he could have said. Her father swung around and glanced at his watch. "At last. Well, hurry on, girl, get your coat."

"But what — ?"

Mr. Cullenden was a gangly raw-boned man with Buddy Ebsen ears and eyes that had seen much. "Your mom had a little mishap, she fainted and your neighbor called an ambulance. They took her to the hospital just to look her over. I'm sure it was just a precaution, she'll be fine. Now you go along with your dad, you're excused for the day."

She tossed him a quick "Thank you," as she followed her father out and down the hall. He was striding along, talking to himself in a mutter.

". . . always seem to happen when I have an important . . . just had a feeling . . ."

"How did you learn about it?" Panting, she caught up.

"Called home, just happened to call home, had a feeling . . . and I needed her to find me an address in Palmyra, so of course there's no answer . . . could have gone out, but I had this feeling. Called Maybell Queal and she went over and found her on the floor, couldn't get her to wake up, so she called the ambulance. Do you know how much an ambulance costs?" The question broke from him like a yelp of pain.

Terry veered off to go to her locker. When he realized she wasn't with him, he came to a halt. "Well, what are you lollygagging around for?"

"I need to get my coat."

"Always something. What was it, what did you say, what went on there at breakfast to make her so upset she passed out?"

Terry's nerves spasmed. "Mother was still asleep in bed when I left for school. I didn't even see her." *More likely you two had a fight last night and it made her sick.* She climbed into the old Dodge, square and sturdy like its owner.

"It's this whole audition thing," he was saying. "All the grief you been giving her over which damned piano piece to play." Henry seldom used profanity, and never when Marjorie was around, but it was in his blood. His father was a crude old man. The one time they had visited the farm up in Iowa, Gramps had used a wealth of words that were new to her, most of them to do with the bodily functions of the farm animals. Terry remembered her mother's mouth drawn into a tight knot. She understood that it was the nature of the Millers to be vulgar, and like her mother, she forgave it. But she wished he wouldn't speak that way to her, as if she weren't worth being treated politely. "You didn't even come home after school yesterday, you shoulda seen her, she was out of her mind!"

That's not true. Mother knew I had a volleyball game I couldn't get out of. "I have to take part in intramural sports to make the honor roll. She understood that."

"Don't you talk back to me, missy, you're not too big for a touch of my belt." He threw the car in gear and they rocketed out of the school parking lot. With a wild swipe of the wheel he swerved around a streetcar that was discharging passengers.

Ohmygosh, he could get a ticket for that.

Phin would never let her jerk the gears around like this. He had made her practice for hours, driving about the neighborhood in his rattletrap jalopy that he called The Heap, looking off out the window while she narrowly missed the odd cat or parked bicycle. He wouldn't take her to get her license until the rhythms of clutch and break were smooth and effortless.

Henry put the wheel over in a sudden left turn that made the oncoming cars honk furiously. They shot into St. Luke's parking lot and braked so hard she lurched forward onto the dashboard. "When we get in there you make sure you convince her this audition-crap is coming off just dandy." Piling out of the car, jerking his coat around him. "Tell her you're going home and practice your head off, you got that? Going to be a lulu of a concert arteest." The scorn in the words telegraphed the news: that her father was well aware she had no talent.

It was a shocker to Terry. He had always gone along with her mother's illusions, forked out money for the music lessons, even though they cost two dollars a session. Putting on an act all this time — why? To avoid arguments? Because he was trapped in a responsibility, a kind of life he never wanted? Maybe he knew he was a travesty and it was killing him. The questions reeled through her mind as she trailed him into the hospital.

Through the back door they stepped into a world of smells, heavy chemical aromas and earthier drifts of bodily odors — Terry's mind shut down. She didn't see people slumped in wheelchairs with a bandaged leg propped up or anyone in a tattered robe being led to the bathroom by a crisp antiseptic nurse. In the elevator there was no orderly carrying a tray of repulsive instruments of torture, and on the fourth floor no group of doctors smelling of ether, dangling stethoscopes around their necks. At one doorway a man in a white coat waited, gold-rimmed glasses and gray hair combed across the bald spot.

". . . going to be fine . . . slight concussion from the fall, nothing serious, but we want to keep her a few days, run some tests . . ."

"How many days is a 'few'?" Henry Miller was going on about the cost of a private room, while Terry slipped past.

"There's my sweetheart." From the bed Marjorie beckoned to her, drew her down for a quick kiss. "Don't be nervous, dear, I'm perfectly fine. Sorry I gave you all a scare. Just a touch of vertigo. Maybell sort of panicked, I'm afraid." But there was a bruise on her forehead that shone dark against the pale, pale skin. When Terry hugged her, the shoulder blades were fragile as match sticks under the blue hospital gown.

I've got to bring her a pretty nightie, she should always look pretty.

". . . school, honey?"

"Mr. Cullenden excused me. Don't worry, I'll get the assignments from Dixie and do my homework . . ."

"Mainly, she's going to use this afternoon to practice the d-d-the piano." Henry Miller went around the far side of the bed to plant a quick kiss on the pallid cheek. "You feeling better, toots?"

The silly nickname brought tears welling. Terry turned away fast. Her father used to call her mother "Toots" in the happy days before the Depression. There had been a ragtime song, *"Toot-toot-tootsie Goodby."* He hadn't minded it all so much then, having a family, being tied to a job. He was manager of sales in those days. But when the layoffs began, the company let a flock of travelers go and made him take to the road. Turned him into a travesty.

". . . silly, them keeping me here over

night. All because I neglected to eat enough lately, haven't been getting my spinach." Marjorie made a little face. "I will immediately correct that."

Miller nodded grimly. "And we'll just change a few more things while we're at it. From now on, you are going to rest and let us do the chores. We don't need to have this happen again."

"I can do the cooking," Terry offered, *and maybe get out of a few scales.*

"No, you will not," he snapped. "I'll take charge of the kitchen. I've done plenty of k.p. in my day, that ought to be good for something now. Your mother will be the sergeant and I'll be the dogface." He gave Marjorie a mock salute that made her giggle.

Now it came more clearly to Terry, why he was so crusty. This was his fault. They'd had one of their arguments and this was his way of apologizing. Phin had told her once that his folks had spent most of their time yelling and apologizing. They'd actually gone to a movie the night before his dad walked out forever. A wave of warmth broke over Terry — room hot, stifling — needed fresh air.

"Darling, what's the matter?" A mother's instinct.

"It's nothing. This awful place — I think

I'll walk around a little."

"Henry, take the child home. We don't need two of us with the tizzies. Go to the piano, dear, practice some Hanon, it's wonderfully stabilizing."

When the cold clean spring breeze hit her, as they walked back across the parking lot Terry took a deep breath to cleanse the odors of sickness from her lungs. It gave her a nudge of guilt. Embarrassed, she said, "It's nice that they are taking such good care of Mother."

"Oh yeah, real nice of them at fifteen simoleans a day. Which doesn't include the doctor's bill, we'll be helping him pay for his big fat house out in Ladue Village. Real nice of him to look in on her tonight, at five bucks a peek."

So much? Terry was appalled.

". . . get ready for this damned audition . . ." he was still raving, half to her and half to himself.

"I wish," she began cautiously, "I wish I could talk her out of it. I don't think I'm good enough to make an impression on the music director anyway."

"You can say that again," he growled. "Well, forget it. I did my best to talk some sense into her last night: I told her, what difference if the girl gets into the program this year or next? But Marjorie wants to impress those got-rocks people in Richmond, show them what a hot-shot pee-anist you are, so that's what you're gonna be." Yanking the car over, he made a wild turn into the Loop and parked behind the market, backing and jockeying the big Dodge into a tight spot.

Terry started to get out, but he made a short negative gesture. "You stay put. I'll get the grub, I will cook it. I'll take care of the kitchen. You, young lady, will play the God-damned piano."

Swallowing hard, she felt her face turning red with shame, at the tone of his voice, at the profane words. Fed up with all the polite talk, his patience was coming undone. It frightened her. There was a kind of desperation in it.

It's the money. He's scared of not being able to pay the bills. Of course she had known that for years, but now it became an ominous reality. *If I could help, if I could bring in some pay from a job or something . . .* Something commercial, like Dixie's designing clothes or Ozzie playing football. With a pang she suddenly missed the big booby. By now he was off at some Naval training camp in Florida, another piece of her life flown away. In a world of frustration she sat amid the afternoon rush, streetcars clanging, people hurrying past on the sidewalk. All of them knew where they were going, what they had to do.

They had to figure it out for themselves. Why can't I?

Then her father was back, lugging two brown grocery bags which he chucked in the rear seat. Wedging himself and coat behind the steering wheel he labored to get them unparked. Silent now, looking a little calmer, he might be receptive to a suggestion.

"I've been thinking," she said, "I would really like to help out with the bills and stuff. I might be able to get a Saturday job down at Sonnenfeld's . . ."

"Are you out of your head?" He glared at her in such fury, she shrank. "I handle the bills in my house, I, me, I've been doing it ever since you were still drooling in your oatmeal, my girl. I can manage just fine. You stick to your Beethoven, that's your job."

At home, he wouldn't let her carry either sack, took them both into the kitchen and dumped them on the table. Strange purchases, a piece of mutton, a big gross cabbage.

Mother never buys coarse foods, the odor

makes her ill, she says.

Filling the stew pan with water, he dumped the meat in — hadn't even taken off his coat. Sliced a slab off the cabbage and added it, chopped a big onion into quarters and threw them in, dowsed it all with salt, put a lid on and stomped out of the kitchen with a sort of grim satisfaction. As if he had won a victory over spoon bread and scalloped potatoes and veal birds.

Terry put away the rest of the groceries, a bag of coffee, but no tea for her mother — they were almost out of tea, and Marjorie claimed coffee was bad for you. In a white package of butcher wrap she found a great wedge of yellow rat cheese. She broke off a chunk — the taste was blunt and oily, none of the tang of Cheddar, but she liked it. The pot of stew over on the stove was beginning to bubble, making a smell that was pungent, but it stirred her appetite. Mutton, cabbage and onion, a whole new cuisine. *What kind of seasoning beside salt and pepper?*

An odd thought slanted across her mind. *I'll bet Rudi Klein would know.*

FIVE

The root beer float did it. Like a trigger, it detonated all the questions, the confusion, the shock left over from what had happened last night. In a heat of panic Terry took the straw out and slurped it straight from the glass, the big dollop of ice cream bumping her nose. This sweet favorite drink that she and her mother had always shared since she was knee-high . . . her throat closed, eyes blurred, *I am not going to cry!*

"Here —" Across the marble fountain top Dixie handed her a spoon. "What's the matter, Ter'?"

"Coming down with a cold." Terry snuffled and sucked and struggled with a terrible impulse, to tell, to tell somebody all about it. "The truth is . . ."

"Hey, Dix, could you help me with these boxes?" From the rear of the pharmacy Mr. Dribbin's voice summoned.

"Right away." Laying aside her soda-jerk

apron, Dixie went. It was only her second Saturday working at the drugstore, but already she seemed different. *Not so smart-mouth, not so sure of herself, not quite Dixie. She's already ten steps toward becoming a —*

Back behind the fountain now she put on the apron again. "So, you were saying about the truth?"

"Nothing."

"How's your mother?"

"Came home from the hospital this morning."

Dixie eyed her with a frown. "How long now until you fly off to that audition?"

"Ten days. Don't remind me."

"You still having trouble with the Grieg thing?"

"Going down for the third time."

"Did you try talking to your mother? I know it's not easy, I gave up a long time ago trying to really talk to Mom, but with yours it might work."

"If I even mention how I might not be such a great success on the piano she starts to cry." Can't afford that, certainly not now. Not since last night. She shoved a nickel across the counter and picked up the white sack with her mother's pills in it. The medicine and the *Saturday Evening Post* had already been put on their account.

As she walked home under the hot spring sun, with the crabapples starting to burst their buds and cardinals out house-hunting in the elm trees along Delmar, the world seemed despicably happy. Terry shuddered. In her mind the day was dark as midnight. Or, actually, it was eleven o'clock last night when their lives had taken a change for the worse.

She had wakened to thumpings, rustlings, weighted footsteps in the hallway, back and forth. Slipping out of bed, she had eased her door ajar in time to see her father march past in his pajamas, slippers making the soft *queep queep* sound, arms piled with a stack of underwear, socks, shoes, which he carried into the guest room across the hall. In a few minutes he went back down to get another load — shirts, coats, pants, his shaving kit and alarm clock perched on top.

He's left her. He moved out of their room and left her alone.

The thought still squeezed her heart until it hurt. She'd been ready to demand some answers this morning, but when she'd got up he was gone, even though it was a Saturday. *He doesn't need to work Saturdays any more. The Depression is over, everybody says so. He just wants to get out of the house!* And when she thought of asking her mother what it was all about, her insides twisted into a harsh knot. *NO.* Still asleep, such a fragile creature bundled into the blankets this morning, even though it had been a warm night.

The brick bungalow halfway up the hill took on a haze of misery to her squinted eyes, an aura of disaster as she rushed up the front steps and almost barreled into the postman who was coming down from their porch.

"Sorry, Mr. Letweiler."

"That's okay, Terry, young folks are always in a hurry." A huge Santa Claus of a man, his face was already taking on its summer shade of red. "Glad to see your mama looking better. Just gave her a couple of letters that made her happy."

"Postmarked Virginia, I'll bet."

"One was from Delaware. By the way, where's Queals at? Mail is piling up in their box."

"Oh, sure, I'll get it. Mr. Queal took Maybell with him to a sales convention in Memphis."

"Well, they're lucky. They can go anywhere

they want, got no kids to tie 'em down, just pick up and leave."

The words struck Terry a fresh blow. She stood watching the man lumber off down the street. *He's right, of course. Kids are a nuisance, they're expensive and burdensome and a trial to their parents.* Sometimes it gets too much and men like Isaac Berensen just take off. First they move to the guest room and then they don't come home at all.

Just as well, she thought, *that I've decided not to get married.* It was news to her, she wasn't conscious of having made that choice. As she grew up, she had always secretly hoped there might be somebody who'd want her, in spite of the fact that she wasn't pretty, didn't have a "line" like some girls. Now it was becoming clearer that having a husband was a mixed blessing. The images you dreamed up long ago, of a cozy cottage with a fire place and a front porch and a man, a faceless hero who adores you and so forth, seemed like kid stuff. What marriage really amounted to was a lifelong indenture with the word "obey" prominently featured. She wasn't even sure how those vows pertained to s-e-x, but the whispers around school were disquieting, that a wife must submit to this hateful indignity that men enjoyed, bear his children dutifully. Ever since she'd grown old enough to understand what men and women did together, it was almost impossible to imagine her delicate, dainty mother being required to submit to her father's earthy demands. There must have been a time when they had fun, of a sort, or they wouldn't have got married. How long since the youthful pleasures had faded? Now all that was left was the drudgery of life under difficult circumstances, for better or for worse, the words plain and unequivocal. What a bondage for a proud woman . . .

Thinking such grievous thoughts, it disoriented her to come in the kitchen door and find her mother sitting at the table, smiling. Face pink and healthy — *it's the rouge, she has on too much rouge, it makes her look like a china doll.* Marjorie glanced up from the letter she was reading. No cosmetic could have put the delight in her eyes. "Darling! I have the most wonderful news."

The letter from Delaware — *who lives in Delaware?* Yes, Eudora James, best friend and roommate from those long-ago days at school in Washington, D.C., Gunston Hall, finisher of proper young ladies. In tales of school days, the two girls shared such escapades as making midnight melted-cheese sandwiches on the hot radiators in their room, trying out for the drama club, and walking in the rain down on DuPont Circle. Terry had heard the stories all her life.

". . . wrote her a few weeks ago. She lives on the Eastern Shore, you know, since the Admiral retired, they have a huge estate, he comes from a fine family — Navy all the way back to the Revolution. Anyway, her oldest son, Tommy, is at the Academy now and . . ."

Oh no, oh no!

". . . first classman, a few years older than you, I think he's twenty-one or two. Which is nice, it's good to be introduced into the social scene by a man who knows what he's doing. And believe me, my dear, those middies are taught every amenity in the book, including how to dance divinely. So I told her I wished you could get up to Annapolis at least one weekend this fall, and here it is: your official invitation." She waved the lavender page triumphantly.

"You fixed me up for a blind date?"

"Well, not all that blind. I mean I know

his family. And if he's anything like his father he'll be a handsome young devil. Mostly, I just wanted you to have the experience, the absolute magic of a visit to the Academy. A formal dance in Dahlgren Hall is like stepping back into history — the pageantry, the magnificence of the gowns — Good heavens, we must buy you something suitable!"

Even in full wince at the prospect of being launched into unknown territory, Terry had enough of her wits to recognize an opportunity. "Wait a sec. I have something I have been meaning to show you. Don't move, I'll be right back."

Racing off, she took the stairs two at a time. *Never be a better moment.* Up another flight to the attic, she grabbed the red velvet gown. Back in her room in front of the vanity she dropped her clothes in a pile on the floor, the slip too, bare from the waist up and there was nothing in the mirror to justify the bodice of that glorious dress, but the scrim did its work, made her look as if she had a bosom. Face too pale beside the vivid material — she thought of the secret box of rouge she'd bought, but decided against it. *Let's don't spring too many things on her at once.* Rubbing her cheeks vigorously she got them to pink up a little. Now, the black leather pumps — even in high heels the skirt of the gown brushed the floor. Picking it up in both hands, she went back down-stairs cautiously, wobbling a little on the extra two inches.

At the kitchen door she stopped, watching tensely as her mother's mobile features were shaped and reshaped by a race of emotions: shock, denial, rejection, then slowly turning to acceptance and, in spite of her, delight.

"Terry Miller, you're a knock-out!"

Rushing to hug, she almost stumbled on a lot of red velvet. "I didn't know whether you — well, actually I didn't start out to buy it. You mustn't blame Fran. It was hanging there on the wall in the dressing room and I kind of bullied her into selling it to me. I had enough allowance money and I thought I might need it some day."

"Of course you will!" Marjorie giggled now like a conspirator. "We won't mention it to your father, of course, but in a year or two — well, maybe sooner. I don't know, Annapolis has very strict rules of what's acceptable and proper. It depends on what kind of dance you go to. But whenever it comes, you will need the right accessories. We must get you some long white gloves —

those matrons look at every detail. The boy wants to be proud of his drag. That's what they call their dates, 'drags.' I'll have to fill you in on Annapolis lingo. And customs. Don't ever snatch off a middie's cap and put it on. If you do he's honor-bound to kiss you." She chuckled at some memory. "For now, we need to shorten the dress so you don't trip on it. Get me my sewing basket, dear."

A familiar ritual, standing on the kitchen chair while her mother measured with the long wooden yardstick. Mumbling through the pins in her mouth she went on, "I suspected you had some kind of secret, been very mysterious lately. I thought you and Dixie might be hatching some plot."

"She's the one with the plots. Do you know she's got a job working at Dribbin's Drug Store? Every Saturday. So I wondered, why couldn't I get an after-school job? My grades are better than hers, and next summer I could maybe work full-time."

"At the drugstore? Your dad would have a fit."

"No, I was thinking of the library. You know how I helped out last year with the shelving, which only paid twenty cents an hour. Now they need somebody on the desk, where I'd make more. I really wish I could earn some money, my allowance doesn't stretch all that far and there are things I need to buy." *Like a car of my own.* The thought bounced out of her subconscious like a rubber ball. Terry had been trying to give up all hope of that.

"Well, the library is respectable enough — turn, dear." Her mother's hands tucked and pinned. "But you haven't forgotten you need to practice the piano, harder than ever to be ready for Gloucester next fall."

"If I'm accepted into the music program."

"Oh, I'm sure you will be. And if you need to buy a few more clothes, I have some spondulics tucked away in the cookie jar." Mother had been saving "spondulics" all through the Depression, a few pennies here, a dime there. "All right, now slip out of that and I'll get to work on the hem."

As the dress slithered down into a soft mound around Terry's ankles she was suddenly conscious of her body, bare except for panties.

Marjorie was appraising her with a bemused smile. "You're going to have a lovely figure, my dear. Now go get dressed, your father might decide to come home for lunch." She began to measure a length of red silk thread from her basket, biting it off with sharp little white front teeth.

My father, my father, my father, a wordless misery flooded Terry's head as she got into normal Saturday clothes, gingham shirt and wool skirt. The awful questions kept bubbling up, it was a temptation to take advantage of this rare moment of intimacy to ask them. Going back down to the kitchen she tried to frame an approach.

"Do you really think Dad might come home? I don't understand why he keeps on working so hard, now the Depression is practically over."

"He doesn't trust the President," Marjorie commented.

Two nights ago he had gone on a rant: "The reason we've got this *prosperity* is because old Franklin D. Rooty-toot decided to make weapons by the boatload, give 'em to England, and who's going to foot the bill? You know darn well, it's the taxpayer. We're paying for their war over there, and you mark my word: we'll get dragged into it yet. Mister FDR is itching for a fight. Of course he never seen a front-line trench, with gas creeping across the fields, never got caught in a rolling barrage. What does he care if good men go over there and die in the mud? You want to see a real depression, wait until the houses begin to hang black flags in the windows."

Now, cautiously, Terry said, "Dad seems so — I don't know — miserable. We used to all be sort of happy, didn't we? Mother, why did he move his things down to the guest room?" She hadn't meant to blurt it out like that.

Marjorie's graceful fingers faltered, then went on with the even rhythm of dip and stitch. "He's just being solicitous of me. He was afraid he would disturb me when he gets up early to go to work. I told him I don't mind, but I believe it shocked him, the other day, when I went and fainted. It was just a dizzy spell, but now he's being over-protective."

Terry didn't believe it. What she had decided was that her father couldn't stand the closeness of that master bedroom, with all the windows shut and the heavy aura of Evening in Paris cologne on top of the smells of the medicines and the bedclothes. Even she didn't relish going in there. *Those vows also say: in sickness and in health, but men don't ever think they'll really have to put up with an illness. They expect a woman to be beautiful and — and competent and useful forever.*

"Mother, tell me about men." Another blundering question that hid the real problem troubling her. *Tell me about marriage. Tell me about your marriage, and why it's going wrong and what can we do about it?*

Marjorie's smile was a little wistful. "It's hard to accept the fact that your child is turning into a woman. You wish they'd stay a baby forever. Now, soon, your life will get more complicated as you meet new people off at school, new boys. Those lads will be drawn to you even if they never see you in this dress. You're an attractive girl, my sweet. Maybe not a classic beauty, but your bones are well defined, your eyes are expressive, your whole lively personality is written in your face. It's a good face, my darling, and one that will stand out in a crowd like a diamond in a bowl of peanuts."

Terry was flustered by the compliment.

"So, I guess it's time to warn you," her mother went on slowly, "about the pitfalls of being popular. You must enjoy yourself without being lured into an improper kind of pleasure. Men have persuasive ways, and unfortunately their morals, when they are young, give way to their physical impulses."

There it is — s-e-x. That's all it is, a physical impulse, and because they lure you, all of a sudden you find yourself married. But what's so wonderful about it? Nobody ever says. "So how do you know when you're in love?"

"Hard as it may be, you must try to be objective when you meet a person, decide whether he's a true gentleman, whether his intentions are honorable. It isn't easy to make those judgments, but I'm sure you can do it. You have a good head on you, and I've tried to teach you the right and wrong of things. If you are confused, just go cautiously, don't leap into a serious relationship. There will be plenty of time for that later. These are your days of joy, they shouldn't be too full of problems." *Time for those later, too.* The implication was there.

"When you were my age, did you have a lot of beaux?"

Her mother knotted the thread carefully. "That was a different time. There was a war on. It changes everything. Your emotions are so stretched, the world is so different. You are torn from your normal life and find yourself wearing a Red Cross apron and doing hospital chores you never dreamed. Life hurtles along so fast — Thank God, that's all over. A lot of brave men made it possible for us to live in peace, we'll never go to war again. You'll never have to learn the awful anxiety, the pity, the anguish that you feel for the fallen — it's almost too much to be borne." Her slender body shuddered.

Pity? Is that what drew you and Dad together, you felt such pity you had to marry him, and that's why it's coming apart now?

"But in any day, no matter what the climate is, the main thing is to go slowly with your suitors, don't be too quick to choose."

As you were? You rushed into it because he needed you.

"But how do you know?" She came back to the big question again. "How can you be sure which is the right one?"

"I don't think I can tell you darling." Marjorie put the sewing things back in the box and closed it. "It's a feeling you get. Until that happens, make sure you wait. You do know what I mean by 'wait,' don't you?" A very faint tinge of genuine pink came into the cheeks behind the makeup. "I needn't tell you the disastrous results that can occur when girls give themselves too soon."

Is that what happened? You — you — did you get — and had to — and he felt he had to, and now — no wonder he doesn't like me a lot. The revelation was so devastating, Terry was speechless.

Everything she knew about pregnancy came from *Gone With the Wind*. The book had been forbidden by all their mothers when it came out, so they'd kept it in a locker at school, passing it around furtively and whispering over some of its passages. A bunch of the girls had spent one whole study hall discussing how the word "whore" was pronounced, until Dixie set them straight. "You leave off the 'w'."

"There you go, darling. Tuck this away in the trunk and dream about it. Some day" — Marjorie's misty eyes were a little sad — "some day write to me and tell me how it felt to wear it to a great ball. Don't leave anything out."

"I will, I will. Thank you."

"Now, I think I'll go up and rest a bit." *And there goes my chance to ask her about the one thing I need to know: are they going to break up? Is he likely, some midnight, to just pack his stuff and leave?*

As Terry heard the faltering steps mount the stairs, she shuddered with the question, too dangerous to ask. As if any slight shift in the wind could make the whole house of cards come down.

SIX

Too far, too fast. Nine hundred miles from home — it felt more like nine thousand, as they drove northward through Virginia on a bright April morning. Terry felt as displaced as if she'd landed on another planet — in all her imaginings she had never pictured jungle. Never envisioned such dense forests, towering pine trees that dripped gray moss and wore monarch butterflies as big as flapjacks high in their branches. Below was thick underbrush where the occasional cardinal sprinted like a crimson dart through stands of dogwood with blossoms so large they looked as if they might swallow a small bird whole. The illusion of savagery was very strong.

In fact a deep aura of violence seemed to haunt this corner of the world, memorialized by the rows of bronze historical markers that lined the narrow highway. Battles — she could glimpse a few words as they drove past in her grandmother's big town car. The driver, a uniformed servant, had seen her efforts to read the messages and pulled over at a turn-out.

"Would you like to look at some of these, Miss? This country has the blood of three wars on it," he said, a dignified man with gray hair and skin the color of the bronze itself. "So many battles there's hardly room for all the epitaphs."

"It's fascinating," Terry answered him politely.

"Thank you, Jeremy," her mother added, "but I think we'd better not linger right now. We have an appointment at the school, so let's keep going."

Eyes bright and expectant and nervous, Marjorie had come alive. She'd been a different person from the minute they'd set foot in the big mansion on the outskirts of Richmond last evening. With the family crowding around, smiling faces everywhere, chatter in soft southern cadences, she had taken on color and excitement. A happiness.

Terry, on the other hand, had felt the full weight of the long day heavy on her shoulders. The plane ride had gone fairly well, but it took some concentration to get used to all that space beneath you. At one point she realized: *Mother is scared.* Very pale under the makeup, Marjorie was gripping the arms of her seat.

The flight attendant had noticed, too. Looming over them, she'd asked with genuine concern, "Are you folks feeling a little rocky? Can I bring you a drink of water? Or we have ginger ale if your stomach is queasy." Aged thirty-five or so, a sturdy woman with heavy legs that braced against the bouncing of the plane, she wore on her lapel a pin: RN. Terry wondered what it would be like, to have a job that took you into the sky every day.

And with that came a new thought: *I bet I could learn to fly. Maybe easier than piloting a car — no traffic up here.* But then the plane hit a big invisible pothole and tossed them around. The stewardess, coming back along the aisle, never spilled a drop of the juice she was bringing.

"Just a little turbulence. Don't be concerned. The DC-3 is the safest plane ever built and the pilot is very experienced."

After a while the bucking stopped and the air seemed to smooth out like an ice rink on which they skated smoothly. It was wonderful, to hang 5,000 feet in the air while below, tiny cars crawled along a highway and farm women hung out their washing behind miniature houses. A school with a football field, a graveyard with tiny headstones — it was like a vast diorama.

Later in the afternoon huge thunderheads towered above a range of mountains, while below, the world was dark and wet. Up here they coursed an airy highway between stacks of cumulus clouds that took on hues of gold and red, like castles of great mystery. As the sky grew cool and dark a line from a poem came back to her.

". . . saw the heavens filled with commerce, argosies of magic sails, pilots of the purple twilight gliding down with costly bales." When she'd had to memorize it she'd thought it was pure fantasy.

Then the plane began to settle toward a distant city and she thought of Phin, his buoyant ironing board, and felt a pang of homesickness. Not Marjorie — she was looking forward out the window, her heart in her eyes. This *was* her home, more deeply than any other.

Coming back to the big old mansion on the outskirts of Richmond, she seemed to strengthen and grow brighter. It was a celebration, at which Terry felt herself an outsider. The talk was broadly accented, the food too rich, infused with spices she didn't recognize, swimming in real country butter.

After a few bites she felt sated. Mostly she felt smothered with the hospitality.

"We are all so thrilled, my dear, that you have been granted a special audition . . ." Grandmother Hamilton, powder and perfume and pomade, her white hair piled high, she was the image of the family matriarch, regal, kindly, serene. And Aunt Celestina, so unlike Marjorie, a plump pudding of a woman with a tiny high voice. "You'll love Gloucester, Terry. Your cousin Lindell attended there." And Great Aunt Zenobia, with a nipped nose and a tone like old parchment ". . . been hearing about your good grades . . ."

At one point someone said, "Where's Reddie? I can't imagine what's keeping the boy."

That got Terry's attention. *Ah, yes, don't forget Uncle Redford, darn him and his chopsticks.*

"He went to the Hunt Club meeting this morning, but he should have been home by now."

When he did come, it sparked an instant memory in Terry, surprisingly vivid. A handsome man with flowing mustache, his face was slightly crumpled now by time, a few tiny veins in the Hamilton nose. But the bearing was still debonair, the chestnut hair rampant, cravat a bit askew, dirt on his jodhpurs.

"Sorry to be late, but the new filly spooked at a snake and went down rather hard, had to be led home at a walk. As a hunter she'll never be worth much, too short in the stifle. We probably should sell the poor beast for dog food. Sis! You look ravishing. And who is this lovely young creature?" Seizing Terry's hand he bent and touched it with his lips leaving her speechless and blushing.

After supper, at their urging, she gave them a rendition on the piano, a silly recital piece, "The Rustle of Spring," no unreachable chords, just a lot of flashy arpeggios, show-off music. Then Uncle Redford had insisted they play a duet, dragging out some sheet music, a romantic little sonata which he played rather badly. When they were done he turned and swept her into his arms, kissing her full on the lips.

"We have a true concert artist in the family," he boasted loudly, as if that excused the gesture. It was all she could do to refrain from wiping her mouth. It was a relief when her mother had decreed they must go to bed, rest up for the audition. They had adjoining rooms upstairs, she inheriting a four-poster with a feather mattress that was too soft, felt as if she were being swallowed whole. The tall canopy above gleamed pale in the half-light from the window where the moon was out full all over the gardens. It had been early hours of the morning before she'd dropped off into dreams of keyboards and untested music and an austere professor who held a rule ready to whack her fingers if she missed a note.

Shivering now inside her spring coat, she almost wished she'd brought the tatty old fur, but Marjorie had proclaimed it a disgrace, so she pulled the blue unlined wool around her tight. Grandmother had been more perceptive. As they were leaving the house she'd said, "It's really quite chilly for this time of year. We have so many coats, wouldn't you like to borrow one?"

At which Marjorie had drawn herself up, chin in air, you could almost see a ribbon wreathing around her, like the escutcheon in the genealogy book with the family motto on it: *Nulli Secundus.* "We'll do just fine, thank you."

Looking ahead up the road avidly, now she was searching for the first vestiges of a campus. "That looks like a hockey field. I was the left guard for the Gunston Hall team. Eudora James was our center. Oh, what victories we celebrated. You would have loved Gunston, my dear. It's a shame they don't have a music department."

They began to pass dormitories now, tall brick buildings that looked ancient. The Phoebus Theater was shabby, but elegant as an old opera house. Its marquee bore the big news:

Coming April 30th
Gone With the Wind

Only a year behind the rest of the country. A town hall, a bus depot and a hamburger shop, The Hot Shoppe. *Where do people go to have fun?*

"It sort of looks like a ghost town," Terry said with a shudder.

"Well, it's Easter vacation, dear. Which reminds me, we must be extra appreciative to Professor Wolff for giving up part of his holiday to hold this audition."

Mind your manners. It went unspoken. How could you forget them when you're togged out in blue velvet with a lace collar. The silk sheath with the comfortable raglin sleeves that she'd got from Fran back in February had been deemed too sophisticated. This was an old recital dress that made her feel like somebody out of Dickens. He would have loved these college buildings. That ubiquitous pink brick, square, tall, plain, with rows of unorna-

110

mented windows, they stood on three sides of a small quadrangle of grass, much worn from the feet of students coming and going. On the fourth side a large edifice stood, topped by a low dome.

"That's the Music Auditorium, Miz Marjorie." The chauffeur spoke over his shoulder. "Shall I let you out there?"

"Thank you, Jeremy, that will be fine."

And Terry thought: that's the tone they used when they talked to a slave back in the old days, gracious but impersonal. As they walked away up the broad marble stairs, she glanced back and could picture the man atop a coach, holding the reins to a team of horses. "Do you know Jeremy personally?"

"Oh, certainly. He and his brother have been with our family since he was a young boy. Hurry on, dear."

Voice vibrating with tension now that the moment was upon them, Marjorie was wound tight as a ball of yarn. Yank at one loose string and she might unravel all over the floor, Terry thought, and braced up, determined not to be the cause of it. As they topped the long flight of stairs she paused to look out over the little town. There wasn't much to see, off the main street. In the distance she could make out the roof of the depot, so at least the place was visited by civilization in the form of a train. Then she turned and followed her mother inside under a frieze of sculptures, a bas relief that depicted people dancing, emoting, playing ancient instruments.

Nothing antique about the grand piano. *What a beauty!* Terry marveled in spite of herself at the grace of the big Steinway on the stage at the far end of the vast rotunda. A magnificent room with parquet floors and damask draperies at the walls of windows, she could almost hear echoes of grand balls and huge receptions. A first-class hall for a third-rate town.

Marjorie seemed impressed by it too. "You're going to need to work on your strength of presentation," she murmured. Their foot-steps echoed as they walked across the empty chamber. "This must be where they hold the Music Department's annual reception. Just think, next fall you'll be here, you'll be part of all this."

"I — uh — I don't really feel ready for such a — you know — I mean I wouldn't mind at all waiting 'til my sophomore year to get into the program."

"Nonsense. Time is a precious commodity, we can't afford to waste a minute." Her mother sounded so grim, Terry was startled. "Where's Professor Wolff? Why isn't he here to meet us?"

"We're twenty-five minutes early." Terry wished they had stopped to read a few more bronze markers. *Two miles west of here General Longstreet's forces met a brigade of Federal Cavalry under General John Buford.* That put a perspective on all this.

Marjorie was heading onward, heels clicking on the parquet, heading for a doorway that led to a long corridor broken by regularly spaced doors, all of them closed. Practice rooms. From the near distance came the muted sounds of a flute rendering scales, thin and somehow mournful.

Somebody couldn't get home for the Easter holidays. Next year, that will be me.

At the far end of the hallway a door stood ajar, leaking light and sounds of movement within. As they paused in front of it they could see one of the students in there setting up folding chairs near an upright piano. Dressed in cords and a brown turtleneck sweater, the man was slender and raffish, russet hair hanging about his ears. Then he noticed them and straightened. No student. The youthful face was shadowed by years of hard living. The smile, though, was boyish as he came over to greet them.

"Mrs. Miller and daughter? Yes, come in, how do you do. I'm Max Wolff." He made a short bow that reminded Terry of Rudi Klein. Trace of the same accent, too, though much more refined than Rudi's. "My dear ladies, you are early, how very good of you. Come in and seat yourselves, please."

Marjorie went into the room, moving stiffly, as if she couldn't accept this, the piano with the water stain on top and the yellow keys, pedals that were worn down with years of heavy-footed *fortissimo*. Wolff read her expression perfectly.

"I know it has a humble exterior, Madam, but the action is very good, and I have just tuned it myself. I like to use a practice piano for auditions. In a more elaborate setting there can be a temptation to over-execute."

Or in other words, you can't put on a lot of airs in a little cell of a room on a hacked up piano, you have to stick with the music. Terry understood.

"Will you try the piano stool for height, Miss Miller?"

She slid onto it, uncomfortable in the gushy velvet dress. "It's fine, thank you."

Her mother set the music before her, and then under the insistent eye of Professor

Wolff took a seat. Aware of the silence growing louder in the room by the second, Terry flexed her fingers, took a deep breath and attacked in a crash of sound. Almost as if once removed, she saw her stubby hands clawing at the keyboard, seizing the big chords ineptly, raking them aside and driving on to the next page, trying to dominate the rippling theme, *go at it as hard as you can* . . . After a while a very gentle hand on her shoulder brought her to a halt.

In the small room the vibrations remained, ricocheting around like spent ammunition. She was aware that the professor was talking to her mother — she tried to focus. He was saying he needed a private interview. *Why is he going on with this farce? He knows I played lousy. Yes, Mother, it's a vulgar word, but I was very lousy.*

"Miss Miller, will you come with me, please?"

Resigned, Terry stood up, glanced at Marjorie and froze. *She knows. She really, finally knows the truth, this time she listened. She heard it.* The delicate face was sheet-white under the rouge. Stiffly she made a small motion with her hand: go on, the man's waiting.

Automatically, like a metronome on the

tick, she followed Wolff back along the corridor to the rear of the building where he led her into a narrow cluttered office. Clearing a chair of a pile of exam papers, he held it for her, then hitched a hip onto the desk. Being informal, friendly, the better to impart bad news.

Terry looked him firmly in the face, hadn't realized his eyes were red, actually the tawny color of a fox. Behind him was a bookcase full of sheet music and bound scores, La Traviata, Requiem Mass by J.S.Bach, The Art of the Fugue. On the piano in the corner was a collection of Beethoven's Sonatas. She looked at those hands resting on his knees, long, powerful fingers, he could probably play the Waldstein without dropping a hemi-demi-semi-quaver. Talking to her now . . .

"Thérésa?" Giving the name a continental lilt.

"Yes, sir."

"As I said, when I interview an applicant for the music program, after the audition I always ask a rather embarrassing question. So please don't think I have singled you out. The answers tell me more than any other evaluation I could make. It's this: What did you think of your own performance just now? As a musician, how would you rate

116

yourself?"

Without hesitation she answered. "I think I sounded like a person without a lot of talent trying to play a selection that's way over my head. I know my fingers are too short to handle those big chords. I can play fast and light and do trills pretty well, and if they had let me play Chopin it would have come out better. I don't mind practicing pretty hard —"

He stopped her with that mild gesture of the hand. "This is obvious to me. The amount of effort that went into your rendition of the Grieg must have been monumental. It goes beyond just the urging of a teacher or a parent —"

"My mother never makes me do anything," she told him defensively. "She just — believes so much. She's positive that I will be a concert artist, and I can't bear to disappoint her. She isn't well, she's been under a lot of strain. She's counting on me to be accepted in the music program here next fall. I know that's not a very great reason, but I feel like — I mean I had to — I mean, whatever it takes, you know? I mean it's my *mother.*"

As he sat there listening, something changed about Professor Wolff, no more the fox. With sober consideration he seemed to be rearranging his mind, a world of kindness clouding his eyes. *He's lived a hard life, but he isn't bitter, like Rudi.* The glimpse of truth flashed through her head like a small goldfish in a turbulent pool.

Beginning to nod, as if to himself, he had made up his mind. "I applaud your honesty, and your spirit. The trouble is, you have been poorly taught and badly advised — with all due respect to your esteemed parent. So, for me it is impossible to say at this point what underlying talent you have, because it has been distorted and pressured, forced into unnatural patterns. There may be more of a musical spark than is apparent. I am tempted to see whether I can discover it, but right now I have more students on my fall schedule than I can handle. Every hour of my time is crammed with the needs of advanced musicians who have possibilities of a future on the concert stage. That being said, I want to assure you that there are many things for you to learn beside the keyboard technique that will make your entry into the program worth while."

"You mean — you don't mean —"

"Freshman or not, I am accepting you into the department. That way your mother will be happy and you may even enjoy it at times if you are willing to pursue the classroom work and forego the personal attention I'd like to give. What do you say? Will you be patient about this? Work for me if not with me?"

"It's — it's more than I ever expected." *And I am about to do a silly thing and cry.*

He tucked a handkerchief into her hand. "When you are ready, come down and join us. I will give the lady our good news." He left her alone and she heard him walking back down the hall as she wiped away the tears of reaction and disbelief.

By the time she joined them Wolff was explaining to Marjorie that she had a most remarkable daughter and he was looking forward to having her in his classes. Stunned, confused, she was trying to thank him.

"I have only one request, which I trust you will take in the spirit of an experiment," he went on. "I believe her teacher is on the wrong track. I feel that Thérésa can continue through the summer on her own, scales, exercises and maybe a little Mozart. Concentrate on tone and precision, rather than technical brilliance, yes?" This last question directed to her, with a look so full of warmth it seemed like a brotherly embrace.

Oh yes, she wanted to say, couldn't get the words out.

"Okay!" He spoke the word gaily as if it were an embellishment to be followed by timpani. "I will see you next Fall."

Then they were back out in the sunshine, walking down the long flight of marble stairs to the limousine and the faithful Jeremy.

On the way back to Richmond Terry was gripped by a silent perplexity. She had been sure, as she sat down to talk to the Professor, that he was framing a polite refusal. Whatever had turned him around, she couldn't say, but it had converted them into conspirators. She had a hunch it might lead to other things, but that didn't really have to be faced until next fall. Right now — *At least,* she thought, *Uncle Redford won't have to sell me for dog meat.*

SEVEN

Noblesse oblige. At some point in the past her mother had tried to explain what the words meant, a sort of shimmering ideal that well-born people were honor bound to be noble, kind, strong in adversity. It seemed all too vague for a child to understand, but today it made a certain kind of sense. When Terry glanced sideways at those delicate fingers gripping a handkerchief to death, she had an inkling of the cost in will power of maintaining one's composure under shock. Marjorie stared straight ahead at some fixed point in the future, a future that did not include concert halls or glory, but she didn't turn a hair. No sign of the struggle to accept a whole new world. Wincing with guilt, Terry turned back to the window, staring out at the tangle of forests, the bronze markers erected to fallen heroes. Words came back to her from a textbook:

"The tree of liberty is nourished by the blood of patriots." Who said that? Patrick Henry, or Thomas Jefferson? Grandmother Hamilton would know.

The regal little figure was poised on the steps under the grand portico of the old mansion, waiting to welcome them home. "What happened? Tell me every detail." Then her smile came slightly ajar as she turned to embrace Terry.

"It was — all — very nice." Not much of a liar. Terry's face felt as if it were made of wood, like the balsa from which she had carved a totem pole in Girl Scouts, not very tough wood.

"I think it was most successful," her mother was saying too brightly. "She has been accepted for early entrance into the music program."

"Did you meet the head of the department? Did you like him?" The matriarch directed this at Terry.

"He liked me." She carved a smile. "He said he wanted to find out what I'm capable of," or something like that. "Already gave me an assignment, to start playing Mozart." Some nice easy little pieces.

But she must have sounded convincing, because Grandmother Hamilton relaxed. If not a roaring triumph, there was enough good news to propel the family into a celebration. They liked to put on parties, these Virginians. Roast goose with Smithfield ham on the side, candied yams with marshmallows, a corn pudding with soft-boiled eggs baked inside. The asparagus had been plucked from the back of the property, and one of the house boys had found some fresh mushrooms in the woods. Potato rolls and salad greens were followed by a dessert and topped off with a brief appearance by Great-Grandfather Hamilton.

In his nineties now, they'd told her that "Dadda" was in poor health. But that night he joined them, carried downstairs in his wheelchair by Jeremy and another brown-skinned man of shining pleasant face. Frederick, the companion and nurse saw to the old man's needs, feeding him rum cake and ice cream, respectfully wiping the ancestral chin.

A large, lumpy caricature of a patriarch, scrawny arms and wattled neck, his faded blue eyes peered at Terry hard, and though a bubble was forming at the corner of his toothless mouth, there were traces of a younger face that had been craggy, arrogant, even fearsome. By right of seniority he dominated the scene, the others built a whole conversation around him, supplying his side of it adeptly when there was no visible response.

"Dadda, do you recall the time we found those bones?" Uncle Redford's face was alight with the memory. "We were out there near Turkey Island," he explained to Terry — the others had obviously heard the story many times, smiling in anticipation. "Duck hunting down on the river, we started to set up the blind in a thicket of live oak, and there under the grass were bones scattered around. Human bones, ribs and a femur and a military belt buckle. No way to tell whether he was North or South, probably was wounded in the fighting at Malvern Hill and crawled away to die. We looked all over for a skull, but didn't find one, just those few loose bones."

"What did you do with them?" she asked, realizing she was supposed to cue him.

"Well, we talked it over, didn't we, Dadda? If he was Northern we would have just put him in a hole in the ground. But we decided he might have been one of ours, and if so, he deserved a proper burial. So we went back to the truck — remember that old green International? Well, we had our blind there and our guns, and a case of good Kentucky sour mash. Remember that,

Dadda? Anyway we figured that case was about the right size, so we unloaded the jugs and put in the bones and just drove them over to Seven Pines Cemetery. The caretaker didn't know what to make of it, but he promised he'd see they were taken care of. Never did get our duck that day, but I guess we did our bit for the Bonny Blue Flag."

And slowly a miracle: the old man's gaping mouth broadened into a gummy grin. A murmured cheer went around the table. "Oh, well done, Reddie!" "Dadda remembered!" "Very good, fill his glass again, Frederick."

Even Marjorie was smiling, with infinite sadness. *Noblesse oblige.*

Later, upstairs in her bedroom, Terry felt a wordless need to hold her mother tight, beginning to understand a little of her heritage, this family tree that she was so proud of. There alone, the two of them clung together for long minutes filled with love and relief that the wretched day was over.

Stepping back at last, Marjorie said fervently, "My darling girl, I am very proud of you. You have done marvelously well." Not talking about music, this was much more. "The family loves you, and they're aren't easy to please. Now I feel confident that they'll be happy to see you whenever you want to come here. In time of trial, when I am far away in St. Louis, you can turn to this place as a sanctuary."

Terry hesitated. She wondered, weren't they going to speak of the calamity of that audition?

But her mother had already begun to re-arrange the reality. "I believe you will do beautifully with Professor Wolff, even if he does need a haircut. I won't fault him for that. He behaved like a perfect gentleman, and he's absolutely right about Madame Ar-quette — I never did feel she was good enough for you. We will get some of the Mozart concertos when we get back, he's a lovely composer. Everything is going to work out fine."

If we don't talk any more about the concert stage, Terry warned silently. She said, "You'd better get some sleep now. That plane leaves pretty early in the morning."

"You're right. I'm tired." Moving across to the door of the adjoining room, she opened it. "Oh good, Jeremy remembered. I asked him to leave me a little brandy, to help me nod off." There was a cut-glass decanter on the table beside the bed. "Sleep well, dearest. We'll talk more tomorrow."

But not about a career in music, no more of that. Terry shivered as she got into her flannel nightgown. With sundown came chilly drafts in the old house. Crossing the Persian carpet that had once been opulent, she closed the casement window, then stood looking down at the garden. Under the silver gloss of moonlight it had a shimmering loveliness, like a scene out of a fairy tale. This whole place should begin with "once upon a time."

Or maybe "there once was a mysterious old house," which right now was settling for the night, full of creaks and poppings. And footsteps . . . from out in the hall came a shuffling sound, then the knob of her door turned an inch at a time. Terry stood frozen as it opened enough to let Uncle Redford poke in his head.

"Ah, good, you're still up. I saw the light under your door." He slipped in quickly, a rakish figure in a black silk robe, his light hair tousled. He was holding up a bottle and two glasses, cleverly clutched in one hand. "I thought you might like a nightcap."

"Uh — thank you, but Mother doesn't allow me to drink spirits."

"Ah, dear sis, I love her to death, but she's a trifle conservative. I doubt if she realizes how mature you are. Quite old enough to partake of a bit of champagne." Deftly he poured the golden liquid into the glasses — *straight out of a Charles Boyer movie,* Terry thought fleetingly. "Every girl comes differently to that moment when she becomes a woman." He invested the word with full ramification, his hazel eyes glinting in the glow of the bedside lamp as he advanced toward her.

Terry took a couple of steps backward. "Uncle Redford, I don't think —" *I don't think Mother would like this.*

"Call me Reddie," he insisted, still in that soft, secretive tone. "We're not really strangers, you know. Our fates have been bound together over the centuries, a bond forged by this hallowed soil. You were by my side when I fought off Powhatan. You were there when I was one of Washington's 'family.' You stood by me when I was wounded at Yellow Tavern, that sad day when we lost Jeb Stuart. We've been through a lot, you and I, my lovely, this is but one of our enchanted lifetimes."

"How come I don't recall any of that?" she asked, refusing to take the glass he pressed upon her.

Setting it aside, he emptied his own. "It's

because you weren't raised in the aura of great history. How did such a superb rose grow among the weeds of the middle west? So perfect a woman should have come from Virginia." He invested the word with the same reverence her mother did. "You should have long silken hair and pearls at your throat."

"Well, I know this bob is a mess, but Maybell Queal had this new perm machine she needed to try out . . ."

With gritted teeth, Uncle Redford managed to chuckle. "Your naïve charm is a delight. It only enhances my need to know you better before you flit out of our lives."

"Uh — I'm very glad you like me," she said, the words coming out stiff and suspicious, even to her own ears. "Right now, though, I need to get some sleep so I'll be ready for the trip home . . . a-a-aack!" The muffled squawk escaped her as Reddie, in one swift move, caught her in his free arm, holding the glass of champagne to her lips.

"Try it, just one sip. Come on, my dear, you are too fine to be a tease." The intimacy of the tone brought a flush of heat rising from her knees up, as if she were getting a fever.

Trying to break lose, she said, "How —, how am I supposed to be a tease? I didn't mean to, certainly." *I didn't invite you in, I didn't lure you on — isn't that what a tease does?*

"Oh you may put on an act for the others, but it doesn't fool me, that demure little dress, the schoolgirl shyness."

"I can't help the dress, my mother happens to like it." She was beginning to resent his strength and his insistence. "I don't think she'd like what you're doing right now, Uncle Redford."

"Her head's all taken up with visions of you as a concert artist. I see you somewhat differently." His breath smelled heavy with the champagne, so close to her face she couldn't get away from it. "I see a nubile maiden under the silly clothes, pretending to the old conventional ideas, waiting for a lover to liberate her." He set down the glass and began to fumble for the buttons at the back of her neck.

"Stop that!" she said, more forcefully than she'd intended.

For a moment he did, stepping back far enough to untie the knot in his sash, letting the black gown fall open. In a single searing instant she saw hair growing thickly down his front to a gross nest where stood — *ohmylawd! It's huge! Nobody ever told me It was red! Like a great ugly raw carrot!* Backed up against the bed she had nowhere to retreat.

"You see how I trust you?" he murmured. "I offer you my body and soul. Let me show you the mysteries of my heart." He pulled her close against him, she felt his lips thick on her face and through her nightgown she was painfully aware of *It.* In a flare of repugnance, she tore away from him and flung herself in flight across the bed.

He followed, his long, bare shanks pumping as he bounded over the soft mattress while *It* bobbed up and down. Coming up short against the door to the next room, she clutched the knob. "Mother's asleep. I don't really want to wake her, but if you don't leave me alone, I will."

Breathing hard, he came to a halt. With an irritated grin he sighed. "No, I think we'd better not wake Marjorie. That's not part of the game, my dear. You don't know the rules yet, but there'll be time. Good old Gloucester, it's not a great school, certainly can't touch William and Mary, but it has the advantage of being near by. You'll be able to come to us on weekends. What a time we'll have, you and I."

Does he mean what I think he means?

"Next fall," she said, "I will be studying hard, really hard. Good night, Uncle." Hand still gripping the doorknob, she was quaking inside, but her tone was tough.

Reddie belted his robe about him. "Au revoir, my sweet." With a wink, he gathered the bottle and glasses and let himself out as deftly as he had entered.

On silent feet Terry rushed to set the chair against the knob. A little French chair with needlepoint upholstery, a priceless antique, no doubt. Nothing less will do to brace the door against a lusty uncle, not in Hamilton House. She choked back a giggle. But then caught sight of herself in the mirror, angry eyes, cheeks flushed. It was no laughing matter.

So much for sanctuary. She tried to imagine coming down here for a weekend next fall, or worse, a whole holiday like Thanksgiving. *Not on your life.* Only then did she realize that she'd been counting on having a friendly retreat from school if she needed one, and she sensed that she might. Well, that was out the window. *Doggone it all, what ever happened to noblesse oblige?*

It was a long ride home, with the plane bumping wildly, Mother looking pale and spent. Finally, apologetically, she said, "I'm really feeling quite unwell. I believe I'll just have a taste of brandy." Dipping into her reticule she brought out a thin silver flask. The smell of the liquor drifted across, reminding Terry of Uncle Redford's hot breath. She had to look out the window hard to get her own stomach under control.

Now, with the magic gone and the expectations finished, she just wished the flight could be over. When they finally drifted lower, she could look down onto the broad waters, smooth blue, smooth brown coming together, the meeting of the two great rivers well defined when seen this way from above, and for a moment she was touched again by the sheer beauty of flight. Under the late sun the confluence was a thread of colors, flowing together like polychrome silk around dozens of small islands. The big river looked so solid you could have walked across its surface if you didn't know about all the treacherous undercurrents.

Virginia was a thing of the past — and future. She didn't begin to understand its mystique. Maybe she would learn to love it as her mother did, but for now she'd tell anybody: *I'm from Missouri. You've got to show me.*

EIGHT

To explore our "hidden potential," to discover "hidden opportunities" to beware of "hidden pitfalls.". . .

As the audience applauded the young man on stage, Dixie gave a muffled snort. "I counted seven 'hiddens,' " she snickered while he bowed and batted self-consciously at the tassel of his mortarboard.

Terry hadn't been listening to the valedictory. She was thinking about her mother. In the hospital again. No panic, this time. She had just admitted to being a bit dizzy this morning and they had taken her down in the car, left her there while Henry brought his daughter back to school.

"I don't really care about all the graduation stuff," she protested, only halfway lying. It seemed kind of an anticlimax after the exams, the posting of the honors list. What really preoccupied her thoughts was the fact that her mother hadn't even come down to breakfast the day of the horrible Chemistry final, too hard asleep to give her a good-luck kiss. Now, days later, Terry still felt a vacancy of heart, a terrible puzzlement as to what it all meant.

Ever since the Virginia trip Marjorie had seemed removed from reality. Not exactly a travesty, she was more like a facsimile. Terry had learned the word when she was about ten and wanted to send in a coupon for a birthstone ring. It had to be accompanied by the top from a Grapenuts box, or a reasonable facsimile thereof. A look-alike, only a copy of the real thing. The moonstone in the ring had been a facsimile, too, milky glass with a chip in it. It was disturbing to think of Marjorie Hamilton as just an imitation of herself. Didn't hover during piano practice, didn't get excited about clothes for school next fall, just moved through each day with a faraway look on her face. She didn't eat much and usually left the dinner table early. Henry had taken to reading the paper at meals. There was a lot of unspoken tension between them, so much that neither had noticed Terry's birthday.

Not that it mattered. Birthdays are kid-stuff. By the time you're eighteen you should get over such sentimentality. And yet one person had remembered. Grandmother

Hamilton had sent two checks, one for the birthday — $15.00 — and one for graduation for $30.00 along with a beautiful antique cameo pin. "Congratulations on your wonderful grades and your successful completion of high school." Terry had put the note with a few other special keepsakes. It made her warm to think of it, or maybe it was those two checks in her purse. *Why does money make the world so much brighter?*

Dad could probably explain it. He was worrying again about doctors' bills, those shots they were giving Marjorie to "build up her blood". Nobody would explain anything, Terry fretted. *They won't even let me hang around her room. . .*

"You will go and get your damned sheepskin." Her father looked as furious as if she'd flunked all her courses. "I'll wait in the car, I've got some orders to enter. I'm not going to sit around while a bunch of Jew-kids march across a stage."

What it was, she thought, her father had never graduated from high school himself, and somehow her achievement sort of shamed him or belittled him. It made her sad. All the Jewish parents sat there proud enough to pop their buttons while their sons and daughters got the diploma.

Some diploma. As they all filed out of the auditorium, Terry looked down at hers again, no imposing piece of parchment like Phin's, just a leatherette folder with a framed printed form that had a blank filled in with her name and — "Oh no."

"What?" Dixie craned to see. "Oh my gosh, they spelled your name wrong."

They'd left the "h" out of Therissa. She shrugged it off. The writing was plain old Palmer Method, no fancy script with curlicues. For curlicues you have to go through college.

In a kind of fog Terry found herself in front of her locker, had stopped there automatically, though there was nothing left inside. What happened to all the books, the papers, the tablets and assignments? Where did the shreds of childhood go? The not-so-great memories . . . the time she forgot her history paper, the C-minus she got in Chemistry when she was a sophomore, and last week, what *was* the answer to the sixth question on the Trig exam?

Nearby, Dixie slammed the door of hers with a loud metallic clang. "Good riddance to all this baloney!"

"You're supposed to leave the doors open," Terry murmured. They had announced it a few minutes ago in the auditorium: *Students will immediately clear out their lockers, leave the doors open and return the keys to the hall monitor.* Staring down at the key in her hand, reality came crashing in like a condemned building being demolished. It was truly all over, high school was done. Students were milling in a ragged line around the monitor, gabbling in tones that ranged from happy to smug to arrogant.

". . . haf accepted been to the Stanford University in the gr-r-r-eat state of Califor-r-rnia." Rudi managed to sneer at having made it into one of the best schools in the country after less than a year of study, the rotten little genius. His black gown hung open to reveal beneath the inevitable dark wool suit and red bow tie, and he wasn't even sweating. "So," he was saying, "it is to New Yor-r-rk, then, you are goink?" Only came chin-high to Dixie, but he held himself as if he towered over them all.

Dix contributed to the illusion, she seemed to shrink in his presence. She had told Terry once that Rudi scared her to death. "He's seen horrible things and he's not even afraid of life." Smiling now obsequiously she said, "Yep, I'm on my way in a few weeks, going to take the big city by storm. Next time you see me I'll be design-ing clothes for all the posh society women."

"Goot. Chust be sure on the sleeve to sew the Star of David, so the gentiles vill know who to spit on." His grin was like the angry grimace of a mean terrier. "You'll see. Your gr-r-reat Pr-r-resident is not the troops sending over, this big country shouldn't get dirty the hands in zomebody eltse's fight. Ja? But soon he vill sorry be. Gr-r-reat Britain cannot forever stand alone."

It was the same thing the papers kept on about, the editorial writers all saying the United States must do more to save En-gland. Across the hall was a recruitment poster: JOIN THE NAVY AND SEE THE WORLD. Terry thought of Ozzie, missed his big pink-cheeked face in the crowd. *He should have been here today.* She'd got one postcard from him, some place in Florida, Pepsicola? That couldn't be right. It was a training camp, and he'd said he liked it a lot. Scrawled a final SWAK at the end, not too original, except for the three strange symbols: Circles with X's inside them. Something nautical? There'd been no return address, so she couldn't even answer the card. Darn it, she'd rather have him here today than this smarty-pants refugee.

". . . . stor-r-rm tr-r-roopers vill soon be marching down Delmar Boulevard, goose-step, *Heil Hitler!*" Rudi flung up his stiff arm so suddenly Dixie jerked backward and landed on Terry's toe.

For some reason, it triggered all the resentment inside her, the frustration, the impatience with the little brat and everybody else. Randomly she said, "I don't have time for this!" Breaking out of line, she charged past the monitor's desk, flipping her locker key at him as she went. "That's for one-twelve."

"Hey. Wait! You can't just —"

"What are you going to do, give me a demerit?" She snapped the words over her shoulder as she pushed through the outside door and down the broad front steps for the last time, the mortarboard under her arm, black gown swirling around her ankles as she ran for the car. The old Dodge was breathing exhaust fumes as it idled. Henry Miller had it in gear before her door was closed.

As she started to wriggle out of the gown, he said, "You leave that on, girl! Break your mother's heart if she don't see you in the black doo-dads, after all the years she's been working on this."

As if it were her mother who had memorized the irregular verbs and struggled with the stupid theorems. Terry bit down on her lower lip, not going to say a word to this man who seemed such a stranger nowadays. As if he hated the world at large and his family in particular, stuck with them, full of frustration. She could feel it coming nearer, the split. She'd already figured one thing out: they were probably just waiting until she left for college. *What if I don't go? Would it delay things for a while? Or make it all worse?*

He pulled up and double-parked at the side door to St. Luke's. "You can jump out here. I'm going downtown, I've got to go to the Mercantile before it closes."

"The bank is closing?" Ever since those fearsome days in the Thirties, Terry had been nervous about banks, any institution which has all your money and is so vulnerable it might "go under."

"It closes every day at three p.m." Stupid. The word was implicit in his tone. "I got to take some out of savings and put it in checking. Doctors cost an arm and a leg." He snorted as if he'd made a joke. "Sometimes take off the wrong one if you don't watch out. 'Prep him for surgery —' " He was speaking in an odd, artificial chirp. " 'This one's a belly wound, skip him, he's not going to make it.' Bloody little gods, they know it all. 'Send this one down to Ward B, he's shell-shocked.' Couldn't give a damn."

People were crowding past, honking at them. She had her hand on the door handle when he came back to normal with a jerk.

"Wait a minute. You can give me the graduation check, I'll deposit it to your account. Well, what's the matter? Your rich gramma sent you a check, didn't she?"

"But Dad, I need that. I need to buy stuff for school next fall." *I need to feel in charge of that money, I'm old enough, he can't make me give it to him.* The unruly thought rampaged through her mind like a wild animal. "It's my present, it's mine."

"You got the gewgaw she sent, that's a present. This is money!" He held out his hand. "Hurry on, we're double-parked."

And I will hand the "gewgaw" down to my children, but right now I need the cash. Yanking the door open, she scrambled out. "See you later." Running up the stairs she burst into the dim, odorous world of the hospital. There would be a horrible scene later, she almost hoped there would. She needed desperately to let go some of the steam bottled up inside. *But not now, forheavensake!* Leaning against the door to her

142

mother's room, she tried to get her breath back, while nurses passed on soft feet, glancing curiously at the black gown. *Right now Mother needs me. I have to put up with — anything, everything. What would she do if I just took off and left?* Because that was the alternative, to run. To run away, for good. The idea didn't shock her as much as it would have six months ago. *Only who'd do the cooking? Who would help her shop, who would she listen to Vic and Sade with all summer? Darn the socks together . . .* A tidal surge of love almost swamped her, she had to fight back tears as she eased open the door.

Propped in bed, Marjorie was working the crossword puzzle, the paper laid out on a lap-table. Without makeup her face was white as the pillows behind her, but the lusterless eyes took on a spark of pleasure as she saw the graduation gown.

"Oh, it's over. Did it go well?"

"I guess so." Terry clapped on the black mortarboard and tossed her tassel with a grand gesture. "I am now an official high-school graduate."

Marjorie smiled, eyes swimming with tears. "My little baby's all grown up."

"How are you feeling."

"Better, I guess. They gave me a transfusion. Said I wasn't getting enough nutrition," she sniffed into a hanky. "So stupid. I'm sorry, I seem to ruin everything. I really wanted to be there today, but my knees were so weak. Where's your dad?"

"He had to go" — *don't remind her how much all this is costing* — "down to the office. He'll be along later."

"There's no need. They aren't going to let me come home tonight, want to run some more tests. I feel like a pin cushion." She glanced down at her arm — a dark bruise marked the spot where the needle had gone in.

"So what shall we do? I could read to you, or we could play a little rummy or —"

"Actually, I think I need to take a nap. You run on, sweetie. You need to practice, next fall isn't far away now. Do your Hanon, concentrate on getting the tone." But it was obviously hard for her to summon any enthusiasm. The truth lay there between them like a patch of mud, slippery, ugly, to be skirted around. "Don't worry about me, I need to think — about a lot of things. The hospital is a good place for that, no distractions, everything so neutral." The thin voice faded, her eyes closed.

She didn't stir as Terry eased out the door,

disappointed. Anger began to creep in — *he did this, the way he's been acting, it's ruining her.* Resentment made her almost sick, as she rode the bus home, the rented robe folded in her lap. Or maybe it was just the fumes from the traffic. The whole world was a bad smell today, summer heat already rising, the sky a haze of smoke from the factories over in Illinois. Walking into the familiar confines of home, she sniffed the air — *he's been smoking a cigar. He knows she hates it.*

Folding the robe away in its rental box, she put it by the front door, then hurried across to grab the ashtray with the odorous butt, on through the house and out to the back to dump it in the ash pit. That was getting full too, smelling rank. Dad should have burned the trash long ago. As if her senses were sand-papered, she went back to the kitchen, glaring at the mug on the sink drain. A heavy piece of cheap china, suitable for the black coffee he liked — Marjorie never touched the stuff, and she certainly wouldn't drink out of a thick clumsy cup like that. Terry washed it and put it on the shelf, scrubbed the sink and the counter top, and felt a fraction better. This was exactly what she should do: clean the house right down to the baseboards, make it fit for a delicate woman to come home to.

I'll start with Mother's room.

Days since it had been touched. The house maid who used to come weekly was gone now, couldn't afford her, Henry had said. "With school out Terry can do the chores, save us a few bucks." In a tone that indicated he thought she should be good for *something*. And it was true. What else did she ever do to earn her keep around here?

Grimly, she gathered dust mop and vacuum cleaner and hauled them up to the master bedroom. When she opened the door a stale miasma emanated from the shadows, human odor camouflaged with Evening in Paris, and under it something sour she couldn't name. Rushing to open the draperies, Terry raised the window to let in sunlight and warm breeze. Even the city's summer aromas were better than the air inside. She hauled the sheets off the old four-poster, a smaller version of those antiques in Virginia, and took them to the top of the stairs, tumbling them down to be tallied and sent to the laundry later.

The scent around the bed was slow to dissipate. She got the furniture oil and began to wipe down the thick posts of burl walnut.

The story was that she'd been born in that bed. Terry couldn't picture it, her delicate mother reduced to a sweating, laboring creature in horrible pain — all so she could live. Again that tidal wave of love swept over her. And as she leaned closer to oil the headboard, a sheet of burl walnut beautifully swirled, her foot struck something below that rolled away. When she bent down to look she saw that it was a bottle.

Down on hands and knees she brought it out — empty brandy bottle giving off fumes that made her gag. Didn't smell like the elegant stuff at Hamilton House, this was raw and cheap. And when she peered farther under the bed she saw others, three more bottles back there rolling on their sides. In a daze, Terry sank backward onto the floor.

Slowly the clues fell into place, out of a chaos of confusion came comprehension. All the forgetting, neglecting, retreating into her room, hardly eating, the loss of interest in anything or anyone — this was the answer. How long had it been going on? Ever since the trip to Virginia? Or earlier . . . maybe it began when Henry had changed rooms? Or was that the reason he'd moved out? Terry felt muddled, her mind in a fog of confusion through which one ter-

rible certainty persisted:
My mother is a drunkard.

NINE

It was as if she had been playing her hardest in a tough game and suddenly found she was on the wrong side, among strangers. How to act, what to say in the face of grinding confusion?

Terry roused to realize that she had been sitting in her room for hours, letting a stream of memories flow over her, muddied now by a lot of ugly questions. Dirty suspicions: *All this is my fault, I wasn't good enough. I ruined her dream. Maybe their marriage went bad because I'm such a disappointment. Such an expense. Which is why Dad is beginning to hate me. Maybe he's right, about some things I guess I am kind of dumb.* But the realization didn't fill her with the humility it should have. In fact, Terry felt a stirring of anger.

She glanced around at the little-girlie room with its pink candy-striped wallpaper, the rosebud quilt on the handsome bed. Another transplant from the mansion in Virginia, it was a walnut four-poster complete with a canopy, *except I never was the canopy type. I don't feel like a little princess. I don't really belong to that family in Richmond.* The face that looked back at her from the vanity mirror was even-featured, high-boned, with a wide mouth, rebellious brown eyes, *I look more like those people up in Iowa, Dad's folks.* Certainly no beauty, as Marjorie Miller had once been.

She could hardly bear the thought of her mother, wasted, gaunt, lying down there waiting for tests to show how badly the alcohol had spent her body. *What can you do with a drunkard? No wonder Dad looks desperate.* But Terry couldn't summon up the proper grade of pity for him. He could have prevented this somehow. Maybe he should have told her in the beginning: "Marjorie, that girl doesn't have an inch of talent, so don't build all those fantasies about her." But no, he waited until the awful truth became undeniable.

Still, she shouldn't have given up on me. I did get pretty darned good grades, I graduated. I made the music program. I'm going to that school. The least she could do is keep up her end. She's the thread that holds the family together. All these years Dad has provided the food and clothes and shelter, now she owes it to him to stay sober, at least cook his dinner.

Terry pulled her scattered thoughts together and got up. Stiffened by resentment, she went out into the hall again where the cleaning implements still stood, hauled them back downstairs to the closet, *and let those bottles lie there under the bed, may she never know that I saw them.* Glancing in at the piano she shuddered with loathing and hurried past to the kitchen.

The fridge yielded a half casserole of scalloped potatoes and the end of a pork roast. No dinner feast for the graduate, no cake for the birthday girl. It was cry-or-get-mad time, and she was already halfway to mad. Terry dumped the stuff in the oven and banged the plates onto the yellow checkered oilcloth. As soon as her father arrived, glum and brooding like a storm about to break, she retrieved the food and slung it on the table fast. Before he could get a word in, Terry was seated, dishing out the potatoes.

Rule of the house: no arguments at dinner. Marjorie had made such a fetish out of it, they'd got in the habit of obeying the commandment. In silence they ate, though it obviously cost Henry a lot, bulging with unspoken words. Doggedly he cleaned his plate, *remember all the starving Chinese.* It had been a cry throughout the Depression to remind people not to waste food. As they finished, she braced herself, nourishing that flicker of anger like a castaway hovering over the fire that keeps back the wild animals.

The minute she stood up to clear the dishes he was on his feet too. "Now then, young lady, you and I are going to have an understanding."

She got out the pan, filled it with hot water, added soap.

"You may think you're pretty big stuff, got your scrap of paper from that school, but it don't give you — turn around and look at me! — the diploma don't give you license to sass your dad."

I never said a disrespectful word. Terry laid aside the dish rag and turned to face him.

"I want to know: what was the idea of walking off today when I told you to give me that check?"

"I'm sorry if I was rude, but I heard the music starting, I didn't want to disrupt the processional by being late. There wasn't time to talk about everything then. It's not just the graduation check, it's my whole bank account. I'm grateful you kept my money safe all these years, but now I really need it . . ."

She saw she had startled him by taking the initiative, by making it sound logical. The brown eyes blinked rapidly, the mouth came ajar. In one moment their relationship had skidded into a different position, like a car on ice, wheels spinning madly. It took all her effort to keep looking him in the face as his square simple features showed signs of fracturing.

"So you will now decide what you need?" The words exploded through the fissures. "You don't care for any more guidance from your elders, eh? Got it all figured out? You ever been to a bank? You ever write a check in your life? Ever keep a balance? Oh, you know how to spend the stuff, but do you have the faintest idea how money is *made?* And don't spout that job in the library, that's chewing-gum change."

Summoning every ounce of patience, she tried to speak evenly, though her voice was on the verge of cracking. "Dad, it's only three months until I leave for college. I need clothes and I have already spent my June allowance. I didn't want to ask you for more, I thought that's what my savings are for. I need to go shopping, I need bus fare, I have to eat lunch downtown and all that. I just want to spend what's mine. I thought you'd be glad I was going to pay for it all with my own money."

Getting redder by the minute, he spoke thickly. "Oh, we'll spend your dough, all right, but we'll do it my way. No fancy duds that cost a fortune, no silly stuff. We'll make a list and set down prices, which you can charge to my account and I'll pay it out of your savings. That's how we're going to do *that!*"

"But you don't have accounts at all the stores. We buy my shoes at Famous Barr and my underwear at Scruggs, and I have to shop around to find a new coat, the old one looks like it's been in a cat-fight. Mother was so embarrassed she wouldn't let me wear it in Virginia."

"You leave your mother out of this, young lady!"

"I know, obviously she can't be with me every time I go downtown and neither can you. But you could trust me, I'm not going to buy anything expensive."

"You don't even know what that word means, little girl. Wait til they hit you with the school stuff — books and gym suits and lab fees up to your ears. I may not be a college boy, but I've known a few. I know what it costs to go to one of them hoighty outfits, and I ain't about to let you arrive there with no funds. So just hand over the check."

Terry felt bile rise in her throat. "That's my very own graduation present, the only one I got and —"

"Oh, you'll get your watch. It's down at the office, the girl didn't have time to wrap it up yet. And I had a few other things on my mind today. So I don't need you acting up now to top it off. Gimme the damned check."

"Dad! I'm not some little kid any more. I'm eighteen, as of last Monday, which nobody also noticed —"

"Feel pretty put-upon, do you? Did it ever occur to you your mother is sick?"

If you want to call it that, okay, but I saw the bottles. "All the more reason I have to have money to do my own shopping. I'm practically grown —"

"Oh yeah, I got that message, but let me tell you, as long as you live under this roof you are my responsibility, and that means you do as I say."

At that point, everything seemed to boil up and spill over. "Okay," Terry heard the incredible words distinctly, "okay, I will leave. I guess I'm really just a burden, another mouth to feed. Like you say, I need to learn to make my own money. So I will." Her feet took her out of the room and up the stairs, but the ankles were weak and the knees shaking as she waded through heavy waters of fear and dismay.

Throwing stuff into the old canvas bag she'd used for field trips, she moved around the room blindly, snatching up nightgown, toothbrush, underwear, socks. Rushing past the mirror she caught a glimpse of flushed face and tangled hair, *take along some scissors.* She picked up the sweet-potato plant, putting out a new green shoot — *you can't take that, silly.* But she put in some silk stockings and high-heeled pumps. *For job hunting, I've got to look like a grown woman, no bobby socks.*

Pausing for one final scan of the room her eyes fell on the framed glossy photo of Errol Flynn over on the mirror of the vanity. Good-looking devil, smiling his sardonic smile that she used to think was romantic. Now he just reminded her of Uncle Redford. Into the wastebasket. Purse with wallet and driver's license, and the two checks. *How do you cash a check?*

At the last minute she held the charm bracelet in her hand. Her mother had added a charm every year, as a birthday present. She dropped it back in the jewelry case. *What will she do without me?* The question had been hovering, she looked it in the eyes and didn't blink. Marjorie didn't need her, didn't even want to be around this wretched creature who would never make the Hamiltons proud. *She must really loathe me, to have to go and get drunk!*

Crushed out of shape by the thought, she grabbed up the canvas bag, running downstairs in a headlong rush and out the front door, leaving fragments of her father's voice behind.

"Terry Miller, get yourself. . . . this minute . . . hear me?" But the words came from far behind, where a whole structure of obedience and effort and loyalties had collapsed. Leaving it all in shreds, she ran on until she was out of steam and had to slow to a walk.

When the red haze cleared she emerged into a lovely summer's eve, with a warm wind blowing and the sky turning dusky. She found herself walking down Delmar, past beautiful homes where the wealthy Jews lived surrounded by lawns and gardens and sheltering hedges. In the twilight the yellow glow from the windows was warm, a sign of families gathering after supper to listen to the radio or play rummy. Maybe read the papers. Women knitting . . .

I knitted my father a muffler once, blue wool, he really seemed to like it. But then it sort of stretched, longer and longer — I never was good at knitting, couldn't keep my stitches tight. Not really good at anything, face it.

The street lights seemed to fog over, but Terry blinked the moment of weakness away. Forget mufflers and kites and doll houses, they were just a way to kill time in the Depression when you couldn't go anywhere, do something that didn't cost any money. *When he gets over being mad, Dad's going to be very happy that I'm out of there, he won't have to worry about me any more. Left alone in the house, maybe he and Mother can come back together, if they ever were together.*

That was a question she'd never solve. It was time, Terry thought, to face her own future. *Maybe go to New York, steal a trick on Dixie. She was working the evening shift at Dribbin's Drug, making fifty cents an hour now. But she's never run away. For once I am ahead of her. Except I've got to think where I'm going to sleep tonight.* Would the "Y" rent you a room and let you pay for it the next day after the banks open?

Deep in her new plans, she became vaguely aware of a blat of horns loud enough to make her glance around. Cars were stacked up behind a familiar jalopy that was inching along beside her. *Phin, go away.* But he was leaning across, setting the door ajar on her side. "Give you a lift?"

For a second she resisted the temptation. *When you run away from home, you should do it all by yourself.* But the Heap was panting pitifully as if it had run to catch up, and after all, she and that car had been through a lot together. She put a foot on the running board.

"Did my father send you to rescue me?"

Phin shook his head. "He called to see if you were over at our house. Sounded upset. Looking for you was my idea. You need to be rescued?"

"No!" Against her will, Terry climbed the high step into the front seat, avoiding the wayward spring that had halfway burst through the cushion. Phin shoved the gear forward hard   first gear didn't work, he had to gun the engine to get them back into motion. "Actually," she said, "I've left home."

"No kidding? How does it feel, good or bad?" Just professional interest, Phin was always curious about experiments.

"It feels — necessary."

He considered that, watching traffic now, nursing the clutch at the stop signs, but never relinquishing his focus on what she'd told him. More than anything else could have, his silence affirmed the fact — that she had made a major decision in her life, for better or worse.

I ought to get out of the car right now. He is going to somehow talk me out of this without ever seeming to! He'll poke around . . .

"How does your mom feel about this?"

"Uh . . . let me off on the next corner, I can get a streetcar there . . ."

"Hey, what did I say? Your mother doesn't know. Right?"

"She's in the hospital again."

His head came around in a jerk. "What for? What's wrong?"

May he never learn the truth. "Who knows? She gets these dizzy spells." *Which happens, so I've heard, when you swill a lot of booze.* In her mind, Terry used the coarse language deliberately, it helped convert the hurt to anger. And right then, fury was all that kept her going.

"This is going to hit her pretty hard," Phin observed, no blame, no passion.

"I don't think so. When I went to see her today, she sent me away. She's been off of me ever since I turned out to be a lousy second-rate pianist."

"Aw, I don't believe that." The Heap coughed discreetly and Phin turned his attention to his gas meter. They had reached The Loop where buses and streetcars traded passengers, a place of shops, groceries. He swerved into a gas station and up to the pumps, cut the engine and dug in his pockets to bring out some small change.

"Wait a minute, I could buy," she offered. "I raided my piggy bank before I left." Delving into the tangled contents of the canvas sack, she felt for coins.

"I've got it. Three gallons," he told the attendant. "Listen, Bunch, will you stay put while I make a couple of phone calls?"

"Two-and-a-quarter," she was counting, "two-thirty-five, forty, fifty, seventy-five . . ." When she looked up he was over in the phone booth, a crooked silhouette, sagging loose-jointed against one wall of glass, his back turned. *He's calling my mother!* Terry had her hand on the door handle. *Or maybe he had a date and he's calling it off. Don't jump to conclusions.* The truth was she could use some advice. Phin obviously would know how you go about cashing a check.

He hung up and took the receiver down again. This time the message of his posture was different, straightening, stiffening as he listened with his chin out. Finally talking in short sharp thrusts, not like Phin. *He never gets angry.* Coming back now, tilting a little more than usual, skinny and warped as a burnt match stick. He *was* mad. Slung himself into the front seat and got the Heap running without a word. As they joined the flow of traffic along Delmar, the city ahead was banked across the evening sky, towers of light against a luminous gray — the only time of day that St. Louis was ever beautiful.

Abruptly he said, "I called Ruth Ann. She works at St. Luke's, you know, she's a nurse."

"No, I didn't know." *Nurses get paid big money, no wonder she drives her own car.*

"She's on night shift this week, I thought maybe she could tell me about your mother, but she's on a different floor. She asked around, one of the others said your mom is resting comfortably, all tucked in for the night. So I guess we better not disturb her."

"I could have told you that. Did they say

162

what's wrong?" Terry held her breath.

"They don't talk about patients, they're told not to. Ruth Ann said she thought she was a little run-down is all. She'll be going home tomorrow. So then I called your dad — don't get sore! I had to. If I didn't tell him that you're okay and you're with me, he was going to call out the cops to look for you."

"Can he do that? Phin, I'm eighteen years old as of last Friday!"

"Happy birthday. But until you're twenty-one you're technically a minor."

In appalled silence she sat, picturing the awful scenario of police officers hunting her down, dragging her out of the YWCA, taking her home by force . . .

"I gathered from what he said that you had a fight about the savings account thing. I don't like to be disrespectful, but I had to point out that you're old enough to be given your own money to spend. And why not now when you're still at home? Better than waiting to give it to you after you leave and there's nobody to ask for advice. I don't think I got through to him, he kept raving along. Told me some day I'll find out what it's like to have to support a family. Your pop doesn't care for me, for some reason."

"You're too smart. Remember that time

you explained specific gravity to him?"

"Well, shoot, I was just making polite conversation. Seemed like a thing we could discuss, him being in the ink business. I tried to pick a subject he'd be interested in."

"But he isn't. He doesn't know all that stuff about viscosity."

"Oh sure, he's got to. It makes a difference in how an ink prints. It would be part of his sales pitch."

"He's memorized the words and he's got a little table he uses, but he never knew how it worked, because I asked him to explain it once and he told me to shut up. He never went to college."

"Lord-ee. I must have come across as a cheeky know-it-all kid."

And a Jew. Phin was so innocent he didn't seem to realize there were people who don't like Jews in general. "Next time you see him, ask him to explain Social Security and how it will wreck our society, and by the time he gets through telling you about that you'll be a 'pretty decent young fellow.' "

Phin made that chesty sound that was half chuckle, half groan. "Anyway, I had to promise him I'd bring you home — when you get good and ready. Bunch, I don't

164

blame you for skipping out, but it's just a little too soon. You need to have a plan. And you need to discuss it with your mom. She's got a lot of common sense. She's a good one to give advice."

Memories of that polio year were never far beneath his surface. Terry could still remember the time he'd hit rock-bottom. After months laid up in bed he had exploded with frustration, picked up the dishes from the lunch tray one by one, and fired them at the bedroom wall as hard as his measly arms could throw. While Terry and Dixie crawled around like six-year-old elves, gathering up the crockery shards, Marjorie had sat on the bed, holding his hand, talking him down in her own quiet way. Lending him a new stock of patience in a voice filled with love.

The memory put a crack in her hard shell of resentment. *Mother has always been ready to comfort everyone else. Now maybe she needs a little of it herself. Who knows what she's had to put up with? Not just the music thing, but Dad getting weirder every day.*

Marjorie had explained it to her once, "It's what happens in a war. The shock of shells going off all the time made his brain sensitive, the way your knee feels when you've scraped it. So don't blame him if he gets a little strange, it means he's hurting in some place that doesn't show." Still, for her to give up and turn to brandy now, it was as if she'd left her family behind to go off into a hazy world of alcoholic drift. Terry wished she could discuss it with Phin.

She glanced across at him to catch a glimpse of some private trouble of his own that screwed his brows up. "You got problems too?"

"Yeah."

"Okay, give. Come on, it's your turn."

He heaved a sigh. "I just — well, there's a big gap between what I should do and what I want to do, and I hate that."

"You mean at school? You said they were interested in your project."

"Yeah, but I shouldn't be spending any more time in college. I ought to be out helping bring in some dough for the family. After years that I've been sponging off Mom, letting her do it all, I should be out there looking for a job. I hoped maybe they would give me the Fellowship money early. I could use some of it to buy the things we need most, but I learned today that doesn't come through until next fall when the new term starts."

"Well, you got the refrigerator." That had

been his graduation present, he had insisted to his mother it was the only thing he wanted.

"Yeah, but we need a new furnace, the roof is leaky. Damn, I hate money."

The words struck an echo in Terry's heart.

They were almost to Grand Avenue by now, and all at once she knew what he was thinking. He felt in his pocket, but she spoke up first. "I've got enough for tickets."

Grimly, Phin swung a hard right and put his foot down. The Heap lurched forward as if it had been prodded, passing a leisurely Oldsmobile, rattling along streetcar tracks, through a canyon of bright lights, theaters, people channeling into The Fox for a first-run movie. And ahead, above the rest, the gaudiest sign of all:

TUNE TOWN

TEN

Phin had found the dance hall years earlier out of necessity. In high school by then, he had exchanged his crutches for a cane, against doctor's orders. Rebelling against all advice to take his life slowly and rest a lot, he set off on foot to test and stretch and command his warped muscles. All those weeks in bed had robbed him of the natural rhythms of motion, his steps were awkward and barely under control. But he had a hunch, some primitive sense drew him toward the sound of the boogie beat. Following the music that reached out across the wilds of Grand Avenue, he sought out the lair of the jitterbug. Crooked music for a crooked back — he was too young to be admitted, but he got in. He was too inept to attract a partner, but the unattached women who hung out in the place pitied him — for a while. He learned all they had to teach and began to invent his own customized steps, crazy and lopsided and challenging. Somewhere along the line he lost the cane and never acquired another one.

So tickled with the place, he took Dixie down before she was old enough, ferreted her in through the back door from the alley. Never could understand why she would turn up her nose at it. "Uncouth" was her favorite word about then. She informed him it was low-class, grungy and disgusting. Phin suspected the truth: Dix didn't have much ear for music. Terry was a different story.

This was so different from the mechanical notes she was forced to play on her piano she reveled in it, much as he did, to mend and heal the tatters of her self confidence. Music that boosted, that gave you a kick in the ribs, music that made your feet sing. She was a natural hoofer. Phin told her so and thus it must be true.

Over the years that followed, Tune Town had been their refuge whenever the going got tough. The time he had failed to convince his adviser to let him accelerate his courses at Washington U. The test she had flunked in physics, in spite of Phin's coaching. Whenever times got grim, it had relieved her frustration to slam around the floor to some totally idiotic tune. After the disastrous recital where she had wrecked Chopin's Black Key Etude, she had thrown herself into the "Flat-foot Floogie," giggling and chanting, *"Floy doy, floy doy, floy doy."*

So tonight it had been an automatic re-action, with stress beginning to overload their world, for the two of them to seek the old panacea of stomp and sway. Music was bursting the seams when they got there, bulbs glittering, smell of popcorn. Terry doled out the last of her change and they were swept through the door into the frigid depths of the place, which was air-conditioned enough to make you shiver. Hanging on the sidelines they waited for the South Side crowd to finish a polka, hefty Germans pumping elbows to "Roll out the Barrel." Up on the bandstand, an accordion was accompanied by a bass fiddle, cornet and a set of drums that sparkled like a kaleidoscope.

Dixie doesn't know what she's missing, Terry thought. *It does you good to be vulgar occasionally. To lose yourself in a crazyness. As Phin says, when you dance they can't tell that you're limping.* As the polka crowd retired toward the tables around the sides of the room, she followed him onto the dance floor. In threadbare cords that came high on his bony shins and not much sleeve on the T-shirt to inhibit his long arms, he was always garbed for action, but she had just been lucky to come away tonight in the perfect dress, an old green gingham with a full skirt, scuffy sandals. *Let them play something fast, please!*

The squeezebox sounded a long chord, the lights turned to cherry red, and the bandleader, a pudgy young man with his hair greased back into a ducktail, yelled one word into the microphone: "Drumboogie!" Cymbals clashed and Phin grabbed her hand to spin her with a flip that made her skirt flare.

The change that always came over him was radical. It was as if his lanky frame came unbolted, everything loose and dangling. The brainy face got savage under the mop of light hair, his stance was that of ancient manhood approaching the rites of spring. As the cornet screamed he appropriated his nymph, turning her this way and that, under and over and around and out and back, almost threw her away, but his hand was there to snatch her at the last minute, then suddenly set her free — *Git!*

Released, Terry made up her own moves, dancing in place, arms high, body sinuous as grass in the wind, twitching her hips with the ageless innocence of a vestal virgin in a rain forest. Meanwhile the primitive worshipper was all around her, advancing, retreating, bringing her fire as jungle drums shivered the air. Captured again, she grew compliant, was rocked and swung and finally lifted and set down reverently as the cymbals ended it all with a crash.

And around them Tune Town is thunderous with a vast ovation, stamping and whistling — Terry marveled how it always happened when Phin danced. Never the same moves twice, always experimenting, always creating, he communicated something to the others with his strange body that drove them wild. He had no idea why, always looked surprised. Blinking at the crowd, frowsy and sweating and diffident, he draped an arm across her shoulders.

"That felt okay."

Furies spent, they collapsed into a chair at one of the tables. Somebody set down some drinks. "On the house." Cokes in frosted bottles, nothing ever tasted better. In silence they sucked at the straws and breathed a while. Then, for no particular reason, Terry raised hers. "To graduation." Hard to recall that it had happened only this morning. She felt as if she'd been out of school for years.

Phin clinked with her. Two weeks ago he had been valedictorian at his own coming-out, stood up on stage in the stadium at Washington U. looking awkward and insecure, the mortarboard squelching his wayward hair, the black gown hiding his tilt. His voice had been soft and hesitant until he began to speak of the future. Then he took hold of the microphone and made them listen to all the things that would come — marvels that would be within the grasp of everybody, like better furnaces run on natural gas, washing machines and air conditioning in every home. He told them about a new invention called television that would bring moving pictures into their living rooms. But it would all come at a price — they would have to find new power sources to run the marvelous toys. Harness the energy in the wind, the sun itself. Tap into the heat under volcanoes, make electricity from the earth's own elements, such fantasies that Terry's imagination burned out. How could one mop-topped head think of all that? And now he'd be going on to post-graduate school, what was left for him to learn?

"So what's this experiment you're working on at the lab?"

"The short answer to that is, I'm trying to

find the weight of something that's too small to see." He made a face as if it were ridiculous. "Don't know why I think I could manage something nobody else has ever done."

"Why is it important?"

"Bunch, there's a new world coming — remember those newsreels about the World's Fair, a 'Century of Progress'? All that fancy stuff runs on electricity. All we've got right now are coal and oil and they're going to be gone one of these days, we keep using them up so fast. So I'm just trying to help us move into the next fifty years of inventions."

"Do you reckon they teach that kind of thing at Glow-cester College?"

"That's a school of arts and literature, as I understand it," he said. "Which are also important. Anyway, you won't go there forever. Just put in a year and then you can say, 'I tried this, and now I'd rather —' It helps to have a 'rather.' "

"Yeah, I know. That's my whole problem, there's nothing I really want to do with my future."

"You will. Something will trigger a snapshot: you'll see yourself as a nurse. Or a teacher, or a journalist like old Nellie Bly. You could even be a politician. President Roosevelt has a woman in his cabinet. Or maybe you'll just end up as a mother with a bunch of kids, that's probably the most important job in the world."

Oh yeah? Then why don't you settle for being a dad and work in an office all your life? Because it's exciting to try for some great goal. The lack of a Great Goal had been a dark spot in her mind for years, every time she saw Dixie bend over a sketch pad and come up with a design for some new-fangled fashion, or when she'd read about Amelia Earhart flying around the world, or see Lana Turner signing autographs. Terry had looked into her cavernous self in search of any glimmer of that kind of talent and found nothing.

"I guess I could be a cook, I kind of like to cook. I don't get all excited over it, but I don't mind whipping up a pie. And my biscuits are almost as good as Mother's."

"Give it a chance." Phin tipped up the Coke bottle to get the last drops out. "Considering all that's been going on in your life, I bet you haven't had a quiet moment to just think."

The notion was totally foreign to her. What thinking Terry did was while she was walking to school, mostly about the quiz on Friday.

"Sometimes," he went on distantly, "I sit

up in the sun room and watch the Rock Island Rocket go around, and my mind begins to click like it's on a downhill track, faster and faster."

"You're lucky. You don't have anybody telling you what to do."

"I don't know, I kind of miss that." He looked out at the crowd, waltzing now, most of the couples out of step, not the most popular dance at Tune Town. "I ever tell you? The night I was born my ma said my papa stayed up 'til dawn, walking up and down the room, holding me, saying how I would be named Phineas, Lord knows why, and how I was meant to do big things. He had plans for me, great plans. I wish I knew what they were."

"He'd probably try to turn you into a banker or a doctor or something. Parents always want to influence you."

"Everything in nature influences everything else. It's what makes the world go around, all those atoms bouncing off each other, creating reactions. It's what shapes you, being bounced. You want to influence me? Go ahead."

"Okay. I've decided you are wasted on a life of science. You were really meant to be a choreographer. Let's see you compose a new ballet." By now the band had struck up a rhythm on the drums again.

The leader grabbed the mike. "Beat me, Daddy, eight-to-the-bar."

Hours later, Terry let Phin walk her up to the front door from which she had burst only hours ago. "If he starts in about that graduation check again —"

"I doubt if he will. You gave him a scare."

Henry Miller was waiting for them. The door opened a second before they got to it. He stood there looking drained of rage, dull with weariness, confusion. For a minute the puppy-brown eyes searched his daughter's face in a kind of bewilderment, as if maybe he missed those kites and mufflers too. Quietly, he said to Phin, "Thank you for bringing her home."

When they were alone the silence thickened with unspoken words. Terry could hardly bear to look at him. "I think I will go to bed." Very formally.

Her father made a small gesture: *wait.* "I've given the matter some thought and I believe you are old enough now to handle your own finances." As if he had invented the idea. Holding out a small red folder he went on, "This is your savings passbook. It's been in my name, but tomorrow we will create a new one. You'll have to come down to the bank and give them a signature card. Then you can deposit or withdraw as much as you like."

Speechless, Terry opened the pages, scanning the long column of figures down to the final total. Four-hundred and seventy-two dollars and sixty-one cents. Weakly, she said, "Thank you."

"I'd advise you to be careful how you spend it. Like I said, college will take more dough than you think. Of course, if you run short maybe that Hamilton outfit will help you, but I can't. I'm tapped out, hospital bills, pills. Life can be rougher than you'd ever believe."

"Yes sir," she said mechanically. "I will — uh — make out a list, I'll budget everything —" That figure, $472.61, it was finally sinking in. He'd saved every cent for her. There was a strong impulse to fling herself on him, to hug and kiss and make the sadness go from that sagging face. But by then he had already turned away.

ELEVEN

She had come into a new place, a world that was indifferent and lonely and exciting, because she could choose her own direction. And pay her way. Terry stood in her bedroom with the ringing quiet of an empty house around her and a curious hope within — that things might work out after all. Maybe her despair had been premature. This morning they, her mother and father, had left on a trip together.

It had all happened so fast. On top of her disillusionment over the bottles and Marjorie's indifference had come the big fight with her father and his sudden capitulation. The red bank book was now in her jewel box in the bottom drawer, but its figures simmered in her heart. Then her mother had come home, warm and loving again, almost herself, but frail. Henry had announced that they were going to take a little trip to Minnesota. And when Marjorie suggested they ought to include Terry, he had said, "The girl is old enough to take care of herself." A slight twist of the lip suggested his skepticism, but he really didn't care, and that was okay. The main thing was that the rift between her parents had lessened, maybe was even on the mend.

"Of course, I'll be fine. I'll take care of the laundry and burn the trash —"

"Stay away from the ash pit," he ordered. "There'll be time enough when we get back."

"Okay, okay. I'll clean the house and lock the doors at night. You have a great time." *A second honeymoon,* but she didn't say it aloud. Maybell Queal was honking out front to take them to the train station. *I could have driven you there!* But Terry didn't want to precipitate a whole new crisis with her father. She needed to prove her responsibility first, build up his confidence in her.

Standing in front of the vanity mirror she eyed herself critically. It could have been an illusion, but she thought she looked older. Felt older. Right then she couldn't resist an experiment. The makeup kit had been her first purchase with her own money without anybody's strings attached. Using the eyebrow pencil, carefully she traced a new line over her plucked brows, an arch which she darkened at the crest. It wasn't quite Claudette Colbert, but almost. *Now some rouge . . . lipstick . . .* She'd forgot to buy a lipstick! Racing down the hall to the big bedroom, she found the top drawer of the dresser empty. Of course. Marjorie had taken her makeup with her. *Okay, I'll buy one.*

That certainly came under the heading of school supplies. She would keep an orderly list of what she spent (without being too specific) and show it to her father later, demonstrate a certain wisdom. The challenge had been there ever since the night she'd almost run away. Those hours had given her a whole new perspective. She had taken a plunge into unknown waters, and even though she had climbed right back out, she knew she could do it again. Even better now, with the bank book. And in an odd way it had cleared the air between her and Henry Miller. He seemed relieved to have resolved the crisis. Now he treated her with distant formality, as if she were a person he hardly knew, but it was better than those furies. Pretty soon, he seemed to be saying, she would be out of sight, out of mind. It gave her a pang, but there was some comfort in neutrality.

Now, if he would patch things up with her mother, Terry thought, they might actually be a sort of family again. Maybe the two would share the big bed once more. Pausing at the guest room she glanced through the open door and saw, beneath the bed, his slippers. In a rush she went over and grabbed them up, dithering, as if she could somehow run after the car and restore them to him. Minnesota is a cold place, the mental image of bare feet touched her heart. All at once her eyes were swimming with tears. She sank onto the bed and cried as if she'd lost the world.

Big baby, they aren't even on the train yet, and you're wailing like an infant! Couldn't help herself, for a few minutes she sobbed, feeling the old love she'd had as a little girl for a father. There was no way they would ever get back to the closeness they had all felt through the Depression. That time was gone, never to return. The words sounded old-fashioned and melodramatic, like something out of Sir Walter Scott, but they were true. Novelists knew how to express these feelings of the heart. She was still sniffling when the phone rang.

"May I speak to Miss Therissa Miller, please." The deep voice was invested with authority.

A sudden montage of accidents, misdeeds and miscellaneous pitfalls reeled across her mind. "This is Terry Miller." She tried to rally her usual telephone manners, but she was too confused to grasp what he was saying.

". . . our mothers, bless 'em, like to control us . . ."

"Excuse me, who is this?"

"I'm sorry, I do tend to plunge right in. I'm Tommy James." He had said it before, she realized, as he went on speaking more slowly now. "From Annapolis and all the seven seas. My mother went to school with your mother."

"Oh, yes, now I know. I just couldn't — I wasn't —"

"You weren't expecting me to pop up on your doorstep. Neither did I. But coming back across country from visiting friends in California, I decided to stop off for a day with a cousin of mine who lives in a place called LaDue Village. Do you know of it?"

Just the ritziest suburb in the St. Louis area. "Yes, sure. It's not too far from here."

"So my cousin informs me. Which made me think perhaps we could get together, sort of play a trick on our parents for once. My mother does love to control the action, so I have a little game sometimes, to put one over on her." He was talking along as easily as if they were best friends.

Even befuddled, Terry recognized true sophistication when she saw it. Something she didn't have, she knew, as she struggled to keep up.

"So what do you say? Shall we slip off on a date now, so we can confound them all later: 'As a matter of fact, old dear, I met Terry last summer,' and so forth?" He sounded amused, his chuckle had overtones that reminded her of Uncle Redford.

Terry shook off the thought. "Actually," she heard herself say, "we don't have to 'slip' anywhere. My parents are out of town. I'm free for anything." Mirroring his tone, her voice was gracious and tinged with humor. "I think it sounds like fun."

"Great! How about I pick you up around six o'clock, so we can make an evening of it? Wherever you want to go. My cousin has loaned me one of his cars."

One of his — ? "How nice," she said. "Six will be fine. See you then."

Putting the phone down she stood and replayed the whole conversation. When her mother had spoken of the "midshipmen" at the Naval Academy she had pictured young boys in sailor suits with baby faces and crewcut hair, sort of nautical versions of Ozzie. That image hardly stood up to the easy aplomb of the man on the other end of the phone just now. Tommy James sounded as if he could master a ship or a car or a girl with one hand tied.

A long shiver ran down her spine. But she collected her emotions and went into the bedroom to consider what was available in her closet. What kind of date? It didn't really matter. She had to dress her best, if she was going to match this man step for step. After four tries, she settled on the silk party gown with the raglin sleeves, the one she hadn't worn to the audition. It definitely made her look older, and it was light weight, just right for an evening in June. Full skirt in case of dancing — she felt a bit of unease at the thought of going body-to-body with someone she didn't know. That voice on the phone had sounded too military to be musical, *I'll be lucky if he can fox-trot a little. Good grief, I look pale.*

Bending toward the mirror on the vanity, she pinched her cheeks. It had always worked for Scarlett O'Hara. In Terry's case it just made her face look blotchy. *Anyway, I've got to have some lipstick.* Skinning out of the dress, she put on her gingham skirt and blouse and headed for the door.

The warmth of high noon struck home as she stepped out into the sun. Perfect weather, great for practically any kind of date — *he's going to ask me where I want to go.* The Muny Opera would be safe. Music under the stars, a stage bright with dancers in full swing — The Student Prince was playing this week. *Watching an opera you don't have to make small talk. You sit there and listen, for hours. Pretty dull, what are you scared of?* A sense of experimentation crept into her like a dare. *How about the Admiral? That romantic top deck?*

At the foot of the hill, she turned in at Dribbin's Drug. With its new air-conditioning on it was practically chilly. Over at the fountain, Dixie looked up from the movie mag she was reading and gave a casual salute. Terry returned it, wandering toward the glass display of make-up products, aware that Dix had followed, curious.

"I need some lipstick," she said, without turning. "Pink Passion, I like that one."

"Better you should use plain old apple red, you're as passionate as cotton underwear," Dixie observed. "Anyway I thought you weren't allowed to wear lipstick? What will your mother say?" She always managed to put a little fishhook in the word "mother." She hadn't asked Fran's permission in the last five years — about anything.

"My folks are out of town, on vacation. Sort of a second honeymoon." Terry made the announcement casually.

"You're kidding! They left you alone?"

"Mm-hm. And I've got a date for tonight, so I need to get a lipstick. I already have everything else, rouge, powder, eyebrow pencil."

"What date? With who?"

"Blind date. That son-of-a-friend-of-my-mom's. You know, I told you about him."

"But that was for next fall."

"Well, he's here in St. Louis, came through on his way back to Annapolis from somewhere, and asked me out. I think I'll take that Cerise."

"A college boy! And a sailor, to boot. My God, you can say goodbye to your virginity."

Secretly shocked, as usual, by her friend's frank tongue, Terry managed a shrug. "Well, we all have to climb out of the nest some time," she said. "Did Phin tell you I ran away from home the other day? Would have made it, too, I was almost to the bus station when he caught up with me. He convinced me I should stick around for my mother's sake. She hasn't been well. But it's just a matter of time until I take off on my own, now that my father's turned over my savings to me. I could buy a ticket to anywhere."

"Like where?"

"Oh, I don't know. Maybe Hollywood. Anyway, this is a good time to start practicing my sex appeal." Terry was startled by her own words, as reflected in the wide-sprung eyes of her best friend who was staring speechless.

"Ter', you don't know what you're getting into. Men are deadly. Especially some guy who's going to be gone tomorrow. You let him invade your innocence and you'll be sorry."

Terry had an idea what Dixie was hinting at, but she didn't want to frame it in words, even mentally. Innocence was what got lost in those books they read in the secret confines of the Berensen living room when no one was home, books like "The Sheik."

" 'Sorry'," she said, "is staying at home all safe and sound the rest of my life. How much is the Cerise lipstick?"

"You don't want that, it's the wrong color," Dixie wrenched her focus away from the big picture down to the detail. "You've already started a suntan, you need something with more orange in it. Tangerine is all the go right now, since that song came out." She unlocked the cabinet and retrieved the lipstick . . . "Hold out your hand — see? That blends in with your skin tone."

Impressed, Terry said, "You're right. I'll take it. It will go great with the blue silk."

"No! You're not going to wear that? It makes you look like a nun or something. This is the moment to put on your sharkskin." It was a purchase they had made off the expired will-call rack at Sonnenfeld's, while Fran dithered . . . *way too old, hon!* A sophisticated little white sheath with a flirty jacket, the dress had gone into hiding in the trunk, hanging there forgotten until now.

"So you really think it's alluring?"

"First step to that little cottage with the picket fence."

Terry had once thought that was the ultimate future, marriage, kids, the bridge club on Thursdays and supper on the table at six o'clock, *how was your day today, honey?* Shuddering, she said, "I gave that up." Along with all the bickering and hard feelings and eventually d-i-v-o-r-c-e.

"I'm glad you've seen the light. So if you don't want to submit to all that, you don't feed the kitty. Wear something frumpy, leave off the lipstick, and if he starts to pitch the old woo, dampen him down by doing something uncouth. Like a burp or a yawn."

Terry didn't know whether to laugh. "Did you ever do that?"

"Me? Would I ever be so dumb as to go out on a date? With a boy?" Dixie looked so horrified they both broke up in giggles.

"Well, I've got to bring this off for Mother's sake. And it may come in handy next fall, to have a 'steady' up at Annapolis when the Hamiltons start asking me to come down to Richmond on weekends."

"You're going to get serious with this guy?"

"No, no. But I can pretend to them that I am. It will be a great excuse. They're all Navy people, they'll think it's wonderful if I'm tied up with an Annapolis man."

"Watch out you don't get caught in your own net. I hear those academies teach seduction as a minor course. Come on, I'll ring this up and we'll have a float. On the house. At the pittance Mr. Dribbin pays, I figure he owes me a float or two."

If seduction (whatever that meant) was on Tommy's mind, the sharkskin dress wouldn't discourage him. Smooth as milk, it fell in perfect folds to the hem, which

Terry had shortened to a couple of inches below the knees, at Dixie's instruction. It let her show off the new nylon stockings to perfection. And the bright striped bolero jacket, trimmed with gold ball-fringe, was positively sexy. If she could have put her hair up, or let it fall around her shoulders the image would have worked better. She felt her curly locks, but they were still too short to crop. *I've got to do it before I go off to school, though, I cannot appear there looking like a brunette version of Little Orphan Annie.*

At quarter-to-six she took off the makeup for the third time and tried again, just a little rouge this time, a touch of lipstick, dab of powder on the tip of her nose which was beginning to shine with nervous perspiration. *What's the worst that can happen? Anyway, he'll probably be too smart or too short or too rich and snooty, Ladue Village, my de-ah!* Grabbing her little white silk clutch purse, Terry went downstairs, refused to go to the window to peer out, retreated to the piano room. *Should I be playing something? Maybe if I knew any pop music. Certainly not The Rustle of Spring!*

And then the doorbell rang.

TWELVE

I hope he doesn't smell like styptic pencil. Poor Oz, you could suffocate. . . .

Terry opened the door and stopped, transfixed. Struck by the late sun, Tommy James stood in a gloss of light. Tall, brilliantly white in a uniform with gold on it, his hat under his arm, leaving the dark wavy hair gleaming undimmed, he looked as if he had just stepped out of a parade. There was a glint of humor in his eyes, which were the blue of a gun barrel — the big service revolver that Henry Miller kept under his mattress — the color of war, yes, this was a warrior.

"Terry?" He held out his hand, warm grip, firm enough to telegraph respect. Not exactly handsome, his face was too hard-boned, the nose had a jog in it as if it had been broken at some time and the eyebrows were uneven, one cocked higher in surprise. "Good grief, blind dates aren't supposed to be this beautiful."

A jolt of inner electricity brought Terry out of her paralysis. "You're right, this has got to be a mistake. Do come in, Admiral James."

He joined her in a chuckle. "Sorry if I appear too nautical, but the truth is, after years at the Academy I've outgrown all my civvies. Didn't want to buy new, just for a few weeks' leave."

Yes, those shoulders definitely wouldn't fit into the meager shirt of a mere college kid.

"Anyway, I leave it to you to decide where we can go that I won't draw too much attention." He was still kidding. "There must be some place that's a favorite of yours. This is one big handsome city, at least as seen from a plane."

"It wasn't always beautiful." She found herself talking easily, about the clean-up efforts that had sand-blasted away years of soot from St. Louis after they passed the smoke ordinance, *and what am I doing, babbling about civic improvement on a date?*

"A very historical town, too," he was saying. "Great rivers coming together, a natural hub for the exploration of the west."

And now she had no trouble at all deciding what they should do. "If you'd like to take a closer look at the old Mississip' there is a paddlewheeler that offers an evening cruise, down the river and back, dining, dancing —"

"Plus a top deck with a great view," he added. "The Admiral, right? My cousin told me it was a prime place for a date. Shall we set sail?" He was escorting her to the vehicle parked in front of the house, a swanky golden thing with the new stream-lined look and chrome all over it. A Lincoln Zephyr. Terry had never seen one up close before. Handing her in on the passenger side, he went around and got behind the wheel, resting a white-gloved hand on it.

"M'lady, you have the conn."

Afterward, Terry could hardly recall that ride through Forest Park and on down into the old town along the waterfront. They talked — about history. She was glad she'd paid attention to old Kettler, she could add to the conversation such tidbits as the fact that the first streets of St. Louis were laid out by a teenage boy, young Pierre Chouteau, who was left with just a work crew over one hard winter and by spring had the beginnings of a small city half-built for the families which came upriver in 1765 to provide a trading post for the mountain men. It had always fascinated her that out of the wild prairie a town had appeared almost full-grown, with homes and warehouses and a church.

"They just forgot one thing," she added, "namely to grow any food. For the first few years the town was snickered at and called 'Pain Court.'"

"Short of — bread?" He liked it. He liked everything about her, it was plain in his eyes whenever he glanced away from traffic and took another visual bite. Once they were on the Admiral he took charge of the conversation, commenting on the use of steam to drive the huge pistons, the same power that still propelled ships at sea. "But that's all changing," he added. "Soon they'll be experimenting with new energy sources —" Halting in mid-sentence, he gave a rueful laugh. "What am I doing, talking to a lovely young woman about the future of nautical propulsion? Bad form, old boy."

"I don't mind at all," she said truthfully. She was beginning to relish this kind of conversation, not to mention the grilled channel catfish entrée. She never knew the food was this good in the river boat's dining room. "I've recently been told I should learn to know more about this future I am about to inherit."

"Sounds like a graduation speech? I'll be

195

going through that next June." His strong features were high-lighted by the candle that flickered in the globe of red glass in the center of the table. It seemed to add a different dimension to his eyes. "Wish it were sooner, we're needed out there in the real world right now."

"You mean, as naval officers?"

"Right. The shipyards are turning out all kinds of craft faster than we can man them. We ought to be putting them to sea, patrolling the shipping lanes."

"To keep the Germans from sinking the freighters?" It had been in the papers a lot lately. Her father had seethed over it. *If the Germans torpedo just one of our destroyers, we'll be in the dad-blasted war faster'n a greased pig. Old Franklin can hardly wait for it to happen.*

"Or maybe we'll take the fight right to them, see if we can't rid the North Sea of this pack of subs."

"Then you think we should get in the war?" She said it cautiously, but she was tempted to have a really good argument. Never could with her father or her teachers or all the older know-it-alls of the world. But here was a man who not only talked straight, he listened.

"Yes, I do. I think if we don't get into it pretty soon England will go under."

"But we've sent her so much ammunition and so many planes."

"Who's going to fly them? They're short of pilots, short of ground troops, they've been decimated these last few years, they're just staggering around trying to hold off the end. That country is barely glued together by Winston Churchill, but he can't do it alone. If Britain falls, we'll be alone in the world, and it wouldn't be pleasant, I can tell you."

"One of the boys in my class, a refugee from Austria, says that we could have storm troopers marching down the streets of our city. I thought he was kidding."

"Jewish, no doubt? They've seen the worst of it first-hand. Hitler wants to rid his country of the Jews permanently."

Terry had heard someone else say that, but it seemed so inconceivable. "Why? Why would they want to? U. City is a Jewish community and our schools are better than any other suburb in the city. We pay our teachers more."

"And there's the point. The Jews run things their own way, set their own priorities and set out to control the finances wherever they live. Money is power, and

Hitler can't stand to have anyone else claim power over what happens in Germany. Or the other countries he's invaded. Doesn't it make you burn a little to think of him owning Paris, for instance?"

"Well, yes, I guess. But war is such a terrible thing. My father got shell shocked in the Argonne. He still suffers from it. He says if we ever do anything stupid again like getting into a fight over there, we'll kill our best men. We can't afford to do that twice in twenty years."

"The doughboys took some heavy casualties," he admitted, "but the totals weren't all that high. Not like the decimation of the English and the French who really did lose a generation of their youth. We're better prepared and better trained than they were. Anyway, I don't see that we have a choice."

"There's a big ocean between us and the fighting."

He smiled, a kind of grimace. "Oh yes. We were out on that ocean, my classmates and I, on our summer cruise recently. And what do you know, right there off the coast of Virginia we sighted a U-boat. Gave chase, but we lost her."

"You — chased — What were you going to do if you caught it?"

"Well, you always hope they'll get reckless

and try to engage. It would have been good experience in battle tactics."

"I thought you could practice shooting at dummies." She had seen it in the newsreel recently, Naval vessels booming away at a sort of fake boat with a white flag on it.

"Drones," he nodded. "Which is okay, but it doesn't teach you evasive tactics. You don't really know how you'll react until you see an enemy torpedo coming at you. It's sort of like playing dodge-ball with the ship."

"What would you — I mean if they did shoot, what — ?"

"We'd try to depth-bomb them out of the water."

"Er — wouldn't it — thank you," she said to the waiter who had set a piece of lemon pie in front of her, "wouldn't it bother you to send a bunch of people to the bottom of the ocean?" And if the question was naïve, she thought, so be it.

He raised those cold blue eyes to hers. "When an enemy is firing their fish at you, you don't mind hurting their feelings, not at all." Then, with sincere relish, he tasted his pie. "This is really very good food, you know?"

It was, indeed. Terry felt as if she had entered a whole new world where she might, possibly, hold her own. She hadn't funked out, and he hadn't belittled her questions.

"It's natural for you to feel a distaste for the idea of war," he went on. "It's hard on a woman, staying home while the men are off fighting. But can you think of any other way we'll ever stop a maniac like Hitler from dominating the world?"

Terry had never felt so complimented — he was actually waiting for her to make a suggestion. "Couldn't we boycott him or something?"

"That's what got us into this mess. After the World War everybody ostracized Germany, bottled them up like a bunch of rats in a cellar. They were starving, their money wasn't worth the paper it was printed on. But even rats fight for their lives, and if they grow big enough they can strike back, even start recovering territory."

"Like Scarlett O'Hara after the Civil War — 'I'll never be hungry again,' — and she went after them all with a vengeance." Terry shut up, abruptly, feeling she had probably sounded shallow. Fighting men don't get their insight from going to movies.

But he was nodding. "Exactly. We're up against a desperate nation, or they would never follow a man like Hitler."

It put a whole new slant on the problem.

Why didn't anybody ever explain all that to me? More questions rose in her mind, but she saw that he'd had enough. He was paying off the waiter, shoving back from the table.

"Why don't we go and explore the rest of this marvelous boat?"

On the deck above, a combo was in full swing, people dancing. "Shall we take a quick turn?" They were playing "Deep Purple" as he guided her expertly into the milling crowd. Glad that Phin had taught her the ballroom steps, Terry felt a twinge of guilt to be dancing with someone else, but it was fleeting. Phin was off tonight with Ruth Ann at some wedding dinner of a friend of hers. Probably dancing himself. *Don't you dare do the rain-forest thing with anybody but me.* Then she had to smile a little, at the childish thought. Life goes on, and so does the lindy. She did a couple of fast steps, Tommy picked them up and spun her expertly, they were moving in a heated counterpoint as the band closed down.

"Wow," he said, a little breathless. "Now I know I'm dreaming. A blind date who can really dance."

"It's all in the lead. Do they teach that at the Academy?"

"Matter of fact, they do. You'll see, when you come up there — all the fellows are at home on the dance floor. You haven't lived until you've attended one of the big balls in Dahlgren Hall. Let's do some more exploring."

He meant the top deck, of course. A sudden shiver ran down her spine, as she screened all the whispers she'd heard in the gym locker-room about the smooching that went on out there under the stars. By now she knew that she would have no trouble standing him off, no need of Dixie's subterfuges. He'd never go farther than she wanted. The thing that had made her quake inside was the sudden realization that she wouldn't mind, wouldn't mind at all, if — something happened. In the pit of her stomach a tightness, a kind of tingle of anticipation was made more acute by not knowing exactly what was involved. No boy — much less a man like this — had ever wanted even to kiss her.

Holding her breath, she followed him up the winding stairs and out into the warm summer night brilliant with stars, extravagantly strewn across a black velvet sky. The breeze was laden with the strange odors coming off-shore, mossy trees and marshy sand banks, you could imagine it was the smell of the wilderness as it had been two hundred years ago. The face of the river stretched out on every side, with only a distant scatter of lights to indicate the eastern bank. Illinois was in another world.

Tommy had gone to the rail. For a few minutes, the boat took over as the object of his interest. They were turning around, getting ready for the laborious return trip upstream against the current, the big paddle churning the water hard. Over on the far edge of the glow shed by the boat, the brown face of the river looked like chocolate sauce, boiling around its eddies.

"That's a mean-looking current," he commented.

"A lot of people have drowned in the Mississippi. It isn't very deep, there are a lot of snags right under the surface."

"I wonder what the draft of this boat is?"

"Only about six feet I think. Maybe eight or ten. It's totally flat on the bottom. There was a piece on riverboats in the paper not long ago. The main danger in the old days was that the boiler might blow up if they put on too much fuel — they used to pick up wood at the landings along the river. When the boats would race, they'd just keep building up the fires until there was too much steam."

"And — boom! Poor devils, having to swim for shore in that water." He glanced around now, and she noticed the dark shapes in the dimness of the starlight, people in deck chairs. He found one — a sort of double-seated recliner that required a closeness. Terry wasn't sure she was ready for it. Swift thoughts of Uncle Redford had to be quickly put down. *Don't ruin things by being prissy. This man isn't a letch.* All the same, she shivered as she accepted the seat beside him.

"That's a kind of chilly breeze. Come here, I'll warm you up." With an easy-going gesture he laid an arm around her shoulders.

Her problem, she thought with a panicky amusement, wasn't the chill. It was the heat that had begun to rise in her like a sudden fever, a flush of awareness, of his body tucked against hers. *But not like Uncle Reddie, nothing remotely like Uncle Reddie.* Or was it her own reaction that was so different, the way her heart hammered inside her, the sensitivity of her skin to his touch? This time she *wanted* to be held. Closer . . .

Almost absently he began to stroke her hair. "We need to make some plans. For next Fall. Our 'blind date' is all mapped out, a football game in October, followed by the Saturday night dance and so forth. But I'm thinking we should plot our own course, if you agree? What I propose is that once you get off at school — Gloucester, isn't it? I've met a few people from there — it's not too far to Annapolis, about a three-hour bus ride. As I understand it, you may have trouble getting away from them, they're pretty old-fashioned about rules and so forth."

"My mother's going to write them a letter, giving permission for me to go up to spend that weekend with you. I might get her to make it broader, to include possible invitations that might come along at the spur of a moment, you know?"

"Perfect. I wouldn't want you to get in trouble by sneaking away."

"It would be hard to do without them knowing. Students can't even ride in cars without the permission slip from the Dean. I'll bet when the school was first founded, if you told the merrie olde students they couldn't ride their horses you'd have had a whole new revolution."

He chuckled at that. "Actually, it seems to be a current convention — we're not allowed to drive, either. In fact, I'd put our regs up against yours any day. We can't even have a dance without chaperones, they line up along the walls like harpies. But there are ways around that. We'll manage a private moment or two . . ."

What's he doing with my hair? He had taken off the bandeau and extracted the bobbie pins, and now was nesting in the awful curls, his breath warm against her neck.

"Lord, you smell good."

So that's why Mother always puts sachet behind her ears. She had done it force of habit, but she hadn't put any *there*. His free hand was roaming her knees, finding its way under her slip. *Should I let him do that?* What did Dixie always say? "Relax and enjoy it." Terry felt stiff as a board. *How can you relax when every move he makes is winding you tighter and tighter.*

Slowly he drew back and peered down at her in the darkness. "Terry, is it possible you've never done this before?"

His perception left her monumentally grateful. "Uh — yeah, it's — all sort of new — not that I — I mean, don't stop." In the darkness, she blushed hotly.

"I'm sorry, I just supposed — you seem so grown up. You rise above the school-girl mode like a kite in a windy sky. That's okay, we'll just have to go a little slower. I'm willing to bet my stripes you didn't make any preparations."

*Preparations? For what? Does he mean —
yes, that's what he means!*

"Unfortunately, neither did I. Never dreamed we'd hit it off so quickly. This whole evening has been a revelation. Not to worry —" he nibbled her neck — "our time will come. This just gives us something to look forward to."

Swallowing hard, she said, "You — don't have to — stop on my account." *What's got into me?*

"Well, that's very generous of you, my darling girl, but we can't afford any mishaps. Might end up ruining both of us."

In a flash of memory she recalled a conversation between her mother and the cleaning woman who was moaning over her daughter. "Pore l'il thing got overtook by a sweet-talkin' man and before you knows it, she got one in the oven." It took on a whole new slant.

Tickling her ear with his tongue, Tommy held her closer. "Pleasure deferred can be all the better. Next fall, you will hear me howling a wolf call all the way from Chesapeake Bay. I must remember to thank your mother for sending you to that funny little school. In fact I have the highest respect for mothers. My own, I'd better warn you, is a juggernaut — in the nicest way, of course. She's a pretty lady with a grip of steel. She likes to make my plans for me, the way she engineered our date. But whether she'd approve of us as closer friends, who knows? I think we'd better not tell either of them of our future intentions."

"You think your mother wouldn't like me?"

"She'd be very impressed. That's the trouble: you would loom as an obstacle to her master plan. See, her big guns are trained on marrying me off to the brass. Nothing less than the daughter of a rear admiral will do. Doesn't want me to languish as a j.g. for long years. Never mind, I can handle her. I will pretend it's a big chore, escorting the little freshman from Gloucester. She'll never know that you and I —"

The rest of the thought got lost like the wake of the big paddlewheel. Time and place were left behind, rational thought, self determination. As the darkness ruled Terry was submerged in a deep incoherence . . . *Don't do that, don't — yes, do, please go on, do, do it. What's happening to me?*

THIRTEEN

In the aftermath of that night on the river, she kept her own close counsel. For some reason Terry couldn't share it with anyone, especially not Dixie. At some point a secret door had been opened to a torrent of wind that had blown away all her preconceived ideas about conventions and proper behavior, leaving her inner rooms in confusion. Until she could figure it out for herself, she drew her mental clothing closer, even if it made for a lot of inner heat. The weather didn't help.

Sultry that day on Berensen's back porch. Buggy, too, with a whole population of mosquitoes, flies, June bugs, gnats. It was so normal for summer in Missouri that Terry didn't even notice, but slapped and fanned absently as she stared up at the afternoon sky, thick with yellow overcast.

"So come on. You had this great dinner and you danced and then . . . you went up the stairs onto the top deck . . ." Dixie sprawled in the hammock her pixie face twisted in an evil grin. "I suppose everybody around you was spooning?"

Terry focused on a leaf on the old elm tree at the back of the yard. It hung absolutely motionless in the humid air.

"Hey, girl, give!"

"I don't know what everybody was doing, it was dark." Whatever had happened between her and Tommy James, to call it "petting" was to cheapen it. The memory of that short intense time was so personal Terry held it tight in her heart, not to be discussed, to be diminished by mere words.

"Aw, shoot, you're being enigmatic. Phin, she's being enigmatic."

"So let her alone." From the doorway behind them, he came slowly onto the porch. Something in his curt tone sounded out of tune. Terry twisted around to look at him. And why was he wearing the awful brown tweed suit on this afternoon that was hot enough to bake biscuits without an oven? A fine sheen of sweat on his equine features, he was holding two ties — one a hideous green-and-black pattern, the other raw yellow. "So which looks like a serious minded young scientist?" It was supposed to sound humorous, but there was too much gloom in him to be overridden.

"You cut your hair," Terry accused.

"Can you tell? Did I leave slice marks?" He felt of his forelock which he had chopped straight across so that it resembled the edge of a thatched roof over his eyes, which today were the green of bread-and-butter pickles. "Maybe I should put more glop on it." Some kind of oil was holding down the top, but the wild tufts were trying to lift anyway.

"It's a mess," Dixie said flatly. "Sit down there. I'll get the scissors and neaten it up."

"So . . ." Terry made a guess. "You're going to a funeral."

"Yeah. His own." Over her shoulder, Dixie spat out the words as she headed into the house.

"Cut it out, Sis." The snapped-off words were so unlike Phin, it gave Terry a sense of real disaster.

"What's happened? Major calamity? The University burned down, the city is under attack? A touch of Armageddon?"

He sat down on the step, his face ragged with eyebrows and jaw-jut. "Death in the family." He jerked a thumb in the direction of The Heap, which stood over by the shed which had once been a stable. Its hood was up, its organs excised and lying on the ground around it, while arteries dangled over the edge of the engine cavity and dripped onto the bare earth.

"Carburetor again?" she ventured.

"The fuel line ruptured yesterday down in the middle of Big Bend Boulevard, a guy had to give me a push just to get to the curb. I taped it up and managed to get her home, barely. The pump is shot, the distributor is on its last legs, the engine needs a ring job and she needs new tires all the way around. You know what tires cost these days, with rubber so scarce?"

"It's the fault of the dirty Japanese." Dixie, returning. "Wrecking all the rubber plantations in southeast Asia, burning down the silkworm trees."

Terry didn't follow. "Well, I know, I read the papers, but what's that got to do with — ?"

"Point is, there'd be no use fixing the fuel system, even if I could scrape the bucks together. The Heap is done-for." Phin hung his long arms over his knees and endured the snip of the scissors, as if it heralded his imminent execution. "It's time I got a job and started pulling my weight around here."

"Only I'm not going to let him do it," Dixie vowed angrily. "I've decided. I am the one who should get down to business. I can get work at Sonnenfeld's. Mom said there's an opening in the coat department, winter coats are big in summertime. You get a good commission when you sell a bunch of dead minks to some rich bitch. Oh, shoot, excuse me." She had let the scissors get too close to an ear.

"It's nice of you to offer," Phin told her, "but you can forget about it. You are going to New York on Friday as planned."

"*This* Friday!" Terry sent her best friend an accusing look. "Were you even going to say 'Goodbye'? " Privacy about men was one thing, but to sneak off into the world forever with no warning — that was outright treason.

"I was coming over there later today, honest. Don't be sore, Ter'. I was just superstitious, afraid to talk about it because I might jinx it. I had this hunch it would never really happen, and I was right. It's over. I am not —" to Phin — "going to let you ruin your life."

Terry was still fumbling with too much news all at once. "But can't Phin take the bus for a while? It runs right down to the University."

"Mom needs to do grocery shopping," he said, "and I have to get to Webster Groves for night classes, I can't let Ruth Ann chauffeur me around. She's got her own family to take care of, she's supporting them on her salary as a nurse. She makes me feel like a piker, hanging out in classrooms and labs."

"Well, okay, so you work at Banner Ironworks all summer, make enough to —"They had advertised for a chemist to run tests on their castings, they made sewer covers. Dull work, but it would bring in a few bucks.

"They withdrew their job offer when they found I was going back to school in the fall. They need somebody permanent. Everybody wants you to be permanent."

"Like really *really* permanent," Dixie said through her teeth. "He's going to indenture himself to damned Monsanto Chemicals for five years."

Phin frowned. "Sis, just because you're going to New York, it doesn't mean you can talk like a gangster's moll. It makes you sound cheap."

"Monsanto?" Terry struggled to keep up. "You said you would never work for them, after they made you that offer last May."

"I know. But they pay big bucks, and they told me any time I changed my mind I could still have the job. So I've changed my mind. That's all. You finished, Sis?" He stood up. "I've got to get going."

"They will take his brain," Dixie made a morbid gesture with the scissors, "and cut it up into little pieces which they will sell for big profits, while he stays shut away in the laboratory, a prisoner forever."

"It isn't a life sentence, five years isn't that long," he said lamely.

Dixie scowled, her ugly little face ferocious as a troll's. "They make their key people sign a contract. Every thought he has will belong to them forever, every new idea or development. He'll never see a penny from his own discoveries."

Appalled, Terry shook her head. "They can't do that! I mean, nobody would ever sign away their — their mind?" But she saw the truth in his eyes. He was putting on the yellow tie, but the real sign of servitude was the wing-tip shoes. *They look like my father's!* It gave her a pang so sharp she almost doubled over. Slumping on the bottom step of the porch, she tried to catch her breath. But it had been the birth-pain of an idea. So big an idea, she doubted she could handle it. Of course, if she did, it would be the brain child of all time.

Wait now, don't rush into it, think about the details, how will you put it to him? Getting up, she moved across the yard to stand beside the defunct vehicle. The others followed wordlessly, gathering around it in memoriam. Phin touched a fender: Rest in peace.

Very carefully Terry took the first step. "I wish I knew more about cars. Ever since I can remember, I've wanted one of my own. I even thought I might get one for graduation, but it costs too much, of course. At least — how much do they cost, Phin?"

"A whole lot. And prices will probably go up, the way the country is cutting back on production, making more planes and trucks for England. Takes a lot of steel, arming for war." Then with an effort he addressed her question. "You could probably get a good used car for three, four-hundred bucks. Of course it might as well be a million as far as I'm concerned."

"At least if you had the money you could buy one." Terry sighed. "I can't. I found that out last week — I called some dealers, but when they learned I'm under age they wouldn't even talk to me. Did you know you have to be twenty-one to sign a contract?"

"When did you come into wealth?" Dixie inquired sourly.

"Last week. My father gave me my savings book. There's over four hundred dollars in it. It's supposed to be for school clothes, but I already have most everything I need, so I thought I might get a car — stupid dream."

"What do you need one for anyway?" Dixie glared at her. "You told me you couldn't even ride in one, off there in Gloucester."

"Oh, I just wanted it for this summer, so I could drive around and have some fun, something to think back on next winter." Terry gave them a wistful smile. She turned to Phin. "I don't suppose you could pretend to be my father, I mean in that suit and tie and polished shoes."

"Afraid that's out," he glanced down at his haberdashery grimly.

As Dixie met Terry's eyes, a change took place visibly, her thin face sharpened. To Phin she said, "Couldn't you pretend to be her guardian? Long enough to sign some papers?"

"You're talking legal documents," he shook his head.

"Doggone, it seems like there should be a solution to a simple problem like that." Terry dangled the word "solution" like bait. "Desire plus money equals car, right?"

Dixie was nodding. "I'm going to make some lemonade, and then we'll sit down and figure this thing out."

"I'll do the honors," Phin offered. "I'm the only one allowed to dispense my graduation ice cubes." It still tickled him that the refrigerator made ice when he wasn't looking. Disappearing into the dim kitchen, he left a silence behind.

"You're on the right track," Dixie whispered. "Just leave it to me."

"You'll make him suspicious."

"No, I won't. I'll just say —"

There was a tinkling of glasses as he brought the tray out and they retreated to the shade of the porch.

"I just had a thought," Dixie pondered. "Phin, why couldn't you take Terry's money and buy a car and give it to her?"

"Won't work. If she turns up with an automobile her father will hit the roof and we'd both be in the soup. He could sic the cops on me for corrupting an innocent minor."

"She could keep it here."

"Or better yet," Terry said, "we could form a partnership. It would technically be your car, but I could use it in the daytime when you're down at the lab. Then you could have it nights and weekends. Park it here, nobody would know. Why wouldn't that work?"

He was shaking his head again. "I am not going to touch any of that money, Miss Got-rocks. You'll need every bit of it when you get off at school. You don't know how those fees and charges add up, not to mention books and football tickets and sheet music and all the rest."

"Drat!" Terry set her glass down with the bang. "For two cents I would skip the whole college thing forever."

"Phin, I'm surprised at you!" Dixie frowned down at him as he hunched over his lemonade on the top step. "You usually are ready to help out a friend."

"Only this time, she's the one trying to help me out," he said sagely. "Bunch thinks she's putting one over, but I can see right through her. I would never take money from anybody, it's bad policy, especially with a friend."

"But it would only be a loan." Terry burst out in inspiration. "Just until your fellow-ship comes through in the fall. Then you pay me back and take the car and mean-while we both would have what we need."

"Perfect!" Dixie pounced. "And you won't feel guilty about causing your best buddy to commit suicide next fall when she has to go off to college. It's an act of mercy, to make someone's dream come true, even if only for a couple of months."

"And if you don't, Dixie is likely to go to

work at Sonnenfeld's and give up her life-long dream, too, you know how she is," Terry accused.

Phin eyed them aghast. "You two are something else! When did you cook this plan up?"

"I can just picture it," Terry narrowed her eyes to peer into realms of imagination. "Every day before I go to the library, I could take her out and drive and drive, have her back in your yard before you come home in the afternoon, and nobody would know the truth. A great secret collaboration."

"This country is founded on partnership, people owning shares in a project, everybody benefits." Dixie stood before them gesturing in the best style of their social science teacher.

"Oh, for crying out loud," Phin snorted. But there was a leak in his skepticism now, a trickle of uncertainty.

Red roadsters with chrome wire-spoke wheels are the stuff of dreams. Reality was a blue Hudson coupe with a small dent in the right front fender and only 30,000 miles on the speedometer. Phin had checked out the engine and pronounced it sound. The price was right: $369.00. Which left enough in the bank account for last-minute school purchases. But who could think of money when faced with the magnificence of a hood ornament in the form of a bird with a lion's head? Or maybe a lion with wings, the salesman said he thought it was a griffin. Phin wouldn't settle for that. He proclaimed that, as a mythical beast of prey, it should be spelled "Gryphon."

As they grouped around it in Berensen's back yard, nothing had ever looked so beautiful to Terry. Even Dixie was keyed to a level of excitement unusual for her. And Phin's long face finally broadened into a grin.

"I must be crazy to go along with this. Gawsh-darn, you girls will rule the world some day." With a quick swipe, he unlaced the wing-tip shoes and kicked them off, right one, left one, to reveal bright red socks that Terry recognized as her Christmas present to him last year. Feet flashing he went into a wild conga around the back yard.

On an inspiration, Dixie seized the broom and made a xylophone out of the porch railing, while Terry grabbed the watering can and beat it like a bongo, infused with a kind of madness. The world was coming apart, her family had flown, she had ventured to the edge of danger last night. But this was a greater wonder: of having achieved the impossible:

I solved a problem that stumped even Phineas W. (for Woodrow) Berensen.

FOURTEEN

Too fast, everything coming at her too fast
— Terry felt giddy, a little afraid and yet
oddly detached, looking at herself once
removed: *there's a girl who owns a car.* Make
that *"young woman."* The word itself was
unnerving and wonderful, implying a maturity which she knew, down deep, she had
not earned. But even the awareness of that
made her feel years older. It was confusing
to leave security behind and head off into
an unknown where she would make her own
decisions, spend her own money (an awful
lot of money) and could choose her own
path. It had only been three days since she'd
been a child. A protected state in which you
can relax and be guided by an adult world,
a stern custody, but reassuring. Children
can relax. But little kids don't own automobiles with gleaming hood ornaments.

The other day after the joyous celebration
had calmed down, she had poured a cup of

lemonade over the grill and pronounced: "I christen thee Gryphon." Phin had hastened to swab it up with a damp cloth, of course, wouldn't want the glorious chrome to lose its shine. He hovered over the car like a fond father, trying not to show it. Trying to sound old and practical.

"I believe I'd better drive us to the station, parking may be tight down there."

Terry was just as glad. She was not great at maneuvering a vehicle into a small space, and the Gryphon was a couple of feet longer than the Heap.

"Well, I certainly would feel better," Dixie announced a bit unkindly. "I'd hate to be killed before I even make the train."

So they found themselves elbow-to-elbow that Friday in the dusk of late afternoon, Phin at the wheel, handling the car with authority as he guided it through traffic, looking very cool in spite of the heat. But Terry noticed the way his hand rested on the gear shift, fondly, as if encouraging a son. She was glad they had saved Phin for posterity. Her own personal happiness was seated deep in her skirt pocket, where her hand was clenched around her own car key.

Tomorrow before the library opens, before the folks come home, I can take her out and drive her, race her, let her romp, solo. No Phin to say, "Ahem, if I were you . . ." or Dixie to snort around, "Don't let the beast go to your head."

As they rode in silence, unspoken thoughts vibrated across the front seat. Dixie was a stranger, clinging fiercely to the huge handbag on her lap, a great big embroidered thing that could hold as much as a small suitcase, what did she need all that room for?

Terry said, "When I ran away from home I almost took my sweet-potato plant."

"What? Oh. Well, don't sneer, this purse has all the necessities of life in it." The upthrust chin put an end to that train of thought.

"I'm not sneering. I'm just envious." Terry hadn't intended that confession.

"You're envious of *me?"* Dixie gave a curt laugh. "And all this time I've been wondering how I can catch up to you. I mean, you've been charging off into the future like a speed demon. Running away, even if you did change your mind, and now staying alone in your house for a week, going out with strange men on the riverboat, buying a car . . ."

"Well, for petesake! You're the one who's

225

going off forever to a big city and become a great fashion designer and never even told me you were leaving so early . . ."

"My aunt and uncle wrote, they need somebody to help out at the bakery. Their clerk went off and got married suddenly, and I could use the money, even if it isn't much."

"Free room and board amounts to a lot," Phin commented. "And you'll be on the scene for a while before you have to enter school. You'll know your way around."

"It sounds fabulous," Terry sighed. "I wish I had some sort of talent, to go and make a career for myself."

Dixie gave her a sidelong glance. "I figured you thought it was sort of silly of me, drawing a bunch of dumb pictures like I'm still playing paper dolls."

"*Why?* Why would you think that? I never said — I never even dreamed such a thing!"

"Of course she didn't," Phin added and to Terry, "Don't mind Sis. She's a little off-balance about now, the way you feel when the train takes that first bump forward and you're not ready for it."

Darkly Dixie said, "I'm ready. I've been ready all my life."

He was parking now, jockeying the Gryphon into a tight space with inches to spare. *How can I learn to do that without putting a dent in a fender?*

Dixie had her hand on the door handle. "What are we waiting for?" She lurched out onto the sidewalk and headed with quick steps for the towering lights of the old station. Phin grabbed her suitcases and they followed.

Inside the vaulted waiting room Terry shivered. The place always spooked her, to listen to the echoes of clicking heels, hushed conversations, all caught in the arches high above where a thousand goodbyes were trapped forever. She hurried on after the others out into the train yards where, under the lighted sheds, huge locomotives chuffed and hissed steam. One was coming in slowly, gliding with just a soft click of wheels, backing in so that its club car eased up to the stop at the end of the track. Another train was heading out, monster wheels grinding and slipping under the weight of the long string of cars, dull gray Pullman cars, people at the windows.

Halfway down the platform they found the right section, and a porter received the luggage in an act of finality that struck all three of them dumb. Dixie squared her shoulders under the beige jacket she had made herself, her dark hair pulled into a chignon topped by a little straw boater. Hand on hip, she cocked one white pump at an angle.

"Well, look out New York, here I come."

"Gosh, I'm going to miss you." Terry blurted it out in the heat of last-minute distress.

"Yeah, you will. In fact I don't know what you'll do without me to guide you, fashion-wise. So I'm leaving you a reminder." Dixie dove into the big handbag and took forth a parcel wrapped in tissue paper, shoving it into Terry's hands. "There'll be times when you want to wear that red velvet gown and it will look too naked, so you can throw this on." A length of violent-pink silk with a few lovely crimson flowers embroidered on it — only Dixie would know how to put the two shades together.

"You made this yourself?" Terry marveled.

"Used up all my embroidery floss on the fringe." The elfin grin flashed. "Wear it in good health." With a swift peck on Phin's cheek, she turned and climbed the steps into the Pullman car and was gone.

They turned away, both aware that Dixie would never do anything as mundane as to wave out the window. Walking back through the station Terry held the scarf like a treasure.

Phin sounded almost cross as he said, "How do you do that? I swear, I have tried, but I can't cry. Seems to make people feel better, but I can't get the hang of it."

Sniffling, Terry snickered. "It has to come over you, like sneezing."

When they reached the car he seated her behind the wheel. "You haven't had any experience driving at night. Maybe you ought to practice a little while I'm around to offer advice." Then, getting in on the passenger side, he added, "I'm real big on advice. I wish somebody would give me some."

Hardly noticing the words, Terry fought down a touch of panic as she tried to plan how to inject the car into the crush of traffic around the station, a torrent of headlights coming both ways.

"Watch for the stop sign on the corner back there to turn red," he said. "That will hold up the flow long enough for you to ease out into the lane."

Of course. Nerves steadying, she gave it full concentration and managed to pull it off, but she was still headed in the wrong direction. Couldn't turn right, the mass of the station blocked that way. So work yourself over into the left lane, put your hand out the window to signal a turn . . .

"Okay." She took a long breath as they got oriented westward again. "You said you needed advice? About what on earth?"

"Don't look straight at the headlights," he warned. "Keep focusing on your own lane and don't follow the car in front too close. It's nearer than it looks."

She jammed on the brake.

By the time they got to Kingshighway she was getting slightly nervous. So many lanes of speeding cars, people honking at her because the lights had turned green, whole banks of lights extra brilliant in the thickening dusk. In a lunge she put the Gryphon through the intersection and escaped into the depths of Forest Park.

"You in a hurry to get home?" She was thinking, she had darned well better practice this night-driving thing some more, here where it was calm.

"Not me," he answered remotely. In the glow of the dashboard his face was all bones and shadows. Looking off out the window, his mind was far away in some different time and place.

Paying full attention to the winding roads of the park, with their far-flung street lamps, Terry began to get the feel of it, the quickness of looking at the sparse traffic and back at her own lane without getting blinded, the spatial mystery of the night as compared to the bright obvious day. In the course of her zigzagging she came to a major boulevard that curved away toward a monument alight up on the hill. Last remnant of a once-vast World's Fair, the Art Museum was a minor Parthenon, hanging above its lagoon, its columns up-lit, its portico majestic. Proud St. Louisans had been showing the landmark to their visitors for years. Its two large parking circles offered a view out across the whole city — a favorite spot for the college crowd, cheaper than the top deck of the Admiral for nightly hankypanky. Terry nosed the car into a parking space overlooking a vista of stacked lights, pretty as a postcard.

Staring out at St. Louis from this eminence she felt a shiver of pride: *my city.* Tommy had said it was beautiful from the air — he should see it now. In a wave of nostalgia, she thought: *a good place to call home.*

Beside her Phin viewed the dazzling display and sighed.

"So tell. What are you worried about?"

He hitched his hip into a more comfortable position. "Got the electric bill today."

"Was it that bad?"

"Two dollars and twenty cents more than last month. The refrigerator," he explained. "You don't think about that when you're buying the thing, just the cost up-front. You forget what it takes to run an electric motor day and night."

"But you're saving on ice."

"Oh, it's worth it, don't get me wrong. Food doesn't spoil now, and the vegetables keep fresher. Everybody ought to have one, and that's the problem." He waved vaguely at the city. "All those people with refrigerators and radios and phonographs and vacuum cleaners, they're going to eat up our energy reserves, we'll have to make more and more electricity. In a few years we'll be running short of coal and oil and gas to fuel the power stations, have to build more dams up and down the rivers, put up hydroelectric plants, run thousands of power lines across the country, and it still won't be enough."

Terry was silent. She could see why you might be a little concerned about it, but surely they wouldn't run out of fuel for a couple of centuries. Just like Phin to think ahead to future generations, he was always talking about "fifty years from now," a time which seemed so far-fetched she could hardly imagine it. Of course, Phin was happiest when he was in a stew about some problem he couldn't solve. "You having trouble in the lab?"

"Yeah. My experiment. My big doggoned discovery."

"Doesn't work?"

"I don't know. I can't go ahead until I get funding. And when I have to wait around, I get nervous — there isn't that much time that you can afford to waste any of it."

She remembered other days when he had felt this way, wiped the equations from the blackboard, tore up the schematic diagrams and crumpled them into the wastebasket with mutterings and grinding of teeth. They were always way over her head, but she always offered. "Tell me about it."

"It's the most complicated thing in the physical world, and yet it's so simple . . ." Digging in his pocket he held out a hand with a couple of marbles lying in it. Two glassies, one bigger than the other. "Watch this." With a quick move he tossed them onto the seat between them. "Did you see that? The heavier one landed farther."

"Uh-huh." Terry had become aware of muffled giggling in the next car, marveling as she suddenly understood exactly what was going on over there.

"Now that doesn't sound so important, but suppose they were so small you couldn't see them, even under a microscope. Knowing that principle, about the difference in weight, could help you isolate the two sizes. If I can just prove that, I could follow it on down the road to a future where poor people can live better and sick people can get well, supply power for all the fantastic new inventions, never run out, cost almost nothing."

"Sounds right down your alley. So this is your post-grad project?"

"Trouble is, the University only has limited facilities. It takes new equipment even to test the theory out. Lots of money. Which is why I'm going to Chicago next week — they've got a lab up there you wouldn't believe."

And the Gryphon will be all mine for a while! It wasn't a very generous thought, she tried to subdue it. "How long will you be gone?"

"Just a few days. I want to see what they're doing and talk to a couple of their professors. If they think I'm on the right track, maybe I can apply for extra funding. I've got to convince them . . ."

A great goal. A thing you could work your heart out on, all your life. "I wish I wasn't so dumb," she said, half to herself.

Phin came around abruptly, staring at her in the darkness of the star-glow. "Good grief, Bunch, the way you figure things out, the way you analyze a situation — you've got a great mind."

It shocked her speechless.

"You just haven't had time to develop your own thinking yet, it's all been taken away from you with this music business. You don't want to disappoint your mother, but pretty soon you'll have to make her face the truth: that the piano isn't your future."

"She already knows it, ever since last spring. Of course, she still wants me to go to Gloucester, but that's because my grandmother's paying for it. She doesn't care that it's all useless."

"Let me tell you: your first year of college, it's pretty much a waste of time anywhere you go. Freshman studies are the same, everywhere. By the time it's over, you may have discovered what you really want to do with your life. The picture at home may change . . ."

It could. They might be together again, this trip may solve everything, and soon they'll be alone, they won't be concentrating on me and what I do. If I just don't ruin things between now and September.

"They're coming home tomorrow."

"What time? Will you have a chance to come over and drive Mom to the grocery in the morning?"

And there goes my wild solo ride around the countryside. "Sure," she said. "Maybell Queal is going to pick them up at the station around noon. When are you leaving?"

"Taking the Wabash at eight-forty-five."

A sudden thought struck her. "Where did you get money for a ticket to Chicago?"

He chewed his lip, she could see him squirm in the dimness. "Don't get sore. I had to sell the Rock Island Rocket."

It brought an odd jolt in the region of her heart, a rush of memories, of laying the tracks, putting in the scenery, engineering the trestles, installing switches. The little electric signal light.

"If it's any help, it went to a good home. Ruth Ann's younger brother has been dying for a train, saved his money for years. And I'm going to help him set it up, so it will be done right."

So it will sort of be kept in the family, if he marries Ruth Ann eventually. For some reason, the thought didn't help.

"Sorry I didn't discuss it with you, but I

was afraid you'd talk me out of it. Wouldn't have taken much, just one of those sighs you just gave."

Terry swallowed her feelings, a big lump of them. "That's okay. We're not kids any more. Like you said, everything changes." *Us, most of all. Dixie already trundling off eastward, Phin going north, and I — am going nowhere.*

The silence in the car deepened. Across the sky a meteorite left a bright slash before it burned out over the city.

FIFTEEN

She had the speedometer up to fifty miles an hour and it still didn't help her escape, not totally. The joy was there, the hungering for the rush of the wind, the heady feel of the wheel. But even as these sensations rose in her they couldn't overcome the darkness of heart that lurked like a cloud of smoke pollution over her happiness. For a few hours Terry had forgotten the fears, but now they were back, even more bitter because of hope unfulfilled. The "second honeymoon" hadn't worked.

When she had asked her mother if they had a good time, the beautiful lavender eyes filled with tears. She had casually inquired of her father whether he had done any fishing, and he'd stared at her as if she spoke in a foreign tongue. *What on earth happened?* This morning Marjorie was still abed; when Terry had tiptoed in with a tray of tea and shortbread all she got was a soft snore from beneath the covers. On the night-stand in plain sight was an empty brandy bottle. Leaving the tray on the table she had eased out of the room, feeling sick from the fumes of failure.

Henry Miller ate his breakfast like a blind man and trudged out to the garage, lugging his heavy sample case. He was late making the rounds of the small Missouri towns along the river. In a shuddering amusement she pictured the look on his face if he should be driving down Lindbergh Boulevard and glance over to see his daughter at the wheel of a snappy blue coupe with a hood ornament of a winged lion. And yet there was a time when he had loved a handsome car too. He had once driven around the block in a tall yellow roadster that belonged to one of his friends. Afterward, he had lifted her onto the front seat and let her honk the glorious horn — *Ah-oo-gah!*

So long ago. These days he couldn't seem to allow himself to be happy, as if it made him feel guilty. *Why not buy a few things that other people are getting — one of the modern washing machines that runs on electricity, put it in the basement and we wouldn't have to send the laundry out. Wouldn't that be a saving eventually? Or even a tall Victrola that looks like a piece of fine furniture.* Waste of money, he'd say. It all had to do with money — the lousy rotten Depression had ruined everything. And yet, while it was going on the family had been close, standing together against the specter of destitution that the whole country faced, pinching pennies and making a game of it. *Only now, isn't it time to move on?*

The needle was edging upward, 53, 54, 55. . . farm land streamed past, the breeze was full of the green smell of kitchen gardens, a drift from the bottomlands, rank and fertile. On an impulse, Terry turned onto a gravel secondary that would take her closer to the river. Rich acres of young corn spread on every side, already shoulder-high. In a few weeks it would be taller than a man on horseback. The layers of silt laid down by centuries of flooding made the crops grow to giant size and sweetness. She passed a clapboard farm house with a barn and a pasture where cows chewed and stared at the apparition of the car with interest.

And then, there it was, the old Mizzou tangled in its islands, redolent of mud and rotting fish and history. Ghosts lived along these banks. She could picture leather-clad men poling their boats up the current,

Lewis and Clarke headed for the huge blank places on the map, followed by a whole migration of mountain men, traders, trappers, finally settlers. *Dad should have been a pioneer, a rancher, raising cattle out west or something.* This morning when he had picked up his satchel there had been a set to his jaw that spoke of duty and damnation. The way he must have looked when he faced the enemy's guns in France. But why, with prosperity everywhere, what new shellshock had turned him into a facsimile?

What do I know about how hard it is to support a family? To be responsible for other people's lives? Subdued, she turned the car around and headed for home.

The library had become a refuge. Especially now that she had the place all to herself from twelve to four. Sommertime, not much activity, Miss Wharton had made her a desk assistant. To work alone, to have a key of her own, to answer the phone and send out overdue notices, it made Terry a little proud. *You'd think they would see it at home, I'm making my own spending money, sixty-seven cents an hour.* Of course Marjorie had looked distressed.

"My dear, when will you get to the piano? Afternoon was always your practice time?"

But she knows it's all a farce. Doesn't she? Did she forget that awful audition? Terry realized she had not the slightest clue as to what her mother really thought these fractured days. But there was no doubt where Henry Miller stood.

"You mean after all the money we spent on lessons you're going to let it go, just so you can stamp out a bunch of *books?*"

There was a time when his angry tone would have hurt. Now, Terry accepted the fact that they were all playing a game with no winner. She went to the job with relief, and a certain satisfaction. It was a thing of her own making, she could exert some decision over what she would do next: call people about the reserved books? Or make cards for the new fiction stacked behind the desk?

It was one of the benefits of library work, to be the first to open the pages of some future best-seller. Lytton Strachey had produced a huge tome, a biography of Queen Victoria. How long it must have taken to research and write, Terry couldn't begin to guess. She set it aside — the cataloguer would have to assign it a number from the Dewey Decimal Code. She glanced through a new novel, "The Keys to the

Kingdom," all about religion. An unwelcome subject in the Miller household, her father had announced grimly that if there were a God he wouldn't have let the War happen.

She picked up a smaller, tighter volume, written in spare, direct language, "Inside Europe," by a man named John Gunther. She thought she ought to read it, what with everyone concerned about the fighting over there. If she was going to keep up with Tommy James next fall she had better bone up on current events, even though they didn't really interest her. Poland, Austria, she wasn't even sure where they were. It had been two years since she took European history in school, and most of that had only clung to her mind long enough to pass the final. It seemed an awful mess, those little countries all hating each other.

As she began to scan Gunther's opening words, she became aware of a customer moving up to the desk. Her glance registered only a burly figure in a white sailor suit, cap cocked low over one eyebrow. "Can I help you?"

"Yeah, you could kiss me 'hello.' " The cheeky face split in a familiar grin.

"Ozzie!" Terry tried to get oriented — the Navy had redistributed him. The belly was flat, the chest broader, the pudgy look translated into hard muscle. But the real change was subtler, the self-confidence of that stance, the deviltry in the eyes that used to be such an innocent blue.

"You look good enough to eat, babe."

Babe? "Uh — I — it's good to see you. I thought you were off in Florida or somewhere."

"Training camp's over. Got my orders, I'm headed west to San Diego. Wouldn't you know — with the real action in the Atlantic I'm headed the other way. But them's the breaks. Anyway, I got a one-day layover here to say goodbye to my ma and my girl." He winked hugely, leaning an elbow on the desk to bring him inches closer.

Terry eased back. "Well, it looks like the Navy suits you, huh?"

"It's okay. At least you don't need to worry about them split infinitives. You got buddies — that's how you really start learning about life. Get to know how to hold your liquor, cuss with the worst, and broadside the broads. You get my postcard?"

"Yes, I did, and I'd have answered it, but you didn't put on a return address."

"No, I mean did you *get* it?" He picked

up a pencil and on the pad by the phone he drew one of those symbols, an X with a circle around it.

"Well, sure . . ."

"Nah. You didn't. You never had nobody give you a French kiss." He began to move around the desk as he spoke, anticipation in his eyes, the glee of a stranger. "You don't even know what that is? It's what you give your O.A.O. That means 'One and Only', sweetiepie. Guess I could teach you a few things now."

Trapped in the angle of the desk, Terry glanced up at the clock. Three forty-five, fifteen minutes until Miss Wharton was due. Why that should matter? Her breath was coming faster, she felt slightly suffocated by the looming bulk of this man she really didn't know. She could smell the cigar smoke on his breath.

"Uh — listen, I'm on duty here. My boss expects me to get these books processed before she comes in, which is pretty soon now . . . Oz, cut it out!"

He had taken her by the arm, drew her toward him easily. "Don't play hard-to-get, toots, it's not nice. All these months I been saving this just for you." With a lunge he tried to plant his mouth on hers, but she jerked away and it landed on her neck.

Heaving inwardly, she fumbled blindly for a weapon, hand closed on a book, and she dropped five pounds of Queen Victoria on his shinbone.

"Oww!" Stepping back, he bent and rubbed the area. "You did that on purpose."

"When a man forces himself on a lady, she's entitled to defend herself."

"Force? I never — whatdaya mean 'defend'? Gawd, Terry, you don't need to defend against me?"

"I asked you to stop and you didn't."

"Aw shoot, everybody knows girls don't mean it when they say 'no.' Geez, I been looking forward to a smooch for a long time."

"But why? Ozzie, we never did any necking before you left."

"I was just a kid then. We both got older. Pretty soon I'll be seeing some action, I hope. I'm ticketed for one of those big battlewagons, feeding the long guns. Man, I can't wait. But meantime I thought we'd have a little fun. I got my dad's car and a pocketful of pay. Let's go out tonight and paint old St. Loo a few shades of red, white, and blue. I'll take you to dinner at the Park Plaza, maybe we go for a ride on the Admiral? What do you say?"

The thought of being with Ozzie on the

top deck of the riverboat made Terry sweat, under the light summer dress. Beyond the windows the day was prickly with electricity, not a breath of wind stirred the trees. "I can't do it. My dad's out of town and my mother's very ill, she can't be left alone. Right now Maybell Queal is sitting with her until my shift here is over." *How easily I lied, I never used to do that with a straight face.*

Strolling back around the desk, Ozzie eyed her, exploring his back teeth with his tongue. "You're giving me the brush-off, damned if you ain't."

In the silence a growl of thunder was heard. The sky beyond the windows had a menacing greenish undercast. *I don't want to hurt his feelings.* As she hesitated, Terry heard the sharp click of heels coming down the hall. Miss Wharton was early to work, hurrying in at full-speed, gray hairs sprouting from her bun. A thin, ascetic woman with the face of a nun, she was waving a copy of *The Post Dispatch.* "Hitler has invaded Russia. Can you imagine that!"

Frowning, Ozzie took the news sheet from her with its black banner headlines. "Gawd-a-mighty."

Is that good news or bad? Terry said, "I thought the Russians and the Germans were on the same side?"

"Not any more! Hitler's finally made a mistake," the librarian crowed. "He took on the people who licked Napoleon, and they'll lick him! Anyway, it will take some of the pressure off of England. All the panzers are lined up along a thousand miles of Russian front, ready to roll."

Ozzie handed her back the paper. "Hot ziggity dog. With Hitler's forces divided we could stomp him good, if old FDR would just get off the can and send our guys over there."

Miss Wharton frowned at him sharply. "The President will never commit our young men to die on foreign soil, and you watch your language young man."

Ozzie flushed and for an instant Terry saw the Oz of yore, diffident and sheepish. Then he squared his shoulders and cocked his head. "I bet we're in it by next year. If we don't, Europe's finished. Franklin don't want that, I bet. The Rooskies will kind of distract Hitler for a while, but they can't fight like us. I just wish I was going to the Atlantic, there's going to be a shooting match pretty soon."

Suddenly Terry could picture him, standing stripped to the waist, glistening with sweat, seizing the giant shells and ramming them into a huge gun, the way the newsreels showed the training exercises. Only then there would be real bullets flying, submarines sending their "fish" through the hostile seas. *Maybe I ought to go out with him, it's his last leave . . .*

"Uh — listen Oz —"

At that minute a sudden blast of wind swept the library, scattering charge cards everywhere, flinging a barrage of rain against the building. Miss Wharton rushed to man the fortifications in the reading room, while Terry ran to close the windows in the children's section. For a few minutes they fought a brisk skirmish.

When they got back to the desk, Ozzie was gone.

Sixteen

The glorious day, that first crystalline sky and cool sunny morning of Fall, it seemed almost sinful to be gloomy. At least she was not the only one. Over on the passenger side of the car, Phin was in a brown miasma himself. When she parked in front of Washington University, he didn't move.

"You worried about something?" she guessed.

"I'm mad at myself. I really messed things up."

"Chicago?" She was secretly relieved he had decided not to transfer up there. She wanted to think of him as here where he belonged, in the big sun porch at his study table, wearing that ratty green sweater. To be a point of reference for her own identity, as her life was flung about in strange arenas.

"Yeah," he sighed. "Chicago."

"Well, I'm sorry it didn't work out, but —"

"I thought it would be okay. Mom was going to marry the hat salesman, he'd be around to take care of her. But they had a big split-up and they aren't seeing each other any more. So — she needs somebody, she doesn't even know how to drive a car. I have to stay here — it's the least I can do, with her working so hard. Trouble is, I did the paper work for the transfer, and now the Fellowship money is screwed up. We don't know where it is, but I haven't got it, and I can't pay you back the loan and it's driving me nuts."

"Hey, it's okay. I've got plenty to get started in school, over seventy dollars." Actually $70.29. "And I get to feel like the owner of this gorgeous automobile for a little while longer."

"It will always be yours," he said, but the words came absently. More going on under the unruly thatch than he could say. "Are you sure you don't want me to take you to the train? I could skip my afternoon seminar."

"Thanks, but Mother already asked Maybell."

He was silent a moment longer. "You know —" he hitched around to face her — "if you ever get in some kind of jam you know you can call on me. I mean the kind of thing you can't talk over with your folks."

"I am going to try my best not to do anything like that." She laughed, but it didn't come off.

"And if your bank account gets below thirty dollars, you tell me right away. I mean it. I'll get you some money somehow."

Yeah, take some lousy job that picks your brain and ties you down.

Unfolding his long legs, he stepped out into the sunshine. "Well, good luck, Bunch."

The nickname caught her in the heart. As she watched him go up the walk, tilting a little to the left, Terry felt as if another thread that connected to her known life had been snipped off. Only a couple more to go. Getting in gear, her movements automatic by now, almost as smooth as Phin's, she turned the Gryphon homeward one last time.

Parking in Berensens' back yard, she took the key from the ignition and placed it reverently on the dashboard. The end of summer, the beginning of a new chapter. No tears, commit yourself to slavery for the next nine months so that when you look back later you can take a little pride in the fact that you went through with it.

Climbing the hill for home, she went around to the side door, let herself into the kitchen, and was floored to find her mother waiting at the table, sipping tea. Her face brightened into a smile that Terry hadn't seen since they got back from Minnesota. Dressed in a flowing peach-colored negligée Marjorie looked as ornamental as a china figurine. And if there was a drift of brandy it was covered by the fragrance of her sachet.

"There you are, darling. I'm so glad you're home. I didn't know where you had gone — not the library, I called them. Then when they said you had resigned your job I realized, of course, you wouldn't be working on the very day you're scheduled to leave for school. I feel so silly sometimes — I don't know where my head is."

"You're never silly." A kiss on the powdered cheek. Suddenly Terry felt an impulse to put her head in her mother's lap and pour out all the troubles, the uncertainties, the questions. To confess every secret. "I just took Phin over to school. He could have driven himself, but he knew I wanted one more trip in the car. He lets me drive his car — he taught me how. I have a license." It flowed out as naturally as the air.

"Why, Therissa Miller! You clever little gal! How wonderful." Make-up covered the dark circles under her eyes, but the best cosmetic was the luminous pleasure that shone from them as Marjorie looked up at her daughter. "How is Phineas?"

"Kind of low. He's not going to school in Chicago after all, and I think he's disappointed."

"A very dutiful young man. Probably thinking about his mother — she would be lost without him. Fran is a courageous lady, but it's hard for her to be alone in the world. We are extremely lucky to have your father," she added soberly.

"I know." *I'm glad you still think so.* Terry felt her way cautiously into the subject that had long been taboo. "Is everything okay — with you-all? I was afraid the vacation in Minnesota didn't work out."

A subtle change came over Marjorie's look, like a shadow across the sun. "Yes, Minnesota. It was very — interesting. Now tell me, are you packed and ready?"

"Just about." *Packed yes, hardly ready.* Terry poured herself some tea and pulled up to put elbows on the table, the way they used to sit and talk girl-talk. "What about you — are you feeling better these days?" *Please tell me you're going to stay away from the brandy!*

"I had a good night's sleep. Some mornings it's hard to get out of bed, but today I wouldn't want to miss a last visit with my sweet child. I'm sorry I haven't been around much these past weeks. I wanted you to know that I appreciate all your work, cooking, keeping the house going. You've turned into a very responsible young woman."

"I don't feel a whole lot like a woman," Terry blurted. "I don't know a thing about men."

Her mother looked flustered. Amused, a little sad. "And you're beginning to wonder about those feelings you get."

"I don't know what I am expected to do. Ozzie dropped by the library last week on his way to the west coast. He's going to sea on some big ship. Anyway, he tried — I mean, he didn't exactly get fresh, but he wanted to. I wasn't sure what I should do, I mean he tried to kiss me. Listen, do the French people have a different way of kissing?"

A faint tide of pink flooded her mother's face under the makeup. Cautiously she said, "The French are — uh — a licentious people, or so I've heard. They may very well take certain — uh — liberties that are not acceptable in our own society. I wouldn't worry about it."

"Maybe Dad would know?"

"I think not. For all the 'oo-la-la' he talked

about, I doubt if he had any contact with women in Paris. He was far too damaged by the war. You do know how serious it was, the shell-shock. It addles the mind in ways that leave scars on the soul. That's why sometimes he flies into a temper, his patience is very thin. He's full of torn edges inside, due to that dreadful war. Dear Lord, I do pray we don't get into another one."

"Ozzie is dying to go and fight, he likes to shoot off those big guns."

"Oh yes, young men have that instinct for combat. You'll find plenty of it when you go to the Naval Academy. Which reminds me . . ." She set down her cup and started to get up, then sank back. "You go and get it for me, it's on the desk in the front room. A letter that I wrote to the Dean of Women at Gloucester, asking her to permit you to leave school whenever you are invited to the Academy. I assured her I had absolute confidence in the propriety of the situation."

I wish I did. The fact was that just the thought of Tommy brought on a strange feeling of recklessness, the desire to experience him in what-ever way he wished. Only if he wants to go farther than he should?

"Mother, I was wondering. How do you know . . . what do you do when a boy . . .

when you get serious with a boy?" *For pete-sake I can't say the word "sex" to my own Mother!*

"You're referring to romantic encounters — how far they should be permitted to go. You'll be fine, my darling," Marjorie said it with a wistful smile. "Trust your own sense of values. You know you want a clear conscience on your wedding night — all the rest is a great game. Sometimes men can be very persuasive, but I think they like it when you outwit them. Without hurting their feelings, if possible."

Or other parts of them — I wish I could have dropped Queen Victoria on Uncle Redford's shin. You can't outwit a maniac.

"And don't forget," her mother was going on, "that you will be inviting a lot of attention in that red velvet. I thought it was way too sophisticated for you, but these past weeks you have blossomed into a much older person. When I was your age we were just a bunch of silly coquettes. You're beginning to have a lovely mystery about you, my dear."

Terry swallowed hard — the nicest thing anyone had ever said to her.

"But when the time comes for you to wear the gown you will need something to complete the picture. In the living room, on the desk along with the letter, you will find a box. Bring it on in here, will you, sweetie?"

Terry recognized the black jewel case, of course. As she picked it up her heart did a flip. *This is an inheritance, the kind you only get after somebody dies!* Taking it out to the kitchen, she gave it to her mother, who handed it back.

"It's time for you to have these. Up there at Annapolis they will evoke a different kind of respect — not everyone has such a family treasure. Gives one a unique glow."

"But these are yours, you should keep them, you'll be wearing them again." Terry fumbled wildly, not wanting a bequest, not for a long time. Under her mother's patient smile, she managed to get the case open, to stare at the Hamilton pearls. She'd done it often enough in the past, but now she was gazing down at them as someone old enough to wear them. Wondering if she could ever hold herself proudly enough to be worthy of this lustrous, perfect string.

"I discussed it with your grandmother when we were in Richmond," Marjorie went on, trying to sound matter-of-fact. "We agreed that you should have them now, while you're young. Not just Annapolis, but there'll be dances at the college too, the reception at the Music Department, maybe a recital." No more talk of a concert career, but Marjorie permitted herself a tenuous compromise. "You are doing very well with the Mozart. It has given me much pleasure to hear you practicing. I think Professor Wolff will be good for you. You did like him, didn't you?"

"Yes, I did." Terry was surprised to find it was true.

"I'm glad. At least your studies will be enjoyable. Who knows where it will all lead? Every experience is valuable to you later in life, one way or another."

Holding the pearls in her hand, marveling at the sensation — they felt warm, as if they had a sort of life of their own — Terry sensed a different kind of responsibility than she'd ever known. *Noblesse oblige?* She laid them back on the black velvet lining of the case, then went around the table to gather her mother in a careful embrace. It was like holding a crush of chiffon in her arms. "You'll be with me every minute I have them on."

"I will, I'll be thinking of you. I wish I could see you conquer a room full of strangers the first time." The blue eyes were suddenly bright with tears.

For Terry too the world had become a blur. Long moments they clung to each other in a fullness of heart that was shadowed by a kind of desperation. Impossible to put words to it, or to the fear that came over her in a wave. Then she smelled the faint odor of brandy and things settled back on keel.

Mother, if I ask you now, would you give it up?

But Marjorie was saying she had grown a bit tired. ". . . take a nap now . . . good trip, darling . . ."

Terry sat, spent with emotion, as she listened to the soft steps retreating up the staircase very slowly. *Goodbye, Mother.*

After a while she went on up to her own room and opened her vanity case, put the Hamilton legacy inside and locked it. Not going to let it out of her hands for an instant on the train, to be booted around with the other baggage. On the bed she had left her traveling clothes laid out. Now she put them on, the russet-colored gabardine suit, the new brown pumps, a tricky little hat, like a hunter's with a small feather in the band. Pausing a minute before the vanity she frowned at her image in the mirror.

Before I wear those pearls this hair has got

to be cut off. Almost shoulder length now, the frizzle was all out on the ends. Just take a minute to snip it, but she hesitated. There would be time at school to deal with that — maybe even a beauty salon in the dumpy little town. Better not make a botch of it herself, not with Annapolis looming.

Snapping the locks on her suitcase, she picked it and the vanity case up and ran downstairs. In the kitchen, she grabbed a quick sandwich of left-over fried chicken, a sliver of peach pie, last of the season, and what was Henry Miller doing, turning the Dodge into the driveway at this hour? With a sudden sinking, she had a hunch.

"Therissa!" Even before he'd closed the front door.

"I'm out here, Dad." Going to meet him, trying to hush his racket. "Mother's asleep . . ."

"Thank the Lord for small favors. I hope she never learns what a ninny she raised for a daughter." He was waving a sheet of paper — Terry recognized it, a bank statement. She'd gotten one herself the day before, testifying to the fact that she had closed her account.

"Didn't think they'd send me a copy, did you?" Beside himself with rage, lips drawn back, he snarled, "After all the advice I gave you, after I trusted you to take care of your savings, and you swore you were old enough to handle them — you go and do this! Squandered it all."

"Uh — it really wasn't wasted — I mean, I did have a lot of things to buy and I was glad I could use my own money instead of yours." She made a useless effort to put a good slant on it. "I still have seventy. . . ."

"You want to tell me what this big lump sum of $369.00 is all about? Eh? Did you buy a house maybe? Purchase a car? Invest in futures?"

Yes, Phin's future. But she knew better than to talk about a loan. Her father got apoplectic at the mere word. He never borrowed, never lent money to anyone, not even his own sister who had needed help paying the mortgage on the family farm a few years back. Somehow she had managed to save it without his assistance.

"Okay, look, I will be very frugal from now on —"

"Frugal? You won't have a choice, you little idiot. Green as little apples, you don't know diddly-twat about the world. Call yourself a grown-up just because you stayed alone in the house for a few days, flounce around, throw your savings to the wind. Well you'll find out how tough things can be when you run short of the old moolah. Because I won't help you, I can't. I don't have any extra cash, none at all. I will keep on sending you your allowance, but that isn't even going to pay your laundry bill. You'll have to go crawling to those — those *Virginians.*" Storming out into the kitchen he went to the refrigerator and got out a bottle of cream soda, wrenching off the top.

"I won't —"

"Oh yes, you will. And you'll find out the hoity-toity Hamiltons will charge you a high interest fee — they'll just want your whole life in return." He drank the soda as if it were medicine. "Every move you make, they'll remind you it's thanks to them. Why do you think we scrimped through the Depression without any handouts? It's because there's nothing as low as being in debt. As you will soon find out. Well, that's your bed, you'll just have to lie in it. Get your suitcases out to the car, I'm taking you to the train. No, I told Maybell I'd do it. We owe her too many favors already. Now hurry on, git!"

Terry seized her bags and rushed from the house. The force of his rage had shaken her, because she had a sneaking hunch he could be right. *No, it won't happen, Phin won't let it happen. He'll get the Fellowship money any day now and pay me back for the car and I'll have plenty.*

All the same she was unnerved, forgot to take a farewell look at the house, just found herself being driven down Delmar so fast she could hardly say goodbye to the scenery. Past the Loop, and there went the Tivoli Theater, they turned right into the Park and through it, on across Kingshighway. *Remember when I first drove the Gryphon at night? Yes, Dad, I bought a car.* Tune Town looked defunct without its neon flashing. And then they had pulled up in a no-parking zone in front of Union Station, engine idling as a redcap came to open the door.

"Well, go on, give him the luggage. By the way, you're expected to tip him twenty-five cents for each bag. Try not to make too much of a fool of yourself. Goodbye."

"Goodbye." She said the word with such cold calm, it startled her. All she could feel was relief to be out of the atmosphere of fury, to watch the old sedan roll away through traffic. As she followed the redcap through the huge, echoing station, she walked with the ghosts of summertime, Phin, Dixie . . . She had only had one

264

postcard from New York, a touristy photo of Dix atop the Empire State Building with the whole city beyond, chin up, elbows tight, rigid with excitement.

They were out in the yards now, with engines everywhere, breathing, hissing steam, the air alive with the groan and clang of preparation, people shouting thin words at each other below the steps to the Pullman cars. All this had been someone else's scenery in years past, you watched them climb on and you went home. Now, it was hers, all this chuffing power, the impetus to hurry along, keep up with the redcap. When he'd handed her bags up to the porter, she had two quarters ready and dropped them in his brown cupped hand.

"Thank you, ma'am. Have a nice trip."

Called me "ma'am." To him, at least, I am ready to get on that train.

■ ■ ■ ■

VIRGINIA

■ ■ ■ ■

Seventeen

Why, she wondered, would a college set out to diminish you? From the minute you arrive you're treated as if you are worth nothing. All the sense of orientation that she had managed to achieve on the train ride, the self-possession, the rhythm of growing up — it all came under attack the minute she walked on campus. Freshmen must curtsy to the statue of the Duke of Gloucester in front of the Music Hall; freshmen may not use the gardens to study, freshmen must wear a beanie in the school's colors, slime-green and banana yellow. Freshmen must turn their lights out at ten-thirty. Freshmen may not . . . freshmen are required to . . .

For two weeks Terry had fought to find any sense of dignity. Only now, tonight, could she feel it return as she stood and viewed herself in the mirror. The red velvet dress gave her grace; the pearls gave her power. A flaw in the looking glass rendered her undulant, but it couldn't hide the regal stance which seemed to come with the gown. Her chin, she had got from Mother. It brought a smile to her lips, to think that she had inherited something worth more than the pearls. There stood a Hamilton, if only for tonight.

No piled curls, but her hair was looking better now. The local barber had cropped it short in a boyish cut with loose bangs across her brows. Actually the curve of it was almost stylish — Dixie would have approved. But it was the pearls that set her in a different dimension from the tacky little dorm room. They sneered at the awful floral curtains, disdained the yellow chenille spreads on the pair of beds, and totally ignored the threadbare hooked rugs. Actually, the whole school was beneath the dignity of the Hamilton legacy. That necklace carried an aura of grandeur from another day when it had graced the throat of some southern belle who had probably danced with Jefferson Davis. Or even earlier, adorned a daughter of the Revolution — who knows, it could have been admired by George Washington himself. The notion filled Terry with an uneasy awe. Suddenly she decided that they should not be wasted on a mere gathering of students at a dinky reception in a backwater school like Gloucester College. Taking them off, she put them back in her suitcase and locked it before her roommate emerged from the bathroom in a gush of steam.

Willetha Plunkett of Norfolk, Virginia, five-ten, two-hundred pounds of naked flesh that was pink as a peony from the hot shower. Standing hipshot, she surveyed the red dress critically. "You gonna wear *that* to the big hooraw?"

"No, I thought I'd go for a horseback ride in it." Terry felt the recurrence of an antagonism that had started the first day she had walked into the dorm room to find herself engulfed in Plunkett photos, all of horses, pinned on every wall — snapshots, pictures torn from magazines, one huge blowup of a group of riders amid whom Willetha herself stood beaming in curls so floribunda they managed to look red even in a black-and-white picture. Above her own bed, the one in the corner farthest from the window (the other having been preempted already), was pinned a glossy portrait titled "Man O' War." Conscious of being watched, she had removed it from the wall, along with several others from her side of the room, and stacked them neatly on Willetha's desk. Opening her suitcase, she had taken out a framed picture of an elegant automobile with the hood ornament of a gryphon. Phin had borrowed Ruth Ann's new camera, his shadow slanted across the lower corner of the shot. Using one of the left-over nails on the wall, Terry hung it, amid a wealth of empty space. In the deafening silence she turned and eyed her new roomie.

"My name is Therissa. You can call me 'Tris.' "

The mountainous girl drew shreds of hurt feelings over her wounds and said coldly, "I'm Willetha, but I prefer 'Willow.' What's that supposed to be?"

"That's a car," Terry informed her kindly. "My car. In Missouri we've kind of out-grown horses." *And this is my half the room, so don't take liberties.*

Now two weeks later they had progressed to a point where antipathy had become tempered by grim reality: They might as well accept each other, there being no alternative, but the undercurrents of hostility were as near the surface as snags beneath the eddies of the old Mississip'.

As Willie toweled her mop of flaming locks she said, "I guess you're the only freshie invited to the big to-do over at the Music Hall. Your folks must have a lot of pull, huh?"

"Actually, no. I got accepted early into the program by audition. I played for Professor Wolff when we flew here last spring." Terry threw the line away — Dixie couldn't have done it better. Delving into a drawer she got out the embroidered scarf. The minute she draped it around her shoulders, she knew it was right for the moment and place.

When Willetha emerged from the depths of the towel there was a gleam in her blue eyes. "That shawl is down ra-a-aght swanky. Seems a shame the effect's gonna be spoiled by the beanie."

It lay on the dresser like a dead green-and-yellow varmint. Terry picked it up, considered it a moment, and flipped it in a careless arc at the desk, where it skidded off onto the floor in the corner.

Willy was grinning. "If you don't wear it, the Student Court'll make you scrub the steps of the rotunda with a toothbrush."

"They're welcome to try. See you later."

Heavy shadows outside, it was the only time when the college took on some illusion of beauty, with the lights from the dorms pricking holes in the dusk and the glowing dome of the Music Hall looming, the focal point of all paths. Terry picked up the skirt of the gown, holding it high to keep from getting dirty. The walkways of the campus were of broken brick and weeds damp from the recent rain. As she passed a dark corner, starting up from a bench a group of students confronted her. Dimly she could see their letter sweaters, smell the aura of smoke from forbidden pipes.

"Hey, hey, what do we have here? A little freshie all dressed up for the big party. Don't she know it's off limits to small fry?"

"Yeah, and notice what's missing?"

"I do believe I don't see the hallowed headgear."

"The lady is beanie-less."

"What's your name, earthworm?"

"If you're talking to me, my name is Therissa Miller and I've decided not to wear your ugly little cap." Her posture straightened —*shades of Mother, she always gets taller when crude people get too close.* "Please get out of my way."

"Well, now, listen to that!"

"Bold little scudder, ain't she?"

"Young thing, you're going to come along with us."

As they started to move closer, Terry felt a rush of anger that was like a foot on the accelerator. She hardly recognized her own voice. "If you touch me I will report you to the Dean of Women." Walking straight at them, she made them give way.

After a few instants of stupified silence they called after her. "You'll be hearing from us."

"You better show up at Court tomorrow afternoon. Or else!"

Or else what? I'd better find out. As she marched on up the steps of the hall her fury subsided leaving lopsided heart-beats. Trying to steady them, she paused just outside the doors. That moment of rage had left her spent and scared. It was a temptation to turn and run home — if she could be sure she wouldn't bump into the sophs again? Then a voice seemed to rally her: *A Hamilton doesn't retreat.*

Empty and homesick, she opened the doors to find the big hall bathed in brilliance. Glittering chandeliers all alight tonight put an extra gloss over the parquet floor, bright now with evening gowns, dotted Swiss, silk, a few gaudy taffetas that rustled and showed sweat marks under the arms. The smoothness of the velvet gave her comfort as she walked down the receiving line, shook hands with the President of the College, an elderly man with a huge Adam's apple that bobbed reflexively when he glanced at the unsupported bodice of her gown. He wished her a happy school year and passed her on to the Dean of Women.

Miss Patterson — there had been much correspondence with her, but this was Terry's first meeting. She found herself face-to-face with a dimpled lady, aromatic of powder and sachet, soft as a dumpling in a pink lace gown, but those small blue eyes were sharp. "Therissa Miller. I am glad to meet you at last, my dear. We are all very impressed that you convinced Dr. Wolfenbach — excuse me, Dr. Wolff, he wants to become as American as possible — that he should accept you into the advanced program. You should be very proud of yourself."

"He kind of bent over backward, I think he liked my mother." She pressed the handshake as firmly as seemed polite. Something in her face had alerted the Dean, though.

"I sense that you have a problem, my dear."

"Yes, ma'am, but I don't suppose this is the place to discuss it." She summoned a smile and moved on down the line.

Around her a babble of voices cluttered the middle air. ". . . told him I am very sensitive to e-flat, it positively sets my teeth on edge . . ." ". . . in the sixth bar of the second movement my A-string snapped. I could have gone through the floor . . ."

". . . the cadenza is very muscular . . ." Briefly Terry wished Dixie were here. *She'd know exactly what sort of flap-doodle remark to make to this crowd.*

There'd been another postcard from New York, just to welcome her to the school. Dixie was attending night classes at the Art Students' League, having tons of fun. For a minute Terry longed for her acutely.

"You look troubled, my dear." Dean Patterson had followed her over to the far side of the room.

"I was just trying to memorize it all to describe to my mother," Terry told her. "She has dreamed about this for a long time."

"Well, I'm sure she would be most happy with you tonight. You look lovely." Those round cheeks had earned the lady the nickname of Dean Pittypat but she had none of the dither of that character. Beneath the gentle voice was the strength of steel. "Tell me what's bothering you, child. Sometimes it's easier to discuss in an informal setting."

"Yes, ma'am. All right, I do have a problem. I hate to lie to my mother. She thinks I'm pursuing my musical education, but I can't even sign up for a practice room. I understand why it's policy to give the first choice to the upper-classmen, but I need a piano to run scales, keep my hand in."

"Yes, I can see that it would present a difficulty. But it's one that only Dr. Wolff can resolve; he's in complete charge of the music program. I suggest you get an appointment with him and discuss it, he's very approachable. How are you getting on otherwise?" Her glance took in the unclad state of Terry's head, with a trace of smile.

"Well, that's another thing I should ask you about. There seem to be a lot of rules, and I don't know whether — I mean, is the beanie thing a part of your official regulations? Or is it just some student custom? I wouldn't want to do anything that would get me in trouble with the school, but the truth is, I don't have time to play games with a bunch of silly sophomores who get a kick out of hazing freshmen. It's going to take all my time and energy to make my grades and improve my piano technique. That's what I came here for."

The Dean's mouth drew up into a rosebud of suppressed amusement. "I can see your dilemma. The beanie would have struck a dissonant note to a very charming theme. But I have to tell you: some teasing is part of the college experience. Most of us rather cherish our memories of it. Of course, how you handle it is up to you. I never interfere with that kind of student activity."

"Oh, good! Then if I tell the Student Court to go take a jump, you won't write my mother that I'm making trouble? She isn't well, I wouldn't want her to worry about me."

The Dean's face softened. "I'm so sorry to hear that. And of course I won't write her anything about you without discussing it first. But I should mention that those who choose not to fit in can become rather lonely."

"I'm used to that, ma'am," she said respectfully. "When you're one of only a few gentiles in a Jewish high school, you don't socialize a lot. All I want to do here is get musical instruction." She glanced across the room as Max Wolff was making his way through the crowd toward the stage, where the Steinway grand stood open. "Is the Professor going to play tonight?"

"A small recital. He was a very popular concert pianist in Europe. We're lucky to have him on staff. You'll see what I mean."

This was a far cry from the disheveled young man who had sat across from her in the office and tossed her a lifeline those long months ago. Dr. Wolff wore his tuxedo as if he'd been born in one, his slender figure the picture of confidence. Long hair silken in the lights from above, his strange young/old face was full of zest as he bowed to the crowd, a gesture that conveyed a swift image of great gilded halls.

She'd been to plenty of concerts as she grew up, her mother dragging her down to the Auditorium to hear Rubinstein or Horowitz. Secretly she had thought solo piano programs a bore. But Max Wolff brought a whole new dimension to the art. Those hard, slim hands touched the keys intimately and spoke a few soft words over a dead princess that Ravel had once loved; then told a bright anecdote that George Gershwin wanted to share with close friends. That was followed by a philosophical comment from Eric Satie. The final conversation was so musically witty it was stunning, with Rachmaninoff in a debate over a certain theme with Paganini. The arguments rose so heatedly that when the thing was over and dismissed with a snap of the fingers — a joke — the audience went wild.

Terry found herself pounding her palms to a pulp. For the first time in her life she wished that she had the gift. And was never so sure that she lacked one. She couldn't even imagine playing like that, not even with twenty years of lessons from this man, who now stood modestly accepting the applause.

The minute he stepped down from the stage he was engulfed in a throng of students. She didn't see him again.

Strange how the bright strains of music even kept her awake, later, until finally it was muted by the softer rhythms of rain gusting against the window of the dorm room. She slept at last, until other heavier sounds roused her, the puff and heave of Willie at her pushups.

". . . eighteen . . . nineteen . . . you better rise and shine, Treece, we got that game with the William and Mary freshies at eight o'clock . . . twenty-three . . . twenty-four . . ."

"It's raining," Terry groaned.

"So what? That just makes field hockey more fun . . . get a little muddy . . . twenty-nine . . . thirty." Willie flipped over onto her back and began leg lifts.

"Some day your students are going to hate you." Terry rolled out from under the covers.

" 'Course they will . . . seven . . . eight . . . y'always hate your gym teacher."

The bathroom was occupied by one of the girls from the opposite half of the two-room suite. From the shower came a thin warble. " 'I won't dance, don't ask me, I won't dance with yooooo . . .' "

Terry glanced at the clock over the door, a gruesomely large clock to remind you of the total domination of your time within these halls. Fumbling with the buttonholes, she got her gym suit on. Stubby fingers — a flash of memory brought back the sight of the Professor's graceful hands curling around the embellishments of Rachmaninoff.

"Well, lookahere." Willie was dressed and already on her way out the door, stooping to collect a scrap of paper that had been shoved under it. "Seems to be for you."

Terry unfolded the sheet. It was a summons to appear before the Student Court that afternoon at two "to answer charges of infractions against the legendary traditions of our noble school." Tossing it aside, she belted the green suit with its ballooning knickers that gathered modestly below the knee, talk about legendary — *and I had to pay $15.00 to buy this throwback to the last century.* Squirming into the yellow oilskin slicker that was practically a requirement here *(another ten bucks)* she drew the hood up over her head. It was two minutes to eight when she left the room on the run, fuming over the silly business of skidding around a muddy hockey field, trying to bash the shins of some equally disgusted William and Mary freshman.

Along the hall and down the stairs, she burst through the back door in a rush, headlong into the arms of a man. In sheer self-defense Professor Wolff caught her and held her, looking as if he had just unearthed her from an excavation. He himself was natty, in a vast black weatherproof cape and floppy brimmed hat that shed water as neatly as the beaver from which it derived. Careful not to tip any freshets onto her, he released her and stepped back.

The boyish smile belied the tiny lines around the mouth, as he said, "Miss Miller. I'm glad I ran into you. Our Dean of Women tells me you are concerned about your lack of a practice room."

"Oh — Hi, Professor. Yeah, it's my mother again — you remember her? Well, she keeps writing and asking —"

"About your piano practice, yes. I have made some arrangements. Check with my office assistant and he will give you a time slot. It may be rather early in the morning, but I can see you are up to the challenge."

"Oh, thank you." She found herself smiling back broadly, facial muscles welcomed it — hadn't used them in quite a while.

"Sorry I haven't had time for a conference with you yet," Wolff went on, "but I have to get the advanced classes oriented on their projects."

Terry nodded vigorously. "I know. I don't expect —"

"However," he drove straight on to the point, "it occurred to me that you might be willing to accept a little informal tutoring. I am inviting you to visit my cottage. Every Saturday afternoon I have invited a few students over to have — what is that delightful phrase from the jazz world? — a 'jam session'? We will meet at one o'clock. Not today, but beginning next week. I live down the way on the Richmond Road, you can't miss it, the house is a loathsome shade of pink." His shudder made them both laugh.

"Thank you! I'll be there."

"And do give your esteemed mother my warmest regards."

Terry gulped down a knot in her throat. As she watched him stride off through the rain, she was thinking: *This is the second time he's hauled me out of the deep mud.*

EIGHTEEN

This thing that had happened at breakfast
— nothing in these past weeks had shocked
her so much. With distant church bells tolling, Terry slogged through the massive
Sunday morning quiet on campus, trying to
rearrange her head, to create a whole new
pattern of relationship. Until a little while
ago everything had moved along predict-
ably. The Student Court, yesterday afternoon, had been a solemn comedy, sitting
stony-faced, after she had presented them
with her beanie, gift-wrapped, labeled: *Rest
in Peace.* As she left the tribunal they had
uttered dire warnings. Terry just waved
goodbye.

The hand-printed notices posted on the
bulletin boards this morning had been a
little less impressive than she'd expected.
"OYEZ, OYEZ, TAKE NOTE THAT THE
FOLLOWING NON-PERSON IS TO BE
OSTRACIZED:" Just an ordinary sheet of

notebook paper, hastily drawn, but it had attracted attention, so that when she sat down at breakfast in the refectory, the other girls at the table had gathered up their trays and started to leave. All but Willie.

Her loud country twang arrested their movement. "Well, aren't ya'll the stupid fools?" Bare of beanie, her hair seemed to glow redder than usual. "You think the sky's gonna fall if you don't bow down to them sophomores? Who elected them to boss us? Tell us to do this, do that, or else we gotta wear our clothes backward or scrub the steps or I don't know what-all? How they gonna make us do that? They want to keep us under their thumbs, they better grow some big thumbs, 'cause there's more of us than them."

Students at the nearby tables had stopped eating to listen. When Willie was on a toot, her language got broader and brighter. "Listen, our folks paid good money for us to come here. What they gonna think if we crawl around on our knees to a bunch of sophs? I mean, what is *Gawd* gonna think? You want to suck around, go ahead, but not me." She dug into her oatmeal with zest, as the refectory broke out in a hive of argumentation. By the time the meal was over a good number of the students had yanked off the beanie and some had even thrown them in the trash receptacles.

On the way back to the dorm, Terry had marveled aloud. "You run a pretty good revolution."

"Ought to," Willie grinned. "My great-granddaddy was with Stonewall Jackson at Chancellorsville. When I think what-all he'd say about wastin' time on them ugly caps — that's why I decided to join out."

What's Gawd gonna think? With the church bells ringing, it occurred to Terry that she wouldn't mind believing in an Almighty, especially if He could help her get her head on straight. In the Bible, wasn't there a Book of Revelations? She could write a new chapter, on how it feels to misjudge people.

On the steps of the Science Building, Terry paused, took off the slicker and shook it, stamped the loose mud off her boots and went inside. She had been aware for some time about the fruit-fly project, but it had taken the events at breakfast to stir her to action. As Willie was leaving for the lab, she had offered, diffidently, "If there's anything I can help out with . . ." expecting to be turned down.

But Willie had nodded in that matter-of-fact way. "Now you mention it, I could use a hand with the formaldehyde."

Down echoing halls, she was followed by the silent footsteps of a growing suspicion — that maybe she had jumped to too many conclusions about practically everything since she'd arrived at school. Especially Willie's conclusions; all that flesh had put her off. Now she was beginning to see that some of it was muscle. The girl played a tough game of field hockey.

In the lab, though, Willie was out of her element, trying to ride herd on a pack of insects. Bending over a bottle, she was dowsing them with formaldehyde; the stink of it greeted Terry as she came up.

"What's the experiment anyhow?"

"Oh. Hi. Maybe you can get 'em to lie down. I swear they're the toughest little buggers ever invented. I got some of 'em knocked out, but the others are havin' their-self a party."

Terry took the rag and refreshed the chemical on it, then held it over the bottle while Willie turned to a row of defunct flies already laid out on a piece of paper. "Point is to find out what color their eyes are, if y' can believe that? It's all a project for genetics, which is what Biology is about this semester."

Terry was briefly glad she had opted for Chemistry.

"What you do is take two flies and let 'em do what comes naturally until you got a hundred or so, then count how many of 'em inherited their daddy's red eyes. Or maybe it's their mothers'. Trouble is, to tally 'em you got to kill 'em. I hope they don't close their eyes when they die." She transferred one to a slide and examined it under the microscope. "One red-eyed little cuss for starters —" She made a mark on the paper and took a second fly. "Stupid way to spend a good morning. They want to prove you get your looks from your blood line? Shoot, I could-a told 'em: I got my grandpa's red hair and my chin is just like my uncle Judah's. Fact is, the Plunketts' genetics got so spread around all over Virginia, you can tell one from a block off. Saw a girl in the dime store the other day, she had Aunt Serena's nose. It don't take fruit flies to prove a thing."

Terry thought briefly of the Hamiltons, how they must have expected her to have the golden hair, the delicate patrician features. She must look to them like a foundling. "You grew these yourself?" Terry inspected the bottom of the bottle where a few groggy insects still staggered around.

"Well, you could say they cooperated. Worse'n rabbits, they are purely sex-crazy." She glanced sidelong at Terry. "Good grief, are you blushin' over a bunch of flies making babies? Comes from being a single child. Me, I got six sisters, and I want to tell you, in our house s-e-x is discussed a lot. That's two with red eyes and three without . . ." She picked up another specimen.

Terry recognized an opportunity but didn't quite know how to approach it. "It's lucky these little bugs didn't have access to — uh — protection."

Willie cut her another look, speculating. "You mean birth control? You been wondering about that? You're not engaged or anything are you?"

"Not — uh — yet."

"Well, you better get those answers from your ma."

"Yeah, except she's kind of shy about talking s-e-x." Terry tried to sound brisk and off-hand.

"Didn't tell you anything you really need to know." Willie was proving to be remarkably perceptive. "And you got that invite to go see some big old Navy man up at Annapolis pretty soon. I hear some hot stuff goes on up there at the Academy. Eleven . . . twelve . . . listen you want to lay out some more corpses on this paper for me?"

Terry took the tweezers and delved among the lifeless insects delicately. "I don't know the fellow very well. Up at Annapolis, I mean. He's the son of a friend of my mother's. I doubt if he'd try to fool around."

"Which means you know derned well he's gonna try." Willie grinned. "I been through all that with my older sis, Veronica. She went with a Marine all last year. They got one thing on their mind, believe me. And mostly they know about 'protection' themselves, they don't want to get in trouble. They can get theirs at the drug-store. With girls it's harder, you got to go to a doctor and get a gadget . . . well, you're not about to do that, I'm sure. Just make certain the guy is covered."

Terry felt as if she were bright red down to her shoulder blades. "Of course, even if he tried something I wouldn't let him."

"You think?" Willie snorted. "Fifteen . . . sixteen . . . seventeen . . ."

Laying out a new row of flies, heels upward, Terry was disconcerted by a whole babble of inner voices. *I think. I can't imagine. I bet I could — but I don't know.* "I guess for my first time I'd like it to be after a gorgeous wedding, in some romantic place with candle-light and all, so you'd have a beauti-ful memory." She had hardly been aware of such a dream. She'd never really followed the train of marriage-thought that far.

"Good," Willie said flat. "Stick to that. Because I can tell you . . . thirty-one . . . thirty-two . . ." her head was ducked over the microscope, "my sister, Rowena, fell off the ladder and the boy went off to sea without proposing, and she converted to be a Catholic, went to confession every day for a month, never could get enough penance."

For some reason in the quiet of the lab, Willie's homespun statements drove home a grim reality as it had never touched Terry before. *Guilt. It seems as though I attract it like a magnet. Lordy, do I dare to go to Annapolis?* Lost in a fog of dismay, she came aware too late.

"Willie! The flies are waking up!"

"What? No! They can't do this!" But they could, and did.

Later, in the rare solitude of her room, Terry let her thoughts gravitate back to Tommy James. She read the letter again, ink-black downstrokes so vigorous they leaped off the page. "I swear I cannot wait to see you!" He sounded as though the memory of their date last summer was still vivid. To Terry it had lost a lot of the detail, the way a pencil sketch gets smudged. But she hadn't forgot the strength of the feelings that had seized her briefly, almost ready to throw away the proprieties she'd been taught, the rules of the world about intimacy, and what was and was not appropriate. *Mother would flip her petticoat.* But then she remembered: her mother was never going to know.

The one letter from home had been short and unsteady. Maybell had taken her to the doctor for a Vitamin B injection. Dad was over in Illinois for two days on his route. The feathery writing was almost unfamiliar, though the expressions of love were real, like the touch of a hand on a fevered brow. She had reread the few lines a dozen times. Sitting at the student desk Terry pulled out a piece of stationery, some pink flowery stuff that Marjorie had given her "to write home, my dear. I will look forward to your letters."

Choosing her words carefully in as much detail as she could recall Terry began to describe the Music Department reception, leaving out all mention of beanies. Dean Patterson had been warm and friendly, the students colorful, the music exciting. Professor Wolff had played Rachmaninoff to end all comparison. He had invited her to come to his house, along with other students of course, for some private instruction. (*If that doesn't bring Mother out of her brandy cloud, I give up.*) The informal class meets on Saturdays so she won't be able to accept Grandmother Hamilton's invitation to go to Richmond for a weekend.

Sitting back, at a loss for further words, she realized the rain had stopped pelting the glass, a bleak sunlight was leaking into the room and something was making a squeal, an incredibly loud noise close at hand. On the third floor of the dorm, it seemed unlikely the racket could be coming from the yard below. Terry went to the window to investigate and found the author of the strident celebration — a frog plastered to the pane like a wet leaf. But small, only an inch long, pale green, so delicate it was transparent. With the sunlight coming from behind you could see a trace of bones, the pulse of a tiny heart. From some depth of lung it was emitting a monstrous noise.

Tree frog — the Virginians were proud of them. Native to the state, product of the deep forests, they could climb trees or light poles or dormitories with their suction toes. Though you would have to wonder why they wanted to. "Watch out," she muttered, "that Willie doesn't grab you and dissect you."

She had to smile at the thought of the fruit flies winging around the lab as she'd left. They hadn't had any luck catching them and Terry was secretly glad. To breed an insect just to kill it seemed a sorry business, even for an assignment. Willie must be dead-set on getting that Phys. Ed. degree to go through with it.

And as she often had before, Terry felt cheated that she never had experienced some overwhelming need to pursue anything to its end. Guilty, too, because it must be a lack in her character. *But how do you manufacture a great dream?*

Maybe I was born to be against things. The old Hamilton rebellion coming out in the wrong century, maybe I need a good war. The thought depressed Terry, so much, she couldn't sustain it. Going back to the letter, she signed off quickly, shoved it in an envelope and grabbed her slicker. The day was sunny now, but give it five minutes and it might pour.

NINETEEN

The sun was out. As Terry walked through early afternoon that Saturday, she felt a deep gratitude for the slanting rays that shafted downward through the dense pine forest on either side of the Richmond Road. It was the farthest she had been off-campus in a month. Professor Wolff had flashed a small smile as he'd said, "I have a special dispensation from the hallowed Lady Dean. My house is within the limits of travel permitted to students without calling down dire retribution."

It was intriguing to imagine what a music lesson from the Professor would be like. All things considered, she should have felt at least a little hopeful, but the day had been dimmed by the fact that there was no letter from her mother in the mail this morning. Just an envelope from her father's office containing a check for her October allowance. The twenty dollars was welcome, with the trip to Annapolis looming, but Terry couldn't help wishing for a word, even a scathing one. She missed their voices.

What are they doing there alone these days? She wondered if maybe the breach was healing a little without her presence as a constant irritant. So many fusses had circulated around her, piano, clothing, schoolwork, money, always money. Maybe with the source of contention removed, Terry thought, the air might be a little quieter? They might even start trying to reach each other again? Every wish ended with that silent question mark.

No point. No point in borrowing trouble or imagining the impossible. She was too far from the scene of action to influence it either way, and probably just as well. They would have to work out their own problems — or not. But she had expected her mother to have been a little excited by that last letter, with the news that Professor Wolff had invited her to his private musicale.

Terry had only seen him distantly at times, striding across campus with the great cape swirling in the rain. The man left her with mixed feelings: awe, gratitude, an impulse to like him, but some innate suspicion made her cautious. In spite of the appealing smile, there was a look of the eyes that disturbed her, a darkness. It was probably due to the war, she figured. Sights he had seen were pasted on his inner walls, never too distant. By now she knew that he had escaped from Austria with the help of the French underground, that he'd had a wife who had been killed when Paris fell. It made the war seem a lot closer than the rantings of Rudi Klein with his grim jokes or Tommy James with his thirst for U-boats. Neither had conveyed any real sense of disaster the way Max Wolff did without saying a word.

A man of inner shadows, he shouldn't be forced to live in a gingerbread house. Pink, he had said, but she hadn't expected this fairy-tale Victorian cottage, complete with curlicues along the roof line and an ornamental garden stretching back to the impenetrable woods. Of course, right here they were not that dense; in the downward striking sun she could see gaps.

Willie had explained it. "Well, shoot, I go by that place all the time, it's ra-a-aght off the bridle path. It sure-enough is pink, I'll say. I heard it belongs to a lady, head of the French Department, who's off in Europe on — what do they call it, a sabbathical? I reckon she rented it to old Wolffie furnished."

The front walk was made of crushed shell and the knocker was a cat's head. At least the Professor looked prosaic enough, holding the door, "Come in, come in." Slacks and blue flannel shirt, long hair scattered, a few strands of gray in it, she could see now. And lines around the eyes when they crinkled in amusement. "Told you it was pink. Let me take your slicker, Miss Miller — it's Thérésa, isn't it?" He gave the name a tilt that almost made it pretty.

From the back of the house strange sounds penetrated, a clarinet scolding, answered by a viola, an argument which the cello took over with deep authority.

". . . have a confession to make," Wolff was saying, "I sometimes use these workshops to try out my own compositions. It's good for the students to sight-read new instrumentation, and it's my only chance to hear my own work played." A shy sort of pride in the words.

"Sounds great," she told him, and meant it, but her inner thought was: *at least they'll be too busy to snub me.*

There were five of them, all strings except for the clarinet, grouped around the piano. Wolff slid into place on the bench and gave the keyboard its voice while Terry sank onto a hassock near the big bay window overlooking the garden. The room was bare to the sunlight, she imagined he must have taken down a lot of ruffled curtains. The wallpaper was flowered, blue and yellow and the seat covers on the furniture were blue chintz. Nothing silly about the baby Baldwin, though, it shone with a high polish. So did the music which had taken on new shape with Wolff's return. His long fingers on the keys led the others into a semblance of unity.

Difficult orchestration written in the professor's rapid hand — the girl directly in front of Terry, a cello jammed between her knees, was struggling to keep up to tempo, losing a beat each time a page had to be turned. Terry caught onto the phrasing and leaned forward to flip the page, a common enough courtesy among musicians. The girl made no sign she'd noticed, but when the passage was over and the trumpet burst forth with a few bars solo, she half-turned to whisper over her shoulder.

"Turn sooner next time. I read two bars ahead."

"Right." Terry felt the small circle of this world steady around her. Once more she had been wrong, the advanced students were not unwilling to accept a lower level classmate so long as she made herself useful.

It started a whole new train of thought. When they took a break and the Professor said, "Who wants hot chocolate?" Terry was quick to go along with him to the kitchen, heading instinctively for the cupboard with the pans.

"Are there any marshmallows?" she wondered.

"I never heard of marshmallows in hot chocolate," he marveled. "I see you know what you're doing. Can I leave the refreshments in your hands? I really need to work a little with the viola."

"Glad to help out." She had found a bar of Baker's sweet chocolate. Counting off a half-dozen squares she set them to melt on the stove while she hunted down the milk. It steadied her inwardly, to be back in a familiar setting, doing work that she was trained for.

From the sun room Wolff's voice came distantly. "The term *subito* means . . . well, it's like a sudden change of heart. You go from blustering to persuasion, abruptly, to surprise the listener. Every step you take is to excite or gratify your audience. Remember when you're composing, that's always

301

the goal."

When she brought the tray of steaming cups, they took them hungrily without ever ceasing to listen to him. Now on an explanation of contrapuntus, his store of English failed him. Setting his drink aside he turned back to the piano. "Like this: listen." Beginning with a voice in the treble, he let it speak its theme, then quickly interposed a second, repeating the notes in the bass, followed by a third that inverted the whole idea and turned it over to a fourth voice an octave higher, while Terry paused to marvel: *he's improvising! He just made that up!*

"You see, you want to keep the listener intrigued."

They nodded, nodded and avidly downed their chocolate, to seize the instruments again in a fever to go on with the lesson. Terry had to admit, they were way over her head musically. Sight-reading was one thing, but these kids were playing with a passion, bouncing the intricate elements of the piece off each other with such enthusiasm the room was rocked by it. *This is what college is supposed to be.* It came as a discovery.

They romped so hard he had to stop them. "Hold it, people. Chamber music should be lively, but at all times controlled, yes?"

A riffle of laughter went round the circle. Voices broke out in questions, and they started over, at a more calculated tempo. By four o'clock it seemed impossible that the afternoon was spent. Max shuffled the sheets of music together and stood up.

"It was very good of you to indulge me," he told them. "I have — what is it? — a few clues to how I need to improve the piece. If any of you have compositions of your own, feel free to bring them next time."

Reluctantly they put the instruments away while Terry collected cups and took them to the kitchen. Off toward the front of the house, they were saying their goodbyes, and then he came to join her.

"Leave all that," he invited. "I didn't ask you over to wash dishes, dear girl."

"The truth is, it feels good to be back at work I know how to do." She was trying for a bit of humor.

He gave her a boyish grin. "And you look charming in an apron — in fact it's an interesting variation on the Terry Miller theme. Is she a handy *hausfrau* or is she the Lady in Red."

So he had noticed her the other night. "That was Cinderella at the concert. And I never enjoyed one more. Professor —"

"Please. I am Max to my friends, and that is the reason you're here. A friendly impromptu lesson, so you have something to write home about — is that the phrase?"

She followed him back to the sun room where beyond the windows the afternoon was turning dusky. Rummaging among the piles of music on the piano, he was saying, "I noticed how well you sight-read. Turning pages of an unfamiliar composition, and doing it to satisfy even the difficult Lorraine — that is a credit to your otherwise unlamented instructor."

She didn't tell him that it had always come easy to her, like reading the pages of a book. "I think it must be because I started at such an early age — I was only about six. It's the only part of piano lessons I ever liked."

"Good. So, since this seems to be an afternoon for my self-indulgences, I wonder if you'd find it a bit of fun to play a duet with me. One that I wrote, but have never listened to because I only have two hands. Let's see what it sounds like. Can you decipher my notation?"

As they sat down together on the bench, Terry scanned it, recognizing the theme as the opening of Bach's brilliant *Violin Partita No. 3 in E*. Translated onto the piano, this was a more complex version. Taking the volatile right-hand side, he said, "Ready? One, two —"

The duets Terry had played with Madam Arquette had been athletic matches, to avoid crashing elbows and plunging red fingernails. With Max it was a different game, his hands crossed deftly under and over hers, his touch light as they engaged in a chase up and down the keyboard. Music so rich and joyous, Terry lost herself in the sweep of it, galloping headlong to the finish, fingers tingling.

"Oh gosh! I pushed that too fast!" she breathed.

"But you were having fun." Max was laughing too. It translated his whole face into the image of the man he'd once been, a handsome, happy young artist. "I thought it might happen. I felt there was a joy hidden deep in you."

"It was your arrangement that did it. It was a real pleasure to play."

"I'm very glad. I wrote it for a couple of friends of mine over in Switzerland. We used to have great little afternoon musicales. I feel comfortable now about sending it to them. The world over there is in dire need of some light-hearted escape from all the ugly realities." The excitement faded into his usual pleasant mask.

"Can we try it again — I'll stick to the tempo next time."

"Not this afternoon," he said, kindly. "It would be an anticlimax."

"But my fingering was terrible. I need more practice. If you could assign me a student teacher — ?"

"I think not. You are too precarious. No one handles you but me." He seemed to be teasing, but not entirely. "If you can spare your Saturdays we can get some work done after the others have gone. And no more cooking chores, I promise."

"But I like to work for my keep. I'd love to come again, only not next week. I have to — I'm already set to go off to Annapolis, a blind date with the son of a friend of my mother's," she added hastily.

Wolff's eyes clouded, as if he didn't quite approve, but he only said, "Of course. You'll find the dogs of war rampaging up there I am sure. Young men eager to go to battle, fair ladies giving them favors to wear on their shields. Don't mind an old cynic. You will have fun."

Not so sure of that now. As she walked home along the shoulder of the highway, Terry could hardly remember the interlude of last summer. The silly girlish excitement of the riverboat seemed a long way back in history, especially after a private hour with Max Wolff, who had lived through hell and come out the other side.

It was there in his face again as he spoke of his friends still over in that haven of refuge in Switzerland while the battle raged on every side. She hadn't seen a newspaper since she came to school — none of the other students ever talked about what was going on in Europe. Maybe it was their indifference that made her think harder about it now, or the fact that soon she would be discussing it with Tommy James. No doubt about that — he would be full of expectations, impatient for graduation in June, hoping for war.

War was a word of mixed images. It was Dad coming home shell-shocked, it was Ozzie flexing his biceps, it was Rudi sneering at the kids in French class. It was the President talking about lend-lease, and the boy on the train who had sat beside her for a while coming east. He was from Ohio, a draftee, sullen and resentful of the fact that he was being forced to waste his life in army service for two years. To picture him bravely facing bullets was incredible. In fact, the whole idea of this country ever fighting the Germans was beyond belief. The polls taken last summer showed that eighty per cent of the people in the country were against getting involved. Even if Roosevelt was as perfidious as her father thought, he would hardly dare go against that much public opinion.

So you're safe here, Max. Terry wondered why she should even care, but something had happened this afternoon, sitting there shoulder to shoulder with the man on the piano bench, she had felt a warmth that was more than skin deep. For a few minutes they had been partners, they'd shared an elation that was like a bond, a kind of fellowship that had never happened before. A few moments with Max Wolff had suddenly made life bearable, even though it raised some uneasy questions. Forget them! She walked faster, smiling.

I hope he writes some more duets.

TWENTY

Uneasy dreams. She and Max Wolff were racing from huge red-eyed fruit flies through the rain to find Mother, never quite in sight, but sudden scenery of ships and ancient buildings mossy with tradition, green lawns where haughty women, friends of Grandmother Hamilton, looked down their noses while the men in uniforms drilled with toy guns and a band played "Anchors Aweigh." Groggy and tired, Terry dragged herself out of bed, looked at the clock, and began to scramble wildly. Her clothes were already packed, thank heaven. Forget breakfast. Running down the hall, suitcase banging her leg, she pulled up short at the monitor's station.

The girl, a chubby waxen blonde, was talking to an upperclassman with an Honor Society pin on her lapel. They were pleased to ignore Terry until she broke in on their chattering. "Could I please have my mail?

I've got to catch the nine o'clock bus?"

They stared as if she'd spoken a foreign language. The monitor checked a paper, found the notation that a mere freshie was indeed to be absent from campus this weekend, and stared again, but handed her a clutch of envelopes.

"Thanks." Riffling through them as she ran, she found no lavendar ink, no spidery hand. With the bus loading, Terry snatched a ham-on-rye at the counter of the all-purpose student store and carried it to her seat. Before she was settled the driver closed the door and they began to roll. Three envelopes, one from Dixie, one from Grandmother Hamilton, one from Phin. The sandwich was dry, she was finding it hard to swallow, some constriction that had to do with the tears in her eyes. *How could she not answer my last one, about the music lesson?* "I played a duet with Max Wolff, a little contrapuntal thing that he composed himself . . ." *If that didn't stir her interest a little, what would?*

And then resentment melted down into anxiety. *Maybe she's sick?* But surely if that were the case her father would have written. Even though he had dismissed her from his life, he wouldn't cut her off from her mother if anything serious were the matter.

Marjorie didn't even know about the bank account, his fury, his contempt. Of that, Terry was positive. He kept all financial matters to himself.

I was wrong, of course. I should never have bought the Gryphon. But she couldn't really work herself into a state of guilt. Anyway, the letter from Phin undoubtedly contained payment for the loan. She opened it first — saw that there was no check enclosed, then tucked it under to save for last while a little tremor of nerves began to shiver inside her. Her total worth, at this point, consisted of twenty-two dollars in the bank and three-fifty in her purse, plus her return ticket from Annapolis. Briefly, she almost understood her father's grim preoccupation with money. *If you don't have it, nothing else works.*

Maybe her grandmother was sending her a little present, just to have fun with. She tore open that envelope, but all it contained was a note, elegantly penned on the handsome paper with the embossed Hamilton coat of arms. The family is wondering when they will see Therissa. Surely classes don't take up every weekend? "Remember that Jeremy can drive up and get you in a matter of hours. We would love to see hear all about your new life." *She must not have got my let-*

ter about taking private instruction on Satur-days from the head of the department. "It would be good, too, to have some news from your mother. I haven't heard from her lately." Terry jammed the letter in her purse and opened the third.

From Dixie. The familiar writing made her homesick, those ink strokes like chop-sticks, leaning backward with the "t's" crossed on an upward sweep. Dix had concocted the style in Junior High as a protest against the Palmer Method, which she said was insipid. A short note: she just wanted Terry to know she had a new ad-dress. A walkup in a brownstone not far from the school, costs fifteen bucks a week, but she'd be sharing the rent with another student, a girl name of Zoë. Very talented, going into advertising. Meanwhile they are both waiting table at a restaurant near the school. The arrangement with the family bakery hadn't worked out. Still going to Art Students' League — Lord, the city is fun! Got to rush. Terry folded it back into its envelope. What sort of name is Zoë with two dots? Must be one of those artsy types . . .

She turned again to Phin's letter, and as she drew it out something fell in her lap —

a car key on a pink ribbon. She seized it like a talisman, swallowing down a laugh that was part sob. The letter was laid out with Phinnish geometry down the lined tablet page. She could almost see the long knuckly fingers printing his theorem:

He had been glad to get her letter.

He had read it to the Gryphon. Car longs for her acutely.

Its tires are tired of plodding back and forth to the University.

It has to use the windshield wiper all too often to wipe away its tears.

Engine keeps missing — missing its mistress.

It hopes she won't be fickle and jump into some other car, just for the sake of a fast ride.

Not all vehicles are safe, even those approved by the Navy.

Car is unhappy to say that the foolish boy, Phin, has still not received the grant from the government. The paperwork must have got lost between Chicago and St. Louis. He worries about her — he's running pretty short himself. He hopes she is making out o.k.

Sends her the key (Ruth Ann supplied the ribbon). It will always be hers no matter who owns the car. Please wear it over her heart and remember a faithful Hudson coupe, and, incidentally,

Phin

P.S. What is the state of your bank account? I really need to know. You must be running low. Now don't scream, but I thought I might sell the Gryphon. It would bring a good price these days, and I could buy something a little cheaper, you'd have some cash. What do you think?

Apologetically — P.

Sell my car? Never! Terry slipped the ribbon over her head and tucked the key inside her shirt. For a long time she sat staring blankly at those dense woods that flanked the highway, the forests of Virginia, a world away from St. Louis and another life.

And then, she was no longer in Virginia. The bus was stopping at the station in some place called Collegeville, Maryland, a gang of girls piled on, wearing sweaters with the name Saint John's. Most were carrying Navy pennants, though a few waved the Cornell colors. Their chatter was lively and inclusive, none of the cold stares at her that still marked the attitude of the Gloucester students. They were high on weekend excitement, all of them bound for the big game.

Over the back of the seat in front of her a

fragment of chatter rose. "Are you nuts? Of course I didn't tell my parents!"

They were rolling through a grove of apple trees, fruit ripe on the branch, stacks of apples at wayside stands, polished and perfect. Terry wished she had one.

"They think I'm too young to fall in love! They are so old-fashioned, you wouldn't believe it. They think I've never even kissed a boy."

"You're joking."

"I kid you not."

Love? How do you know you're — that way? Terry couldn't conceive it, what it must feel like. Like Jeanette MacDonald singing her heart out to Nelson Eddy "Ah, sweet mystery of life at last I've found you . . ." or Errol Flynn fighting a duel to the death over Olivia DeHavilland.

None of that related to Terry's own reality. The nearest she came to understanding any of it was the scene where Clark Gable crushed Vivian Leigh in a muscular embrace that she tried to fight off — shades of Uncle Redford. But that wasn't love, forheaven-sake! The bus was slowing into the station at Annapolis.

Tommy had mentioned that he couldn't get off to meet her, but she would be taken in tow by "a girl with yellow hair." She wondered why he didn't just say "a blonde"? Then as she stepped down onto the platform she understood. The word "yellow" actually fell short. No more gleaming dye-job ever graced the head of woman. And the pity was, with reasonable hair the girl could have been pretty. As it was, she had to doll up to match the Goldilocks curls, with cheeks a little too pink, lips a lot too red. Waving a Navy banner she was crying in shrill tones, "Over here, kids, over here." Three other girls flocked that way, Terry following.

"Hi, y'all. I'm Georgina. Shout out your names. Cindy, Martha, I know. Who's — oh, you're Joan, okay. Then you must be Terry, old Tom-Tom's drag." Grabbing her by the arm she headed with quick steps on feet that seemed too small for her porky little body.

"You do know you're a drag, don't you?" The sly sidelong glance was wicked.

"Just so long as they don't call me a 'brick'." Terry was gratified to see a glint of surprise in those china blue eyes. She sent silent thanks to her mother for filling her in on Annapolis lingo.

"Oh. So you're a Navy legacy." Georgina nodded. "Well, hurry on, y'all, we don't want to miss the kickoff." Hardly waiting for them to settle into the ancient Caddy roadster, she rammed it in gear.

Down cobblestone streets they rolled past colonial houses in various states of decay or repair, an old town with a strong atmosphere of fish and salt water and tradition. The massive group of ivied halls that was the Academy was pretty much as Terry had pictured it. Of course she had always imagined herself on Tommy's arm, but it all came clear when they crowded into the stadium where the stands were almost full. Across the field a solid mass of Navy blue uniforms made a block, a cheering section.

"Your sweetie-pie is over there somewhere. Hi, boys." Georgina waved vigorously at the distant men. "Here's our section. Make way for the Johnnies, and one escapee from Gloucester College." Forcing the people on the benches to crowd over, she ushered her charges into place and crammed her own plump bottom onto the bench next to Terry.

Afterward, trying to describe it all to her mother, she could only recall flashes of color . . . wonderful Navy band, fifes and drums and tubas bright in the sunshine, swinging this way and that . . . screaming crowd . . . Terry had never cared for football in high school. This was a whole different game, squadrons of tough-looking men pouring onto the field, fierce contests at the snap of the ball. *I yelled so much my throat was sore by half-time. And then when we won . . .*

The "we" seemed to come naturally that afternoon. When the game was over they flocked together through the early evening shadows down to a coffee shop where hot chocolate drove off the chill. When the men joined them, the world spun a little faster.

Tommy was taller than she remembered, wearing an air of authority that made him seem ages older than she was. Those gun-metal blue eyes quickened when he saw her, in her rah-rah fedora hat with the short feather in it, the hot bronze of her best wool suit. She saw her image in his look of approval. For a minute his hand rested on her shoulder and left the tingle of electricity. Then Georgina deftly maneuvered him into the seat beside her. *She has a crush on him,* Terry realized in a flash of recognition.

"This is great, I can look at you better. No need to ask, that funny old college must agree with you," he was saying.

But any conversation was lost as the spate of game talk began, dissecting the plays, reliving the strategy. They take everything so seriously, as if it's a big deal to plot the right moves. It isn't just the winning pass, it's the winning campaign, assault and victory, sink the enemy. Under the table they were passing a flask. When she refused it, Georgina was quick to notice.

"Reckon you don't know it's an old custom around here to belt a little Jim Beam with your friends when the team wins."

"In Missouri we invent our own customs, including the right to say 'No,'" Terry answered mildly.

"Oh shoot, I thought you came from a Navy family," Georgie shrugged.

"Actually we are. An ancestor of mine served under Admiral Farragut." Impatience, a recklessness began to override her natural caution. "But Missouri traditions go back a good deal farther. St. Louis was a thriving city before the Naval Academy was even founded." It didn't exactly tickle the men. Tommy's glance was sober and wary.

"St. Louis." Georgina began to worry the bone. "I remember that town. We went through there once on a train. Big dirty city on a river that's the color of doggy-poo."

"That mud," Terry informed her, "is Missouri gold. Ask any man who farms the bottomlands. And the river has a few attractions of its own."

Tommy congratulated her with a smile. To Georgina he said, "Our first date was boating on that river, and I can tell you, it was something to remember. You haven't lived until you've seen the Mississippi from the top deck of a stern-wheeler under the summer stars."

Georgina's smile froze in a grimace of desperation. Abruptly she seized Tommy's cap off his lap and jammed it on her glittering locks.

"Now this is a piece of tradition that the mudwumps never dreamed of."

With open irritation, he shook his head. To Terry he said, "Old custom, if a girl puts on your cap you have to kiss her." He gave Georgina a swift, angry smack on the cheek and retrieved his headgear. "Do you know you're being a pain?"

"Well, you can moon around over the scenery," she said, "but I tell you one thing about those boondocks: folks out there never heard of a world where there's a war on. All they know is chickens, and my land, they do squawk when you say anything about going out and saving the world from Hitler. Our poor dern President had to invent lend-lease to keep England from sinking, when we should be over there fighting side-by-side against that paperhanger."

Out of her depth, Terry secretly floundered. What paperhanger — did she mean

Hitler? It didn't matter, war was male territory, the boys took over.

"At least now our convoys will be armed," someone was saying.

"Did Congress pass the bill?"

"A couple of weeks too late." Tommy was frowning into his cup. Sober looks were exchanged around the table, a secret that even Georgina didn't know.

"Where's Keno?" she asked. "Why isn't he here."

"Didn't feel too much like partying." Again the men traded glances.

"He's probably studying. He's about to bilge. He was unsat in Steam." Tommy downed his drink, making a face, too much liquor.

"Damned shame to lose a good officer over a subject that may soon be outdated."

"Steam? Outdated?"

"Some day it will be as obsolete as a windjammer. Weren't you there when the fellow from Princeton lectured on the new power source? Right now we should be studying the atom if we want to keep ahead of the Germans."

Terry came to inner attention. Phin had talked about atoms. She hadn't understood it, couldn't picture invisible bits making up everything in the universe, but they had something to do with power. A memory came back: that night on Art Hill he had talked about lighting a whole city, all the new inventions, tossing those marbles.

It was almost dark outside the little coffee shop. Georgina began to squirm into her coat. "Enough war-talk. We got a dance to go to tonight. Come on, sugar," to Terry, "you're staying with me."

"I'll get her over there," Tommy said curtly. "You just make sure the room is ready."

This time the hurt showed a little in those wide-sprung eyes. "Why sure thing. Only just don't expect old Tom-Tom to carry your bag, honey. It's against regs." She flounced off, followed by the other girls. And it was true, they all lugged their own overnight cases while the men strolled along, kidding, laughing now, the somber mood overridden. But not gone.

Walking beside her, Tommy was silent. His fingers warm in hers, he was still heavy with a troubling thought.

"I hope," she said, "you're not sore because I wouldn't drink with the rest of you? Because that's out. I don't touch liquor for any reason. If it's expected at this dance tonight — ?"

"Good Lord, no." A nervous laugh. "The

punch will not be spiked. The Superintendent of the Academy and his wife will preside in person and the watchword will be 'protocol' in capital letters. Which reminds me: You're a marvelous dancer, Terry, but we need to keep a lid on the lindy."

"Or else — what? They sew a scarlet 'L' on my bodice?"

"No, on mine." He spoke lightly, but the undertone was serious. "Every time the brass notices a middy for any reason, it goes onto the books, a minus or a plus. If you want to get ahead in the Navy you hope you get most of the marks on the right side of the ledger. Once a man gets labeled a 'queer fish' he seldom makes it onto the bridge of a ship. War is a team sport."

"Well, war . . . I know it's very popular around here. But if Georgina wants to make an issue out of it, I will tell her: I am a pacifist."

They were climbing a cobbled street flanked with tall old houses, most of them in a state of disrepair. "Don't let Georgie get to you. She's had a hard life. Her father was killed in an accident while he was on a tour of duty in the Mediterranean a few years ago. Her mother has to make ends meet by renting rooms."

"Okay. I'll try to be polite."

"Only if you want to, it's not Georgina I'm concerned about. Tonight at the dance there will be officers listening who'd prick their ears up at any isolationist talk. People who may become important to my career once I'm out of here. So could you sort of bite your tongue about your anti-war sentiments?"

"You mean you're not allowed to have private opinions?"

"And neither is my date, unfortunately. Price you pay when you enter the service." They had come to a stop in the shelter of a stairwell leading down from a dowdy townhouse. Even in the darkness she could see that the shutters were in need of paint, a gutter hanging loose. "Of course," he was going on, "I don't personally object to a free spirit . . ." the words were mumbled against her cheek. For a few moments there was nothing around them, no thought, no words, just the closeness and warmth of their bodies clinging together, his breath mingling with hers, lips on her eyelids and cheeks and then . . .

I don't think . . . I'll tell Mother about this kiss. Vive la France!

TWENTY-ONE

Dahlgren Hall — majestic old pile of a building, so grimly prudish clad in its ivy. But inside, blown wide open with color and noise and elegance, it over-powered you. The walls were hung with a myriad of flags, huge, brilliant, flags that had flown from the mastheads of ships down the centuries. Above the heads of the milling crowd they made a kaleidoscope of color. Below, an equal display of uniforms, stunning gowns, the glitter of instruments at one end of the ballroom, where a combo was setting up on a bandstand. Terry was stunned by it all.

"It's like a movie," one of the other girls burbled. "Like it came right out of Hollywood." The ultimate inadequate compliment. Filmdom never could have captured the aura of towering antiquity in this ancient arena. Echoes of history were so thick they overwhelmed the babble below.

Still speechless, Terry unbuttoned her

black velvet wrap and let it slip into Tommy's waiting hands, aware of her naked shoulders and the warmth of the pearls around her neck. She saw herself mirrored in his wide-eyed expression as he hung there a minute, staring at the Hamilton legacy. Doug had to nudge him. They went off to the checkroom with the wraps while the girls preened self-consciously, shooting envious looks at the red velvet gown.

Georgina was zipped into a tight yellow taffeta that already showed creases across the rear. Fingering her bubble-beads, she snickered. "Don't you wish those little bitty old pearls were real?"

Terry looked amused. "If they weren't real, my great-grandmother would hardly have worn them when she danced with Jeff Davis." *Where did I come up with that tall tale!* And yet it might be true. She knew her mother would have enjoyed it. With misty eyes, she turned away to stare blindly at the scene around her. *Oh, Mother, you were right, this is something I wouldn't want to have missed!*

The Navy in all its glory, tall men crusted with gold braid, arrogant clever women in satin, white gloves up to their elbows, hair piled high to show off the pendant diamond earrings. Their faces were beautifully devised of rouge and eye shadow and snobbery, these officers' wives, scanning the new crop of girls as if they judged a herd of brood mares. Their casual glances raked Terry and her pearls and came back for a second look. Approval. At the sight of Georgina, they winced visibly.

"Old biddies," she muttered, "always looking down their noses. Only reason they tolerate me is I'm Doug's sister and they dote on him. He's good boy, he takes care of me, even if it means he doesn't get a date of his own. But he could, he's every bit as charming as old Tom Tom."

Terry doubted that. Doug's simple cheeky face was skim milk next to Tommy's rugged features. She was still confused about what she hoped might happen tonight — or tomorrow. That kiss in the entryway awhile ago . . .

"Well, it's just too bad you missed it." Something in Georgina's intent look alerted her, some fishhook of meaning in her prattle.

"I'm sorry?"

"I was just telling you about the ring dance. Didn't your sweetie fill you in on that? The third-year boys put it on every fall. They set up this big golden ring in the center of the dance floor and the middies walk their O.A.O. up there to stand in it while they put their class ring on her finger. It's a big ceremony, almost like getting married, which they can't do until they're graduated. So they settle for this — it means they're bound."

"That's nice," Terry said absently — the boys were back now.

Tommy glared at Georgina suspiciously. "You look like a cat with one paw in the birdcage. What you been up to? Telling tall tales to my girl?"

"Aw, lay off Georgie," Doug protested mildly. "Everybody knows she's just a kidder. C'mon, toots, let's dance." He led her onto the floor.

Tommy handed Terry a small white folder with a braided loop to go over her wrist. "Got to confess, I'm guilty of gross conduct. I signed every line of your dance card. We're supposed to share with our dear classmates, but I wanted to be with you as much as possible."

"I'm glad." Inadequate word. As Terry came into his arms, she felt a new respect for close dancing. Body to body, she was guided expertly through the rhythms of a Glenn Miller tune. "A String of Pearls."

"I asked the orchestra to start off with that

one," he confessed. Moving her gracefully through the grapevine, he muttered under his breath. "One thing I can't do is stop fellows from cutting in. Hi, Pete. This is Peter Wells, who may have you for one moment, no longer."

The young man smiled smugly. "And I'll make the most of it." Another adept partner.

"Do they really teach ballroom dancing here at the Academy?"

"Absolutely. Along with other social graces, like how to get a lady in and out of a car, seat her at a table, all that good stuff. My, you do know how to follow a lead. Where did old TNT find you? Did he say William and Mary?"

"Gloucester College."

"Not possible!" Then he flushed pink. "Sorry. I just never met anyone from there who had your grace and beauty. Didn't mean to disparage your alma mater."

"It's not my alma anything," she told him. "My family sent me there because they have a strong music program, but I don't intend to stay long."

"You're a singer!"

"Pianist."

At that point Tommy was back. "Sorry, old buddy, but I need to know this lady better, and there's not enough time." The light words were underscored by some hidden energy that made his eyes harder than usual, the color of the barrel of one of those cannon out in the yard. "Here come some other stags. Let's wander over to the refreshment table."

When she had been presented to the Commander's wife, presiding over the punch bowl, Terry made a few cautious responses to the lady's perfunctory questions. The name "Hamilton" rang a bell. Easy to impress these people, she thought, as he moved her off to one side. Still looking troubled, a little grim.

"Have you had bad news?" she asked.

A curt nod. "I'm sorry. It's awful form to talk about a disaster on an evening like this." Downing a cup of the pink drink, he made a face. Then, as if a decision had been made, he went on. "But it's equally impolite to let your date wonder why you're down. Truth is, I just learned that a friend of mine died on the Kearney." And when she looked puzzled, he said, "You haven't read the papers today. One of our destroyers was hit by a torpedo off the coast of Iceland. By some miracle she wasn't sunk. But there were heavy casualties. Arnie was one of them." Then in a burst, he went on angrily. "God! I wish I were out in the North

Atlantic right now!"

Terry absorbed that silently.

"Oh shoot, I didn't mean it the way it came out. It's just that I can't wait to nail those Nazi bas— excuse me again. I'm forgetting all my manners. But I can't help thinking, if I had entered the Academy a year earlier I would be out there on the high seas, lobbing depth bombs at any U-boat that came in sight."

His intensity was disturbing. It put into context the artificiality of all this glitter. She thought, the frivolity must frustrate the men when their hearts were out there on a cold ocean in a life-and-death struggle. When they'd taken their pledge of allegiance it wasn't to a service, or even a country — this was a religion. And that applied to their women, obviously. Those frigid faces of the wives were a testimony to the same code, hide the personal grief, carry on the tradition. To be married to an officer would be to take double vows of love and honor and especially obedience. 'Til death do us part.

She came out of her daze of discovery to hear Tommy say, "You impressed the brass tonight. You hold yourself like a princess."

"Just a lowly Daughter of the American Revolution," she told him. They were back on the floor now, swinging sedately to the long, lazy strains of "Sleepy Lagoon." "What would have happened if I'd asked the Commandant about the polls that show Americans at 80% against getting into the war?"

"I shudder to think," he said with a wry grin. And then another middie was cutting in, a gangly boy introduced as Hiram Williams.

"Ah, at long last I get to meet your fabulous Kate," he said gleefully.

"You've got it mixed up, Hi." Tommy spoke fast. "It's Bill Kennedy who has a Kate. This is Terry Miller."

"Oh. Sorry. Welcome Terry." He whirled her away so fast she was barely able to keep up.

"Who's Kate?" she asked. "And why is she fabulous?"

"I purely don't know. I've just heard about the lady — scuttlebutt. Got the names all wrong, as usual." Flustered out of his skin.

"Everybody's a little absent-minded tonight." She tried to help him out. "I just heard about this ship, the Kearney? You must know the people on her."

He nodded, suddenly straight-faced. "Some of them were just a class ahead of us. Arnie Easton was a special friend of Tom Tom's, spooned for him when he was a plebe. That means he was like a big brother.

332

Reckon I better give you back to him — he needs all the comfort he can get tonight."

As Tommy took over, the band gave its signature tootle and the musicians set down their instruments to take a break. He drew her aside into a deserted corner near the stand, the big glittering drum set at rest for the moment, a limp handkerchief draped over one of the music racks.

"I owe you an apology," he was saying. "I never did lie very well."

With a flicker of amusement, she told him, "Don't worry about it. If you're dating some girl named Kate, it's none of my business. There are things you don't know about me too."

"It was my mother's idea. She takes a lively interest in my social life. Kate happens to be the daughter of an Admiral — Mom's always on the lookout for anything that will give me a boost up the ladder of command. It was never all that personal. She's just another nice girl."

But did you kiss her that special way? Do you kiss them all like that?

The music began again and the evening flowed on. But after the band played "Goodnight Ladies," Terry felt a little let down, not sure why.

The trip back to the rooming house was a

total disappointment. With Georgina and Doug tagging along, she was squirming with frustration, which Tommy seemed to share.

He whispered in her ear, "Tomorrow will be different. See you after chapel."

And by then I hope I have it figured out — what I feel, what I want to happen or not happen.

The bed was too soft. She wallowed in the comforters, wondering if it was a custom throughout the south to get half smothered while you slept. She tried to write a mental letter to her mother: *It was everything you promised and more.* The splendor was indescribable. But equally so the dangerous pulse of power she had sensed. She wondered if she could handle that, day in, day out, if — "if" being a big word — if it ever came to that? Suppose he turned serious, wanted a commitment from her. *Would I like being a Navy wife?*

There was no answer to that. All she knew was that she wanted those strong arms around her, to hold her sheltered against all the storms of this new and dangerous world she had entered when she left home. She wanted him to love her, she wanted to be closer to him that his own skin, a thought that made her dizzy and embarrassed and oddly reckless. *Grow up, girl,* she advised. *These men are worldly, they like their girls sophisticated.* The word haunted her through long hours of sleeplessness.

By dawn she was in a ragged mood, and so was the day outside. A cold front had moved in, drawing a veil of haze across the sky. Behind it the sun was only a silver ghost. After the Sunday morning service the congregation had filed out of the beautiful little chapel while it still echoed with the deep voices, singing the Navy hymn.

The air was raw as Tommy took her by the elbow and walked her across the lawn to a spot overlooking the Severn. The river was the color of slate beneath the overcast, its dark waters flowing off to Chesapeake Bay and then that vast ocean, across which a mortal conflict was going on.

"Any further word about your friends aboard that ship?" she asked.

He shook his head. Then abruptly, he said, "Arnie was a good man. If he had to go, this would have been the way he'd have chosen. But damn it — !" Then without real apology, he added, "I'm sorry, I just feel so helpless." Glancing down at her, with a slight tinge of resentment he went on,

"Doesn't this make you at least a little less tolerant of the Nazis?"

Startled, she turned to face him. "Tolerant? Where did you get the idea that — I mean, I grew up in a Jewish community, I know refugees personally who were hounded out of their homes forever. It's absolutely revolting! But Europe is a long way off. If we get into a fight thousands of miles away, it would be just like the Great War. We stopped it, but we lost an awful lot of men. And some who came home — Well, all I ever said was, I don't think those countries are any of our business."

"Tell me this: Suppose a gang of hoodlums comes into your nice neighborhood and begins to kill off good people right and left. Maybe the fighting is over on the next block, but would you stand by without raising a hand? If the Nazis are allowed to swallow England, our country will pay a terrible price. Hitler will own Europe and the Japs will own Asia, and where will we look for a trading partner? They can run us from long distance just by their combined economic power."

Terry thought about the fact that tires had suddenly become almost impossible to buy, a matter of some concern, since the Gryphon's were getting worn down. She thought of silk stockings, almost gone from the market. You were at the mercy of some country who had a monopoly on the materials. She hated that. "But the Japanese are a little country on a bunch of islands, they must need what we have to sell, too. They can't push us around, as big as we are? I mean a bunch of barbarians?"

Tommy made that sound between a snort and a laugh. "Those little 'barbarians' have produced the greatest fighting plane ever built — the Zero. They have advanced weapons, aircraft carriers, and they're highly motivated. They need more land. They're aggressive as a pack of wolves. But they're not our main worry right now, it's Hitler spreading his swastika all over Europe." Then he broke off, "There I go again. Probably boring the wits out of you."

"Oh, please, really! Don't treat me like a mere girl." Terry had enjoyed the sense that for a few minutes they'd been on an equal level of conversation. "I live in this world, too, you know."

His look delved into her eyes. "You're right. You should have questions. You, people in general who are not in the military, are not being told the whole story. Some of it is top secret, classified information. I mean if you knew what the German scientists are doing it would make your skin crawl. And their experimental weaponry — but that's all hush-hush. Just take my word for it, they cannot be allowed to win."

"Why cover it up, then? If it's all that bad, maybe the country wouldn't mind getting into the war."

"Not my call. Maybe you could write your congressman, demand to know the truth." Heaving a sigh, he said, "I love you when you speak your mind, and I wish we could really just let the bars down and go at it. But the truth is, all I want right now is to go over to Sleepy Suzie's and —"

"Who?"

He chuckled. "One of the rules of this place, you can't go inside a house with a date unless there's a chaperone present. So Suzie is a good sport. She's got a big old place, and her husband is posted to Manila, so she's there all alone. Every Sunday, she holds open-house and then goes off upstairs for a long nap, so we get to — you'll see." He was drawing her along with him, down a side street.

Right then Terry was holding to a word she thought she'd heard. Love? Trying desperately to read between Tommy's lines, she thought it would only be minutes before she'd have to make a decision. They were going up the walk to a rambling colonial mansion. Inside, the hallways were dim and the rooms even darker, blinds pulled nearly shut. On the floors, in the corners, dark forms nestled together, murmuring or silent except for the occasional muffled giggle.

Tommy fashioned a nest of cushions behind the sofa in the gloom. As they settled into each others' arms there was no war or argument or even thought. Just warm, intuitive touching, searching, caressing bare skin.

Softly he muttered, "What the Devil is this?"

"It's my car key."

Shaking with silent laughter, he buried his face in her shoulder. "I've heard of girls carrying mad money, but a key to a car that's a thousand miles away — ?"

Then the words were lost in kisses as they clung together. Terry shivered at the touch of his hands — *where did he learn that?* — everything racing too fast. She wasn't ready, she needed to think. *And that — my Lord — he's exploring places never before known to man.* Instinctively she seized his hand, to help or to slow him down, not sure, and then —

Suddenly her belly was full of ice, a chill that crept up her like an ache.

"What is it? What's the matter?"

She couldn't tell him, but in the moment she had gripped his fingers it had struck through her confusion like a gong going off. His ring hand was bare. That telltale glint in Georgina's eyes — "It means they're bound. It's like being married."

"Terry, what are you doing?"

Buttoning my buttons.

"What the — ? Where are you going?"

Good question. Good question.

TWENTY-TWO

The red of the live oaks had flared out like a spent match, leaving the woods around Gloucester a somber, shadowy moss-green, as if the forest had gathered itself close against the coming of winter. Winds gusted cold now, smelling of wet leaves underfoot and dank undergrowth, as the rain changed to mist. The chilly miasma struck through the yellow slickers and even seeped in the cracks around the dormitory window frames, which had done their share of warping over the decades. Swathed in a wool robe on top of her warmest pajamas, Terry tried not to shiver, mindful of her penmanship as she wrote a careful note that might pass Grandmother Hamilton's critical inspection.

"I received a letter from Mother yesterday. She has been very busy with her Red Cross work." Well, she used to be a volunteer years ago. "She asked me to send you her love and tell you she will write soon." Lame. But what else could she say? The little scrap of violet note paper had been a total disappointment. Only four lines, one of them blotched with ink as if the pen had reeled a little:

Darling child,
I am so pleased that everything went well at Annapolis. I knew you'd love it. I assume you'll be going to Richmond over Thanksgiving. Give everyone my love. Sorry I haven't written but I've been so (blot). Remember I will always love you.

Mother

That last sentence made her tremble with questions, as if her mother were expecting to go away or disappear or something. Or maybe she knew she would soon be abandoned, turned over to the County Welfare? Where do they put drunkards? Not that her father would walk out if he were in his right mind, but those last days at home she was afraid his brain might blow up, shut down, twist itself out of shape. The violence she felt in his rage, the coldness of his dislike for her as they parted — if he could write his own daughter out of his life, he could leave a tipsy wife. Maybe he even wanted this excuse, or else why did he buy her the brandy? That question had eaten at Terry for weeks. Her mother wasn't well enough to search out a liquor store. But all that was nothing she could discuss with her grandmother.

Gripping the pen tighter she tackled the hardest part of the letter. "It's wonderful of you to want me to come to Richmond for Thanksgiving, and I'd love it, of course. But we have a concert coming up that weekend. Our Chamber Music Group is performing at a hall in —" make it far enough away that no prideful Hamilton might show up unexpectedly — "in New York City. So I'm afraid there won't be any time after I get back, even for a quick trip to Richmond. Exams are scheduled for the very next week, and I really need to study. I'm sure you'll understand. Thank you for inviting me. Love . . ."

The lie sounded thin, it wasn't as good an excuse as she'd hoped for. She had intended to use the news of a new romance in her life: a handsome mid-shipman insisting that she spend the holiday with him. Terry heaved a deep sigh of regret and disillusion. That farce up at the Academy still sickened her. To be plucked up, enchanted, in a whirl of emotions, only to be dashed by the truth

— not that she could blame anyone but herself. Expected too much. Took it for granted that his feelings for her were serious. Stupid!

That note he'd written, which had only arrived yesterday, was a final piece of deceit, the bold black penmanship defensive and a little angry.

Terry, darling, what happened?

Why did you rush off last Sunday? I don't get it — I loved our weekend. I want to do it again. But you were suddenly a stranger, all that warmth turned cold. What happened? Please enlighten your dismayed — Tommy.

Tommy who? The handsome attentive escort, or the boy who was cheating on his O.A.O. while leading a silly little freshman on to believe he was interested in her? Not that he didn't have every right to belong to somebody else, but to conceal it was horribly embarrassing. The collapse of the fantasy had left her empty and sad, but chagrin overrode everything else. Thank heaven nobody had asked her how her trip had gone. Nobody but Max Wolff.

On Monday he had stopped by the practice room where she was furiously hammering Hanon. "You do try hard to stretch those fingers," he'd teased a little. Then with a closer look, he wondered, "How was your trip?"

"Fine. Actually, it was rather boring."

"Sorry to hear that. I missed you Saturday. And unfortunately the group won't be meeting again until after the Thanksgiving Day concert." That was the first she'd heard of a concert, a real one to be held in Philadelphia. It didn't include freshmen even as page-turners. "Once that's over —" he hesitated. "Well, it may be against the rules for us to have a private lesson at my house, but if you don't mind overlooking a few conventions I wondered if you'd like to come by the following Friday for a leisurely afternoon of music? Or do you have other plans? Of course you do. Everybody goes off somewhere over Thanksgiving weekend."

"Not I," she said grimly. "Thank you, I'd love to come."

He stood there, frowning, speculating. "Something went very wrong up there in Annapolis, didn't it?" Then another quick retreat, "I'm sorry, it's none of my business."

"That's okay. I don't mind admitting, the whole thing was a total bust."

Why did she think she heard him murmur

"Thank God!"? Actually, he made the proper sympathetic noises. It must have been her imagination.

In the days that followed it seemed to her that he was around oftener, taking a renewed interest in her education. Making up odd little assignments: "Here's a challenge for you, Thérésa." He always gave her name a foreign twist that made it charming. "Take these and see if you can convert them into a three-voice fugue in the manner of Bach." A few bars of music in his own hand. A few days later he'd handed her a book of Christmas carols. "I'm in need of an arrangement for the choir. I want to make 'Adeste Fidelis' sound bright and happy instead of the usual dirge. See if you can't — what's the phrase? — pep it up. We'll be giving a little concert the week before you all go home for the holidays."

All go home? But will I? There isn't enough money in my account to buy a ticket as far as Cincinnati. I can't imagine Dad will send me money for the fare. Mother would think of it if she weren't lost in a bottle. The thought always shocked her, even now after she should have got used to it. A sense of remoteness from her own childhood, a feeling of guilt, that somehow she should be home, trying to put things right. It all took itself out in resentment when she opened the note from Dixie. Dashed off in a flurry of excitement:

I'm on my way to a gallery opening, very posh, had to make a new dress, black silk sheath, quite nice if I do say so. This is an affair where the big-time artists will show up, I was lucky to get a ticket thanks to my darling Zoë. So, I'm off to savor some Braque, spiced by Klee and iced with Kandinsky. More later, Dix

Terry ripped it up. Shoving the other letters in a drawer of the desk, she became aware of somebody close behind her. Looking around, she received a jolt.

Willie stood there, ready for the Harvest Ball. The Phys. Ed Department always threw a big bash for its students at Thanksgiving time, and Willie had been thrilled to be asked by one of the boys, a football player. Terry just hoped it might be a lineman, somebody hefty enough to move the girl around the dance floor. The box with her evening gown had arrived last week, a gift from her dad, whisked away into Willie's closet as if it were precious. Now she was bedecked in the thing, and Terry's impulses had to be stifled under a wooden mask.

Fathers can be cruel, even the ones with kind intentions. Dreaming of some petite little girl, he had bought Willie a gown designed for a fairy child. White, with pink rosebuds all over it, and tiny straps that made those muscular shoulders look like captive balloons. Terry inspected her gravely — if she even smiled, she knew she would go off into a gust of horrid heehaws.

With tarnishing eyes, Willie nodded. "Looks pretty silly, huh?"

In sudden indignation with parents Terry stood up, wanting to clench her fists at the whole lot. "Of course not. It's a beautiful gown. It just needs — something." And abruptly, she knew what. Going to her dresser drawer, she rummaged around and found Dixie's scarf. Draping it around the bulging shoulders, she stood Willie before the mirror on the closet door, both of them speechless. The drape of the pink silk gave grace to the arms, fringe camouflaged the tightly packed waist — it actually gave Willie an aura of style.

"The red goes with the rosebuds," she said, with awe. "I'd-a never thought of that." Then, "Isn't this the shawl your dear friend made you?"

"She called it a stole. That's okay, I'm happy for you to wear it."

"Well, then, thank you." Very formally. Willie gathered the small beaded evening bag that looked as though it had been made for a child and looked squarely at Terry. "You know, Treece, you could come to my house for dinner on Thanksgiving. We got such a big family, one more's always welcome. All my sisters would be real happy to meet you, and there's plenty of room for you to sleep over. I mean if you'd want to?" Nervous, afraid she'd be snubbed.

With genuine warmth, Terry said, "That's the nicest offer I ever had. And I appreciate it. But the truth is, I really need to study for that Chemistry final. I just can't remember all those elements. And actually, I'm not real good company right now."

"I noticed." Willie nodded soberly. "Any way I can help?"

"I'm afraid not, thanks. It has to do with my mother — she's not well and I'm worried. I wouldn't want to throw a wet blanket over your holiday. But thank you anyway, it means a lot that you would ask me."

"Yeah. Well, we got to stick together, us freshies." Willie's face bloomed into a broad and genuine grin.

■ ■ ■ ■

By the next Thursday morning, Terry almost regretted her snap decision to turn down the invitation. But she really didn't want to go to Richmond, the thought of a house full of Willie look-alikes left her feeling stifled. Besides, she had this stupid idea that maybe her folks would call. Wouldn't the holidays remind them, of a time when they all used to be together, wouldn't they miss her a little? As the day wore on, of course, she began to make excuses: they thought she was at Hamilton House. Or they were probably out at one of those parties Dad's customers always threw at this time of year — plenty of drinks, good food. She wouldn't mind some really good food again.

The dinner the refectory served to the handful of students left at school was as festive as supper at an orphanage. Lukewarm turkey and runny cranberry sauce, gummy dressing and limp salad plunked down hastily all on one table. The kitchen help was obviously in a hurry to go home to their families. After the meal, Terry went for a walk, wandered over to the stables and took the bridle path idly, not really intending to go far. She was surprised when she glanced across through the trees and saw the pink cottage. All quiet and deserted. It gave her a pang to think of the gang up in Philadelphia, making music together.

For some unknown reason she felt lonesome for Max. Nothing all that personal, but it had been a comfort to know he was somewhere nearby in case of need. *If it wasn't for our music lesson tomorrow, I could walk away from this place. Be gone for two days before anybody noticed.* But he would, and he'd been very kind, and it was a crazy idea anyway. *Where would I go?*

So, if life serves you lemons, make lemonade. Who said that? Will Rogers? Or maybe W.C. Fields? The thought reminded her of that afternoon on the back porch of Berensens' house, with Phin and Dixie and a childhood slipping away. I'll probably never make lemonade again, but I could certainly enjoy cooking up a good meat loaf. I haven't had one in three months. These southerners were brought up on spoon bread and Smithfield ham, never heard of German dishes. A thought came creeping in like a thief in the night:

I wonder if Max likes meat loaf?

TWENTY-THREE

The Phoebus was displaying a poster of coming attractions: "Next week, the unforgettable strains of Sigmund Romberg's operetta "New Moon." She had seen it last year in St. Louis, a great musical. It would be worth viewing a second time, but Terry was counting every nickel and dime these days. The trip to the grocery store had cost $2.76, leaving her with a couple of ones and some change out of her last five-dollar bill. The bank account was down to thirteen dollars with ten days to go before she could expect her allowance. If it came.

St. Louis, her last known world, seemed a million miles away at this point. She felt as if it might have all disappeared when she wasn't looking. The only reality was Gloucester College and a pink cottage and Max Wolff. He was back, the battered black Essex was parked in the driveway.

At the sight Terry felt her pulse quicken,

some emotion she couldn't name. Warmth flooded into her, as if she'd sighted a familiar landmark. *So pretend this is "home." Why not?* But it didn't work. You can't have a home without love. Or was that word another booby trap, something dreamed up by the fiction writers? Something that silly girls babbled about on a bus. Romance a concept to sell tickets to a movie show? Did anyone ever *feel* the way Nelson Eddy looked when he gripped Jeanette Mac-Donald's hands and sang "Wanting You"? A scene so intense, and yet it was completely fake, a product of the silver screen. So maybe love was fake, too, just a catch-all word: "I love your dress," or "to love, honor, and obey," until marriage grows cold and you want to move on?

I'm never going to get married. It was a not a sudden decision, the thought had been growing on her. So why didn't it make her feel better, to have her mind set firmly? Knees hollow, she walked up the path of crushed shells to the house. The oval of glass in the front door brought her face-to-face with herself and she suddenly realized how thin she was. Eyes large in the framework of brow and cheek, hair growing long again, untamed licks sprouting around her ears, that awful in-between stage where it's too short to put in curlers. She would like to get it cut again, but the barber cost thirty-five cents.

As she hung there, half-tempted to run home, Max appeared beyond her reflection, through her own image she saw his welcoming smile.

"Come in, come in." He held the door wide. "I wasn't expecting you so early. I was going to come to the dorm and collect you up — is that right? — no, pick you up." Long hair tousled and shirt open at the collar, he looked newly arisen, but genuinely glad to see her. "You are bearing gifts?" He eyed the grocery sack curiously.

"It's — mostly for me. I hope you don't mind," she blurted, against her careful rationale. "I just got really hungry for meat loaf. I miss cooking, I did a lot of it at home, so I thought —" She thought it was pretty cheeky of her to assume he'd let her use his kitchen.

But Max only seemed delighted. "How great! After all that turkey — I must tell you I am not a great admirer of turkey — a meat loaf sounds superb. Do you use tomato sauce?"

"No! Did you want — ?"

"I detest tomatoes in meat loaf."

"I make it the German way, with onion

and sage and —"

"Say no more. I am in heaven already." He ushered her into the living room, a den of ruffles and flourishes with a grandfather clock in the corner. Hanging up her coat he went on, "How did you do yesterday? Was the campus deserted? I imagine everyone's gone for the week end." Talking too much, the fox-colored eyes a little shy, Max looked younger than usual. "We may be a bit out-of-bounds, you know, having our private lesson here, but if the lady Patterson gets the wind of it I will get you off the hooks. Is that the right word? I am enchanted by American slang."

"I'm not afraid of the Dean," Terry told him. "I've already sort of crossed words with her. She didn't put me in any dungeons. I think she likes me."

"Good. A fine woman, but so incredibly Victorian. All these rules that the school has laid down, they're quite ridiculous. In Europe youngsters your age would be living in garrets, subsisting on black bread and wine, sitting in cafés until dawn and arguing about life and death and love and Chopin. How else can one mature?"

"I guess we seem pretty backward to you."

"In some ways. But in others — ah, there's the great anomaly! This country has done wondrous things with inventions, experiments, producing radios, movies, the tall buildings, the fast cars. You are so full of the pure joy in the newness of your gadgets, it's a charming kind of innocence. Dangerous, too, because you are pretending that it will go on forever, this unthreatened world you live in. Like a giant toyshop." He took the sack of groceries and led the way to the kitchen, still chattering over his shoulder.

He's nervous, Terry realized. *He's making up conversation like a boy on a first date!*

"What did you bring us? Let's see, apples, wonderful, I love your apples. So big and sweet and full of juice. Ah, good, ground steak, it will make a great loaf. I actually didn't eat much yesterday, I spent most of my time tinkering with the piano. It was woefully out of tune. Rye bread, for the stuffing — I have never used rye, but why not?"

"You'll like it. Oh, gee, this feels good." As she tied on an apron.

"Yes, a kind of therapy." He spoke more slowly now. "I imagine you were lonely yesterday."

Don't you dare go weepy! She said, "Yeah, I was homesick, I guess. I hope you have an egg?"

He got one from the refrigerator in the

corner, then hitched a hip on the stool by the sink, watching as she began to mix the meat and bread. "Leaving the parental nest, it's quite a step for anyone. There's an awful emptiness, a sense of displacement until you find your balance in some new setting. Not made any easier by the world changing around us so rapidly."

"Or by not really liking the new place a lot." *Except for you.* She almost burst right out with it. "Coming here helps." *Watch yourself, don't take too much for granted, the way you usually do.* But the closeness of the room was a temptation to kick over the barriers and find some level of friendship — he must want it too. He looked perfectly comfortable perched on the stool.

"Your authority with onions is impressive. I just wish you may some day find yourself in equal command of the keyboard." Teasing her, with warmth in his eyes and a diffidence. "Have you ever tried any dill? Just a trace." Reaching over to one of the cabinets he found a bottle.

"Sounds good to me." She finished her mix and shaped the loaf. "Now a slice of bacon across the top."

He barked a word in German that she didn't know. "You're a magician," he translated. "You must have learned from a German cook."

"My grandmother's recipe."

"Upper Danube, I'd say."

"Lower Davenport, Iowa," she told him smiling.

With the meat in the oven and the potatoes on to boil, she went to investigate the dining room and found table settings in the high boy. *He never invited me to go this far.* But he was in the spirit of it, finding the napkins, filling glasses from a pitcher of ice water, ceremoniously.

"Actually," he confessed, "I was going to invite you to lunch at the Hot Shoppe. Not a bad little — what's that marvelous word? — eatery. Of course we would have had to walk. This ridiculous prohibition against the automobile. Why don't they allow you young people to accept rides in a car? You're old enough to be driving one yourselves."

"I do," she confessed, as they migrated out to the music room, with aromas of cookery beginning to invade the house. "I have a car of my own at home."

"No? I am impressed. So young to be in charge of a powerful machine. But there's no reason why you shouldn't. Your reflexes are at their best, your eyes are quick at your age. It's only the judgment that needs developing. How fast do you go in your automobile?"

"I'm a careful driver, but I've had her up to fifty-five." *And there's no feeling like the whip of the wind in your face, the scenery flying past.*

Reading her look, he nodded. "The joy of it, I can imagine. It's the great gift of this land, that there is such freedom and such pleasure everywhere. After Europe, it's like being on a different planet. No threats to the future, no tragedies, at least not nationwide ones, no killing fields. You just keep building your cities, higher and higher, streets full of stores, so many things to buy. All houses have bathtubs and gas-fired stoves, even in small towns like this. Do you know that in many villages in Europe they don't even have electricity. Here you can turn on the light with a switch. Sit down and read a book, too good to be true." The thought seemed to sadden him.

"Well, there's a catch to it," she said. "I have a friend who's afraid we'll run out of electricity some day. Too many things like phonographs and radios, he says we need to find new ways to make power without burning coal. In St. Louis we had an awful problem with soot. Of course they cleaned it up, they're cutting down on smoke from all the factories."

"And what do the factories make?"

"Lots of stuff. Shoes, mostly, and Budweiser beer and Purina dog food."

Max shook his head in wonder. "Dog food. A special food for dogs. It would make my friends in Zurich astounded."

"It's mostly horse meat. We have a lot of stock yards, too, they smell pretty bad when the wind's from the wrong direction." Terry was feeling almost embarrassed by the plenty that she'd always taken for granted.

"Not to apologize," he said, with that swift comprehension. "It is no crime to be optimistic. To wander through the toyshop unsuspecting."

"Un— ?"

"Excuse me. Wrong word. Unsuspicious? Unaware of dangers impending. I would say naïve, but that has connotations of stupidity. Americans aren't stupid, they are just hopelessly trusting. Too much trust in one's own luck is a dangerous thing."

"You mean we might get drawn into the war?"

"Oh yes. I know it seems distant to you, but to me it's always there, right over my shoulder. This is the ugliest war ever fought, ruthless destruction. The Nazis are trying to wipe out a whole race of people. Acquire an empire, by spending a generation of men.

Which makes the rest of Europe sacrifice their own young warriors. I feel a sense of guilt, that I am not fighting with them."

"I'm glad. That you're not!"

His lips quirked as if he found her amusing. "The decision was not mine. There were others to consider." And the subject was closed. "Anyway, I hope your President will continue to stand tough, as they say, against getting you involved, but I am afraid he will fail."

"He'd better not! We elected him to keep us out of all that."

"Incredible, the whole idea of electing one's own government. It just isn't done anywhere else. To go to a place and vote — it's one reason I came here, the kind of country I would like to be part of. To raise a family in." Again that shadow crossed his face, but he shook it off. "The other reason I came, of course, was for the music. This country is a haven right now for the world's best musicians. You have produced some great composers yourself."

"We have?"

"Absolutely. Copeland, Ives, especially the late Gershwin. In fact, I've been thinking that an acquaintance with George would be good for you. In his work you feel the pain of youth, of loving and losing, of loneliness in the middle of the night. Come on, let's try some of it out. Here's one of his easier pieces." Seating her at the piano he set the sheet in front of her. "Try this."

She could read the notes, but hardly believed them. The combinations were dissonant and the beat syncopated unexpectedly, in a way that wasn't quite jazz. "What does 'rubato' mean?"

"That is the correct question for Gershwin," he told her enthusiastically. "You reached for it right away. Rubato is an invitation to the pianist to take liberties. To make the piece a little bit his own. Through this passage you can forget the inner metronome and 'monkey around' with the rhythms. Faster or slower, however your emotions prompt you."

It was a whole new concept to Terry. "Tell me how."

"No, no, no. That is exactly what I must not do. This is your chance to — how shall I say — put yourself in the driver's seat."

That, she understood. And with her imagination wheeling free, she ran through the passage impulsively. It didn't work. The diminuendo came too soon and the following allegro stumbled. "I really messed that up."

"So. Next time you will try it differently.

No harm done. The pleasure is in the experiment. And when you get it right, like magic you will discover the beauty of the shape Mr. Gershwin wanted you to discover." His face was alight with fire now, so warm she wanted to hold out her hands to it.

"Play it your way," she urged.

And he did. Not just that page, but on through the whole piece, giving a twist here and a skip and jump there, chords off-key and sour and sweet. A glimpse of what music could be, if you had the touch. *Mother wasn't so wrong to wish this for me.* It brought a surge of emotion that cut across her heart like a rip tide.

"Hey!" he broke off in mid-phrase, peering at her anxiously. "What's this? I could have sworn that you never cry."

"I'm sorry." *Lord, what did I do with my handkerchief.* "I was just wishing my mother could have heard this."

Max was offering her a clean one. "What is it, liebchen? Something serious. Your mother is ill?"

He's too smart, he can read my mind. "I'm worried about her. Her last letter was kind of shaky. And I didn't hear from home yesterday, I was sure they would phone me. I keep wondering if they forgot?"

He shook his head firmly. "I could never believe that. The mother I met would hardly neglect her little virtuoso."

"I'm a big disappointment to her. Ever since the day of the audition she has known I'll never be a concert artist. It's all pretend now. We make believe that I'm a musician, but we both know it isn't true." To speak it aloud was to twist her heart again, and she had to hide in the depths of the handkerchief.

"Reality," he was saying, "is a difficult commodity. But the love, that was not counterfeit. She adores you. If there is a problem at home we shall find out about it. Better to know, eh? We will, as they say, just give her a call, yes?"

"On the *telephone?*" All her life Terry had been in awe of the high toll of communication. Every phone bill that came in caused her father to explode. And as for long distance, the few times her mother insisted they call the folks in Virginia Henry had suffered visibly, his watch in hand, ticking off the minutes: one, two, three . . . Ring off!

Aghast, she watched Max take the receiver from the hook, heard him speak to an operator. "We want to talk to St. Louis, Missouri please."

Terry came to stand beside him, trembling

at the prospect that in a minute she would hear her father's voice — what she could say to him? Never mind, just to find out, to feel a touch across the miles. It was a woman's voice asking, "Number please?" Hesitating, she gave it. And listened to a distant phone ring, and ring and ring. At last the lady was back again. "There is no answer at that number."

Stiffly, as if her parts didn't quite fit, she put the phone down and came back to the piano bench to sit. Even in the Depression, her father had never worked the day after Thanksgiving. All the offices were closed. She couldn't imagine where they would be. In a burst of fright her mind raced off through thickets of possibilities — accidents, separations, vanishings —

Max had an arm across her shoulder, firming her back to earth. "Don't imagine the worst. We will put the call through again later, that's all. I've another fellow I want you to meet, Eric Satie. Don't take him too seriously, he's a whimsical sort." But after a half hour of effort, they both knew it wasn't working.

"Maybe a bite to eat will settle your nerves?" he suggested.

"Oh my gosh! The meat loaf." From the fragrance in the air, she could tell that it was done. And oddly, it did help her settle inside, to serve the food, to see the appetite with which he tackled the meal.

"This is excellent," he commented between bites. "You are a remarkable young woman. Not just your housewifely accomplishments, but the grace with which you deal with situations. You have a dignity that reminds me of — someone I knew. She was brave too. Caught in a war. But there are many kinds of conflicts and the lesser ones create wounds just as deep. Let's try that number again."

But once more there was no answer, and by then it was two in the afternoon. Different time in St. Louis, of course, but the fact remained that the house there was vacant — even the ringing of the phone sounded empty.

"It's going to be a long weekend," he mused. "For both of us. Campus deserted, all activity halted in mid-stride. It's even hard to think about next week, exams, concerts coming up, they all seem in limbo. So I had an idea, but it does involve a little risk. If the lady dean found out she might banish you back home — which could even be a blessing, no? This school is no place for you, Thérésa." As always, he adorned the name with accents like small jewels.

"No. I mean yes, it could be a blessing to be ordered home. Anyway, I don't mind taking chances any more." *What does it matter?*

"I've thought that you really would benefit by hearing more of our great pianists. Dame Myra Hess is playing a concert Sunday afternoon in Washington, D.C. For you to go there in my car would constitute a serious breach of rules. Maybe get us both kicked out, as they say. But if we pull it out — I mean pull it off? — it could be a marvelous experience. Are you game?"

"I'd love that." Terry didn't even have to think twice. To ride in a car again, get away from the boundaries, not just school but the walls of her imagination that loomed.

"Thank you," he said soberly. "Thank you for trusting me." In a strange and gentle gesture, he took her hand, turned it over and kissed the palm.

Flustered she looked into his eyes and glimpsed a deeper dimension than she'd ever seen there before, a probing look that asked some question, maybe not of her, but of himself. Beautiful eyes, right now they were the color of cream soda when the sun comes through it. Max Wolff had something in mind, and she couldn't even guess what.

Terry almost forgot her troubles, as she

pondered that look all the way back to the dorm.

TWENTY-FOUR

In 1370 — or was it 1371 or 1375? — some time around there the Black Plague devastated Europe. One sentence from the textbook stuck in Terry's mind: "The streets of London were deserted, and a terrible silence hung over the city, broken only by the tolling of the death knells." It came back to her now as the bell on the Catholic Church began to ring for nine-o'clock mass that strange Sunday morning of the holiday weekend. As Terry walked the empty streets of Gloucester Town, she could almost picture the terror of those medieval people as they lost neighbors and family to an unseen killer.

What if something like that could have happened to St. Louis? An outbreak of cholera — it did once a century ago. Suppose they both for some reason —

Terry couldn't pronounce the word "dead" even in her mind. Shuddering she walked slowly across the vacant campus, trying to invent a scenario that would account for their absence. She had a terrible impulse to go get on a train for home at once, but that was crazy, of course. Her total worth was $5.23, plus the quarters in her pocket. All day yesterday she had held them in her hand ready, each time she'd called home from the pay phone in the down-stairs hall of the dormitory. Only to hear, over and over, the hollow sound of the phone ringing in an empty house.

They just went somewhere for the holidays. You'll feel silly tomorrow when you get them and they're perfectly all right. No need to tell me their plans; they would have thought I'd be okay, with the Hamiltons so nearby.

And for a moment Terry was tempted. One call to Richmond and she would be surrounded by her family, with all their love. Their pride. Their darling "Reddie." They would never believe he could be capable of any wrong. If she retreated to Hamilton House there was bound to be a terrible scene.

Somewhere a steeple clock struck its hours with a distant ghostly clanging. Terry crossed the street to the post office. She had written Phin, as a last resort. Could he please drop over and check on her mother? She hated to ask. Not that he would mind, but she could hardly bear for him to learn about the brandy. "Maybe the phone is out of order," she'd said, "but I can't seem to reach them."

Except the letter won't get there for days. I could call him . . . But suppose Fran answered the phone. Sunday was her day off. She'd get all excited and run over and find out that there was some reasonable explanation after all, and then she'd tell everybody how that poor child got in a terrible panic over nothing. Terry shook off the temptation to hear a familiar voice.

Continuing on down the street, she paused. In the window of the drugstore was a poster, a Norman Rockwell illustration of one of President Roosevelt's "Four Freedoms." A painting was of a family around a table with the mother bringing on a roast turkey — it made Terry think of her one visit to Dad's home, the farm in Iowa. It had been a disaster, with Mother sitting on the sidelines, looking like an expensive piece of cut glass in the middle of a second-hand store. Granddaddy Miller was a rugged, hard man with stubby callused fingers, while Grandmother was thin and tight-lipped. Terry had seen a resemblance to herself even then — she'd only been about ten years old. *Could they have gone there for the holidays? Maybe Granddad is ill, he has a bad heart. He could have died. That would be reason for them both to take the trip.* It was the most plausible idea yet, a sign that there were unexplored possibilities.

Terry felt a sudden twinge of hunger. She had skipped the desolate refectory this morning. Turning in at the drugstore, she made her way past tables piled high with used textbooks for sale and the little booth that sold bus tickets, closed now. At the rear there was a lunch counter where a solitary fry cook read the Sunday comics, leaning against the unlit stove.

"I'd like a cup of soup and a grilled cheese sandwich, please."

He glanced up at her offended. "For breakfast?"

"Would you rather make me poached eggs and cinnamon toast?"

"Gawd, no!" He set the paper aside and lit the grill with a pop and hum of gas. Slapping down a couple of pieces of bread, he reached up to get a can of soup off the shelf. "Tomato okay? It's all we got."

Sweating inside the yellow slicker, she

unzipped it and laid it on the next counter stool. Underneath she had on a wool sweater — the wind had been raw this morning, freighted with the smell of snow. She wondered if Max's car had a heater?

As her thoughts veered in a new direction Terry felt a stir of excitement. Off and on all night she had pushed aside thoughts of her parents and wondered about Max Wolff. She was sure she hadn't been wrong — there was a hidden intention about him, an interest more personal than professor-to-student. She had never felt this close to any other teacher she'd had. In fact when they sat close together on the piano bench she was very much aware of him as a man. The muscular arm beneath the shirt sleeve, the subtle expressions of mouth and eyes as he played — the joy that underscored the scars of a hard life.

As she left the drugstore she shivered, put the slicker back on. A chilly mist lay over the town and the forests. But inwardly a warmth was driving off the cold of premonitions. She was beginning to look forward to the day, this one day on which she could relax. A concert, a forbidden ride in a car, and Max. If he wanted to move closer at some point, she felt suddenly that she was ready for that. This was a decent man. In fact, she had to admit, it was that quality which drew her, unlike the feverish magnetism that had brought her crashing into Tommy's arms. What good was all that passion if it was based on deceit?

Turning away from the main walk across campus she followed a brick path around the quadrangle and over to the horse corral. No one around to notice, just another figure in a yellow slicker, and if they did, so what? *I felt like taking a walk in the rain.* She almost snickered aloud. *Love this raw Virginia air, the suck of mud on my boots, the stink of the stable.*

In the clammy odorous building, she passed between stalls where long-limbed animals paced and snuffled at her, as if they welcomed her company. Who would have imagined that horses could get bored or lonely? Straight through and out the far side, she walked down the bridle path, glancing at her watch. Nine-thirty-five. *I'm early.* But if you're going to break rules, you feel like getting that part over with. Max had said he'd pick her up at the dorm, but he'd been nervous about it.

"I hate to think what the Lady Dean will do to us both if we are caught going to a concert without the royal permission." But his grin was rebellious. A man who had crossed the Alps to escape Hitler was not really afraid of old Pittypat. Terry was tempted to ask him about his escapades, but decided it wasn't the time or place. Somewhere along the line his wife had been killed. Today was for forgetting.

On either side the dense woods dripped and brooded, wilderness unchanged since colonial days. You could almost imagine a Virginia settler riding his big hunter down this path at the "planter's pace." Willie had read a book on the subject, passing along excerpts to Terry as a matter of interest. " 'They developed a special breed to do the pace, which combined speed with endurance in covering the long miles between plantations. It took a very strong horse to carry the weight of a man at that gait hour after hour.' "

Sturdy the ghosts that shadowed the woods. Rousing in a little while she glimpsed a patch of pink showing through the thin curtain of trees. Only ten-fifteen. Maybe he wouldn't appreciate her showing up early. He was out there now in his driveway, loading the battered old green Essex, putting suitcases into the trunk . . . *suitcases?*

That usually meant an overnight stay. Hesitating, she tried the idea on for size. *By the way, how would you like . . . it just so happens . . . pretty late to go back to Gloucester . . . my darling Thérésa, I have loved you ever since . . . in Europe a young woman your age would . . . you have such an ardent soul . . .*

None of it quite worked in her imagination. Terry scrunched her toes in her boots as she watched Max shut the trunk of the car. Then walked forward through the wet underbrush, low branches of the trees showering the hood of the slicker with drops. At the sound of her boots on the crushed shells he spun around, startled.

"Good grief, liebchen, you look like an orphan of the storm. Didn't I explain that I would pick you up?"

"I thought maybe this would be less noticeable," she said, amazed at the candor, the level voice. *Whatever he wants, I'm not going to bumble around. I'm going to do it!*

"Well, at least I can give you a ride back to the dorm. Climb in, my dear. I'm sorry we can't have our concert after all."

"You're not going to Washington?"

"Yes, I am, but on a different errand. I have to discuss some business with the people at the Swiss Embassy. It wouldn't be much fun for you. I'm sorry." He seated her and tucked a blanket across her knees.

"No. I can't go back there, I can't stay in the dorm another minute or I'll go crazy and do something really wild, like get on a bus for New York and never come home." She heard her own voice, rising higher, almost out of control. "I don't care what you have to do in Washington, I don't mind tagging along."

"New York?" His face looked completely boyish in his dismay. "Oh, dear young lady, that's not a good idea. Forgive me, but you are not ready for the big wicked city." Brow etched with indecision he hung above her, the rain pearling his roan-colored hair, his eyes troubled and full of fondness. "Any word yet from your family?"

"No. I tried all day yesterday and this morning. They've gone somewhere and I am going somewhere. I can't sit around another second."

He hung there, troubled, then straightened up and closed the car door. "Wait a minute . . ." Ducking around the side of the house he disappeared from view, only to return, holding something under his trench coat. Getting in on the driver's side, he handed it to her, a copy of Saturday's *New York Times*. "Look at the headlines. They are very bad. The world is about to come into a moment of crisis. England may fall. The Nazis are within a few miles of Moscow. Your president will have to do something almost at once if he's to save the day. When the storm breaks I want you secure in your dorm."

"You didn't stay safe at home, hide in the cellar and try to pretend there wasn't any danger out there."

"But I am considerably older, and I had a plan."

"I have friends in New York, I'll be all right." *I wouldn't ask Dixie for a quick hello.*

"If I take you with me on this junket today, will you promise then to go back to your studies and stay put until we find your parents?"

"Okay." The word *we* put some foundation under the word.

He put the car in gear and backed slowly down the driveway. "It won't be much fun, I'm afraid."

"I don't care. I just can't sit around and pretend everything is all right."

"No. I can see that." He heaved a sigh, as they rolled slowly out onto the Richmond Road, the heater beginning to provide a thin warmth. "I am a pullover — is that the word? — for a brave young lady."

"Pushover." Terry smiled and he smiled back.

"You remind me a little of my late wife. Lena. A wonderful woman."

"I know she died — ?"

"She was killed working with the Resistance outside Paris when the Germans moved in." Too brisk, too matter-of-fact. "Somehow I was rescued and spirited off to Switzerland. Thank God for friends. One of them telephoned me last night, a man who is on the inside of things. He warned me to go see the people at the Embassy today, at once. There will soon be a development. Look through the paper, will you? See if you can find any hint of it?"

"How do you get *The Times*?"

"They deliver it, even here in this backwater little burg. Beside the headlines, what does it say?"

Terry scanned the close-set columns. Another convoy had been torpedoed by the U-boats. The RAF was fighting off nightly raids over London, heavy destruction of the old city. "Where's Stalingrad?"

"Somewhere on Germany's eastern front. The Russians are tough, but they are primitive compared to Hitler's panzers."

"It says here the Japanese have sent some envoys to talk to President Roosevelt, to get him to lift the trade embargo."

"He's been tweaking their nose, refusing

to sell them scrap iron. Will he make concessions to appease them, do you think? Your president is difficult for me to read. He says he hates war, but I sense he really wants to get the country involved. For good reason, a free country cannot exist in a Fascist world. So he builds fighter planes for England, but he says he'd never send American boys overseas. What sort of game is he playing?"

He wants me to tell him what's in the President's mind? "I guess sending them planes is our way of trying to help."

"But they're no good without pilots. The RAF is running out of aviators. The British Army is decimated. Without American manpower the war will be lost, the swastika will fly over all the territory from Tibet to Land's End. I'm sure Roosevelt won't let that happen, but what's stopping him? Is he afraid the people of this country will refuse to fight?"

"Don't worry about that," she told him flatly. "The men up at the Naval Academy can't wait for next June to graduate and go out to patrol the convoys."

"Yes, yes, there are always professional heroes. But to provide the forces needed to stem Hitler's tidal wave it will take factory workers, family men who are used to the concept of freedom. They thrive on your ideal of independence. Even now they are resisting this token draft that requires military service. What if they were suddenly forced into it in large numbers and required to throw their bodies into the teeth of battle? To die? Would they obey? Or would they maybe rise up and revolt, overthrow the government?"

Overthrow Franklin D. Roosevelt? It would be easier to picture a mob tearing down Pikes Peak. "This country," she said, "is not made up of shirkers. Did you ever look at these historical markers we're passing?" They were even thicker along this stretch of highway than on the one down near Richmond. "Each one stands for some battle. Three wars were fought up and down this stretch of land. That last turn-off was to Fredericksburg — twenty thousand men died there fighting over Virginia. And just a little to the north at Antietam another twenty-five thousand gave their lives, both northern and southerners."

"Your Civil War, yes, but they were fighting over personal issues that they cared about greatly. A world war is more remote, more complex and far removed from your gentle country. I am sure Americans would fight if the enemy was in your streets. But you're a long way from the battleground."

"Right now," she admitted, "it doesn't seem as if it's any of our business."

He heaved a long breath. "Unfortunately, it's still my business. My friend who called last night is in the Swiss Embassy. I'm in this country on a Swiss passport. He couldn't talk over the phone, but I gathered that my visa is in jeopardy, he told me to come at once."

The rain had changed to snow now, blizzards of it, dry as feathers. The big flakes scattered in the wind as if a giant pillow had been dumped, whitening the shabby outskirts of the District.

"You mean . . . they might not let you stay in this country?"

"Or worse."

"What's 'worse'?"

"Internment."

Terry didn't understand what the word meant.

"Anyway, that's why we must miss our concert. Maybe after I hear what he has to say we can go and have supper somewhere. Meanwhile . . ."

She sat silent as he drove through narrow streets and finally found his destination, wrestling to jockey the car into a parking space, slipping and skidding in the slush. "I'm afraid you'll have to wait here. I can't take you inside tonight, the security is very tight, they say. I had to have my name on a list."

"That's okay, don't worry about me." Terry settled back in the seat, the blanket across her knees. "This is better than the dormitory."

Watching the fat flakes pile up on the windshield, she had one of those strange notions: that the deluge of snow could swallow the whole city of Washington so that nobody would find it for a thousand years. Like the fall of Pompeii where the ashes came down and preserved everything instantaneously.

The future archaeologist would scrape away the surface: What have we here? A car, part of the rubble of what once was a shining city, reasonably well advanced culturally, prosperous. No one knows how it came to be destroyed. No volcanoes around, maybe it was an ice age that froze it in its tracks. Digging further he would find a calcified mummy, young female, sub-species bonehead. Why else would she be sitting in a car without struggling to survive? Born without much of a will to live, make notes, this may have been prevalent among the populace of that era. Put her in a museum.

A great thick breath heaved in Terry's chest. She was too cold to sigh properly.

TWENTY-FIVE

Hands were clawing snow off the windshield, gloved hands. Max slung himself into the front seat, shedding white flakes.

"God in heaven, I'm sorry! Never dreamed I would be in there so long." The starter ground without success and he let out a Germanic oath. "Come on —" Tried again and the engine turned over. "Poor child, you are turned into an ice maiden. I should have found a warmer spot for you to wait, but I didn't think . . ." He spun the tires to get them out of the snow that had drifted around the car. Not much traffic, the streets of the Capitol were empty. Bursting through lace curtains of white, Max was muttering to himself. ". . . remember a café around here somewhere . . . get something hot inside you . . ."

Cold to the center of her being, Terry huddled under the lap robe, too numb to talk. She'd begun to feel drowsy, *little match girl, no matches.* She was vaguely aware that they had parked again, lights coming through a frosted window.

"Inside, come along." Max was boosting her out of the car, his strong arm holding her up as she tried to get her legs to work. Then they were in a restaurant, only a few people scattered at the tables. He sat her down, tried to help her out of the rain slicker, but she shook her head: *not yet.* Teeth beginning to chatter, and her hands were trembling so hard she couldn't take the cup. He held it to her lips and she drank — never did like the taste of coffee, but it was fueling her inner machinery. She could follow the heat of it all the way down.

"I swear I thought I'd only be ten minutes. Yes," to the waitress, "soup, please."

Chicken with rice, Terry burned her tongue gratefully, able to hold the spoon now, though she couldn't really feel it in her fingers.

"My fault. I shouldn't have brought you along. I am a fool. But you looked so needy standing on my doorstep, and I guess I felt a little needy too." He was babbling. "This was a trip I dreaded to make. But that's no excuse. It was mad of me to let you come. I've been a little mad thinking about you lately, fashioning a plan — what an idiot I am. Never mind that. Miss — ?" Calling the waitress back. "Could we have another bowl of the soup please?"

"What plan?" she managed the words in a strange, rusty voice.

". . . but matters are even worse than I feared." He had gone on talking, to her, to himself. "You feel so distant from the battlefields here in this safe land. I'd almost forgotten what it was like, to be afraid, constantly on guard, to lose the landmarks of your life, everything you've built, not the material things, but the inner structure, the heart. War is more than a devastation, it's evil incarnate."

How long do you have to study a language to learn words like that? Terry tackled the second bowl of soup with returning vigor. Feet still insensate as a couple of blocks of wood, but her hands were tingling, pink with circulation.

"Good. You're getting your color back. I want you to know," he leaned across the table earnestly, "I would never have let this happen if I hadn't found myself suddenly running for my life."

Oh come on, now, I don't believe that.

"Never mind, you're going to be all right.

I must try to explain things in a hurry, my train leaves in a little over an hour."

Terry gulped another spoonful. 'You're going somewhere?"

"Yes. I have to leave the country at once. My friends at the embassy have information — diplomatic sources, they wouldn't reveal, but they learn these things. They say it will only be a matter of a week or so until Churchill will prevail on your President to step in and save the British Empire before it is crushed out of existence. This country must enter the war, like it or not. And when they do, it will be too late for me to get out."

"I don't understand. Where will you go?"

"Switzerland. They went to extraordinary lengths to fix it up for me, that's what took so long. I'm booked for passage on a liner leaving New York tomorrow. God knows how they finagled that. It's odd, I had a premonition this was going to happen. I even packed a couple of suitcases with my music, my papers. Thank heaven for that. What? Oh, yes, miss, the soup was very good. I think we could both use some beef stew if you have it?"

"I don't get it. Why not stay here where you'd be safe?"

"But I'm not. You see, I am a German. Even though the passport is Swiss, I am the enemy. I'm not a Jew, I can't claim to be a refugee from racial oppression. If your country goes to war against mine, I could be interned. Or worse. If your people turn to anarchy all Germans could be the target of crazed mobs." The stew had come, steaming, full of big chunks of vegetables and beef.

Terry attacked it as if she were starving. Even though her body had warmed up, there was a frozen core that still felt numb under the news he was giving her. "We'd never be a crazed mob," she said.

"Ah, you are so full of trust, so sure of the state of law and order here. You've never seen a riot, the look of blood lust in the eyes of men who were ordinary citizens the day before. A mob has a life of its own, a fever to break and burn and kill. I'm glad you have never seen that. But you must believe it, you must be prepared." He shook his head. "I swear you are more innocent than my eight-year-old son."

Spoon on the floor.

When the waiter had brought another, she said, "You have a child?"

"Erich. He's a nice little boy, if I do say so. Now at a school near Bern, costs a mint, as you say. I turned over my total bank account in Zurich, put it in trust for his keep, then came to America to try to — what is the phrase — to make a buck. You would laugh, I paid my passage over here by washing dishes on the liner. Fortunately I've laid away enough from my work here to afford a cheap ticket in lower class on the way back."

"But what will you do over there?"

"Who knows? There's little demand for concert pianists anywhere in Europe. But I will find a way to keep alive. I believe a child needs his father to be alive."

"You could bring him here. This country would protect you."

"Maybe. Or not. Democracy is a fragile shell. With so much power in the hands of the people, everything is unpredictable." Max was forking down the stew as though he were fortifying himself against imminent starvation. "You don't know how a clever orator can manipulate the public mind. Who could have imagined Krystallnacht? Honest German citizens going wild, looting the stores of the Jews, so much broken glass from the windows it earned that terrible name. There have been atrocities all over Poland and Austria and France that your papers never have reported. Whole communities of Jews have been decimated. You are inclined to believe the best of your fellow man, but you have never seen him in a passion of hatred. I pray that you don't." In the grim silence he scraped his plate with the last crust of dinner roll.

Terry couldn't argue, of course, she'd never seen anything like what he described. Words couldn't paint the real picture of men gone berserk. She still couldn't imagine it happening here. *If I had a child, I'd want him to be here. Right in the old U.S. of A. No place safer on earth.*

"You must have missed your son terribly."

Max nodded, wordless for a moment. Then he gave her a weary smile. "So generous, so warm of heart, to try to understand my problems. You are a rare young lady, Thérèsa. From the first day I saw you last spring, so concerned about your mother, trying so hard under great difficulties, I recognized your inner strength. Then when you entered school, I watched the way you held yourself and knew I wasn't wrong. New shadows in your face, a growing maturity, all the symptoms of becoming a marvelous young woman. It's what gave me this strange notion: that in time you might some day be my wife. I think I'd be good for you, and I know you'd be good to me and the boy. He needs a mother. I've never known anyone else I could trust with the job."

Stunned speechless, Terry stared at him.

Under the long scattered forelock, his face was in its aging mode, lines all showing plainly, eyes sad, mouth pressed and patient, smiling a little. "Does that surprise you?"

"I don't — I can't —"

"Never mind. This is not time for hasty liaisons. We'll never know how it would have worked out. But I wanted you to know that my interest in you was not just part of my job. I will think of you often, my dear." He turned away and waved for the check. "I'm afraid we must now go back out into that wretched weather. I have a train to catch."

Take me with you! Even dumfounded, Terry knew that if he lifted a finger she would go. No matter that there was a horrifying conflict in Europe, danger seemed acceptable. What she couldn't bear was the thought of how lonely it was going to be without Max Wolff.

Outside the last daylight was being swallowed in the storm. Along the street, lights hung in halos of snowfall. The wind struck through her for a minute, and then he had her in the car and was trying to get the cold motor to start. As they drove through desolate streets Terry was a tumble of emotions, like a heap of laundry full of garments that didn't fit.

". . . you can catch the five o'clock train and be back in Gloucester Town before eight, in your dorm and safe. Tell them you were at the movies, something. Here —" Driving with one hand he dug in his pocket and brought out a wad of bills. "Take some for your train fare."

Terry looked at the money stupidly. "They're all twenties."

"Yes, I went to the bank on Friday. Go on, child, you don't think I'm going to abandon you here without making sure you can get home?"

Unwillingly she peeled off a bill.

"Take more."

"Twenty is enough." She had only obeyed him because she had nothing but the five dollar bill and change in her pocket.

"Why don't you drive to New York?" she asked suddenly, meaning *we. Why don't we drive to New York?*

"In this weather it would take too long. The roads could be icy, maybe run into accidents. I don't know the way. It's easier to take the train, get off in the heart of the city and hire a taxi to the dock."

Ahead a large building took on the profile of a stately depot. Pulling the Essex up close to the entrance, Max cut the engine. "I may as well leave the keys in the ignition. It will help the police in removing the vehicle. I won't be needing it again." He helped her out and went to get his suitcases from the trunk.

Inside under a big vaulted ceiling they found themselves amid a throng of people. Sunday night, everybody was rushing for home. Coming together out of the storm, holiday travelers looked worn out, impatient, nervous. They made a din like a hive of wasps. Max had brought her up to the ticket booth. Unable to think, to make a move or say the right things, she watched him go and buy a ticket. Two tickets, he brought one back to her.

"This will get you to Gloucester by eight o'clock this evening."

"Here —" She tried to return the twenty but he wouldn't take it.

"At least let me be a little bit of a gentleman. I can't see you to your door, but the gate is right over there, number sixteen. If the weather is bad down south take a taxi to the Hot Shoppe, from there it's only a short walk to the dorm. I pray that your absence hasn't been noted. Here . . ." he tucked in her free hand a set of keys. "Go out to the cottage and help yourself to any of the music. Don't give up on it, liebchen. You will find another teacher. I'm just sorry it won't be me." Drawing her into his arms with a hasty fervent hug, he turned and strode off toward a gate at the far end of the row.

Lost to sight in the crowds, he suddenly faded from reality. Terry almost could believe that Max was a figment of her imagination, a fleeting fantasy she once had. Everything about this day had slipped into the weird dimension of a dream. Her thoughts eddying slowly like ice in a muddy river, she couldn't feel her heart beating. It had stopped somewhere out in the snow-storm. All that was left was a shell that would take the train back to a mechanical life of boredom and loneliness.

Why couldn't I take the train to New York? Just go to that booth and exchange this ticket, find Max, travel a few more hours with him . . . But then what? Go where? Try to find Dixie? Never! Get a job, but where would I stay in the meantime? Need to make more of a plan, get together a little more money. Allowance would be along next week — probably. Dad's secretary is still there, isn't she? Unless he quit his job, and then there wouldn't be any more neat impersonal little checks. Maybe I could get some from Grandmother Hamilton: could I please maybe have my

Christmas present early? I need to buy presents for the folks. Lie, what difference? And you could sell some of the sheet music in the pink house to the student store. Too bad you couldn't sell the car —

The car. Sitting out there at the curb with the keys in it. If someone hadn't already driven it off . . . Terry began to trot toward the exit, not even examining her motives.

The Essex was still there. As she slid into the driver's seat she felt the first glimmer of her old self returning. To turn the key, feel the ignition respond. To drive again . . . almost made it worth while, to go back to lousy old Gloucester. *At least I'll have one great ride.*

She tried the wheels experimentally, felt them slip and grab, got a sense of the snow-packed street as she moved slowly toward a huge intersection ahead, must be a crossroads, several highways converging on the station. Windshield wipers cleared the snow, she saw a sign pointing south: "To U.S. 1" As the heater began to struggle to spread a little warmth, she followed the markers until they took her onto a slushy thoroughfare, major route, a lot of traffic. Couldn't see the signs now, but she was going in the right direction.

Before long she had come through the outskirts and found herself on a road that felt familiar. Highway marker, but it was crusted with snow. Windy out here, the flakes were hard as popcorn, the wiper had trouble flinging them aside fast enough. On either side were the black forests of Virginia, this had to be the road — yes, a green sign: FREDERICKSBURG — 20 MILES. She looked at the gas gauge, but it showed half full. No need to stop, be in Gloucester in an hour.

Dashing through the snow, in an Essex no one wants, down a highway full of ghosts, rising from their haunts. The bronze markers stood like shrouded specters along the edge of the road, picked up by her headlights and then gone again. Another sign, couldn't read it, snow piling on the windshield in spite of the wipers going like a metronome, whip, whip, whip. A one-and-a-two-and — there is a bridge. It came at her suddenly, before she realized that the road was taking a curve. Terry put on brake and felt the car slew around, sliding in a long, graceful arc like a figure skater. Heading for the pylon . . .

Hey, Phin, what do I do now?

TWENTY-SIX

"Pain is a funny thing," she wrote, and almost snickered. Alone in her room at the dorm Terry was aware of stirrings up and down the hall as the others went to class. Almost eight o'clock, it soon quieted down as she considered her assignment, to write an essay for Freshman English. *"You think pain has something to do with a broken rib, a wrenched shoulder."* The highway patrolman had said she was lucky, to be thrown from the car when it wrapped around the bridge pylon. To fall in a mound of snow. To be rescued by a passing truck driver almost immediately. Must have landed on the shoulder — she rubbed it cautiously. *"Bodily damage just hurts. Real pain is different, it's like a nail driven into your heart."* Sounded stupid, but she wasn't going to turn the paper in anyway. It was something to kill time.

The doctor had ordered her to rest for a week at least, until all traces of dizziness had subsided. "She's got a slight concussion, and those ribs need to knit."

"It's a miracle she wasn't killed." Dean Patterson discussed her across the bed as if she were an inanimate object. "Thank heavens that trucker brought her here."

"Here" was the hospital in Fredericksburg. She had faded out as they worked on her and come back to find the Dean bending over her with birdy-bright eyes. It was Tuesday morning by then — she'd lost a whole day of her life. Another one came and went somewhere as her mind tilted and slept. Wednesday, the Dean was back bringing clothes that Terry recognized as hers. "How do you feel, my dear?"

"Pretty well, thank you." And the amazing thing was, she did feel reasonably okay. Except that every time she took a breath the tape around her chest gripped her implacably, and when she sat up to get dressed, her head seemed to swell like a hot balloon. She discovered the shoulder when she tried to get her arm into a sleeve.

"Let me help . . ." the Dean eased the blouse over her head, buttoning efficiently, muttering under her breath. "I will never forgive Max Wolff!"

"We were just going to a concert," she protested.

"In the middle of which he suddenly got called out of the country? On a Sunday afternoon?"

"It's the truth. He stopped at the Swiss Embassy and they told him he had better leave fast. They had a ticket for him on a boat."

"Oh, I'm sure it's true enough. He phoned me from New York to make sure you got home all right. Which you didn't, of course. I was about to report you as a missing person when the doctor called me." The Dean's pleasant face was drawn into taut planes around pressed lips. "Sinful, to leave you alone like that."

"He gave me money and a train ticket to get back."

"What on earth made you decide to take the car, child?"

"I know how to drive. I have a car of my own and I m-m-miss it." A flood of tears was spilling down her cheeks. *Oh, no, oh no. I mustn't let it get started, I'll never be able to stop!* Hands clamped on her wavering mouth, she heard herself making terrible choking noises and grabbed the wet towel the nurse was holding out, burying her face in it.

"Delayed reaction," the nurse said in that matter-of-fact tone. "Let her cry."

". . . maybe should leave her here another day?"

"Oh, I think she'll be all right. It'll be good for her to be in familiar surroundings, provided she rests."

And so she found herself huddled in a corner of the Dean's Oldsmobile, driving through a world of slush. The snow had turned to rain again and the woods were dripping. Nose dripping. Soul dripping . . .

The Dean talking. "I'm sorry to have to badger you, child, but this matter must be reported to your parents. I realize that you don't want your mother upset, but the school must fulfill its duty. We simply have to notify them at once. I tried to reach them yesterday and apparently they aren't home. I presume they've gone somewhere for the holidays. I need you to tell me where they are."

"I — can't." It came out in a wretched croak.

"But my dear, you must. This is a matter of our responsibility to you and to them. Nothing else is as important as that. Trust me."

"I don't know where they are."

The Dean's face had darkened ominously, the current of anger picking up speed. "Theresa, this is no time for hedging. I will be most tactful, I will try to reassure them, but they absolutely must be told that you've been in an accident."

Terry huddled in the heavy woolen car robe that they had draped around her. *If I tell all of it, how I've tried and tried, she's going to get scared too. Then she'll dig into the files and find out about the Hamiltons paying my tuition. They'll send somebody to get me and I'll be under their thumb. I can't let that happen.*

The silence was becoming unbearable by the time they reached Gloucester. Amid a clutch of females, Dean, monitor, Willie, others, she was put to bed in the dorm, aware of scandalized whispers. Now, two days later, she bent over her tablet and wrote: *"Pain is a state of mind, when you think of all the awful things that could have happened, may have happened, and you are too far away to find out."*

Maybe St. Louis had been in an earthquake, the entire city sucked into a vast hole. It helped to imagine the ridiculous because it was so obviously wrong. Terry tore the page out of her notebook and wadded it up.

"You better get that essay done." Willie had come in, speaking now out of the corner of her mouth like a spy. Word had gone out that the runaway was on room-campus, nobody allowed to associate with her.

The Dean had come to confront her once since the return. "I'm sorry to have to invoke discipline on a person who has already been through so much," she'd said, with a kindness that was steely and implacable. "This is not so much a matter of punishment. I want you to take this time to think about your duties to your parents and to me."

I don't owe you a thing. The hospital charges you will put on my parents' bill.

"You know what room-campus means: when you're feeling better you can go to classes and to meals at the refectory, but otherwise you are to stay in your room, no visiting, no talking to anyone. You are incommunicado."

Or what? Terry had wondered, *what'll you do? Send me home? Please do. So long as you pay for the ticket.*

Her allowance would come in a few days. With the twenty Max had given her, she would have forty-five dollars. Not enough to get to St. Louis, but she wasn't sure she wanted to go there, to walk up to the door of an empty house, and then what? Go over to Maybell's house: "Hey, what ever happened to my folks?" She wished Phin would write, but the mails were probably slow at this time of year, some of the trains had been held up by the storm over in the mountains of West Virginia.

Didn't matter. What was becoming clearer with each day, as she got her balance back and the ribs mended, was the idea that had begun weeks earlier as a sort of daydream. Now it took on shape: to buy a ticket, get on a train and go to New York. Get a job and a room and start making a life, like everyone does eventually. When she thought about it, now it felt fairly right. A little risky, but wasn't that what everybody had to do — jump off into the future? Dixie, Max, even old Ozzie took the leap. Have a little faith that you can find work, housework, cooking, *I could wash dishes. My hands don't matter.* She thought of Max earning his way to the new world, those wonderful pianist's hands in soapy water.

By now she could think of the pink cottage without choking up, just an abandoned bungalow with stacks of music that he had given her. Take whatever she wanted, he'd said. Somehow she couldn't face the thought of selling any of it, but there were other considerations. She pictured milk in the refrigerator, leftovers gone sour, beginning to smell.

As the sounds of the dorm died down, she got dressed. Yellow slicker, there were crowds of yellow slickers all over campus, blend in with the scenery. And since it was still raining there wouldn't be any equestrian classes trotting down the bridle path. One more time, and don't think of that walk last Sunday which had begun this monstrous week.

Pain is having done things that are really wrong, like betraying your mother's trust. Never mind that she's deserted you, you shouldn't have deserted her. You had no right to break her rules. Worst of all, you wanted to go farther, be more sinful, it could have happened. For that, nobody punishes you except God, maybe, who is probably the one who cut the telephone wires between here and St. Louis.

That night was restless, the exhaustion cured and no new activity to tire her out. Her mind kept roaming. It had been a disheartening job, to clean Max's GE and put all the spoiled food in the garbage can, but she accepted it as a penance, far more severe than the Dean ever thought up. She made herself sit at the piano and remember the duet. She fingered some of the sheet music and left it. When she had got back to the dorm, she almost hoped somebody had noticed she was gone, that she'd get dressed down further. But no one was around and even Willie had stayed away from the room until bed time.

Shoulder pulsing, she took one of the pills the doctor had given her; it settled the jitters, but left her feeling heavy and dense. In a sodden dream she saw fleeting visions, of her father leading a mule through an ocean of mud, his eyes fixed straight ahead. She kept crying to him, "Where is Mother?" but he showed no sign he heard as he slogged on through the Virginia woods where the Spanish moss hung dripping from the tree branches. So he must have come from Richmond, where the moss grows on the cypress trees and you find bones that have lain unburied for ages . . .

"Treece, get up, come on now." Willie in a whisper, nudging, trying to find a hold to help her sit up. "You need some breakfast."

The shoulder had subsided to a dull

throb, the headache still there but distant. "Aren't you afraid to speak to a notorious criminal?" she said lamely.

"Oh shoot, you know I can't stand that kind of nonsense. Live in the same room with somebody and not speak to 'em? I don't care if they put me on room-campus too, we'll start a club. Pals need each other." The offhand statement, the lift of jaw and toss of red hair, brought tears to Terry's eyes. New subject of essay: *"How can you be so wrong about practically everybody?"*

As they walked back from the refectory the church was clanging its bell again, just as it did a week ago, so it must be Sunday. How can the whole world change in one week? That, she could really write the essay on, how everything was transformed in seven days into a different time and place. A strange, unforgiving place where there was no love, just none at all.

"Don't forget your essay is due tomorrow morning," Willie reminded over her shoulder as she went off to church. Good solid Baptist, she never missed a Sunday.

Terry slumped at her desk. The assignment was to write about human feelings. If pain wasn't really suitable, maybe love would do. *I know so much about it!* Terry sneered at herself and took a deep breath, trying to settle the lump in her stomach. Southern food was heavy, sausage, eggs, grits, biscuits, hot chocolate from rich whole milk — it made her feel weighted down. Still tasting the sausage, she bent over her notebook.

"Love is like glue made of library paste. It holds people together for a while, but then just when you think all the gaps are sealed tight, it starts to rain and the whole thing comes apart at the seams."

Actually, it's a kind of wishful thinking. She had wanted to be in love with Tommy, as you would welcome a dare, one that might be fun. She'd pictured herself being courted by Max, before she found he was looking for a mother for his child. Good thing there hadn't been time for that to develop, she might have said *Yes.* And would it have been all that bad? Probably. Love for the wrong reasons turns out poorly, look at Marjorie marrying poor Henry because he was helpless and needy. Then the union held together by the paste of guilt — a child that had to be brought up, maybe one that nobody really wanted.

"Love is a trap that you can't ever get out of. It's an idea that authors invented so they could

develop plots for their books. Or the screen writers — they had to have some reason to get Jeanette MacDonald together with Nelson Eddy in a romantic duet. It is an exercise for actors to learn, to stare into each others' eyes with all that fake adoration."

Leaning back, Terry tried to think whether she'd ever actually seen love in anyone's face. Maybe when Max mentioned his son. But that's different, you are supposed to be fond of a child. Dixie used to say she "loved" the new fashions. Their rabbi, whom she had met once at the Berensens' house, talked about loving God, but he wasn't all that excited over it. Not the way Phin looked when he talked about his experiments, his face bright as if there was a huge powerful light bulb in his brain.

"You can love ideas, it's sort of one-sided, but they won't let you down the way people do." Unless somehow the equations grow teeth and bite you. Jilted by a theorem — *I'll have to ask him some time if that could ever happen?* Then she slid down a little lower in the desk chair, wondering when she'd ever see Phin again. Suddenly he was as distant as the rest of her old life, all of it erased as if it were a few chalk marks on a blackboard. She tried to picture Berensen's house, the

back yard, the big elm tree with the Gryphon parked under it.

"Loving your possessions is about as safe as you can get. You can be ecstatic with joy over owning an automobile." Until you hit an icy patch of road and the car turns into a crumpled tin can.

Terry stared around the silent room. Beyond the door the halls were full of noise, stocking feet trotted down the hall, people called across from room to room, a radio was going somewhere, playing a symphony. Sunday afternoon at Gloucester, maybe her last one here. As soon as her allowance came . . .

"You can love money, but it doesn't love you back." Her father loved it, or else he hated it, or he was deadly afraid of it.

"Mostly, love is a travesty and my advice is to stay a long way away from it." Terry signed the paper and put it in her assignment folder. Shock the prof. *He's a stuffed shirt, probably never thought of being in love.*

Distantly she was aware that the noise out in the hall had hit a different pitch, more like the screech of panicked bluejays. It crashed into the room as Willie came bursting through the door, lunging over to her desk to turn on the small Philco radio, twisting the dials frantically.

"We're being bombed! Where's the station —" She found the announcer's voice.

"The attack was directed primarily at Hickam Airfield and the Naval docks in Pearl Harbor . . ."

"Where's Pearl Harbor?" Willie swung around on her.

From the next suite, through the bathroom that linked the two rooms, Peg and Mona came running. "My radio's on the blink. What's happening?"

"They broke right into the symphony," Willie yelled. "I was talking to Louise and they cut in with this news bulletin. Shut up, listen!"

". . . waves of Japanese planes are still bombarding the Naval Base, no word yet on casualties . . ."

"The Japanese? How can they be bombing us?"

"Where the HECK is Pearl Harbor?" Willie kept bleating.

Standing a little apart, Terry was remembering. "Tommy said they have the best fighter planes in the world," she said to no one in particular.

Mona swing around, prohibitions forgotten. "Who's Tommy?"

"That boy she goes with up at Annapolis.

411

He told her there would be a war. Terry, where is Pearl Harbor for heavensake?"

"I think it's in the Philippines," Peg said.

Terry was thinking of Ozzie, manhandling a big gun on the deck of a battleship. But he was posted to San Diego, wasn't he? That couldn't be anywhere near the Philippines. Except ships sail across the ocean, it's what the Navy does. He'd be out there on the deck, slinging the shells, loving it. Unless the ship got sunk, but that wasn't likely, a battleship is a big boat. No, Ozzie couldn't get hurt. *Not after I let him go off to war with no XXX.*

"Does this mean we're in a war?" she wondered to thin air.

"Pearl Harbor is in Hawaii!" Willie's voice rose loud across the chatter. "Louise says so."

The place where they do hula dances? Why would anybody want to drop bombs on Dorothy Lamour in a grass skirt?

"It's a lot closer to us than the Philippines," Willie added. "I got to find a map." She was pulling on her boots. "I'm going to the library."

"Don't forget to take off your bathrobe," Terry said absently.

Shedding the pink terrycloth wraparound, her roommate shrugged into a house dress followed by a slicker. Raining again outside, a steady drumming on the window. And against it sharply the strident ringing of a phone, the one down the hall at the monitor's station.

A voice rose in a bawl. "Maizee! It's your folks calling."

Terry's thoughts slewed around in a new direction. If this could lead to a war maybe her parents — *wouldn't they have to call? To see if I'm all right. Even tell me to come home? You don't want to be away from home in a war.*

But it wasn't going to come to that. This country didn't want to fight anybody. This raid was probably a mistake, the Japanese would say how sorry they were. They always said they were sorry, while they took over whole countries in the Orient. Terry never had understood what happened to Manchuria. Should have paid more attention.

She tried to hear what the announcer was saying, but you could tell he didn't know, really. "It is reported that Japanese troop carriers are cruising toward the coast of California . . ." Ridiculous. How could a little country like Japan expect to conquer the United States of America?

Somewhere beyond the room an argument

had broken out, Willie's full-throated tones rising above the whine of the hall monitor's. "For the love of pete, Mary Kay, are you a complete dummy? You can't pull rules at a time like this! That phone call may be a matter of life or death! *Treece!* Get your behind down here, you're wanted on the long-distance."

A great surge of confusion like a wave of fever broke through her body as she ran in socks and terror and relief, shoving her way through the mob in the hall. Because St. Louis was still there, and everything was going to be all right.

"Mother?"

But it was a man's voice. "Terry, is that you? I've been trying to get through — speak to me, Terry."

"Hi, Tommy." Collapsed under a ton of disappointment, she struggled to focus. "How are you?" Of all the stupid remarks —

"I'm great! I'm absolutely wonderful! We've got our war. We are graduating. In five days, next Friday to be exact. I want you here, I want you to come be with me. My folks have reserved a suite in Carvel Hall, you can stay with them. I'll send you bus fare — you've got to come. Please. It's my big day. I need to see you one last time before we shove off."

Those words got a grip on her. *Never again turn down a sailor who's going to war* . . . "Tommy, are you sure there's going to be a war?"

"We're already in it, sweetheart. Believe me. Please say you'll come!"

Or you'll feel guilty all your life.

"Terry, there are three hundred guys waiting for this phone."

"Tommy," she firmed up her voice. "I think you should ask the girl who's wearing your ring."

Silence on the line. Then he said, "So that's it. That's why everything went sour last time you were here. You found out about me and Kate. That damned Georgina! Excuse my language, but I'm going to kill her with my bare hands."

"For telling the truth?"

"But it's not what it seems. It was sort of a scheme of my mother's, to make the right connections, for the future of my career. Kate is the daughter of an Admiral. They're stationed in San Francisco, I haven't seen her since last summer. Terry, it's you I want. I need you to be here. Honey, we're going off to battle." Sounded high as a flag flying from the top mast. "Please say yes."

Weakly, Terry said, "All right. I'll come."

TWENTY-SEVEN

One suitcase to hold an entire lifetime, she thought, and you have to leave a little room for spare socks. The picture of the Gryphon lay flat against the bottom, protected by a layer of letters. *I don't know why I'm keeping those.* They were mostly from Grandmother Hamilton. *When I get to New York maybe I'll write to her, try to explain.* Terry doubted it, though. What could she say? Folding her best suit carefully, she laid it on top of the papers. The red velvet gown? *I won't need that where I'm going.* But she touched it lovingly where it hung in the closet, the rich color blurring before her eyes. *Stop it!* She took three of her best shirtwaists and one wool skirt. *I'll wear the other.*

"What the Sam-hill are you doing?" Willie sounded angry.

In a guilty lunge, Terry whirled around. "Oh, hi."

"You know you're not allowed to go anywhere!"

"Aren't you supposed to be in Biology? It's Thursday morning."

"Went to the lab. It's closed. Our teacher enlisted in the Army. So did half the guys in class. The whole Phys. Ed. Department is totally shut down, not enough people to make up a basketball team, only a few girls and some of them are going to join the Red Cross. I might do that too, only I got to shape up first. Man, I love those grits and beans, musta put on ten pounds since I been here. But you're in no shape to join anything, so why are you packing that suitcase?"

"Tommy asked me to come to Annapolis for his graduation."

"But you're under orders you can't leave campus."

"Come on down to the bus station about ten o'clock tomorrow and wave goodbye."

Willie contemplated her, frowning. "You're not coming back. You're going straight on home and look for your folks, aren't you?"

"Yes. Yeah, that's exactly what I'm going to do. You tell the Dean that, if she asks."

"Tell the Dean nothing," Willie muttered, dropping suddenly to hands and knees. "I'll probably leave, myself, if I can get in shape.

One . . . two . . ." pushups, hard, fast, making the muscles ripple on her hefty arms. "One of these days . . . five . . . six . . . the Army is going to wise up that they need women, too. We can march and shoot and do anything a man can, except pee through a hole in a fence. When they realize they got a big new crop of female soldiers they'll bring us in, you watch . . . eight . . . nine . . . and I'll be the first to sign up."

"You mean you'd go out and shoot a gun, try to kill people?"

"If they're Japanese, darn right." That anger had been in her eyes and voice ever since last Sunday. On Monday when the President had made his speech, about infamy and all that, even Terry had felt the stir to do something, show these foreigners that the U.S. is no push-over. According to the radio, the whole country had rushed to the cause. There were lines at the recruiting offices, all the movie stars were enlisting. Even here in the wilderness the college had announced a rally next Sunday to sell war bonds, as they were now called.

Savings bonds to finance the cost of all that ammunition and stuff. Terry wondered if her father felt maybe a little bit of patriotism in the light of the attack on Pearl Harbor? Probably not.

He'd be more outraged at the President for speaking of gas rationing, even food rationing, meat and sugar and butter — why would they have to ration that? Terry didn't know or care. Her own immediate plans were taking shape now and she had to pay attention. *Pack the pearls in a safer place.*

". . . forty!" Willie rolled over and began to do sit-ups. "Treece, I got to talk to you about something . . . five . . . six . . ."

Terry unzipped the inner compartment of the suitcase and put the jewel case in, packing underwear all around it. *Wonder what they're worth, if you could sell them?* It gave her a chill to consider it, but what good are family heirlooms if you have no family? The coldness in her belly was icier than the weather outside, an inner refrigerator that was always on, even when she was sweating.

"Treece, are you listening?"

"Willie, I want to give you this." She took the embroidered scarf and laid it on the bed that was surrounded by pictures of horses. Actually, horses were okay. To care about a living thing was nice.

"M'gawsh! Treece, you don't mean it." Scrambling over, Willie touched the stole reverently. "But I got nothing for you!"

"I tell you what — give me that snapshot of you with your mare."

"Sure. Of course! I got plenty of those at home anyhow." She rushed to detach it from the wall, suddenly awkward as she handed it to Terry. "But I still got to say something you won't like."

"Go ahead." Everybody else does.

"It's about your English essay. Now I know I didn't have no right, but I figured I'd ought to look it over. You been acting a little loco since the accident. I was nervous you'd go writing something screwy, and you did. Treece, that's a bad paper. Please don't hand it in."

Terry could hardly recall it, some silly stuff she had scribbled a long time ago, last Sunday.

"Love," Willie said earnestly, "is the only thing that matters any more. We all got to stick together, now that we're at war. I mean, I love my friends, I love my sisters, if I didn't I'd just about die. I love my horses and my folks. But mostly right now I love my country." Her voice had crept up the scale, her lower lip was wobbling. "Please tear it up."

Terry moved past her to the desk and got out the assignment folder. "I was mad when I wrote this. I didn't mean it." She ripped it in pieces and threw them in the wastebasket.

"Thank you." Trying to be very dignified,

Willie lumbered out of the room as the tears started to pour down her cheeks.

Terry stood a minute, stunned. She had to get away from this place before she got any more confused. She locked the suitcase. Whatever wasn't in there, didn't matter. At least she was ready, she could slip out of the dorm around nine-thirty tomorrow while everybody was still in class — if there were any classes. Going to the basin she washed her hands and slicked down the haircut. She had kept it trimmed with manicure scissors, it still looked pretty good.

For a minute she had a mental picture of herself and Willie, dressed in uniforms and helmets, charging across no-man's land with guns, strafing the fox holes. Except this was a different kind of war, fought with ships and planes. *Did they fly all the way from Japan across the Pacific Ocean?* Suddenly she wished she could read the *Post Dispatch.* Or even the Richmond paper, but the newsstand at the train depot was cleaned out every day the minute the truck arrived. It occurred to Terry that she did know where she could find a copy of *The New York Times.*

Making sure the monitor was nowhere in sight, Terry stepped into the hall. On the desk by the stairs was the morning's mail. A letter with her name on it, in familiar bold black strokes. She glanced inside; there were a couple of ten-dollar bills to cover her bus ticket. Sticking it in her pocket, she slipped on down to the first-floor hall, which was also empty. Ducking her head beneath the yellow oil-cloth hood, she stepped out into the rain.

Once she was in the woods she slowed up. The thin patter on the floor of the forest, the mist that lay over the land was like a protective barrier, hiding her from the world. She got out Tommy's letter, managed to read it before the ink ran. "Darling girl, thank you so much for coming. Please take this in the spirit of the moment, I don't want you to be out of pocket by coming, I am just grateful you will be here. You will be met, greeted, housed, and loved to distraction by your doting Tommy."

I've heard that one before. She felt a little ashamed, at the cynical harshness of her heart. *Is this what it means to grow up? You doubt everybody, you lose the ability to trust, you can't feel anything. I wish I could warm up!*

The pink cottage was cold, somebody had set the thermostat low and had removed the stacks of sheet music. Probably belonged to the school — she was glad she hadn't taken any of it. Terry turned up the heat and sorted through the pile of papers she had brought in from the front porch. The Monday edition had the blackest headlines she had ever seen. On the sedate front page of *The New York Times* it had the effect of a scream. Tuesday was all about the President's speech to the nation. Wednesday was the latest. It occurred to her there might be a section where jobs were advertised, rooms for rent, but she couldn't find one. They must not include the classifieds in the papers they mailed out of town. *Why should they send big-city ads down to a jerkwater little burg in Virginia?*

Spreading the wet sheets on the radiators, which were starting to click and hiss with steam, she paused to look at pictures — a tall ship of some kind was tilted at an awful angle with smoke pouring out of it. There may have been as many as four battleships damaged, the caption said. The airfield at the Naval Base was wrecked, some planes had been destroyed. The Japanese had done it by sneaking in close with their carriers. The Pacific Fleet was all in the harbor, which meant that Ozzie was probably there. *And I don't even know which boat he was on.* The paper said there were casualties. *Why do they call them 'casualties'? There's noth-*

ing casual about being shot, for heavensake.

Slowly she read the news stories until they began to repeat themselves. The truth was, she realized, nobody knew exactly how bad it was, the attack. They kept guessing, estimating, kind of circling around the few facts they had. But there was no uncertainty about the way the country was rallying to war. *You were so wrong, Max. No riots, not even the need to draft these boys, they can't wait to get in the Army.* Or the National Guard. Older men were signing up to defend the west coast against invasion, patrolling the streets at night where everything was blacked out, stationed on the beaches around the cities up and down California, expecting the enemy to try to land and — what? Capture Hollywood? They were holding air-raid drills, draping black cloth over their windows. It seemed so farfetched Terry couldn't believe it.

And then in a smaller item on an inside page she found the information that all Japanese residents in New York City had been rounded up and put in a temporary internment camp on Ellis Island. *Max, you were right! If they could arrest the Japanese, they could arrest Germans. We're at war with Germany now too.* The thought of U-boats off the east coast was easier to imagine. A shiver went through her, a trace of a very old emotion: *I want my mother!*

Forget that! She had to reformulate her own plans, in light of this new situation. New York was going to be in a turmoil. A bad time to plunge into the big city and make a fresh start, when nobody knew where they were going or what would happen next. Or maybe not. With everybody leaving and going in the Army, there might be jobs open. Some businesses would be closing, but others would spring up. In a few weeks things might be less confused. Right now you could get lost in the shuffle.

I could wait here a while, she faced the unbearable thought. *Or I could get married.*

From the tone of Tommy's letter, he was dead-eager. Terry thought, with sudden clarity, *I could have him if I want him. Waltz him right down the aisle under his mother's nose. I could help his career better than the fabulous Kate. You just need to learn the lingo, how to get along with those uppity officers' wives, cock your cocktail at a few of the generals and rip off a bit of Mozart for light entertainment at the afternoon teas. After a few years old Tom-Tom and I would be presiding over the punch bowl at Dahlgren Hall. So long as you don't make the mistake of ever becoming parents. I'm not the type to rock the cradle.*

I'm better at rocking boats, and I'll just bet I could upset Tommy's mother's canoe.

She refolded the papers and stacked them on the table in the kitchen, turned the thermostat back down, moving automatically, trying to process the new state of the world into which she was about to step. Waiting would be a coward's way. Everything was ordained now, suitcase packed and ready, *I can't stop the clock.*

Squared away by the time she got back to the dorm, Terry was moving fast as she came through the back door and hurtled into the hall monitor. A sallow senior she blocked the way, her heavily braced teeth bared in a grimace of disgust.

"So there you are! You're supposed to be in your room, girl! Serve you right if you missed your visitor."

"Visitor?" the word hissed out thinly.

"I don't know why the Dean is so sweet on you, but she's allowing you to have a guest. He's down in the parlor right now. You even have an okay to leave the grounds, not that you seem to feel the need of permission!"

But Terry was already shoving past her, on the run. *Dad?* How could he be here unless something awful — ? The parlor was a small private room set aside for family gatherings, velvet curtains and antimacassars on the over-stuffed chairs. She stopped short in the doorway trying to get her bearings.

Because either she was seeing mirages or Phin was a long way from home.

TWENTY-EIGHT

In that stuffy brown overcoat he came toward her, tilting. Breaking free of her shock, Terry crashed into his arms and clung there as the world spun around her. She felt like a dislocated joint that had been wrenched into place again, racked by an awful ache of relief. St. Louis was real, she hadn't lost her whole earlier life — the world had been there all along.

After a few seconds she realized that she wasn't doing all the clinging. Phin was clutching her to him as if he needed saving too. Drawing back a fraction she looked up into his homely visage and saw new lines around the mouth. The unslept eyes were freighted with some emotion — not fear exactly, it was more like a terrible dread.

"Phin, what is it? What's wrong?"

He let go of her and drew a long breath. "Oh, Bunch, a whole lot is wrong. Starting with this place. What kind of school is this?

I had to go get sore at some little old lady before she'd even let me talk to you."

Phin getting mad was a novelty. Terry suppressed a grin. "You fussed at the Dean? What did you say?"

"Wasn't very polite. I told her you weren't some immature child to get shut in your room, and if you said you didn't know where your folks are she should believe you and maybe even help out a little in a tough situation, give you the benefit of the doubt, for the love of pete. I kind of sailed into her."

"Well, the truth is I got myself in a lot of trouble lately. Left the campus without permission, borrowed a car that wasn't mine and wrecked it — I didn't know ice was so slick."

He surveyed her, frowning. "You okay?"

"Got thrown into a snow drift. My shoulder hurts and some ribs got broken, but I'm fine, now." She grabbed his arm. "Let's get out of here. There's a Hot Shoppe downtown."

"I could use some coffee," he admitted. Something in his tone . . .

As she led the way back down the hall and out into the drizzle Terry said, "Phin, you didn't do something awful, like sign on with Monsanto, did you?" For him to be here,

430

someone must have paid his way.

"When you go into a skid, you don't put on brake, you turn your wheels in the direction of the skid and try to drive out of it, slowly."

"Phin, you didn't join the Army?"

"Would've if they'd have me, but they aren't taking guys with one short leg." Bareheaded, he seemed unaware of the speckling rain as they crossed the campus and turned down the side street. "Is this the place?" Holding the door for her, he followed into the steamy warmth of the coffee shop and over to a booth by the window. "Dreary darned town, isn't it?"

"And it's always like this, always raining. How's everything in St. Louis?" *And what is he not telling me!* All at once the unknown was a gaping no-man's land and she wanted to skirt it, never to go there. *Just sit here and be glad of his presence.* The girl handed them menus. "I'll have a hamburger and fries."

"Same for me, with coffee." He wasn't anxious to step into that void either.

"Phin, did you come all this way just to see me?" Getting close to the edge of the pit.

"No. That would have been reason enough, but I had business in Washington,

D.C. Flew in there by plane. Then I took a bus down here."

"But how? Who footed the bill?"

He got a grip on the coffee mug and nursed it as if he were freezing. The hamburgers came with a mound of fries. Phin picked one up and examined it.

Tell me! Don't tell me! "Phin . . . did you get my letter?"

Letting out a long sigh he began slowly, keeping everything in order. "I got it all right. Went over to your house that same evening. Place was shut up, dark, paper on the porch, mail in the box. So I thought maybe they went off some place for the holidays and didn't get home yet. But next morning the paper was gone, mail too. So that night I tried again, and this time I waited. About eleven o'clock your dad finally showed up. I don't know what I said — 'Hi, Mr. Miller, how's everything?' He stared at me and right there on the front steps he told me Hitler would never take Moscow because the winters were too cold and a mule won't haul artillery through frozen mud, they've got too much sense. When I could get a word in, I asked, 'How's Mrs. Miller?' and he kind of went nuts. Called me a rotten little kike and told me to get off the premises, went in the house and

432

slammed the door. Bunch, I didn't know what to do. But I couldn't call you until I got some answers." He had twisted the French fry to the breaking point, testing its torque.

Terry sat, as if in a vacuum where time stood still.

"Your father sounded sick in the head. I needed to discuss it with a doctor, so I talked to Ruth Ann."

Awkwardly Terry said, "She looks like a real nice person, that picture you have on your dresser."

"Picture? Oh, you mean Aunt Sarah. She was my dad's sister, died of leukemia when she was only twenty-two. I wish I'd known her. Anyway, Ruth Ann is going to marry an intern next month. I described the situation to her and she knew what the matter was right away. 'I can explain why Mr. Miller's on edge. He's half out of his mind worrying about his wife.' Turns out your mom is in the hospital again, has been ever since before Thanksgiving."

Terry should have suspected that. *And Dad going crazy thinking about all those bills.*

"So anyway, Ruth Ann and the night nurse on your mother's floor, they smuggled me in after hours, since I told them about you and how you needed to know the truth and so forth. I think your mom was glad to see me. She's pretty weak, but she wanted to talk about you, how much she loves your letters. Only she hasn't got enough strength to write any back to you, and I guess your dad didn't think of it."

"I don't exist for him, Phin. Not since he found out I blew all my savings. I didn't tell him about the Gryphon, but he got the bank statement."

"Hoo boy." The French fry ruptured and Phin ate it absently.

"But my mother's okay, isn't she? I mean she's just — well, you don't know, but she drinks a little too much. It's probably the brandy made her sick."

He gulped some coffee and grimaced. "Wow, that's strong."

"Listen, please don't hold it against her, that she likes the bottle."

"I know all about that, it doesn't matter. The truth is there's no easy way to put this: your mom has pernicious anemia. She has almost no iron in her blood and her body rejects it in every form, pills or shots or food. She can't eat much of anything, which is why she drinks the brandy. It helps settle her stomach. But that gave her more problems, liver and jaundice and so forth, and she finally collapsed."

Terry sat with the hamburger in her hand, stuck with it, unable to think. Finally she said, "Well, the doctors are fixing it, aren't they?"

The diner was overheated. Sweat gleamed on Phin's brow, his forelock damp and plastered. "You remember last summer when they went to Minnesota? They were at a place called the Mayo Clinic, the best in the country. Top specialists ran all the tests. No use."

"What — *what do you mean, 'no use'?*"

"It means she doesn't have a whole lot of time left. She just — hold on, Bunch!" He reached across to grab her arm.

Shoulder screamed and she didn't even feel it. "I've got to go be with her."

"Sit still. Right now, you need to sit and listen. Don't go running off cock-eyed."

I don't have train fare, I've got to figure out how to get some money first. Grandmother Hamilton . . .

"Are you listening? If you go busting in on her, looking like a walking spook she'll feel worse, I swear. Bunch, you are skin and bones and held together with whipstitch. Right now she thinks you're happy, you're enjoying some kind of 'golden youth' in this forsaken place. It's what keeps her going. You don't want to take away her greatest comfort."

"If you think I'm going to stay here and just — just write letters, when she — she's —"

"It's not going to happen right away. You need to get yourself together, to where you can put on a good act. Maybe wait until Christmas holidays, then it will seem normal for you to come home."

"I can't. Listen, I was about to head for New York. I've been in trouble ever since I came here. It's like this place is in some backward world where the wrong things matter, like whether you wear a stupid beanie on your head, or if you get into somebody's car. My music professor understood, he said people my age ought to be out on their own and getting experiences in living. Only he's gone now, he went back to Europe just in time, he was a German. Not a bad one, he was a good one, but now we're at war he couldn't stay. So I borrowed his car and cracked it up, and I am all packed and ready to leave this place. I figured my folks didn't care, I didn't hear from them. By now, I thought they were probably separated or divorced — Dad was about to walk out on us anyway, what with mother getting — well, not just that she drank too much, but the doctor bills cost too much. And then I spent all my savings, that really hurt him. So he hates us both, and —"

"No, now you wait. You got that totally wrong. Your Dad spends every extra minute he's got with her. He sits by the bed and reads her the papers, he tells her those jokes that aren't funny, but she laughs anyway. Ruth Ann says she never saw two people so much in love."

Terry's mind slammed to a halt. *In love?*

"So if you think he'd ever desert her, you're wrong."

The word reverberated inside her like a gong . . . *wrong . . . wrong . . . been wrong about everything . . . about people, about the world, about me . . .*

"Terry?" Phin must have said it two or three times, he looked worried.

"Yes. Okay. Just tell me what to do."

"Well, first thing, eat the darned hamburger. You need to put on weight. Then — you're supposed to be studying for exams, right?"

"Actually I was about to take a bus for Annapolis. Tommy James is graduating tomorrow, going off to chase submarines. I told him I'd come, but I won't, of course. Forget that."

Phin frowned at his coffee severely.

"School doesn't know about this?"

"I'm done with them. No point telling them anything, ever."

"Yeah, but they can raise a fuss if you just disappear, maybe get the police looking for a missing person. So what you do is, you go over to see the Dean. She won't give you any trouble. I told her exactly what the situation is, and she looked pretty meek when I left. Tell her you're going up there —"

"No. I don't want to waste that much time."

"Bunch, that man is going off to war. You can't send him away without a goodbye from his gal. It wouldn't be right. Besides, it will be something great you can tell your mother. She loved your letter about the grand ball you went to up there. That's what you need, to write to her positive things even if you have to lie through your teeth about how much you love this place."

No more letters. But he's right, I should go to the graduation. Then I'm going home if I have to borrow the money from somebody. Tommy? Tommy's folks are rich.

"Then at Christmas vacation —"

"Phin, I can't wait that long. What time is left I need to — Look, I will tell Mother that the music department is shut down, the teacher left the country. That's the truth.

438

She'll accept that. Only I need to be there when they let her out of the hospital." She broke off at the twinge of sorrow in his face. "With me to take care of her they will let her come home?"

Slightest fraction of movement, his head shook, *no.*

Terry drew a deep breath, but right now she couldn't think about finalities. She needed to do something. Solemnly she picked up the burger and began to eat, no time for inner weakness. The food had no taste, but it was bolstering her inside. She noticed then that Phin hadn't touched his.

"Why don't you finish yours? You're pretty darned skinny yourself. What else is the matter, what's this 'business' that brought you here?" Suddenly she was on the track of it. "It has to do with your experiment, I bet. Somebody stole it from you? One of those Chicago people?"

He shook his head, but an inner shadow crossed his face. *Fear? Phin never was afraid in his life.* The blue eyes, usually all fired up, were bleak as the sky out beyond the window where it was beginning to snow. "Chicago started it off, the men up there — they're brilliant, way ahead of me. But they liked my lab work, they saw where I was heading with it. Electromagnetic separation of isotopes, takes big equipment to develop it properly. Man named Arthur Compton has been working on the same thing, coming from a different direction. We compared a lot of notes and we've been corresponding, but I couldn't leave St. Louis. Mom needs me. Except now she's going to have to do without me. I got this call from them, these physicists, right after Pearl Harbor. They wanted me to come to this big meeting in Washington. I met a lot of the world's greatest scientists, some of them from Europe — they're Jewish, barely escaped with their lives. It's incredible what's been going on over there. They've been working to split the atom for years. Anyway they're putting together a team to —" He halted in mid-sentence. "I forgot, I can't talk about that. It's what they call 'top secret'. Anyway they put me on their payroll, starting the first of next year. I have to go to Tennessee." He motioned the waitress for the check.

When he pulled out a wad of bills, Terry stared.

"Expense money. They gave me travel expenses. Here, I'm sorry I couldn't get you any sooner. I know you said you didn't need it, but you were fibbing, weren't you? I was about to sell the Gryphon when the war hit us. Glad I didn't have to. Cars are going to be scarce, maybe for years. Anyhow, money is no problem any more. This is all yours —" he shoved the pile across. "I've got my train ticket home, I won't be needing it."

Terry sat stupefied. Tens, twenties, a fifty-dollar bill — she had never even seen one before. Slowly she picked them up, straightened them, the seed of an idea coming to rest in a distant corner of her mind. *This is what Dad needs, to feel like there's plenty.* Meanwhile Phin was getting up, putting his coat on.

"When do you have to leave?"

"One o'clock train. We better hurry along over to the depot." That barren look in his eyes again, as if he saw beyond to a terrible place, a place of death.

The notion wouldn't be brushed away. Terry gripped his arm as they left the diner. "Tell me, what sort of thing will they do with your experiment?"

"I wish I could talk. I am so damned confused."

But Phin was never confused. If there was a problem, he was excited, glad to tackle it, elated to solve it.

"You're usually ahead of everybody else."

"Not this time. The atom can stump the best of us, even Einstein. I met him, by the way. He's not all that happy either." He tucked her under an arm and headed for the train station, the snow beginning to frost the lanky light hair, the shoulders of the brown overcoat.

Wracked with all the bad news, the knowledge of what she was going to have to do, Terry thought she couldn't bear to have him go. And in a kind of revelation, a new concept: *Phin needs me too.* She stood straighter, taking her weight off his arm.

"Whatever your problem is," she said, "we'll solve it. Like you always told me: start at the beginning."

He made a noise deep in his chest, anger, amusement, protest. "The beginning was the first time I ever worked an equation. I can't remember when I didn't want to know what makes things happen. Math was a magic staircase to physics, which turned out to be a whole mystical kingdom I've been exploring ever since. Once in a while you hit a sort of 'open-sesame' and get a glimpse of a new approach to an old conundrum. Like I got this notion of how we could make electricity without using gas or oil or coal. Light up the dark corners of the world. Now comes this damned war and it's all turned upside-down. Instead of 'light up', they want to use it to 'blow up.' "

Without understanding what he meant, Terry knew that it was killing him inside. She wished she could pull off some miracle, the way she had that day she had conceived the idea of buying the Gryphon. To be Phin's fairy godmother: Tess of the Tinker-bells. *Oh heavens, my mind is turning to cottage cheese.*

"Maybe it's not as bad as you think," she offered lamely.

Blinking the snowflakes off his eyelids, he glanced down, holding her with that arm across her shoulders, but tighter than usual. "Remember that day when Sis wanted me to turn the pennies in the jar into gold? And I said, to do that you had to sell your soul to the Devil? Well, I wasn't kidding."

Bodies moving together, they held each other so tightly she could feel the hitch in his stride. And then in the distance the sound of a train whistle spurred them, they began to run for the station.

Twenty-Nine

She had no idea where she was. The train was rocking and clacketing through the night somewhere in the West Virginia mountains. Here and there Terry could see the dim yellow glow of a kerosene lamp up on the flank of the hills. Mine country, dirt-poor, but one hut they passed near the tracks had a Christmas wreath hung in the window. A small town came and went in a flash of red crossing lights as, far ahead, the engine wailed its warning. Then they were plunged into blackness again, rushing through the dark, a capsule of manic merriment.

It was a club car, the overflow of passengers without reservations. Over at the bar a company of men, some in uniforms so new they still bore creases, tried to out-sing each other.

". . . ramblin' wreck from Georgia Tech . . ."

". . . never stagger, we never fall . . ."

". . . helluva, helluva, helluva, helluvan engineer . . ."

Sitting on her suitcase by a window, Terry swayed with the movement of the train. Tommy had done some push-and-shove to get her aboard. Lines of soldiers had been crowding on, filling every spare inch of space. Now they all juggled back and forth like packaged goods. On the floor next to her sat a stout woman in a chinchilla coat, grimly waving a small American flag in time to the singing. Across the way a young girl sat with a two-year-old asleep in her lap. A soldier had commandeered one of the few chairs for her, brought her a Coke. She had thanked him with a terrible politeness as if her mind were in a spasm of fear. All shades of mood shaped the faces of that crowd, but the strongest was defiance, determination. Anger.

"Stand Navy down the field, anchors a-weigh . . ." Terry sang along with that one.

The graduation had been sober, but undershot with excitement. The commencement address had been delivered by the Secretary of the Navy, a plain man, too bland for that great chamber of warriors. Beneath the ancient flags the young graduates sat fidgeting, and when the ceremonies were over their caps exploded into the air like a bomb burst. Afterward, the new Ensigns did what their forefathers had always done: they drove their parents' cars in and out of the gates for the heady pleasure of making the Jimmy-legs salute. If Terry felt it was a bit childish she kept her mouth shut.

Be part of this society, she thought, *and you would keep shut a lot of the time.* In some ways she felt ages older than these boys with their eager faces and eyes keen for battle. She tried not to dampen their celebration with her own troubles. Of course Tommy was aware that something was wrong, so she told him briefly, without going into details. Mother very ill, on her way home, so forth.

Mrs. James had gone all maternal, concerned that her "dearest friend" was in the hospital. A tall angular woman with blue hair and a nose that could have sliced bread, she had been very gracious, but in truth she was anxious about the effect Terry was having on her son. After luncheon at the lovely historic hotel, Tommy gravely made their excuses.

"Got to go, Mom, I'm expected to attend all the parties they're giving, got to polish the old brass, you know." As soon as they were in the car, he had planted a swift kiss on her lips. "It's true, we have to make the rounds. Sorry, there's so little time, so much I want to say. In fact, I'm sorry about a whole lot of things. Am I forgiven?"

Easily Terry said, "I see you're still not wearing your ring."

"Oh, that. Listen, the ring isn't important. To me it was a sort of friendly gesture. I may have had a slight crush on the girl. What matters is that you're here and you're the one I wanted to be with me today, Terry Miller, so please let the thing slide, huh?"

"Sure. I never had any claim on you," she said. "I just resented being used, I felt foolish taking you seriously when all along you had made promises to somebody else."

"I didn't *use* you!" He looked horrified. "For God's sake, I — you — you're the best thing in my life, the most genuine person I know. You don't flirt, you don't simper or go into giggles or tantrums or play little feminine tricks. You make the other girls look dippy. That's why I wanted you —"

"Plus, the fabulous Kate is in San Francisco." She was teasing him now. "It's okay. So hadn't we better go to all those parties where the big cheeses are expecting you?"

The grand old houses of the city were alive with lights in the dusk of late afternoon. Through marble halls the handsome assemblages milled, voices high with passion barely in check. On this one day an Ensign could chat with an Admiral, and Tommy did it well. When he spoke of the new weaponry being developed in Europe, they listened. When he told how the German scientists were said to be working on the atom as a weapon of unparalleled destruction Terry's mind flashed to Phin — that was it! His invention was going to be used to make war, and it was killing him.

Dazed at the discovery, she put in a word. "Does it have anything to do with separating iso— isotopes?"

The silence with which they stared at her was appalling.

"It's just that a friend of mine is working on some new electromagnetic thing —" her voice faltered. She was being confronted by a tall man whose shoulders dripped gold braid.

"Young lady, whatever you may have heard about that, you keep to yourself, understand? The enemy can be anywhere."

A swift mental image of a Japanese butler hiding under the buffet table almost prompted a snicker until she remembered that Phin had been reluctant to talk, even out alone on the street in a snow storm.

Tommy's face was beet-red by now. She swallowed her smile and gravely nodded as if her lips were sealed forever.

But later she got into hot water with a different officer, simply by asking how many battleships had been damaged in the attack. "I know somebody on one of them," she added, with a new pang for Ozzie, wondering how she could find out if he was safe.

The man, who turned out to be an Admiral, gave her a look that a car would have skidded on. "Ensign —" to Tommy — "I believe you should instruct your date on the need for discretion in matters of top security."

"Ensign" had bowed and rushed her off to a far corner of the room. By then he was a little tipsy, the punch having been well spiked. "Terry, please! You really have got to watch your tongue. That guy may be my CO any day now."

"I didn't know it was some kind of secret. I mean the Japanese certainly know how many ships they hit. They were there."

"They're only claiming four kills. They may not realize they wiped out most of the Pacific Fleet. Those ships were sitting like ducks in a row. We haven't got one operational battlewagon left." He sucked in his breath sharply. "For God's sake forget you heard that."

Later on at the train station, by then thoroughly drunk, Tommy had asked her to marry him. She gently refused, didn't even have to think twice. The closed society of the Navy was one into which she would never fit, and she told him so. In a wild rush of regret and relief, he kissed her, one of those marvelous, expert kisses. It hardly brought a twinge of feeling. *Happy marriage to the fabulous one, and lots of promotions. I hope you'll love her.* Only somehow she doubted that Tommy James would sit by his wife's bed reading Robert Louis Stevenson as her life faded.

He might end up a hero, but the true essence of heroism, she was beginning to realize, came without flags or bands playing. To trudge through the mud of a hard life to the bitter end without running away, to stick with someone in "sickness or in health". She'd had time now to think of those words: *Never saw two people more in love.* They had banished her skepticism about love, but Terry wondered if she would have that kind of courage, if there would ever be anyone on earth she could commit her life to, forever.

You can't know that until you know who you

are. This was the conclusion she had reached in the long hours of the train ride. *You can't make up your mind where you're going until you can define the word "you."* For right now it was enough to be heading home. No doubt about her feelings for her parents. She had never cherished her mother more. *And somehow I will square things with Dad.* She had already taken a step in that direction. The seed of an idea yesterday had grown quickly into a plan of action.

When she had called the Hamiltons, her grandmother had been in a high dudgeon over Pearl Harbor. "How dare they attack us, the horrid little monkeys!" Her voice rattled the telephone. "I tried to reach you at school, but they couldn't find you. Are you all right, Theresa?"

"I'm fine, but Mother is not." She told as much as she could, not really understanding all the words — "Pernicious anemia, I think they said. Right now, I'm worried about Dad. He's near the point of a breakdown, afraid of losing her and so worried about the hospital expenses, they've just about eaten up all our savings. So I thought — I'm leaving school to be with her — I wondered if maybe instead of paying my tuition, you could help my father with the bills." The words shocked her as she said

them, but need was greater than embarrass-
ment.

"Of course we will. Don't give it another
thought. I'm only glad there's something
we can do." And now the old lady's voice
had tears in it.

So whether he likes it or not, Terry thought,
*he is going to take the Hamilton money. And
he's going to take me back and let me be part
of this family.* The idea of forcing anything
on her father was scary, but she thought he
might need to be bossed a little, the way
she had all those years. His stern pro-
nouncements had saved her from various
disasters. "No, young lady, you may not go
to an over-night party in Columbia." And
"Yes, girl, you will go to summer school.
You're going to graduate if you have to do
math problems ten hours a day." *Now it's
my turn. I have to make him listen to me. For
Mother's sake.*

Maybe the war would actually help. It had
juggled everybody around until they had to
find new faces, new points of view. This time
they were all in the same boat: nobody knew
what the future would bring.

Over at the piano next to the bar a kid
was trying to play "The Sweetheart of
Sigma Chi" and hitting a lot of wrong notes.
I could do it better, Terry thought. *I'm a pretty*

darned good pianist. A novel thought flared across her mind: *I will probably go on playing, only from here on it will be for fun, like Max Wolff does.* It intrigued her, to think what she might try if she weren't under pressure. She wished she had a copy of that duet they had romped through — the memory made a small cool spot in the heat of inner turmoil. *Music could be like a refuge from distress. People are going to need that.*

With the tipping of flasks and beer cans the noise in the club car was taking on a higher pitch, full of suppressed rage. They were singing: "Well, I wish I was in Dixieland, to live and die for Dixie . . ." The woman in the chinchilla coat was leading them in a fierce soprano.

As the chorus concluded one of the men yelled, "We're gonna kick them Japanese asses!" and threw his glass at the wall behind the bar, where it made a tiny crash.

Don't underestimate the enemy, Terry warned silently. *They just sank the entire Pacific Fleet.*

In the window beside her she saw her image, transparent, fragile. *Got to eat, got to shovel in a lot of food as soon as I get home.* Get stronger, there were decisions to be made, and Dad might not be in a position to make them. *Hurry up, train.*

"The stars at night are big and bright . . ."
(clap,clap,clap,clap)
"Deep in the heart of Texas."

Ozzie used to like that one. He had a beautiful voice, high and sweet, like an Irish tenor. Thinking of him in the past tense made her shudder. Surely if anybody had survived that awful attack, he would. To believe differently was unthinkable. The twist in her heart was so sharp it hurt. She saw in the faces around her that it was happening to everyone. All across the country by the hundreds of thousands people were feeling a premonition of loss, lost happiness, lost freedom, lost pleasure of living. A loss of trust in the old belief that everything was going to be fine.

On the other hand, the war had brought them together in a kind of fierce fellowship. The lady in the chinchilla coat was holding the baby so the girl could go to the rest room. The men at the piano had subsided to listen to one with a good baritone voice singing solo.

"I'll be loving you, always . . ."

Weary to the bone, Terry felt a seepage of tears as the train inched into the yards in St. Louis. Late afternoon, was it only one day after the graduation ceremonies? Everything seemed to be in slow motion.

When they had gone through Pittsburgh they had been pulled over onto a siding for an hour to let several freight trains go by, each one towing a hundred cars, flatbeds with tanks on them, pieces of artillery, trucks painted Army drab, the stuff of war, all moving westward on a priority run, tracks cleared, a troop train right behind them, barreling past with men waving from the windows. In the shabby shanties around the yards windows were decorated with little flags.

Now as they rolled lazily into the train sheds snow was coming down in big flakes. The engine backed the long string of cars toward the platform. The club car would be the first to discharge its passengers. Terry pulled on her coat and gathered her suitcases. Lucky break — to be first off, at least she might be able to snag a taxi. There was no porter to help now. Hauling the heavy bags herself, she backed her way down the steep steps and found her burden lifted, long arms coming from behind. Phin. Of course.

"How'd you know I was coming on this train?"

"This was the first one you could have been on. If you weren't, I'd have kept on meeting them until you showed up." He looked half-frozen and totally glad to see her, the one-sided smile broadened to include his whole face. Dropping the suitcase in the snow he took her into a hug that stabilized her, braced her against that long crooked body. She held him equally tight, drawing strength from him as if filling up at a gas station. She could feel her loose parts mending.

"Mother?"

"She's holding her own. Even a little bit better since I told her you were coming. How was Annapolis?" The words seemed to stick in his throat. He looked strangely anxious, the blue eyes clouded with some important question.

Terry shrugged, it seemed so long ago now. "Okay, I guess. You were right, I needed to go there and finish things up." And suddenly his eyes were alight with the old fire, that Bunsen-burner look. *What did I say to make him so happy?*

"Good." And again, "Good!" In an awkward burst of joy he caught her to him and kissed her on the lips. A different kind of kiss, it had never been practiced on anybody. So new, so fervent, as she kissed him back Terry felt disoriented. Tried it again, more slowly, wonderingly. It was as if she had come into a strange room . . . or rather, it was familiar, but someone had rearranged the furniture. She liked it. She *loved* it. Eyes closed, she clung to him, relished the sensation of having discovered something wonderful.

I need to tell Phin about this!

Drawing back a fraction she looked up, caught him in the same marvelous delight. But he wasn't surprised, as she was.

And the final piece of the puzzle slipped into place. *He's been there all along, waiting for me to catch up.*

ABOUT THE AUTHOR

Annabel Johnson is the author of twenty-three novels, the product of a long and interesting career, which began at a time when the country was young and full of pep and innocence. She had just turned twenty in 1941 when the world changed forever with the events of Pearl Harbor and the ensuing war. It is about that fateful year that she has chosen to write *Last Days of a Toyshop*. The story is completely fictional, but it draws on her own experiences which she remembers vividly.

From the age of twelve, Annabel was dedicated to a future as an author, so that by the time she was twenty she had begun to see the happenings of her life as material for books to come. In 1955 she and her husband Edgar began their co-authorship by writing historical novels of the old West, traveling the country, visiting the scenes of their stories and delving into the research while living in an eight-foot camping trailer, trying to make ends meet on an author's meager royalties. They had no home base, except a certain spot in the Mojave desert in winter, and another site in the National Forest in Wyoming in summer.

In 1966, with the growing success of their books, they settled in Denver, but after Edgar's death, Annabel has come home to Arizona, to continue her career in the desert setting she has always loved. With this new novel she has rekindled the memory of the America of her youth, telling the tale of a girl making the painful struggle into womanhood, dealing with a devastating family secret and learning the intricacies of relationships with the three men in her life. It is a story of personal upheaval, but more than that, the picture of a time that will never return.

MID-YORK LIBRARY SYSTEM
1600 Lincoln Avenue
Utica, NY 13502
www.midyork.org

ww 5-28-13